NANO TRILOGY - III

NANO
TARGETED VILLAGES

WAYNE E. CRISS

ISBN: 979-8-89216-038-4 (Paperback)
        979-8-89216-039-1 (E-book)

Library of Congress Control Number: 2024918265

BookmarcAlliance
California, USA
www.bookmarcalliance.com

HOLLYWOOD BOOK REVIEWS
IN PARTNERSHIP WITH
BOOKMARC ALLIANCE

BOOK REVIEW

Nano Trilogy III
Nano Targeted Villages
by Wayne E. Criss

Nano Trilogy III
Nano Targeted Villages
by Wayne E. Criss

Author:	Wayne E. Criss	**ISBN:**	979-8-89216-038-4
Genre:	Science Fiction /		979-8-89216-039-1
	Mystery / Adventure	**Reviewed by:**	Jack Chambers
Pages:	256		
Publisher:	Bookmarc Alliance		

Nano Trilogy III
Nano Targeted Villages

by Wayne E. Criss

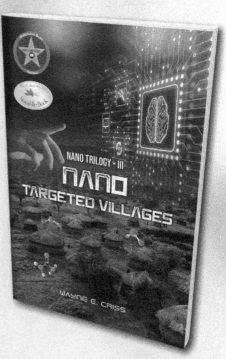

The path of vengeance is one of the rockiest, most difficult paths that one can walk in life. Those who are threatened to be consumed by more often than not lose themselves entirely, and yet becomes the entire reason for their existence. As it was once said, those who seek vengeance should be prepared to dig two graves, for the path of revenge is dangerous and cruel, and will often lead to one's own demise in the process.

In author Wayne E. Criss's *Nano Trilogy III: Nano Targeted Villages*, the battle between the four young men who lost their fathers to nano killers all those years ago and the leader of this group of villains, the Korrectorizer, comes to a haunting conclusion. As the boys, now men, continue their battle, they discover their enemy has developed a brandnew macabre form of nano weaponry, and they begin using it to attack villages around the world and killing hundreds of innocent people. Seeking to finally end the violence and bloodshed these killers have wrought, the men develop their own counter-molecular weapons program, and using the combined nano tech and witchcraft they have honed into skills over the years, they hunt down their enemy in a final confrontation between them and their fathers' killer, seeking the revenge that has eluded them for so long.

The author has crafted a truly gripping and captivating read. The hardships and struggles these young men have faced over the course of three books and the wellspring of world-building the author has done in this trilogy is nothing short of outstanding. The balance between the science and the supernatural elements of the story is still there, and keeps the readers engaged with the narrative fully. Yet in this final chapter, it is the character development that truly shines, for it highlights the men's final confrontation with the Korrectorizer and his band of killers, highlighting both the emotional weight and moral weight of their many years of struggle against the madman and his nefarious machinations. The detail and imagery the author employs in this book helps to add to the tension and heavy atmosphere their confrontations have in the book, and keep me invested thoroughly.

This is the perfect read for those who enjoy trilogies which highlight science, adventure, and mysteries. The book will also appeal to those who enjoy sci-fi and supernatural fantasy elements in the story, as well as suspense and thriller moments and a lot of action. The adrenaline-fueled nature of these stories and the high-octane battles are greatly balanced with the emotional weight of these character arcs and the emotional struggle for the men who have evolved over the course of this trilogy, and finally see their endgame on the horizon.

Captivating, action-packed, and gripping, author Wayne E. Criss's *Nano Trilogy III: Nano Targeted Villages* is a must-read and satisfying conclusion to this action-driven and mystery sci-fi series. The twists and turns in the narrative, including the final fate of the Korrectorizer and the emotional weight of the men facing their futures will bring a heartfelt yet still heart-pounding thriller to a close, and readers will be left eager for more from this truly entertaining and engaging writer.

PACIFIC BOOK REVIEW
IN PARTNERSHIP WITH
BOOKMARC ALLIANCE

BOOK REVIEW

Nano Trilogy III
Nano Targeted Villages
by Wayne E. Criss

Nano Trilogy III

Nano Targeted Villages

by Wayne E. Criss

Author: Wayne E. Criss

Genre: Science / Mystery

Pages: 256

Publisher: Bookmarc Alliance

ISBN: 979-8-89216-038-4
979-8-89216-039-1

Reviewed by: Aaron Washington

Nano Trilogy III
Nano Targeted Villages
by Wayne E. Criss

Oliver Johnson was born in 1998 to a teen mother, in a poor neighborhood in Brooklyn. Despite the harsh living conditions, Oliver Johnson got to make something out of his life - thanks to the help of his mother Kolea, and his uncle, who also played the father figure role. Jordon Johnson, his uncle becomes a key person in his future. Oliver uses every resource at his disposal, wit, and what the universe provides to bring revolutionize things in different parts of the world. *Nano Trilogy III – Nano Targeted Villages* is a science, adventure and mystery book which follows the story of Oliver, who is known as Korrectorizer through his work gets to change the world in an unimaginable way. There is a new nanotech molecular system that is used to finish villages and kill their people. For a long time, the attacks never stop until the sons of the villages say enough is enough and fight back. It is amazing that as they counter, they use high tech weapons, take advantage of the advancement in the military and even apply drones, poisoned animals, and superior molecular weapons.

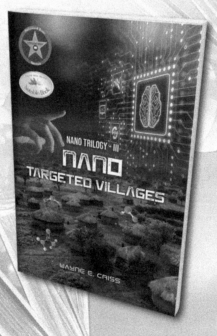

Korrectorizer is mostly at the center of the war, and despite him and his team having the best at their disposal; their adversaries give them a difficult time. *Nano Trilogy III – Nano Targeted Villages* is an awe-inspiring book which reveals to the reader how military missions are implemented, the effects of war, and how politics touch every aspect of our lives. Wayne E. Criss wrote an attention-grabbing novel, having a plot which is captivating and characters who are engaging. The build-up of the story is enthralling, as the book starts on a moderate hype before getting to be electrifying. I love that every minor story can exist on its own even without the main storyline. Wayne E. Criss' writing is moving, the diction applied in the book incredible, and the war jargon instructive.

The storyline could not have been amusing without the characters. Wayne E. Criss's characters are placid, unpredictable, manic, intelligent, and compelling. Apart from Korrectorizer, I enjoyed following characters like James O'reilly, Ms O'keeffe, Amina Adebayo, Asu Oktem, LiJiang, and Dagda Murphy. There is a go-getter element in these characters which made them excellent and appealing. Apart from the characters, I also loved how the reader gets to virtually travel in different countries throughout the world. Reading about nanotechnology laboratories and what goes on behind the scenes was fun and also informative.

Nano Trilogy III –Nano Targeted Villages is a captivating read for those who enjoy action packed novels and an addictive storyline. Wayne E. Criss keeps the reader hooked from the beginning, with his appealing narration and the plot twists in every other chapter. This book is smoothly written. The language, characters, distinct plot, themes in the book and astonishing conversation initiated by the author make it worth reading.

THIS IS A SAM NOVEL
SCIENCE–ADVENTURE–MYSTERY

THE BOOK IS NOT SCIENCE FICTION
IT IS SCIENCE NEAR REAL

Special recognition to Dr. Nur Bilge Criss, Professor of History and International Relations, who has been a leader at my side for the past many years. Her continuous flow and re-adjustment of ideas has allowed me to blend my scientific experiences and knowledge with social understanding. We will continue to blend science and humanity into fascinating near real stories which include living advances in the current century.

PROLOGUE

For the past fifteen-twenty years, Korrector Com I & II companies, using cure-and kill-contracts for conservative industrialists, have been very successful in neutralizing many select high technology scientists. Most targets were eliminated one by one using an organic nanotech molecular system which leaves macabre messages, including the assassinations of the fathers of four young boy musketeers. However, recently the strategy was changed into a military mode by switching to a new cellulose nanotech molecular system which eliminates groups of people in areas, regions, and countries in Africa where there is major political and social unrest.

During the recent few years, a Washington-European International Committee of Nanotechnology Control, four boys/young men from four different continents, and their professional witch friends from the International Witches Conclave, had moderate success in eliminating several of the hired nanotech killers. But now the strategy of the committee has shifted to African villages and has focused on preventing this new style of mass macabre attacks. The African young musketeer identifies, designs, and leads counter attacks against Korrector Com II's frontal attacks in various places in Africa: Nigeria, Morocco, Democratic Republic of the Congo, Niger, and Chad. Most recently major battles occur in both Moslem and Christian areas of Nigeria including Port Harcourt, Maiduguri, Abuja, Lagos, and several outer villages. The Turkish young musketeer identifies illegal monies movement which helps identify the killers. The Irish young musketeer helps fuse nanotech and terrorist international laws into one. The nanotechnologist Chinese young musketeer develops a new counter nanotech molecular system. While American special military drones provide the major weapon which allows for the critical transport of delivery for the Voodoo poisonous snake offensive.

Uncle Dagda and the Turkish and Irish young men identify the founder-leader of Korrector Com II, named Korrectorizer, who was born in a ghetto in Brooklyn, New York, trained as a lawyer-lobbyist on Capitol Hill, Washington, DC, and worked from the British Virgin Islands and Europe. After a vicious psychic battle, he is eliminated, so they think.

MAJOR CHARACTERS

FOUR MUSKETEERS

James O'Reilly [Ey'tuka] – Boston – Irish – Nano-Terror Lawyer

Li Jiang [Tsu'tye] – Nanking/Los Angeles – Chinese – Nano-Scientist

Kefentse Legoase [Na'via] – Johannesburg – African – Nano Homicide Detective

Aykut Turan [Mo'ata] – Istanbul – Turk – Electronic International Banker

Other – Asu Oktem – Istanbul – Turk – Chief of Cybersecurity, (adjunct member of the Musketeers)

O'REILLY FAMILY

Jonathan O'Reilly – lawyer and President of Celtic Inc – Boston

Jackson O'Reilly – lawyer and Co-President of Celtic Inc – Boston

Dagda Murphy – Founder and President of ISAAT, Co-Chairman of Nano-Technology Control in the Division of High Technology, Department Health and Human Services, Washington, DC – James O'Reilly's Uncle

LEADERS OF THE WITCHES

Ms. Banthnaid O'Keeffe – High Priestess of Irish Witchcraft and current President of the World Witches Conclave

Queen Cleopatra – Haiti, the Caribbean, and Central-South America – Haitian

African Queen of Voodoo – Lagos, Nigeria–African

Princess Luminitsa – Centenarian Witch of the European Gypsies–Turk

Priest Quetzalcoatl Totec Tlamacazqui, High Priest of the Aztecs – Mexican

OTHERS

Senator Jordon Johnson, US Senate, Founder of Korrector Com I & II, Washington, DC, and the British Virgin Islands

Mr. Oliver 'Jordon' Johnson, Board Chairman, CEO and President of Korrector Com I & II, Washington, DC, and the British Virgin Islands

Chole Johnson, wife of Oliver Johnson

Mr. John Reasoner – US Attorney General, Chairman of Nanotechnology Control Committee, Department of Health and Human Services, Washington, DC

Dr. William Stronger – Professor and Chairman of the Department of Nanotechnology, MIT, Boston

Mr. Faustino Mariniti – billionaire businessman and merchant, Rome and Milan

Dr. Anneka Andersson – nanotech scientist, Stockholm

NIGERIANS

Aminu Adebayo – Social Analyst in the Department of Health and Human Relations, Government of Nigeria, Abuja

Chimaobi Nkwado – Secretary of the Department of Health and Human Relations, Government of Nigeria, Abuja

Arjana Adebayo – Administrative Assistant to Senator Adelki and wife of Aminu Adebayo

Lieutenant Colonel Nwaoloko – stationed in Maiduguri, Lake Borno area, Nigeria

Adaeze Okonkwo – Administrative Associate of Judge Iherjirika, and engaged to Kefentse Lagoase

Little Kiy – ten-year old village boy who worked for Kef and the Nigerian military as a superspy

Mali–village girl who identified the mode of 'food poison'

CONTENTS

SAM – Science – Adventure – Mystery

1

KORRECTORIZER I

Older brother (Jordon) and little sister (Kolea) were born in Canada to a racially mixed middle-aged couple. Their father was a very skilled Ford auto engine mechanic. The manager of a New York City Ford Dealership, learned about him, invited him and family to the USA to work on Ford car engines. They came, became double citizens, Canadian and American. They settled in Brooklyn, New York. Ten years later both mother and father were killed in an underground NYC-Metro crash. A small amount of Ford Company's life insurance for father kept the two children in motion. The son, Jordon, finished high school and took college courses at night. The daughter, Kolea, ran away and eventually settled in a ghetto-like area in Brooklyn. She refused schooling, but big brother was always nearby and helped her socially and financially.

It was 1998, a sixteen-year old dark brown unmarried girl (Kolea) was lying in a dirty bed in a run down apartment building on Doglus Street in Brooklyn. The apartment had badly worn carpets and furniture, but it was reasonably clean. She was screaming in birth pain as there was only an old woman and her twenty-year old brother helping. The old lady was close by in a wheel chair and shouting directions. The baby was coming, blood was coming, and the girl was trying to get up to escape the pain between her legs.

The brother (Jordon), a big strong athletic male had tied his sister's hands and feet to the corners of the bed. He had boiled water, had lots of clean towels, and was carefully following the old lady's orders. The birth process was happening. There was no turning back.

Neighbors heard the screaming and looked out their windows. Soon a couple of local women, with similar experiences, came to help. Living in a Brooklyn ghetto, there were few secrets. Mothers in the building were already prepared. They brought more hot water, drinking water, a couple of clean nightgowns, blankets, and some sugar cookies.

The brother caught the baby, a boy. He cut the umbilical cord and was cleaning him when the ladies took over. He then collapsed in a nearby chair. The women started cleaning up the new mother, the bed, the floor, and discarding all bloody sheets-clothes-towels in a large plastic bag for later cold water washing. They gave her two aspirin, forced her to drink cold water, re-dressed her, moved her to a corner floor mattress, and laid the newborn on her chest.

The child was screaming loudly, searching for 'food'. When he found a breast, there was suddenly silence in the room as he did not have to be told – 'this is life'. The group laughed and sighed – success.

Kolea, the new mother, was a large strong 5 feet 10 inch and 180 pound un-educated girl who earned minimum wage as a cook in a nearby fast food restaurant. She had been living in this apartment for the past two years with two other teenage girls who ran away when her labor began. The girls were each on birth control, Kolea was not. She got pregnant for the third time. This time she did not spontaneously abort. Now she was a mother. And maybe her friends would return, maybe not.

Therefore, Kolea's brother, Jordon, had showed up when labor began. He was 6 feet 4 inches and 225 pounds, and a locally famous high school football player. He lived only two blocks away, and had already helped deliver two other babies of his male friends in nearby apartment buildings. So, he was an experienced midwife.

He was smart, worked his way through high school by following in his father's footsteps at the NYC Ford Dealership, and was now taking night courses at the Pencertab College. He was studying social and legal management while working as assistant manager at a local grocery-department store. Routinely he helped his sister pay rent and other bills. They were reasonably close as a brother-sister who had lost their parents in a train accident when they were very young. They had been in and out of government care. Jordon's size and football reputation kept them out of major petty crime and local gang problems in the neighborhood. However, this only allowed his sister to frequently enjoy community males—hence the results!

But the new born nephew was genetically HIS FAMILY. They named him Oliver Johnson, keeping their parents and their common name. Kolea did not know who the real father was.

Oliver was a very strong baby. Kolea was a big strong girl and had more than adequate milk. Jordon found an empty apartment in the building and moved the three Johnsons into it. They settled into a fascinating baby-oriented life. Both worked and babied. Every moment settled into their long-term memory banks.

'Mama' Johnson provided the primary baby food, milk. 'Uncle' Johnson, from work, brought home other food and necessary antibiotics. Soon one of the girlfriends returned, so the 'family' moved into an empty three-bedroom apartment on the top floor. Many apartments were empty and 'unrented'. They worked out a three-way shift. The girls worked at a bakery, occasionally snatched food. Jordon altered between school, work, and babysitting.

Life was hard. But they survived the difficult relationships of the general dog-eat-dog interactions which happen in poor neighborhoods where ethnic teenager gangs roamed and stole at random. For adequate security, Jordon organized the nine families who were living in the apartment building, registered everyone with local authorities, received permission to have police security service available using emergency electric signals. It worked better than nothing.

Three years later Jordon completed school-college training in administrative law. He then married his girlfriend, a 22 year old lawyer, joined her father's law firm, entered a college juris doctoral program at James Robert College in the Queens, New York, and moved. He promised to stay in close touch, physically and financially. He did. He definitely wanted to watch, and help, his 'nephew-son' grow up.

A Boy to Man

So, Oliver Johnson was born in 1998, to an unmarried dark brown woman, named Kolea, in the Brooklyn ghetto of New York City. He did not know his genetic father. He had one dark skinned uncle who was four years older than his mother. Mother and son moved to and rented a second-floor condo of a ten-story building on NW 27th Street, near 100 Hester Street where his Pace Elementary and High School was located. The area had less poverty and less moderate housing. Their apartment was well renovated and very clean. They lived reasonably well from mother's washing/ironing clothing for single employed men living nearby, welfare checks, food stamps, Medicaid, and regular monthly 'pieces' of support from his uncle. Uncle Jordon Johnson was now a lawyer who had recently been elected from the 3rd district of the state of New York into the House of Representatives in Washington, DC. The Uncle had married but did not have children. His wife, Micaela, preferred her lawyering. Plus, she liked NYC better than Washington. So, they lived in both places and doted on Oliver when in New York City, who was growing big and strong and smart.

Oliver helped his mother, physically and financially. She had arthritic knees, so had some difficulty on the stairs. Fortunately, a part time working elevator was present. He helped carry most things up and down, especially the bachelor businessmen's clothing for washing and ironing. There was a good laundromat in the basement of the building. And he did pick-up and delivered all on his bicycle, summer and winter. At the age of fifteen, he obtained a delivery van driver's license, and delivered pre-prepared hot meals from Helen's Hot Foods, every day, to eight nursing homes nearby, late afternoon. Oliver cleverly arranged his school day with a breakfast of high protein cereal, whole milk, morning classes, noon lunch at school, afternoon classes, deliveries, basketball or volleyball practice, depending upon the season, and home to study or attend a conference sports game. He usually managed to obtain one of the pre-prepared hot meals, which was not claimed, for a late day snack.

Oliver was a big kid who just continued to grow, always the biggest in class. But he was somewhat gentle, more like a St Bernard.

He established himself as a school yard policeman by settling disputes quickly and rather easily. He was living near his school and had continuous access to all school sports, especially school yard basketball. In his freshman year, he had reached six foot-seven inches, 200 pounds, so this was his favorite sport. He proved to be an athlete, guiding Pace High School to the New York City High School Basketball Championship during his junior and senior years. He was in the top ten percent of his class so he easily qualified for college. With a university sports scholarship and Uncle Jordon's financial assistance, he went on to Hunter College where he entered the law, history, and government program. Within five years, at 24 years of age, he had completed the Juris Doctorate degree, passed the New York bar exam, and was invited to join his Uncle's New York congressional team in the House of Representatives in Washington, DC, to learn how law is practiced from the top down–by the big boys.

Capitol-Hill

Capitol-Hill is in the center of Washington, DC. It is at the crossroads of North and South Capitol Streets and East and West Capitol Streets. This is the point in the USA, the Capitol Building, where all legal drafts are converted into American federal laws. The south side locates the House of Representatives and north side houses the Senate. There are 14 government office buildings nearby. A 200 yard wide National Park area runs, from the long Capitol Building west, and ends at the Potomac River, approximately two miles. The Park contains the Washington Monument, the Lincoln and Jefferson Memorials, 11 of the 20 Smithsonian museums, and is bordered on the south by Independence Ave and on the north by Constitution Ave. The White House, just north and close to the Washington Monument, is connected to the Capitol Building, going east, by Pennsylvania Ave.

Immediately North of the Capitol Building are the Union Station, and the Hart, Russell, and Dicksen Senate Office Buildings. To the East are the Supreme Court Building, and the Library of Congress.

And to the South are the Cannon, Rayburn, and Longworth House Office Buildings. There are 100 Senators, one third elected every two years, serve six-year terms, and work in office suites, each with a congressional staff of 34 in the Senate Office buildings. 435 Members of the House of Representatives are elected every two years, serve those two years, and work in the House office suites, each with a congressional staff of 14 in the House Office Buildings. There are many committee and meeting rooms in the Capitol Building and the various Office Buildings. A final vote to declare a new law is taken in the Senate Chamber and House Chamber in the Capitol Building.

When Oliver first arrived in Washington to work for his Uncle Jordon Johnson, he found a one-bedroom rental condo just a couple of blocks south of the Rayburn House Office Building on E St SW, only a few blocks north of the Washington Nationals Baseball Park. This would be his home for several years, he hoped. Uncle Jordon was assigned a suite of offices in the Rayburn Building. He was one of a working staff of five. Each day he could easily walk to and from work. He even met some neat congressional staff members. Some became good friends. But like him, everyone was tethered to his continuously re-elected member of the House. He was lucky because of the three congressional districts in New York City area, Representative Uncle Jordon was elected from New York State District 3. In the same residential building, there were congressional aides with Congressmen from New York districts 7 and 9. So he immediately had other New Yorkers to work with and learn from.

House of Representatives

During his first years on Capitol-Hill, Oliver began as legislative assistant and advanced to senior legislative assistant. He took to law like a duck to water, did excellent work, and was liked and respected by all government and non-governmental members of Congress. As a junior house staffer, he had two types of duties and work. Congressional duties included daily communication with the Rep, his uncle; interactions with various levels of government personnel;

management of the Rep's daily schedule and travels; monitoring of developing and advancing new legislation in Congress; working with news media on articles, newsletters, and pre-publications; interacting with New York state and local government personnel where necessary; responding to voters' district town hall and community questions; organizing intra-staff management meetings; acceptance and carrying out special assignments for the Rep's Congressional work involved selective political research with regard to current congressional bills on route to becoming laws. For his research efforts he had access to the National Library of Congress, several million congressional manuscripts, all legislative government publications and books, the American Archives—plus unlimited on-line searches. He wrote and edited his own analysis of assigned projects.

There was no time for outside work. Ten to twelve hours a day, six to seven days a week, he was occupied in the office, on the Hill, or running here and there. He was Uncle Jordon's communicator. And he did not have time for friends. Many of them were there only two years anyway—their Rep was elected every two years just like his Rep. So, it was a very busy, and not a very warm atmosphere to live in. Government people came and went, rapidly. Only the non-political people, government employees, were there 'forever'.

Uncle Jordon was re-elected for a third and then a fourth two-year term, and of course Oliver continued to work with him and learn how life is controlled from on high. Physically all offices on Capitol-Hill were at a higher elevation than the offices in the White House or in the East or West Executive Office Buildings. Therefore, it is called on high. The concept was meant to remind the President that the members of Congress were also elected and were his 'equal'.

The current salary plus expenses for Senators were double that of the Representatives. Plus, the employment term was six years, not two. So, Uncle Jordon changed his mind and decided to run for and won the Senate seat from the New York City in the state of New York. Now at least six more years in the political money saddle, his motto was 'Keep your people happy and your business on the move.'

The Senate

The election road opened up for him two more times. The Honorable Jordon Johnson won a second and then a third six-year term from the New York district 3. He was already considered the New York 'Kingpin'. But he was determined to become the New York 'Emperor'. He now had many powerful friends in the New York business, corporate, banking and publishing world. And to those Senators who were close friends, but who had recently lost an election, he donated time and money to help them get re-elected. What are friends for? He liked all of them except those whom he did not like. Such was not law; it was called politics.

He became Head of the Senate Select Committee on Intelligence and a Senior Member of the Senate Committee on Foreign Relations. From this experience he was planning to develop a lawyer/lobbyist firm which focused on foreign trade, sanctions, and corporate enhancement. He would clandestinely monitor the Dow Jones (all 50 companies), S&P (select from the 500 countries), and NASDAQ (select from the techs). He personally would make the selections within the next 3-4 years. But, of course, he would keep his industrial friends in New York happy all the time.

Oliver had moved to the Senate with his Uncle and became legislative director, then Deputy Chief of Staff, and then Chief of Staff. But he had two major responsibilities—manage and coordinate the Senator's thirty-member legislative team; and with the help of two legislative assistants, conduct special research projects. So, he would need two offices. One in the assigned Russell Senate Office Building, in the Senator's suite of offices, just one block north and east of the Capitol Building. He was living nearby, on Maryland Ave NE near Stanton Park, in a nice three-bedroom townhouse, which he had purchased. In this way he could easily carry out both legislative responsibilities, which included research on American versus foreign industrial and high technology trade related to New York's major industries, plus the American military. Thus, he would spend one or two days a week at Fort Meade, Maryland, National Intelligence Agency, a half hour drive. The second office would be in his townhouse where he would carry out other 'quiet' work. Always work-work-work—Young Ladies—occasionally!

Major Industries in New York—

Oliver's routine work load put him in direct contact with the 'big boys' in New York. It was a good learning situation and he had an opportunity to meet and 'get to know' some of the sons and daughters of many of the top corporation managers and CEOs:

Finance, foreign trade, health care, real estate, mass media, journalism & publishing, manufacturing, information technology, textiles, electronics…

Best Companies/Corporations in New York -

His social status took a heavy shot upward as many of the CEO's sons grew up in private schools and had Ivy League educations. So, he had to continuously maintain a lower profile, even when he was taller, frequently smarter, but usually with much less money to throw around. Some of these sons were actually nice guys. He cultivated the more conservative ones and catalogued the more liberal ones – all for future use, including from:

Google, Goldman-Sachs, Ernst & Young, KPMG, Price-Waterhouse-Cooper, Accenture, Deloitte, Barnes & Noble, Citigroup, Mastercard, TIAA, Warner Media, Black Rock, Dow Jones…

The Future

So, Uncle Jordon now really considered Oliver as a son he would never have naturally. He had 'birthed' him, housed, and financially supported Oliver during most of his school and college days. He pushed him in the direction of law and politics, and carefully guided him on Capitol-Hill. He tried to involve Oliver in as many legal learning experiences as possible according to his legally titled position. Now that he was starting to plan toward retirement, he had to set it correctly. When he was gone, he wanted to include Oliver at the center of everything.

During the next few years, he would initiate a new series of evening private dinner parties at his Great Falls, Virginia mansion, located on the Potomac River overlooking the rock-rapids/water-falls. This was a popular suburb for 'successful' lawyers, retired Congressman, and lobbyists. He was going to 'interrogate' a variety of corporation presidents and CEOs who were 'members' of Wall Street. He was developing a list of men/women who had minimal scruples, if necessary, to eliminate the competition however necessary. He would not involve Oliver in this first quest. But in a couple of years, after he had made his pre-list, he would then introduce each of them to his 'successor-son' Oliver. In the meantime, Oliver would have many of the experiences of a part time Senator without having to be 'nice' to voters.

And Senator Jordon Johnson would continue to explore a new method for 'eliminating' industrial competition of clients that could pay the proper price. It was called a new type of high technology, nanotechnology. He had been watching this new science develop over the past few years. He spent considerable time with these nanotech scientists, learning what can and cannot be accomplished with these nanotech molecular systems. And he decided it would be a major player in Oliver's future and his legacy.

Nephew-son Oliver did not understand that his real inherited profession was going to be owning an invisible company that sold macabre death systems all over the world, but at very high profits. That he would inherit an infamous name Korrectorizer. And that the first death (assassination/murder) would be the Czar of American High Technology, whose son he would meet, head to head, only at life's end.

2

AFRICA?

The continent of Africa consists of five ancient Precambrian Cratons including West Africa, Kaapvaal, Congo, Tanzania, and Zimbabwe. These rock-mountain-valley formations resulted from many volcanos in komatiite thermotactic events. It all began around 3.5 to 2.0 billion years ago.

At the end of the Precambrian era, the African episode began 900 to 500 million years ago. This era produced several long-folded geological land belts—today's Mozambique, Democratic Republic of Congo and Zambia, Katanga, Angola and Gabon, West Congo, Ghana and Algeria, Dahomey and Azhagar, Senegal and Morocco, Maurita-ide, north Africa and Arabia, Arabia and the Nubian Shield.

After the Precambrian geologic history (500-200 million years ago), the African and European continental plates closed. This resulted in the formations of the Mediterranean Sea, Red Sea, Aegean Sea, and the shifting of the Arabian continental plate. The latter movements allowed the Kaapvaal and Zimbabwe Cratons to form with large deposits of gold, silver, diamonds, and valuable minerals.

The final shape, high and low lands, wet and dry lands, took place during the Paleozoic Era consisting of: Cambrian, Ordovician, Silurian, Devonian, Carboniferous, and Permian.

The first hominids (archaic humans) were determined to appear about 500,000 years ago. These hominids had a skull anatomy similar to the great apes, were bipedal, and had thumbed hands. They lived both in the gigantic forests and massive savanna areas. Most biologicals occurred at the same time—wild animals, wild plants, and all forms of food stocks.

About 2 million years ago the Australopithecine hominids lived through the southern, eastern, and central Africa. They were one of the first to use stone tools.

Homo habilis, nearly 3 million years ago, created a variety of farming tools and weapons, plus they raised small animals.

Less than 1.5 million years ago, the Homo erectus were taller, walked more upright, and used running speed in war and hunting, but were smaller brained.

Homo sapiens, 300,000 years ago, developed modern behavior patterns, family social systems, and had larger brains.

I. Five Ancient African Hominid Regions

Ancient Egypt – 3100 BCE (lower Nile River)

Nubia – 2500 BCE (upper Nile River)

The Sahel – Sahara Desert

Maghreb – north and north east Africa

Horn of Africa – easternmost peninsula of Africa

II. Ancient Egyptian-African Civilizations

1) Kingdoms of Egypt – 3150 – 332 BCE—

2) Early Dynasty Period – 3150 – 2686 BCE—

3) Old Kingdom – 2686 – 2200 BCE; 3rd through 6th dynasty;
    [Dynasty; genetic unit; Pharaoh=King=Head Priest= Commander of the army – for a man to become a Pharaoh one must be born within or marry into a genetic dynasty; only a Pharaoh has an afterlife.]
    [Gods; more than 2000 gods – RA was sun and creator God—Osiris was god of underworld—Isis was wife of Osiris and resurrected Osiris—Horus was sun god—Seth was god

of chaos and violence—Hathor was goddess of fertility and motherhood—Thoth was god of wisdom—Anubis was god of funerals and the dead]

[Pyramids; 118 pyramids – most were triangular shaped with steps, and constructed with stone such as limestone, granite, and basalt—interior had a few rooms—exterior had no windows or doors – west bank on Nile was favorite pyramid location due to relationship of setting sun and setting life.]

4) Middle Kingdom – 2055 – 1650 BCE; 11th & 13th dynasty; Thebes was capital city; Golden Age.

5) New Kingdom – 1550 – 1069 BCE; 18th through 20th dynasty; inadequate ruling during the 20th dynasty caused a major decline in power.—famous pharaohs including Ahmose I, Hatshepsut, Thutmose III, Ahmenhotep III, Thutankhamun, Akhenaten, and Ramses II.—famous Queens were Cleopatra I, Nefatari, and Hatshepsut.—first of many black pharaohs was King Pian, also King of Kingdom Nubia/Kush; Invasion by Persians and Greeks ended thousands of years of rule by the Egyptian Pharaohs; Imperial Age.]

6) Late Period – 664 – 332 BCE; continued military losses and decline.]

There were several reasons why the Egyptian Kingdoms/Empires lasted nearly 3000 years. The capital cities were physically in the center of the richest regions/areas of the Nile River. They had control of the southern Nile (cataracts and black Africa), northern Nile 15 rivers delta and the eastern Mediterranean Sea, vast Sahara Desert to the west, dominance of the desert regions of the Sinai Peninsula and Syria to the east, a most superior society with international traders, advanced school-able intellect, culture, artisans, and powerful military.

III. Kingdom of Nubia or Kush

The Nile River is the longest river in the world – 4,132 miles. It begins with the equatorial monosome rains near Lake Victoria, surrounded by and travels through the Democratic Republic of Congo, South Sudan, Tanzania, Uganda, Sudan, Kenya, and Ethiopia. The ancient Kingdom of Kush (2450-1455 BCE) surrounds the six cataracts of the Nile and had the city state of Karma as the capital. Cataract one is near Aswan, Egypt. Cataract six is near Khartum, Sudan. The Kingdom was physically located such to control transportation routes down the river (raw materials, ceramics, gold, emeralds, animal skins, ivory, cattle, sheep, and smoked wild game) to Egypt and Europe. While movement of manufactured goods (metal-iron agriculture tools and machinery, military weapons, chariots, wagons) manuvered up the river to the larger cities in central and southern Africa. The people were farmers, herders, and traders. Kings and Queens intermarried with the Kings and Queens of Egypt. Wars between the two empires were common and the dominance shifted depending upon the Kings and strength of the armies.

IV. Carthaginian Empire

Carthage was a Phoenician city-kingdom located in northern Africa (today's Tunisia) and was composed of Sicilians, Libyan Berbers, Italians, Celts, Iberians, Numidians, Nubians, and Black Africans. It was the most powerful kingdom on the West Mediterranean Sea between 810 and 140 BCE. Why? Because it occupied northern Africa and dominated the sea lanes between Malta, Sardinia, Corsica, Italy, Sicily, Gibraltar—the center of the Mediterranean. Carthage, with mixed populations, a government elected from clans of nobles, a selected King and Queen, developed the largest commercial, maritime, and politically stable system in the area. The city-kingdom had its commercial docks and a powerful army-naval base stationed inside a very large lake accessed only via a long, sea channel. Over the years, there were several wars with neighbors. In the third Punic War, the Roman army led by Publius Cornelius Scipio, with help from the

Masinissa army, defeated General Hannibal and his elephants. Scipio went on to destroy this major trading power and then the city of Carthage. Even, Tanit, the Goddess of Carthage who ruled the Sun, Stars, and Moon, and her consort Ba'al Hammon, the Sky God, plus the many other Carthaginian gods, could not prevent the complete destruction of the Kingdom.

V. Empire of Mali

The ancient Mali Empire was founded by Sundiata Keita in West Africa in 1220 CE and lasted until near 1600 CE. During the rule of Emperor (Mansa) Musa, this empire engulfed several neighboring kingdoms, amassed thousands of pounds of gold (probably the largest gold cache in the world ever), and had the largest land army on earth. Mansa Musa was considered to be the richest man in Africa.

At the peak of the Musa dynasty in 1330 CE, the empire included most of the 3600 mile long Niger River which involved Senegal, Mali, Mauritania, Benin, Gambia, Guinea, Niger, Burkina Faso, Nigeria, and several smaller provinces. It contained most of the west African gold mines, salt mines, and agriculture rich flood plains of the Niger River. The Mali Empire controlled land west from the Atlantic, north into the Sahara Desert, south and east to the equatorial rain forests.

Mansa Musa's dynasty controlled more than 500 cities, with 50 million people, 20,000 police force, an army of 100,000 men, and a cavalry of 15,000 horses. Most of the general population were Black Africans. The Mansa was the divine emperor, next came the royal family, then the priests, nobles, traders, farmers, teachers, griots, and slaves.

The great wealth of the Mansa of the Mali Empire came from gold, silver, diamonds, and salt mines dug by slaves, the large powerful army for land control, the large police forces for maintaining tax control, status as Caliph of Islam within the empire (religion was Islam and ancient religions combined).

Over the decades and generations, the Mansa family leaders became less competent and slowly lost the small wars and military power to their neighbors; the empire was slowly dismembered.

VI. Kingdom of Monomotapa and Mutapa Empire

Mwene Mutapa was a Shona tribal leader who began developing the Mutapa Empire in 850 CT which survived until the twentieth century in Zimbabwe. He started by building a stone city (totem) at Wedza in Marondera; and soon thereafter built what is now the famous ancient totem, recognized by UNESCO, the granite walled city of Great Zimbabwe, with his first son. This established a pattern whereby a series of capital city totems were built in six neighboring 'states or countries', each given to one of his children 'king-sons', and developed into a large family-like military totems grouping. The father Emperor controlled the land mass of all totems of all six sons, determined which son and family received which totem, and the sons paid an annual tribute of five large granite stones, 100 cattle, 10 elephant ivory tusks, and a 10% share of taxes on the local trade routes. The father Emperor prayed to Mwari, a god who was agriculture oriented and who controlled the irrigations and rain making systems of the region.

The Mutapa royal families maintained a standing army of over 100,000 men and the capacity to rapidly mobilize an additional 300,000 men. Such a family arrangement allowed the Emperor to monitor/control trade on all land routes within several thousand square miles, horses-camels, cattle-goat-sheep breeding and marketing, elephant ivory sales and movement to the Arab territories, plus valuable minerals such as salt, copper, gold and silver. It covered a land mass of several thousand miles in Zambia, Zimbabwe, Botswana, Tanzania, Malawi, Angola, and Mozambique.

When the millennium crusades in Jerusalem ended in total victory for Moslems, many peoples in the middle east and east Africa turned to Islam, either totally or shared with local ancient tribal religions. Thus did the Mutapa royal families and their followers adopted Islam. Even though the several Kingdom totems were 'genetic', by now there was extensive intermixing of the many uncles, aunts, cousins, grand-offspring, etc. Not all relatives loved each other in the same way nor to the same extent. Hence, introduction of the Moslem male brotherhood helped minimize major disagreements and maintained a stable multi-headed military, therefore a stable 'income' system through the Mutapa empire.

European colonization entered Africa during 12th to 14th centuries. The Rozvi Empire developed from several Mutapa totems on the Zimbabwe Plateau around 1650 CE. Rozvi means warrior nation-kingdom-empire.

The Catholic Portuguese settled into several coastal towns along the Indian Ocean. From here they attempted to colonize the African kingdoms as they were interested in the Rozvi gold mines. King Changamire Dombo and his son Kambgun Dombo fought several battles with the Portuguese military, defeated them each time, and drove them from the Zimbabwe Plateau. The magical powers of King Changamire also helped the Rozvi to defeat the Portuguese in other Shona kingdom areas.

The Rozvi did recruit some technology from foreigners. Such new ideas and methods included enhanced animal hybrid breeding, maximized sorghum and millet corn planting, unique polychrome pottery, development of new war weapons such as solid shields, long bow and arrows, and imported foreign guns. They bred chickens, sheep, goats, and cattle; and experimental interbreeding with camels and with horses. Hunted elephant and rhinoceros, and sold the ivory to Arabs and Indians. Used semi-slaves to mine gold and copper. The armies had excellent military strategists. And the senior leaders developed extensive international trade relations with the Arabs and Indians.

However, during the eighteenth and nineteenth centuries, just as the Dumbo families broke away from the Mutapa families, so did the many 'genetic' kingdoms and empires begin to separate; colonization moved in.

VII. Zulu Empire

Shaka Zulu was the legitimate son of the Ruler of the Zulus, Senzangakona. In 1802 CE he and his mother were exiled, found refuge with his uncle Mthethwa, and fought under Dingiswayo who was chief of the Metetwa. He proved to be an outstanding warrior and was chosen as the new leader-chief of the many Zulu tribes in south east Africa. Over the years he proved superior, developed a powerful Zulu land army, and developed a strong Zulu Kingdom. In 1823 CE Shaka was assassinated by his half-brother, Dingane. This brother appointed himself Ruler-King-Emperor, and killed all of the other brothers and sisters. He continued over the next several years to build a military oriented Zulu Empire.

In 1837 CE the Dutch Voortrekkers signed a treaty with Dingane and settled on land between the Mzimvubu River and Tugala River. During the treaty celebration dance the Zulu attacked and massacred all of the foreigners. Two years later the Dutch recruited and obtained more European foreigners. Mpande, Dingane's youngest half-brother, who had gone into exile, returned, killed Dingane and became the next Zulu King. A new treaty with the English was established.

In 1852 CE, Cetshwayo, Mpanda's son, began a series of wars, in five different locations, in what was called Zululand. In 1879 CE, Cetshwayo's army defeated the English army at Isandhwana. (This battle is considered to be the classic Zulu defeat of a modern European army.) Two years later, Queen Victoria increased the English forces and the two armies, in several battles, fought to a draw. Politically the Zulu people were then separated into thirteen different kingdoms. The English, with nearby Voortrekkers, Boer mercenaries, one or two Zulu kings and their armies, battled the Zulu armies of Dinuzulu, Cetshwayo's son and now King. The Zulu lost. They were again separated into several 'Zulu kingdoms', as established by the colonists. This continued until the beginning of the Republic of South Africa.

Elsewhere, European colonies spring up all over the maps of Africa in the 19th century.

3

BAYLESA, NIGERIA

The little white goat with big black spots came flying down the small rocky hillside, over the big rocks, through the creek, and into a doorless small wood posted fenced area. He headed directly for the plastic pan of food and started gobbling away. One second later a bare footed and naked little black girl pulled up behind him, scolded him, and pulled his tail. Mali, the girl, took his plastic pan of food, turned, and walked away. Two steps later, she went flying into the air. Airy, the goat, had taken revenge as he butted her down, grabbed the pan with his teeth, and took off toward the creek. She popped up and took off after him. But he was faster and was across the creek before she could even reach the water. Would he get away with his food? Three bare footed and naked little black boys were laughing and betting who would win—girl or goat.

Little Ji said, "I will bet 7 pepsi bottle caps." Dako said, "I bet 6 cocola bottle caps as they are worth more than pepsi." And Biti responded, "I have 5 bud-light caps which are worth the most. I bet all of them."

And three little boys were up and had joined the chase over the creek, rocks, and into the forest. Airy had such a lead that probably -no one was going to catch him or win the bet. The smart little rascal was up the rocky forested trail, over a group of large boulders, and out of sight before any of the four could even get to the beginning of the rock climb.

Biti shouted, "You come back Airy or we will never give you any food again, ever."

Suddenly Airy stuck his head out from behind a boulder and said, "BAAAA."

Little Ji laughed and chastised Biti, "Dummy. Don't you know that goats eat everything. Remember he ate your flips last month."

Suddenly there was a series of noises back at the doorless fenced-in area. Airy's two black and white brothers had sneaked into the corner and were eating the spilled food. The boys hurried back to try to catch them. No luck. One went over the fence and the other under the fence and they were both gone before the boys got close enough to even grab a hair. Most African villages were designed with little goats that were faster than little boys or girls. It was fun and games when there was nothing else to do.

But the fun was finished. Mother called out, "Come here, all of you, now", she hollered. And they forgot the goat and came running to her.

Mother, in her bright colored long tent dress, gave out a series of orders to each. "Mali, tonight is October 15, the celebration of the Virgin Festival and I need to prepare certain foods to take to the village center. The entire village will be there, more than 319 people. Go to the garden and bring to me 20 yams, 15 cassava, and 30 small maize. Soon as you return, we will begin to prepare these three foods as they are our contribution. Run and bring the two large kettles. Fill them with water. We will prepare the roots and place the yams in the large kettle and the cassava in the smaller one. The maize will go into the oven later."

"Dako, take the two plastic water jugs and the small wagon, go to the village well, fill the jugs with water, return here and pour the water into our large plastic storage container. Make as many trips as is necessary and completely fill the container. We will need much water for cooking. Start now. When finished with that, light the cooking fires; both the open outdoors roast pit and the clay oven. Then go to the village center and help the older boys round up the plastic tables and chairs from the village huts and carry them to the festival area. There will be someone there to show you how to arrange them in a large circle around the village center. Just be sure that the smaller children's tables are near the serving tables. Children will eat at 6:00, adults at 7:00, and the festival will start at 8:00. Let us help get things ready. Let us go now!"

"Little Ji, go to the village shed, fill the cattle cart with straw and two buckets of oats and take it to the animal corral near our hut, and give the evening feeding to the cattle. It is our turn today."

"Biti, run over to Godwin's house, and ask his mother if she has any chili pepper and peanut powder. I need a bottle of each. Tell her I will pay her back, someday."

And she laughed. When did the villagers ever pay back 'borrowed' foods to neighbors?

"And then go to Uncle Odumegwu's place and ask him how many bottles of his beer does he have available for tonight. I know some of the men will want beer. And then tell me if there is not enough. I will send you to a neighboring village to get some more. We will need around 30-40 bottles."

Biti interrupted. "I saw a strange truck coming to the village from Lagos. The driver unloaded several boxes of dates for the special dessert tonight. If we do a good job, can we have extra pieces? We only get to eat dates at this Osun Festival night, once a year."

The village owned one small truck and two midi-buses to take villagers to neighboring bazaars on Tuesdays and Thursdays, and to bring special produce or building supplies from the larger cities in the area. Plus, there were five privately owned cars. So, the children knew all village vehicles.

"Yes. Now all of you get going, hurry!"

And 4 preschool children immediately went four different directions to obey their orders. If they should falter, each previously had bad experiences with the willow branch. It was not something one wanted to un-forget.

The village was composed of approximately eighty various sized block walls/roof thatched huts, each had grand-parents attending babies in occupancy. There were numerous paths and two dirt roads, one leading from east and the other from west, and both ending in the village center which is nearly three acres in size. There was one deep well on each side of the center area. Several small and large garden areas, plus five cattle, cow, and pig animal lots were located just inside the circumference fence which was composed of tree branches and thorny berry plants. Thus, the animals and edible garden crops were both protected from wild animals. The festival would be held in the center of the village. The entire village was filled with many trees, especially walnut and pecan trees. These were excellent for shade and as edible and commercial crops. Near the village center were huts of the tribal chief and the jujuman/witch doctor.

The village women wore brightly colored long loose dresses and were responsible for the small kitchen gardens, meals, house, and children. Younger men usually went outside the village seeking jobs such that they could bring home a little money. Boys and older men tended the cattle, pigs, and milk cows, larger areas of commercial crops such as maize and cassava, maintenance of village structures, accompanied village girls and women when they went into the wild seeking berries, nuts, mushrooms, and food spices, and then they looked forward to and highly sought once a week hunting excursions. The hunt was a reward for the best working boy of the week. The area was filled with good hunting such as water buffalo, black duiker, antelope, deer, and wild pig. It was also loaded with many predatory animals as bili apes/giant chimpanzee, civet cat, leopard, cheetah, lions, and bonobo.

With such a wealth of nature, a carefully designed village structure, cooperation and share in the work load, Tumba village was certainly one of the best in Nigeria.

Nearly five hundred miles north is the Osun Osgogbo Sacred Grove. It is a sacred forest land on the banks of the Osun River near the city of Osogbo, Osun State, Nigeria. It is the last of the sacred forests which adjoin the edges of the Yoruba cities before extensive urbanization begins. In recognition of its international value, it is inscribed as a UNESCO World Heritage Site. Each year in August, the Osun Osogbo Festival is celebrated as a cultural reunion by thousands of ancestors of the Osogbo Kingdom.

The history is as follows. A large group of migrating people, led by a great hunter named Olutimenin, was being pursued by an army of head-hunters. As they arrived on the banks of the Osun river they had run out of food and famine had begun. At the river side, Osun, the Supreme River Goddess, came to Olutimenin and told him she would save them. Follow. They followed. She saved them. Therefore, today there are thousands of Osun People and many international tourists who attend the Osun Osgogbo Festival.

The Festival is held annually from October 10 to 15. It celebrates the continuation of the Osun culture and focuses on the arts. It includes singing, dancing, drumming, playing of historical musical instruments, wearing of elaborate colorful costumes, speaking in the various Yoruba tongues, recitation of stories and sagas of the past, recitation of popular poetry, and the introduction of famous Osun People who played a role in preserving Osun history, both those who had passed away and those who were still struggling to maintain an Osun existence in Africa, and one that has more than 4,000 tribes and ethnic groups.

The people of Tumba, Beylesa State, are direct descendants of the Osun People. Their interpretation of African history concludes that they are here on earth because their ancestors were saved by Osun, the Supreme River Goddess. They cannot afford to perform a multi-day festival, but they can honor her with an October 15, single day-evening celebration, a large dinner festival, prayers by an official Osun Priest, and the selection and crowning of a young village virgin for the night.

The dinner, singing, dancing, reading of Osun poems and narrating history using the 'old' language, and renewal of their hereditary linkages allowed the villagers to feel the spirits of their ancestors.

—The Festival was so popular it could have continued another day or more. However, the next day there was very little noise. There was a very terrible stench in the air coming from inside the village, and the sky was filled with vultures. No one was moving—man, woman, or child.

WHY?

4

TRIPOLI, LIBYA

Tripoli is the capital and major city of Libya. It is both a Mediterranean seaport and an international land trade center on the north-west coast of Africa, near Tunisia and Algeria. The old city harbor is over two thousand years old and has been conquered and occupied by the Romans (Marcus Aurelius Triumph Arch - 163 CE), Spanish (Red Castle - 1589), Ottomans (Eyalet of Tripolitania -1540), the Arabs (mosque of Gurgi - 1845), and lastly became an Italian colony in 1912. It became an independent country in 1942. The new city outside the old walled bay area has expanded in all directions into the desert. During the past 50 years historic renovation has been extensive and the new city has grown into a four million mega pseudo-modern city.

Modern Tripoli has a major downtown area of official government and tall private buildings, banks, hotels, royal palaces, national and international stores, high tech businesses, high rise residences and condos, and choice restaurants. Center city houses the University of Al-Fatah, University of Libya, the Al-Manar University, several research centers, and the national archives. The suburbs are massive with tech manufacturing, import-export companies, vehicle assembly stations, sprawling shopping centers, factories, and food centers. Housing areas are connected to all.

The Libyan economy depends basically upon natural gas and petroleum. It is a member of OPEC. Most of the reserves are located in south and east in the desert. Libya is 10th in the world in oil and 21th in natural gas reserves. Most of this is regulated and shipped from the north-easternmost city, Benghazi. Government and private sales may be controlled by the Tripoli government in the east; and numerous military outposts in the gas-petroleum regions are under the command of the central government. Libya also has large reserves of iron deposits, gypsum, and silica.

Libya has a solid economy, good relations with most European countries, and special petroleum treaties with Italy and France.

Leilah Shennibi was shopping in the old bazaar shopping center, when a teenage boy grabbed her shoulder bag and ran. She hollered, "Stop Thief!"

But the boy was too fast and took off down a nearby alley. He turned a corner and threw the bag to another boy who went a different direction. In 20 steps the second boy turned right and threw the bag to a third boy who was 10 feet off the ground on a building fire escape ladder. This fellow quickly climbed up two flights to the top of building, hid behind a low wall, sat down, and dumped the contents of the bag on the floor in front of him. He searched through everything, looked and found a fat billfold, silver wrist watch, two gold bracelets, a packet of credit cards, a smart card with one end for car and one end for house, two cosmetic kits, several pieces of clothing and head-scarfs, and other nothings. He looked through the billfold. He then took a handful of American dollars and euros, plus the silver wristwatch and the two gold bracelets. Nothing else was of value. He let out a string of curses, put everything else back into the bag, and threw it down the nearby chimney. He then took off to join his gang buddies at their nearby abandoned garage headquarters. Not good, but not bad. The wealthy looking richly dressed middle age bitch was not as rich as they thought when she had been targeted.

At the Zumurrud Shopping Center, near the Kahdra Hospital in Tripoli, Libya, Leilah and her two friends, Aysha and Khadja, were describing to the policeman the teenage boy who stole Leilah's shoulder bag. Two police had run after the boy but found no one in the alley network where he ran. Ten minutes of looking up and down several side streets revealed that it was a 'perfect' street robbery. They had escaped with the shoulder-bag in hand. A very common occurrence in Tripoli.

Leilah and her friends were shopping for Leilah's daughter's wedding in three days, on October 15. Two boys had grabbed a child in a stroller, pretended to kidnap the child, ran only a few yards pushing the stroller with child. When the mother yelled, they dropped the pretense, left the child, and ran off. While the ladies were distracted, another boy grabbed the shoulder bag and took off. Yes. A 'perfect' street robbery.

They spent 15 to 20 minutes of explaining and arguing about what happened with the police. Finally, the three 'upper class' ladies told the police where to go. Leilah hit a button on her cell phone and in one minute her chauffeur drove up in the limousine, stopped beside the three of them, helped each into the car, gave a fifty American dollar bill to the police to enjoy later, got in the car and headed to their house in Massjed, a distant Tripoli suburban village, 20 miles away. When they got there, they would just go to the pool, have a cocktail, and forget the bad event. Each had experienced such 'perfect' street robberies during their lifetime in Tripoli. It was not a new experience. These kids were well organized.

An hour later they reached their village of Massjedi. As they drove through the 12-foot tall steel gates, past the 12-foot high concrete wall, and toward the Shennibi mansion's front courtyard, Aysha and Khadja looked up. They were good friends with Leilah, but had not often been to her house. It always amazed them. It was Arab modern, with white stucco concrete, three and four floors, more than 10,000 sq. ft., red-brown tile roof, all window and door frames had semi-circle tops and the wall trim was bright red, 4 functional chimneys, and many tall picture windows. Inside there were 12 bedrooms, 10 baths, 5 living rooms/salons/sports rooms, 2 food preparation rooms with 3 walk-in freezers/refrigerators, 3 patios and terraces, one swimming pool, and Turkish rugs or ceramic tile on floors and walls. One salon was a salamlik, wall-side couches with several copper coffee tables, ash trays, and long-stemmed smoking pipes—a man's domain. The third floor housed the living space for 5 servants.

The Shennibi family inherited 90% of one of the largest oil companies in Libya. They were currently still living on a major portion of 'their' land. So, there was plenty of money and this wedding would be luxury plus at the mansion. Commonly, weddings in Libya were held in government buildings with government certified marriage officials. But with special 'arrangements', weddings can take place in private buildings/hotels, or homes. This wedding will be very private at the highly secured Shennibi mansion. Several high-level government officials, Libyan corporate Presidents and CEOs, oil company friends and partners, wealthy businessmen, and several Ambassadors—American, French, and Italian-will attend; and of course, spouses. There will be 55 wedding guests. Plus, an Italian 7-people band that can play modern and classical music.

An hour after the ladies entered the house, changed into sun or bathing suits, depending on the shape of the body, they met at the pool, indulged in late afternoon cocktails, and started discussing wedding arrangements.

Leilah asked, "So what do you think about having the 10 tables for six each scattered here around the pool area. A couple of times in the past we have successfully held dinner parties for more than 50 people. So, if we are careful, we should be able handle 60. I hope."

Aysha said, "Where will you put the band?"

"It will go up there on the small deck-patio area above the far end of the pool."

"And the servants will bring plates of food and take empty plates using that side of the house. Right?" Inquired Khadja. "Any serving food at the tables?"

"A little," Leilah replied. "Several serving tables for side dishes and desserts will be over there." And she pointed to the left.

"What are you going to serve?"

"The Tripoli Grand Royal Foods will cater the entire dinner, including drinks and desserts. Let me see."

She opened her cell phone, tapped her file for wedding foods, and read off from the list.

"The main courses will be, as appropriate, lamb, chicken, fish, and egg."

"For example: lamb casserole, carrots, green olives – Tajine Sfinari Bil Zaytun; Morrocan chicken and almond pie – Bastilla; fried fish with mashed spiced potato filling – Mbatan Kawali; poached eggs in spicy tomato olive sauce-Shakshouka."

"One side table will provide short dishes of couscous, asida, shorba, bureek, filfel, chume, rishda, and several flat breads. Another side table will have desserts such as swirl bread, brie cheese, baklava, hasboosa, and super chocolate truffles confections.—Now that is super delicious, so we ordered extra servings of it."

"And a large side table will have extra drinks of water, red and white wines, and several fruit juices. Because alcohol is not allowed in Libya, and some of our guests are religious and prefer that men and women eat separately, we have tried to provide separate eating tables to accommodate these. Some women, who will wear the hijab, may want to eat separately from men, and of course not consume anything alcoholic. Not a problem for the foreigners, but several of our oil rich brethren must also be made comfortable also. So??'

"We have had this experience of mixing and matching the sexes within the religions, or is it religions within the sexes. I always get confused!"

And the three ladies were getting more and more excited with the wedding drawing closer. It was Leilah's youngest daughter—marriage then babies she hoped. The bridegroom was the son of a Libyan Senator, and was maneuvering to replace his father in the near future. He would need children very soon for political purposes. The other two older girls were both in college and would probably not produce grandchildren soon. But the new husband was conservative and did want many children. So, this one was probably a good first chance for a baby. Leilah was approaching forty-one, and that was Libyan female old.

Khadja interrupted Leilah's day dreaming, "How are you going to move all of that food to the guests at the tables and collect all those dirty dishes and…"

Leilah raised her hand, "We have done this before. We use one waiter per table, one waiter per side table, and 3 extra waiters for general assistance and for emergencies. That totals 18 people moving food to and from 60 guests. It will work."

And Aysha spoke up, "What about security? With all of those very important people, plus the ambassadors—HA HA—you will need a small army inside and outside the walls."

Leilah assured her friends, "Yes, we have been there. There will be one private security, armed, for every two guests—30. OK?"

The two friends thought about all of this careful planning. After a minute of exchanging looks with each other, laughed, and then gave her their permission to 'carry on'.

October 15 came and went. Indeed, the wedding and exclusive high-profile party went smoothly. All guests came, enjoyed the cuisine, music, and the heart-warming joining of a handsome couple who were both truly Libyan. They thanked the Shennibi family for sharing the evening with then, and around midnight returned to their homes.

The next morning, most of the night's guests, were in their homes, but did not wake up. Bodies were warm, but their beds gave off a dreadful odor. From the Shennibi mansion, where all was quiet, a horrible smell rose into the air, and numerous vultures circled the building.

WHY?

5

CASABLANCA, MOROCCO—OPEC

Morocco is an Arab African country. It did not export enough oil to qualify to join OPEC. But it did have enough political leverage with certain Arab members of OPEC, to hold this meeting for the world's dominant oil exporting countries on October 13 and 14. The meeting would take place in Casablanca with its spectacular views of the Atlantic Ocean, extensive Moslem history, and the largest mosque in Africa. Many of the OPEC countries declared it was time to hold this special meeting concerning high technology competition from renewable energy sources such as sun-solar, air movement and winds, ocean waves and tides, extraterrestrial sonic waves, biomass, and geothermal. Some of these Sustainable Energy Systems were already here and the others were just around the corner. They needed to learn more about them.

The Secretariat and Headquarters of the Organization of Petroleum Exporting Countries was located in Vienna, Austria. It comprised the Office of the Secretary General, Chief Executive Officer, Legal Office, Research Division, and Support Services Division. It was organized in Geneva, Switzerland in 1961, but moved to Vienna in 1965, where it currently functions.

Current member countries are Algeria, Angola, Congo, Equatorial Guinea, Gabon, Iran, Iraq, Kuwait, Libya, Nigeria, Saudi Arabia, and United Arab Emirates; Venezuela. Ecuador, Indonesia, and Qatar are lapsed members. However, all current and lapsed members were invited to discuss the new challenges to their, and for some, total income sources. Most countries accepted, but some did not understand the need.

In late afternoon of October 12, two OPEC executives from the Research Division were comfortably enjoying a cocktail in the bar and lounge of the Vichy Celestins Spa Hotel in Casablanca, Morocco. The five-star hotel had 150 rooms/suites all of which were directly on the ocean side and had spectacular views of the Atlantic Ocean. It was being closed down, for security purposes, for the next two days, specifically to house this special OPEC meeting. There would be 40 plus attendees from 12 countries, and several guest speakers. Security was under the control of the Moroccan military.

Fahad bin Abdullah Almubarak from Saudi Arabia, and Saeed Mohammed Al Muhairbi from United Arab Emirates, had just arrived and met to review the two-day program. The two gentlemen were in their fifties, had been educated in Oxford and Cambridge, England, respectively. They were in 'close' contact with their countries political systems. Fahad and Saeed had known each other for several years while working at the OPEC Headquarters. They were each at the top of their management ladders as executive program directors. This important special meeting that was being held outside of the OPEC's annual Executive Meeting was unusual. It was labeled as research. They would have to be careful—politically.

Fahad had just finished explaining how his second son's last soccer match was a 'beauty'. He had scored the winning goal that let the Saudis beat the Egyptians in a three country play off for qualification in next summer's world cup. Saeed only had two daughters so he had little to say. Moslem girls rarely play sports even when growing up in a Christian country. The smallest one was an excellent gymnast, but there was fear about play back if she participated in national or international competition. So, Saeed's family were on hold when it came to girls' sports.

"Girls sporting activities are, among many, 'modernizations' that we need on the peninsula (Saudi peninsula)," spoke Saeed.

"I agree," replied Fahad. "We need many such 'modern' changes. But we have to very careful to whom we make such suggestions. You remember big Ali, he let his wife get a driver's license in Vienna. That was not the problem. It was when she was seen driving the car of a former so-called friend in the Headquarters building. Word circulated and he was sent home to a much lesser management job, out in the desert boondocks. And his friend moved up to his position in Vienna. Sometimes you can get by with talking the wrong, but you can never do the wrong."

And they both chuckled, but with frowns on their faces.

Saeed asked, "Because you are Boss 1 and I am Boss 2, you tell me if you think we are ready for this venture."

"Yes and no," answered Fahad. "If I understand correctly there are some member countries that are considering adding other types of energy sources to their consumption or exports. I am talking about the recyclable energy that we will hear about at this meeting. Plus, some countries who have only 20 to 30 year reserves also want to know what is out there that they might consider as a supplement in the near future. Only those countries that have 50 to 100 year reserves are not interested and are not even coming to the meeting. I think that will become obvious as the meeting progresses. But you and I should be careful when we write our meeting reports; we should not highlight such possibilities."

"I agree," commented Saeed. "My observations tell me similar things. I have a political problem with one of my senior countrymen who is also aware of this and has started taking a stand against 'supporting recyclable energy. Talking about such future energy systems is risky, but supporting them is not a wise thing to do from our employment point of view."

Suddenly a group of meeting participants came into the bar area, so the two executives stopped talking about difficult problems, stood up, and went over to welcome everyone. This was a first and probably only time such a meeting would be sponsored by OPEC, so most of the participants did not know each other. One of the 'hidden' purposes that Fahad and Saeed had in mind was to explore current ideas in the recyclable energy field, plus to also bring together like minded members of OPEC. Everyone was staying, dining, and living in the same hotel for two days. Personal communications should happen in a positive way, they hoped. There should be open exchange of ideas and information concerning all aspects of energy.

The following morning everyone met to open the meeting at 9:00 AM, in the conference room. Fahad and Saeed introduced themselves and explained the meeting format. Today, October 13, morning for exploring recyclable energy systems; afternoon at 2:00

PM, for a little sightseeing. Tonight, at 8:00 PM, a general mixer in the roof restaurant-bar while watching the sun set over the Atlantic Ocean. Tomorrow, October 14, at 9:00 AM, morning for looking at additional recyclable energy systems. In the afternoon after 2:00 PM, if appropriate, small group discussions with speakers, and/or more sightseeing. Meeting officially closes at 5:00 PM.

The first speaker was Professor Walter Wilkens from the MIT in Boston, USA. His topic is to review currently pursued energy sources on/in the earth's systems which can be tapped for human usage.

Dr. Wilkins: "I will briefly focus on the concepts in global energy demand and energy supply. Energy demand is constantly increasing and will continue to do so because of increased world population, increased industrialization, and increased demand for 'comfortable' living and working conditions. We will consider two major types of energy supply—limited or non-recyclable such as petroleum, gas, and coal; and the many types of recyclable energy such as solar, geothermal, hydro, wind/air, nuclear, biomass, hydrogen fuel cells, and extraterrestrial sonic waves. Regardless of powerful thinking or wishing or praying or whatever magic you try to use, the non-recyclable energy supply will diminish with time. Some estimates suggest that these forms of energy will not be available in 50 to 100 years for our great grandchildren. So, if not for yourself, think of your offspring.

The general area of the measurement of the various energy supply areas and the making of energy comparisons is difficult. It is confusing because we use British thermal units, kilowatts, kilocalories, short-long-metric tons, and volumes/weight such as different sized barrels, cubic feet or cubic meters, gallons or kiloliters. And comparing electricity production from oil versus coal versus nuclear versus wind/air versus biomass is very difficult…"

The next speaker was Professor Mikael Hageskog, from Uppsala University, Uppsala, Sweden.

"My topic to discuss is solar energy. The sun was here first. Using the Bible for reference or your common sense, the sun had to be here first. Why? All plants and microorganisms that have chloroplasts and copper carrying electron systems require the sun for life and growth. Plants convert CO_2 to O_2, and use the C atoms to produce sugar/cellulose. Therefore 95% of the earth's oxygen is produced by green plants. Today, if the sun suddenly disappeared, so also would life on this earth. So, life to human beings comes from the sun, not food."

"Many early civilizations used the sun's heat for winter heating and plant extract preparations for food and medicines. Today we have constructed solar panels which are made of monocrystalline silicon, polycrystalline silicon, or thin films of crystalline silicon which can be installed anywhere that the sun shines directly on them. The silicon atom is #14 on the chemical periodic tables which allows it to capture and move its electrons to one another, using the sun's energy, and so create a direct current of electricity. A converter changes this direct current (DC) to alternating current (AC). And AC is the electricity used by all electrical systems in the world. Twenty years ago, the solar panels retail costs were about $500 each. Today the panels retail costs are about $50 each. And it is projected that the retail prices will continue to decrease. Hence in twenty years there was a decrease of %90; in the future it is expected to decrease probably another %30-50. Tough competition, and no rental fees for using the sun…"

The third speaker was Professor Gijs van den Heuvel, University of Leiden, Leiden, Netherlands.

"I will talk about a hydro-energy system that we employ in large quantity in our small country, because nearly half of the land mass is below sea level. I am certain that many of you cannot even imagine this. But if you have a shoreline on an ocean or large water mass, sea or bay, with vigorous waves or large tides, this energy system might be worth knowing."

"Our hydro-system uses a structure called a barrage. This barrage is installed across an inlet from an ocean, bay, or sea which forms a land side tidal basin. It is similar to a bridge in that the tidal water goes underneath into the basin. Every 100 meters the barrage has vertical towers which are electricity generating turbines. The towers have under water directly attached wind mills, or water mills, whose wheels rotate by water flow not wind flow. Sluice gates control entry and exit of tidal water, with the incoming and outgoing of the tides. Thus, the tides, from either direction, turn the wheels and can produce electricity. These are large wind/water mill systems. The propeller blades may be 30-50 feet in diameter"

"In addition, there are tidal fences which are similar but smaller. These hydro fences have smaller capacities for small bay or tidal basin areas. The wheels have propeller blades 10-20 feet in diameter…"

"The underwater turbine is similar to the system in dams placed on rivers which also use water flow through an electromagnetic generating system…"

After a twenty-minute tea/coffee/pastry break the conference continued.

The next speaker was Professor Kelde Nielsen, Technical University of Denmark, Copenhagen, Denmark.

"My area of renewable energy coverage is wind and windmill systems, very easy and very cheap. Not so! Windmills are thousands of years old, and there are many types, each specialized for certain purposes. I will explain."

"Wind is created when there is unequal heating-cooling of the earth's surface. Wind turbines convert the kinetic energy of the wind into mechanical action or electricity. One such mechanical action is the pumping of water. A system used by early civilizations such as the Persians and Egyptians. Or more recently it is used directly to produce electricity, which the entire world now uses extensively. The latter system uses the electromagnetic forces within the rotating general fin parts inside the turbine. The electricity is then immediately sent away from the turbine to be immediately used or stored in a battery system. Hence, wind energy is used directly as mechanical or electrical energy or stored. It does not cause pollution like all of the petrochemical energy sources."

He let that settle for several few seconds. Then he followed with, "Many countries, such as China and the United States, both partially energy co-dependent, use wind mill systems. If you drive through the north-central areas or farming regions of America and you will see wind mills everywhere. Just like driving through south-central America and you will see oil derricks and wells everywhere, which require electricity to function. Someday, the oil derricks and wells will have dissappeared, but the wind mills will always be there. Wind is a non-polluting, recycling energy source that will forever be available to us…"

After Dr. Neilson finished his presentation, Fahad announced, "We can now go into the dining room where they are waiting for us, order your lunches, and in one hour we will meet in the front lobby. For those who want to do a little sightseeing, we have a military secured bus ready to take us to two military cleared locations, the Hassan II Mosque on the ocean seashore, and shopping in the Marakesh souqs. We will then return to the hotel and the evening is yours to choose— dinner and the cocktail lounge on the ocean terrace will be open all evening. Tomorrow we will begin the next series of very informative sessions at 9:00 AM. Thank you and enjoy your short tourism journey."

Two hours later, 36 of the 42 attendees and speakers were standing in front of the Hassan II Mosque and staring at the magnificent white 20 floor building as the tour guide organized the group in a circle around him. Ali spoke loudly so all could hear above the sound of the ocean waves slapping against the nearby rocks.

"The Hassan II Mosque is the largest mosque in Africa and the tenth largest in the world. Its minaret is the world's second tallest minaret at 210 meters or 210 stories tall. The entire structure is totally built with hand carved stone, marble, and wood, and sits on an outcrop which juts out over the ocean. The flooring is a mosaic marble tile design, while the ceiling is of a mosaic inlay of light and dark cedar wood. The interior walls are of several different patterns of pink granite stone and various colors of light and dark cedar wood. Intricately designed interior gates are brass and titanium. And the many ablution fountains are shaped like huge lotus flowers made of hand-carved white and pint marble. The inside allows 25,000 worshipers, while an additional 75,000 worshipers may pray on the outdoor courtyards overlooking the ocean. During certain hours, Non-Moslems are allowed to tour the interior. Arms, legs and heads must be covered."

So, tour guide Ali led them inside such that they could see a magnificent Arab designed building, one which won many international architectural awards. Once inside, several of the meeting participants went to the prayer area on the south-east side of the mosque. They later re-joined the group to again play tourist. An hour later they climbed back into the bus and went shopping.

The Souqs/Souks of Marrakesh in Casablanca is the largest shopping area in Morocco and is composed of numerous alley ways and small streets packed with market stalls which are used by locals and tourists. Merchants purchase and sell everything such as clothes, fabrics, carpets, leather goods, foods, spices, pottery, jewelry, tobaccos, and numerous products which are typical Moroccan products. The limitless souks are divided into various professions where products are simultaneously made and sold, such as basket makers, hardware-metal workers, jewelers, bakers, dessert/sweets confectioners, carpet makers, knives and swords, and more. There are no price tags. The cost of an item is by bargaining and haggling. Rule of thumb is— always counter-offer 1/4 to 1/3 what the vendor wants for an item. If you are not really serious, it can be fun, and cheap.

A couple hours later all had returned to the bus, to the hotel, to the dining room, to the cocktail bar, and went to sleep looking at the mass of stars over the dark ocean.

October 14, 9:00 AM, Saeed looked over the conference room, counted some heads and decided a majority of the group had survived the night and were in attendance, so he decided to begin the last group of talks, first on Sustainable Energy Systems. The next speaker was Professor Dubois Aurand, University Mines Paristech, Paris, France.

"My talk will involve the center of the earth's liquid molten core— geothermal energy. Geothermal energy is simply energy associated with the heat in the earth's center or core. We are currently developing more efficient ways to use this heat as it will be here as long as the earth is here. It is 'forever' as the sun is 'forever.' There are many areas near the surface of the earth where this core heat or energy is available to use. Volcanos, hot baths or hot springs, areas near the equator. Iceland is a good example of a large land mass near thermal heat shuts. We have developed Enhanced Geothermal Systems which are basically geothermal heat pumps. They can be small and simply be used to heat a group of houses. Or large/deep and be used in a binary electric production heat turbine."

"An example of the latter is to drill, dig, or pump earth core hot water toward the surface; heat exchange it with isobutane which has a lower boiling temperature than water; run the secondary superheated solution to a heat turbine to produce electricity; recycle the cooler water into the earth core; no water lost to the atmosphere."

"Another example is to pump, in pipes, surface temperature water down into the earth core, convert it to steam, then bring the steam in those pipes, to the surface located heat turbines to produce electricity. Some water may be lost."

"Several other methods are being studied and each has plus and minus cost estimates. I can talk about these research ideas later with anyone interested in geothermal systems."

"Currently less than ten percent of the world's energy usage is geothermal. It is projected that it will reach near fifty percent within 100 years. Production of electricity can be very cheap with a volcano like easily obtainable source of core hot water. Or the costs will go up depending upon the location and method of extraction of the core hot water source…"

A friendly volcano can make you a very wealthy person…"

The next presentation was by Professor John Ebberline, San Diego State University, San Diego, California, USA.

"Today I will introduce you to biomass and to algae as potential energy sources for mankind. These are two separate areas and I will talk about them as a one and a two."

"One – What is biomass? Biomass is plant or animal materials, frequently waste materials, which can be used for controlled energy production. Examples of biomass include dead or remains of grown crops, wood or forestry residues, wastes from food crops, food processing, animal farming remains, and human waste from sewage plants. Most of these materials were originally produced from fixation of CO_2 photosynthesis in plants, consumption in animals, and the internal CO_2 is then released into the air—recycled—either via microorganisms in nature, or by controlled fire/heat. Biomass power plants burn/heat the carbon sources, and the released heat is used to produce electricity, hence controlled energy production. When properly organized, biomass energy can be an inexpensive form of producing electricity."

"Two – Algae? Algae is a small aquatic organism that, via CO_2 photosynthesis, produces cellulose and oils. Algae becomes an oil storage organism which can be used as a biofuel energy system similar to corn or sugar cane biofuels. There are several types of algae, so growing and using them as biofuels varies. Each type of algae has a formula for growing, harvesting, and cooking them in an electricity power plant. This energy source requires considerable sea water availability and aquatic control systems. But it is indeed an excellent recycling and sustainable energy system…"

The last speaker was Dr. Charles H Baker, Massachusetts Institute of Technology. Boston, Massachusetts, USA.

"I would like to introduce you to the sun's sonic irradiation, produced in a convection zone inside the sun, and vibrates inside from interior side to interior side. It produces sound waves/sonic waves which reach very high amplitudes called hyper sound or microsound."

"In other words, sunlight is really electromagnetic radiation of various wavelengths, 50 nanometers to 1000 nanometers—infrared—red, orange, yellow, green, light blue, dark blue—ultraviolet. We can see much of this 'visible' light, but wavelengths shorter than 200 or longer than 800 nanometers, we cannot see. The shorter waves provide much of the heat for the solar energy systems, discussed earlier. The longer waves create a sonar or sound system in certain sea and ocean areas with high salt content. Research is currently in motion to use this sound-energy conversion for explosive energy to split and separate hard rock such as granite. Early experiments are positive…"

As the meeting was winding down Saheed stood up and said, "It is noon, and our dining tables are ready and waiting for us. I suggest we go in that general direction. I want to give a very special thank you to all of the speakers, and attendees, both of you are winners. This knowledge/information exchange went to many individuals which are only literate in petrochemical energy system; hopefully now some of you are a little literate in some other energy systems."

"Please remember, speakers should be available for general question, answers, and discussion of their talks this afternoon around 2:00 PM here in this conference room. We can organize chairs, with tables if necessary, and remain as long as you want to do so. If you need transportation to the airport or elsewhere, see Fahad or myself, and we will help you contact with the hotel transportation service."

"One last very important item. Moroccans are internationally known for their desserts and candies. They are the ultimate sweet tooth people. The Casablanca Tourism Association is giving a five-pound box of famous Moroccan sweets to each of you. It is packed, has cleared customs, and will be waiting with your luggage. I am sure you and your family will enjoy all of it. But it is so packed that you will need kitchen help to open. Let your wife or daughters help you. Maybe they will reward you. Think of this beautiful city when you enjoy the sweets night."

As participants moved toward the dining room, Fahad Almubarak motioned to Saheed Al Muhairbi to join him as he had received an e-mail message from an 'unknown' source. He had it traced and learned it had come that morning from Medina, Saudi Arabia. It was a nasty message that he needed to immediately share with Saheed. The two of them went into a secluded corner of the dining room, and sat in a small booth for only two people. He gave it to Saheed, who read.

[[You are running on white quicksand in the middle of a very hot desert. The only way out is via black liquid sand. All of our families need only one thing from mother nature, black liquids. Do not try to change our history, or you and your family will not be found in the current writing of our history. STOP: First Warning!]]

Fahad spoke up, "Indeed, in Saudi Arabia, all oil production is owned and controlled by Saudi Aramco, government. It is probably the most profitable company in the world. The oil reserves are second, only to Venezuela, in the world."

"Let me open my cell phone and take a quick look. If I remember correctly, using oil and gas as a primary source of energy in the world releases more than 2000 tons of toxic chemicals into the atmosphere and 100 million tons of polluted waste water into the seas each year. Saudi Arabia has enough petroleum reserve to supply all of Saudi Arabia for 100 to 150 years. So, the problem here is not reserve sources, but will the world switch away from black liquid sand, hence not need that Saudi reserve in the near future. They do not have another established source of energy."

"Other OPEC members are not so fortunate. Listen to this list of proven oil reserves around the world. [OPEC – 80%; non-OPEC – 20%.]"

"OPEC – Venezuela – 25%; Saudi Arabia – 23%; Iran – 13%; Irak – 12%; Kuwait – 7.5%; UAE – 7.2%; Libya – 4.1%; Nigeria – 3.3; Algeria-1.1%; Ecuador – 0.7%; Angola – 0.7%; Congo – 0.3%; Gabon – 0.2%; Guinea-0.1%—major non-OPEC – Russia – 10%; Canada – 6.9%; USA – 5.5%."

Saeed agreed. "Many of these countries currently have the minimum of oil reserves to qualify to join OPEC. But in a few years those reserves will drop below qualification levels. What will they sell? And what will they do for their own energy sources? Cyclable sources? They need to hurry and get involved with non-black-liquid-sand science. This is why many of them are here at this meeting. It is why those countries who rely on the black-liquid-sand as a primary energy source do not want competition with the concepts of recycling energies that we discussed during these last two days. And it is not surprising that some countries and certain people will try to prevent the development of any new energy sources. How far will they go in their efforts to prevent such efforts? Assassination?"

"The concept of assassination originated in our part of the world," responded Fahad. "Remember, in 1090, Hassan-i Sabah from the

Nizari Isma' ili Sect established an assassination training center in the Alamut Castle in Syria. The assassins became very active during the Crusades. Therefore, we should not be surprised that we are being so threatened. Today, killing or assassination is almost common, individually or gang style. The question is what can we do about it. All participants that attended this meeting are administrators at a rank below which or even allows bodyguards. We travel every day on the streets to work. The implied threat in the e-mail points at us and our families. If there are those who do not want us to promote re-cyclable energy systems within our countries, we have a choice. Either we STOP. Or we develop and implement home-office-school security methods and move extremely cautiously in making 'business' decisions."

The two day meeting had brought together men who were focused on energy alternatives for their countries. They could certainly be on someone's hit list. It could be someone who prefers current energy usage, world-wide, to remain unchanged. And these someone could use force to emphasize their 'feelings'.

The day after the meeting most attendees had returned to their temporary (OPEC) Austrian homes and enjoyed their Morocco sweets gifts. Later many family members had bowel problems, and some did not wake up from their night's sleep. Plus, the bedrooms gave off a terrifically terrible deadly smell. And there were a few who did not wake up—ever!

WHY?

6

DEMOCRATIC REPUBLIC OF CONGO—PYGMY LANDS

Central African Pygmies live predominately within a few hundred miles on both sides of the equator in mid-Africa between the Atlantic and Indian Oceans. They are less than five feet tall and forage in the rainforests as hunters, gatherers, fishermen and traders. They have so occupied these lands for over two thousand years. More than a dozen ethnic-tribes including Aka, BaBenzie, Efe, Baka, Mbuti, Yoruba, Wachua, Bambuti, Ituri, Bantu, Bembutu, and Mbenga live here.

Why the short stature? Two reasons – environment and genetics. The pygmies live six summer months of the year in the dark rainforest habitat. There they do not have access to UV light. Vitamin D is converted to vitamin D3 by UV light on the skin. Vitamin D3 is critical for uptake of calcium in the body cells, growth and maintenance of bones. Pygmy children lack milk in their diets and calcium is low in the forest soils. Low genetic levels of growth hormone, growth hormone receptors 1 and 2, insulin-like growth factors 1 and 2, and insulin-like growth factor receptors 1 and 2, are common.

During the six-month dry season most villagers close their jungle huts and leave the villages. Many families go out into the savannah, to lakes, rivers, and seashore, build temporary camp shelters, and seek better foods; forge for wild yams, edible leaves, roots, berries, nuts, legumes, gourds, bananas, coconuts, honey, peanuts, etc; hunt for antelope, small and giant hogs, monkeys, fish, crabs, shellfish, snail, ants. Back in the village they raise livestock such as chickens, pigs, goats. During this time much socializing and trade takes place such as for metal and hunting weapons, gardening tools, metal pots, wooden dishes, cloth, water-proof materials, etc.—In general, they are friends to most neighbors.

This is also the usual time for intra-tribal and intra-regional marriages. There are no marriage ceremonies. The groom simply gives an antelope that he hunted to the bride's family. There is some polygamy for the stronger males.

Most tribes do not vote on 'permanent' leadership roles. The older male is leader of the family. The villagers select a tribal chief. And occasionally a king is chosen during times of stress. The same rules/laws generally apply to everyone. When major problems occur, a small group of villagers are selected. They meet during the night and decide the right-wrong and the punishment, including banishment from the tribe.

Pygmy life is jungle forest first. The forest is the provider and the protector. Therefore, it is sacred. There is only one ritual—the death of a loved one is called molimo. This death celebration occurs over several nights and is composed of feasting, singing, dancing, and playing music with wooden/bamboo flutes. Because pygmy life is basically passive, there are very few tribe-tribe disputes and military style battles. Their reclusive style of living helps prevent negative problems with the 'taller' black Africans, most of the time.

In the United States of America there was an organization called SAVE THE AFRICAN SMALLS. This was a small national organization of normal sized Americans who followed the difficult and continuous deteriorating lives of the African pygmies. A thirty old year single American man by the name of Jersey Botley was working at a local bus repair center in downtown Baltimore. He lived with his parents on Levera Street, and was trying to make something of himself. He had organized a Baltimore group of the Save The African Smalls, and assisted in establishing similar groups in Philadelphia, Washington, DC, New York City, and Detroit. Working with the five pro-African pygmy organizations over several years he orchestrated several fund raisers and managed to acquire nearly three hundred thousand USD to use in assisting the pygmies in their attempts at survival. With permission of the Save the African Small organizations, he planned to go there and collect an native American viewpoint, HIS.

One weekend the American news outlet, CNNC produced a documentary about the mass killing of pygmy black Africans. The stories were that the pygmy males were kidnapped and routed to Europe or Asia and sold as slaves. Women were raped, killed, or adopted as additional wives. While the heads of the children were prepared and sold as shrunken heads to tourists in neighboring Luanda, Angola or Lagos, Nigeria.

Recently, a major militant conflict had happened in the savannah on the edge of the rain forest. A middle eastern country decided that there was gold and possibly areas of diamonds in this region in the Republic of Congo. They hired several tribes of big black Loopers from Cameroon, and sent them to 'eliminate' the pygmies. The world was currently not paying any attention to this terrible news.

After flying Belgium Airlines from Baltimore to Kinshasa, Jersey settled in at the Hotel Blue Shark. He met a French journalist, Honri Atuan, on the terrace overlooking the Kasai River. The men quickly settled into a round of cold Wild African One Beer. They immediately found common interest in trying to assist the small Africans. Honri had published several monographs about the tragedy, but all in French. They were not circulating in the English language world. Jersey had not seen any on them. He immediately requested copies such that he could become more knowledgeable about the local tragic situation.

Honri began a brief explanation, "About 5,000 years ago the Congo Basin had one major ethnic group, the Mbena. Perhaps by 2,000 years ago these split into Aka and Baka groups, speaking Bantu and Ubangian languages. They soon split further into Eastern and Western pygmies while sharing a mixed language. The Eastern pygmies became hunters/gatherers and entered more deeply into the massive rain forests. The Western pygmies became farmer/traders by raising crops and domestic animals. The latter lived closer to the Big People of the savannah on the fringe of the rain forests. The various pygmy ethnic groups did maintain close connections with many common language phrases, common music, dancing, and witchcraft medicines. Tribal treaties and inter-marriage are still common. However, the West pygmies are more exposed to the world of the big black people. They are more continuously harassed and discriminated against, and suffer massacre, slavery, kidnapped women and children. Children are stolen and sent to museums and zoos in Europe and Asia."

He continued, "Today, it is hard to obtain good data or current specific information about these massacres. The big blacks, whoever they are, send scouts into the summer camp areas of the pygmies. They identify those camps with trails or fair roads into the site area, for attack and retreat. The pygmies use local streams and rivers for transportation. The big blacks use only trails and roads. Apparently, the big blacks drive close to a camp in several small trucks and 20 or 30 big blacks are armored with military handguns and INSAS rifles. The pygmies have no guns, only spears, bow and arrows and poison dart blow tubes. During the night they attack and kidnap any physically strong males (for slavery), women who would make good second wives or slaves, and children for the shrunken head market place. All others are killed and left to be eaten by the vultures and hyenas. By the time word reaches the police in a nearby city, and the police forces react, nothing is left to identify or record. Only morbid pictures for foreigners like me, to make and sell to select European and American news media. So, I am guessing that the data you will probably obtain will be similar. You must think of a different way of obtaining your information."

"And what type of approach do you recommend?" Jersey asked.

Honri began several well thought out suggestions—

The next day Jersey began walking the streets of Kinshasa. He was looking for pygmy sized men who were shopping for plastic-water proof over-clothes such as light jackets for both women and children, and other types of water resistant or water proof materials for monsoon summer usage. When he finally found three men who met the criteria, he quickly identified one who spoke some English. He invited them to a nearby restaurant for a cold beer—the common male drink.

During the one-hour conversation the men basically confirmed what he had read and what Honri had told him. He needed to go into the area, visit and talk with the pygmies, and see the situation for himself. With his two cell phones he could record and take pictures of the lives and problems of these small black people. The three pygmies were returninlg by canoe to their village in two days. He would meet them at the docks and go with them to their homes in the jungle and to one of their summer camp-sites. He was excited and ready to go. He stashed his money in the safe at the hotel. Later, it could be useful, maybe.

Early morning two days later, he climbed into a 15 foot long dug-out canoe with five pygmy rowers. Abaeze, the pygmy who spoke fairly good English, sat near Jersey and talked and explained the journey and recent happenings while on route. They started up the Kasai River. Eight hours later they stopped in a small side bay, ate a small pre-cooked meal and some fruit, slept for a couple of hours, re-loaded, and continued for the next six hours. They then turned up the Sakuru River. Six more hours of rowing and they entered Opkaru Creek, then Jaclir Creed. Two hours later they turned into Malidir Creek. Here they rested for a few hours, checked their back trails to be certain they were not followed. All was clear.

Abzeze explained, "Malidir Creek is our creek. It is about two miles long, three feet narrow in several places, and three to five feet deep. Wild vines overhang with many snakes, one large crocodile pond that you must pass through, and three false dead-end creeks. There are several hidden wire traps strung across the creek to prevent entry. And we have scouts located at various locations along the way. The scouts have poison dart blow pipes. I will show you as we go slowly to our homes. This our 'front' door."

And he laughed.

Jersey just gulped and said, "Thank you."

He thought about the difficulty of getting in or out of this little pygmy village. He would have to be on his best behavior. He could easily just disappear here.

After forty minutes of rowing, they ran upon a large semi cleared area filled with large Kapok and Ramon trees, and more than fifty huts constructed with clay blocks, wood logs, soko-branches, and large leaves. All huts were shaped like an upside-down soup bowl. It was the largest Yoruba village in the area, with nearly 400-500 people. Jersey would develop many friends and learn much from them.

The boat came ashore. All hopped out and the arriving villagers were warmly greeted by family members, especially the children. Fathers had to pass the candy test or they would not get the kisses they deserved. Abzeze gave out his small package of chocolate hearts to his daughter, took his kisses, and then took Jersey by the hand and led him into the village.

Abzeze and Jersey walked. Abzeze talked, "The village is clustered in family-oriented huts. We are very family-oriented people. That is why you see small and large huts grouped. These buildings sleep 6-8 or 10-15 people. If we need more space, we just cut down more jungle and build more huts. The famous Chief Mawapanga and his families are located in the center of the village, nearest the large fresh water well. But we do have several large containers which open to catch rain water. They are located in various places throughout the village. Water is never a problem."

He continued, "Because this is March, many families have left the village and have gone 'outside' the forest to establish small camps for collecting roots and berries, growing certain crops, hunting, fishing, and just feeling the sunshine. If you have ever lived for a long time without the sun, you would understand the excitement that the morning sun and evening moon gives you."

And all Jersey could do was grimace and smile.

They walked around the village for a few minutes. Jersey was a rarely seen white faced, tall person in the village. But everyone waved and smiled. He smiled back as they knew he was here to help them.

Jersey asked, "Some huts have several windows, others have none. Why?"

"Good observation." Abzeze replied. "Huts which are used as houses have one or two windows. Those which have no windows are used for storage, and maintenance of livestock. It is often too wet in the summer to raise certain animals, except maybe some chickens, pigs or goats during the drier times. The wet weather certainly does not permit raising cows. That large hut over there is for community meetings of various kinds. We are going to go there now. It is getting late in the day so we need to hurry. The village elders are waiting for us. They want to meet you, and ask why you are here."

Already Jersey was getting nervous.

As they continued walking toward the center of the village Abzeze spoke. "Before we get there, let me explain what is going to happen. We will enter the community building. You will meet the village council of elders and simply explain why you came to see us and how you might be able to help us. They will listen and make a decision—good or bad."

"The Chief will control all final dialogue. So be careful. He is famous for two reasons. As a child he was kidnaped, escaped, hid out in Kinshasa, killed his captors, managed to go to Lagos, Nigeria, attended an English-speaking Catholic orphanage-seminary, and even graduated from it. Later he returned to us and brought a ship load of big guns which we used to drive the big blacks out of this area. However, eventually we ran out of ammunition and guns. Now they are back and we have to drive them away again. We thought they would stay away. They did not. Our Chief has 16 children, is 80 years old, and has not had a baby in the past 8 years. Our lives normally end at 50 years. What are we going to do in the near future?"

The two of them entered the community building. At one end of the large room was a long table. Chief Mawapanga sat at the far end of the table. Seven village elders, Chief hunter, and Chief witch sat along the table sides. Jersey and Abzeze were seated at the far end of the table, away from the Chief. The Chief was a little over five feet tall, bald with many wrinkles, somewhat bent over, had a kindly smiling face, and seemed to be relaxed with this American. He walked with two canes. He had two very large black dogs, sitting on each side of him. The dogs stared Jersey down. This certainly made the American nervous. The group would speak in Niger-Congo dialect. Abzeze would translate.

After all were seated a young lady served cups of boiling water to everyone. Another young lady offered a dish of several types of tea leaves to each of them. They helped themselves, dipped the leaves, and waited for the Chief to speak first. They looked each other over. Then the Chief nodded to the Youngest elder.

The youngest elder stood and began a recital about their tribal history, beginning several thousand years ago. He began, *"Our most recent forefathers were Aka. Aka history began with a god named Bembe who created the entire world—earth, sky, water, forest, animals, and plants. He made a male and a female—Tole and Ngolobanzo. Later he added a brother, Tonzanga. Because Tole had Ngolobanzo, and Tonzanga had no one, Bembe gave all knowledge to Tonzanga. After Tole and Ngolobanzo started to make children, Tonzanga took all his knowledge and went to the moon. Thus, the Aka people began with babies but without a foundation of knowledge from which to build a good life."*

"Our people developed edio/ghosts/spirts who rule the afterlife. There are two special spirits, Ezingi and Ziakpokpo. These spirits are benevolent or malevolent to the people depending on how people act toward each other. In Aka thought, outside the village are foreign malign spirits; nearby and

surrounding the village are not so very good spirits; only within the village proper are the spirits well and proper for a good person to live a good life."

The Chief Wizard spoke up, *"The forest has all the good and vital principles for our livelihood. We know how to easily obtain it and use it. If there are special times or special needs, we have several festivals and rites which we use. That is part of my duties. Before travels, major hunting parties, battles, and major repair after heavy storms, we call upon these extras. The chief hunter, a senior divine healer, and I may use our contacts with one or two major gods such as a zengi or the elephant spirit."*

The various elders each took turns expressing his interrelationships with life in the forest and family comradship. Both the good and the difficult were dwelt on. No one had major negative problems with the current 'administration'.

The Chief concluded, *"Because food and children are two of our biggest problems, the men have special rites for fishing and hunting, especially for wild hogs, gazelles, monkeys, crocodile, and python snakes. While women have special rites involving singing, dancing, and getting pregnant. We have the Mokandi ceremony in the spring to help all of these rites bear fruit."*

And the Chief gave Jersey a quick wink. And then he broke down laughing. As if on que, all of the others broke down laughing. Jersey understood the politics, village or not. And he gave his biggest smile.

After a brief period of time, Jersey spoke out and simply said, "I want to directly help you with the massacres/wars that you are now suffering. How can this be stopped, or reversed? What can I do to help?"

Chief Mawapanga took over and switched to English. "We know that you are here because of the terrible killings of the African pygmy peoples in this part of the Congo. Let me give you some ideas. Come with me."

The Chief stood up, took his two canes and two dogs, and went out the entry door of the community building. Jersey and Abzez understood, got up and followed him. They walked down the street with him for five minutes, and entered a large special designed house with several windows and doors. There were several very nice arm chairs with cushions in the entry room. The Chief motioned for them to sit as they would talk here. A young lady suddenly appeared with three glasses of beer, and dispensed one to each of them. The looked at each other, shared a friendly smile and Chief Mawapanga started off in English.

"During recent years we have moved away from much of our ancestral lands. We have moved almost completely back into the rain forest areas of our lands and the forest protected areas. The savannah is open, flat, with numerous rolling hills. We had planted many nut and fruit trees. And we farmed it for many, many years, wheat and corn. It grows excellent cocoa, yams, and many types of wild roots and berries. All of these are high nutrient plants. Living in the forest we have none of these crops. But now, living in the savannah, we have no protection from the big black Looper tribes, or any 'invaders' who have guns. Our people are afraid of guns."

"The solution is simple. We need to rid the area of these big black war parties. But our political connections are not adequate. And we know there are enemies that want our land and will kill to get it. They think there is gold and diamonds here. If so, we have never seen it. I think not. They just want the land."

"We know these hired killers are on the payroll of western white businessmen. That is why we simply say they want our land. And they are readily supplied with cheap military weapons produced in South East Asia."

The Chief continued. "There are about two hundred military trained invaders out there seeking our summer camps. They are divided into units of twenty-five to thirty. Use of the trails and roads with several small trucks is their 'non-clever' tactic for attack. They fear the streams and rivers, as we know all water routes, they do not. We always set up nearby escape routes by canoes on river banks where we are forging. Whenever we can isolate several of them, we set up poison dart gun and spear attacks. These are always successful."

"Because they have a large number of men, they consistently need a lot of food and water. They must purchase all their food, once a week, from venders in Kinshasa, and have it delivered up river to their camp sites. We know most of the 'locals' involved in selling and delivering that food. It is very easy to 'spike' the food, before or on route."

"Poison? Usually! But because the invaders also know this word, it is common for them to test newly delivered food for poison by feeding to monkeys or human prisoners (pygmies)."

"Yes, we prepare poison from plants, insects, snakes, and shelled water creatures. However, all of our preparations are immediately active. Testing foods for presence of our poisons is very easy and very fast. Give it to an animal. So, this will not work for us. We tried! Yes. It did not work."

The Chief smiled and continued. "But today we have a new synthetic (laboratory produced) poison called nanotech system. It is synthesized in Europe. And, yes, there are several types. I know the distributor in Kinshasa. I have talked with him and he explained to me the characteristics of three types which we could 'try out'."

"There is one type called cellulose nanotech molecular system. It is a liquid and can be injected into any fruit. It is stable for several days at room temperature. When eaten it does not become active in the body for many hours. The activation results in the rupture of the colon, and leakage of intestinal fluids into the abdominal cavity. It causes both internal and external diarrhea. A very messy-smelly-irreversible death. Not nice."

And he laughed. His aged sense of humor?

Jersey gulped and asked. "Are you going to try it?"

The Chief responded, "All I need is one hundred thousand American dollars."

Jersey thought for a minute—'this is why I came here.'

Jersey stood up. The Chief stood up. They looked each other in the eye. Smiled.

Struck a high five. And the Chief said, "Is this what Americans call a win-win?

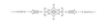

What are weapons?

Weapons are large (nuclear bombs) or small (molecules) and are designed to kill anything that is alive (plant or animal). They can be used by bad guys to kill good guys, and used by good guys to kill bad guys.

Thousands of years ago every army had an armorer who made all of the weapons for that army. The winning army usually captured the losing army's armorer and re-employed him within their army, he was not an enemy. In fact, he was a new important comrade. The better his work, the safer they were.

Has this concept of war changed today?

7

COMMITTEE OF
NANOTECHNOLOGY
CONTROL

On the Monday just before the American Thanksgiving holidays, the US Committee of Nanotechnology Control in the Division of High Technology met on the second-floor conference room in the Federal Trade Center Building on Constitution Avenue in Washington, DC. The chairs at the conference table were full, Mr. John Reasoner, US Attorney General, as Chairman stood up and counted heads and faces. All were present. He called the meeting to order.

The members were:

- Mr. Dagda Murphy, President of ISAAT and Co-Chairman
- Mr. Thomas Bradmier, Director of the Office of Science and Technology
- Dr. William Walker, Chief of INTERPOL
- Dr. William Stronger, Chairman of Nanotechnology at MIT in Boston
- Dr. Joseph Barkley, Chairman of High Technology at the Univ. Chicago
- Mr. Leopold Mueller, Director of the European Bank
- Mr. Harold Thompson, Director of British MI6
- Ms. Harriott Bilmak, private lawyer in international trade

- Dr. Lawrence Batly, Director of Chief Medical Examiner Office, NYC

- Mr. Boursher Femer, Director of ISAAT in Europe

Chairman Reasoner spoke, "I sincerely thank you for your time and effort in working with us to continue to identify and eliminate what we have begun to call Nanotech Killers. This is simply because they continue to use nanotech molecular systems to kill/assassinate selected targets. Most of those targets have been high technology scientists. The killings peaked at near 500 deaths per year in 2032. Since then, they have dropped to just a few each year. This may be related to the elimination of the Equus Transport International, one company thought to manufacture nanotech weapon systems. We can talk more about this later. And of course, new nanodata killings tell us that systems may have suddenly changed."

"You have heard about many of the recent MUSD/Medically Unexplainable Sudden Deaths in several places in Africa. The World Health Organization did an excellent job in the early identification of these deaths. They try to immediately let us know about such deaths worldwide. And in all of these African cases we sent our nanotech literate forensic team. We have much info and data from our efforts which I will offer to you today. We have a lot of what and where and how. We have very little why. I will appreciate it if our committee may want to focus on this latter area as we talk about each case, one by one. Is there a common motive or set of theories?"

"Because all of you have many irons in many fires, I am asking Dr. Stronger to briefly describe the major killing weapon system that we are facing throughout the world, **nanotech-molecular-systems**."

Dr Stronger began a brief summary. "This carefully and very specifically organized group of atoms/molecules are currently used **to cure** certain diseases and also **to kill** normal healthy people. It was first described over forty years ago. And now there are at least 100 scientists designing and producing these complex molecules. The curative direction focuses on single cell diseases, such as the many cancers. The killing direction attacks and 'kills' critical normal cells growing in the body which can result in the killing of the body. The results are assassination or murder."

"A nanotechnical system or nanotech molecular system is usually made of several components. First and most critical is the nanotech component."

"The nanotech component can either have direct action such as a membrane-ase, which can cut holes in membranes, shut down blood circulation to cell/tissue areas, can carry and add heavy 'killing' metals or poison-like molecules to the target cell, can provide digestion protection activity for itself, can electrically short circuit targeted nerve cells associated with key body organs, such as the brain, major nerves, or the heart, and can self-destruct."

"In addition to the nanotech component, a second major component, a homing molecule which will recognize the target, may be used. This is called a monoclonal antibody (MoAB). It can deliver the nanotech component and other attached components directly to the outer membranes of the target cell. It may or may not have specific actions by itself. It may only serve as a specific transport molecule. And, this two-component system must have a delayed action and later under-go total self-destruction after a programed and completed action."

"Overall, this nanotech molecular system can be simply one molecule or a multi-molecule complex with several additional specialized components."

"Because these systems are designed to self-destruct, over the years we have had difficulty in obtaining active ones such that we can copy or reproduce them. Systems designed for cure are simpler than those designed for kill. For cure it is not necessary to have delayed action, nor self-destruct activity, nor multiple activities, nor special transport and storage conditions. Systems designed for kill are always more complex such that any evidence will disappear."

"These, then, are the basic actions of nanotech molecular systems, whether designed for cure or kill. If you have any questions, please feel free to ask them. These are not simple systems. Please ask me now or later, as I want to help everyone develop a general understanding of this new killer weapon that has become more popular, as you will soon see today. Plus, a new one molecule very simple system could soon be used as the latest-newest military weapon system. We will discuss it in detail later during in our meeting."

No hands went up for questions yet. The science may just too much for some non-science-oriented people. Maybe later.

Mr. Murphy took over. "Please keep in mind, even though we have had difficulty in learning the exact atomic structure of these molecules, we have been successful in initiating and implementing new national and international laws and regulatory transportation restrictions. Nanotech molecular systems of any type and their identified precursor chemicals are now all legally similar to components of terrorism. When appropriately informed, any custom/passport control check point officer can challenge entry of cargo or individuals, if they are related to nanotech systems. This is especially true for air, ship, and rail transport. The in-place regulations for terrorism are now also functioning for nanotechnology. We think that this has helped to slow down the number of deaths that we are seeing in the past 2-3 years."

"Another thing to keep in mind, the first diagnostic info we receive is usually from the World Health Organization. They understand our use of the MUSD—medically unexplainable sudden deaths—as the criteria for nanotechnology involvement. In turn they notify us, and we immediately send a nanotech literate forensic team to the site. We have been able to make an on-site diagnosis in two to four days after death. But that is not fast enough to obtain a viably intact or active nanotech molecular system. The scientists producing them are good and very careful; the systems do rapidly self-destruct. We have analyzed more than eighty deaths, and only three good samples did not self-destruct. But we learned much from these three."

Mr. Reasoner spoke up, "During the past couple of years we have consistently identified several MUSDs each year in 5-6 different countries. Each victim was a high-tech scientist. This has been the pattern during most of the last 10-15 years. Only in 2032, when more than 400 scientists were directly killed in the Istanbul massacre, was the 'killing' pattern different. It is also possible that two years ago the Irish Sea yachting accident that drowned the major members of the Equus Transport International, the only known corporation designing, manufacturing, and selling nanotech molecular systems, could have decreased the number of MUSDs. Whatever the reason for the slow-down, we fully expect this to change very soon. Shortly we will explain. Africa seems to have become a newly targeted area."

"First, let me report to you those three recent examples of high-tech scientist assassinations," said Mr. Murphy. "These are the patterns and methodology similar to that which we think the Korrectorizer followed over the past decade."

"Dr. William Knowler, Professor of Aerophysics at the National Institute of Aerodynamics, developed the basic physics for the self-flying drones. He was having dinner, alone, in a Washington, DC restaurant, TGIF. He finished his meal, walked a few blocks to his home on Merideth Street just off Wisconsin Ave. Apparently, he worked on his computer for a couple of hours and then went to bed. The next day a colleague dropped by to pick him up, to take him to a mid-morning conference. They could not roust him, called 911, and with the police they entered, and found Dr. Knowler in bed as a MUSD."

"Dr Mary Jones Potter, Professor of Mathematics at the University of Chicago, who developed the Heisenburg Uncertainty Principle. This mathematical expression is the concept used to evaluate the yes or no of complex ocean-tide flux during areas of rapidly rising ocean temperatures. She was home alone on the Saturday night before Easter Sunday and worked much of the night on a manuscript which had a Monday after Easter deadline. She was planning to go to Mass on Easter evening, did not show up, so two of her best friends went to her house, and using a hidden key they entered. They found Dr. Potter on the floor of her condo as a MUSD."

"Dr. Walter Grandsdown, Professor of Robotics at the Carnegie Mellon University, in Pittsburgh. He developed the microscopic surgical robot used for a newborn's heart surgery, and is now working on a 3-D image analysis for newborn's internal all organ surgery. He was alone at his small Appalachian stone house on a five day leave from teaching. The following weekend he did not return to the university. Police were sent to his mountain house. They found him in his recliner chair—MUSD."

"I can read the info on nine other such cases of high-tech scientists who were each working alone for a short period of time and each became MUSD. They are all similar. Most scientists live within their heads. So, to find them alone in an isolated location is normal. To strike one down, just wait and they will make themselves available. Security! They are too busy. They never have time to be concerned about such things. They are easy targets."

"Mr. Murphy concluded, "Does anyone want to hear any more about the killings of some of our leading explorers of the new sciences?""

"If not, let us take a coffee-sugar break and begin again in 15-20 minutes."

They stood, stretched, walked to the side coffee and pastry table, chatted about how much new was now available to discuss in the afternoon, returned to their chairs, and began again.

Mr. Dagda Murphy began. "Over the years Korrectorizer and his financial supporters-assassins have been fairly consistent in their selection of top-level scientists and eliminating them slowly, one by one. No one has ever been caught, nor has a suspect even been seen near that scientist during the hit time frame. Correct me if I am wrong Dr. Stronger. We have observed introduction of nanotech molecular systems into the body of the victim via the spinal cord/cerebral spinal fluid, oral or stomach consumption, intravenous and intramuscular injections, and consumptions in drinking water and fluids. Correct?"

Dr. Stronger responded, "I believe that is correct"

"Now that we know more about Korrectorizer's scientist designs, we should be able to predict their design based on the mode of entry into the victim's body," said Mr. Murphy. Introduction via the cerebral spinal fluid would not require a stomach digestion blocker. Introduction via the stomach would require a stomach digestion blocker. Yes?"

"Having accepted this idea, later Dr. Stronger will introduce a new type of nanotech molecular system which can go through the stomach and not require digestion protection. It will amaze you! Korrectorizer has some very bright high-tech scientists working for him."

Mr. Reasoner spoke up, "If there are no immediate questions, we will return to the molecular structures of nanotech, MoAB, and associated molecules that make up complex nanotech molecular systems later. But let us first take a look at some of these people who are designing and creating these molecules in their labs. We estimate more than 150 people have been involved in designing, manufacturing, transporting, and distributing these systems around the world, the general focus being to provide for sale various nanotech killer systems. However, there are only 3 to 5 really high-tech scientists that can create original excellent nanotech designs. There are several more that can make very good copies. Choosing from all of these, which we consider quite excellent, ten of them are always high on our killer candidate list."

"Our best success in the past few years resulted from creating such a list, and then investigating those individuals in detail, not just in the laboratory sciences, but also by the monitoring of bank accounts, sales programs, business success, life styles, friendships, etc. Were any of them living beyond their means? Several definitely were doing better than excellent. Dr. Mario Kemps, Buenos Aires, Argentina, Dr Frans Gunter, Munich, Germany, and Dr. Albert Langdon, London, England were spending salaries which did not show on their tax returns. And now they are no longer receiving salaries as they are no longer working in the laboratories. They are no longer working. They are no longer breathing."

And a few smiles broke out among some committee members as they remembered the 'need to know' relationship with four boys and some witches.

"Candidates who were on the previous list, and are now at the top of a new list that we have begun to develop include: Dr. James Walter, Toronto, Canada, Dr. Anneka Andersson, Stockholm, Sweden, Mr. Faustino, Rome, Italy, and Dr. Edward Kline, USA. After lunch we will put forward some new names, give to you the professional work and play history of each; and then we can select, add six more nanotech killer candidates to our new list, and begin an investigation of each."

Mr. Reasoner continued, "I think we have time to cover one more area before lunch. If it is alright with you, we would like to give you more information about this new type of nanotech molecular system that is not digested in the stomach. Dr. Stronger, if you please."

"I left Dr. Langdon to the last because he has recently been a very busy person. We have information and data from two sources that make him a most dangerous man. Dr. Stronger, would you help me here?"

Dr. Stronger replied, "Yes. Give me a moment to put my notes together."

1) "We have learned from his foreign students, with proper financial inducement, that Dr. Albert Langdon, London, England has apparently produced a **new cellulose active nanotech trigger, instead of the usual organic active nanotech trigger. This allows for a new type of cellulose**

nanotech molecular system to become a weapon. The major portion of fiber in our foods is cellulose. Our stomach and small intestine cannot digest it. Only when cellulose enters the large intestine or colon, can it be digested by a digestive colonic bacterial enzyme called cellulase which is produced and secreted by several types of bacteria growing only in the colon, especially E. Coli. Apparently, Dr. Langdon's possible cellulose trigger containing system is activated when so digested. What does it do when active? We think it digests/opens holes in the membrane-walls of the colon and the contents leak into the abdominal cavity and around the anus. If this is so, extreme and continuous diarrhea would occur, both inside and outside the body. But we really do not know exactly how it does work. We are still somewhat guessing."

2) "We followed the shipment of a package containing such a nanotech system via one of McCMetals ships down the Amazon, noted into which villages that it was unloaded and disappeared into the wilderness. We arranged to have a package followed. The package did not require refrigeration. And indeed, yes, within one week, many natives in a small nearby village were found dead, with the symptoms to which I just referred. Reporting it to the police did no good."

"So, this cellulose trigger system appears to be stable at room temperature, must be ingested, probably goes through the first part of the digestion process intact and potentially active, and then the colonic bacterial cellulase activates it when it enters the colon several hours later. The death would indeed be very macabre. And because it is a single unit system, it should not even be expensive. However not all villagers died the same way. Therefore, this possible cellulose nanotech molecule system is still in an experimental state. And if I understand correctly, Dr. Langdon, who did all of the nanomolecular designing in his laboratories, does not share all of his designs with his lab team. So, we do not know the 'secret' or 'exact' mechanism of action of the nanotech cellulose system."

"The last point to be made—Last spring, Dr. Langdon was on the ETI yacht that sank in the Irish Sea. Therefore, he is no longer with us. We do not know if another member of his group can duplicate his work or not. What we do know is that there have been several macabre diarrhea deaths in several villages in Africa in the past few months. So, someone is producing a nanotech cellulose system, and using it."

"OK, that is enough for this morning. Let us break for lunch and meet back here at 1:30 PM. Thank you."

There was a collective sigh among the committee members. No verbal comments were forth coming. What can one say to such a terrible, awesome death?

"A last comment before lunch—I am handing to you a small packet which has the names and info of a new list of candidates. These are considered to have the potential to be of nanotech killer candidate status. Glance through the list and give to me your opinion before we separate later today. We may not have time to discuss each in detail. Question—give me a hand written copy."

With a collective sigh, they split for lunch.

After lunch at 1:30, members of the Committee of Nanotechnology Control, in the Federal Trade Center building in Washington, DC, continued reviewing their discussion on the recent nanotechnology related killings around the world. Mr. Reasoner welcomed everyone back. He sat down and let his Co-Chairman stand and take over.

Mr. Murphy began. "I have most of the data for the next four presentations, so I will review some of this."

"I will present data and information concerning that new cellulose nanotech molecular system which apparently is now being employed by Korrectorizer and his group of conservative industrialists. It presents a completely different set of problems to intercept or stop when compared to the organic nanotech molecular systems that we have been trying to understand and prevent over the past several years."

"During the past few months, a series of unusual MUSDs and several excellent follow-up forensic analyses of the victims were obtained. All of these cases were in Africa. Allow me to discuss four such examples."

Case #1 – Nigeria – "In the small moderately wealthy village of Tumba, Baylesa, Nigeria, nearly 300 villagers were killed by a nanotech molecular system which caused a terrible type of diarrhea."

"Once a year the villagers celebrated the founding of their tribal unit and thanked their ancestors. All other villagers in the area with Osun heredity were also invited to the festival. A large festival meal was consumed, including several special foods. More than 20 types of foods were eaten throughout the long evening. One specific dessert—dates—eaten only once a year at this festival, was purchased from Algeria and shipped to Tumba. This special dessert was consumed during the evening dinner. Our nanotech literate forensic team arrived two days after the killings. They identified unusual macro-cellulose-like molecules in the dates. And from the biopsies of several child victims, a cellulose nanotech molecular system, partially digested, was identified. There were holes in the walls of the colons of several children. Indeed, abnormal cellulose-like molecules were found in the colonic fluids that had leaked into and filled the abdominal cavity—a macabre type of death."

"We have learned that there is a historical ethnic feud between this Osun tribe and a neighboring Malata tribe. The Baylesa police disagreed, so there was no investigation."

Case #2 – Libya – "A wealthy modern Arab family, living on their own historically owned several thousand acres of oil rich desert land near Massjedi, Tripoli, Libya, prepared their desert mansion for the wedding of their number three daughter. In attendance was the entire four generation family, several other oil wealthy families and friends, high ranking political and military officials, and several foreign ambassadors. The wedding took place in their very tall walled double gated, 100 room desert manor house which was clustered around two swimming pools. More than 60 guests, 30 caterers, 20 security personnel and a 7-piece orchestra were involved in an elaborate wedding. Approximately 120 people attended the pre-prepared and catered dinner. The guests sang, danced, drank soft and alcoholic beverages, and enjoyed the food and ceremonies. All guests and workers went home soon after midnight. The wedding family, exhausted, retired, went directly to bed."

"The next morning there was a terrible odor hovering over the mansion and numerous vultures circled the area. Very few people moved around. Most were dead, but still warm. Upon checking it was determined that many of the guests who went home also did not get up, for similar reasons. Two days later our nano literate forensic team arrived. Luckily, three bodies had been refrigerated. Biopsies were tested on those victims available. But most victims had already been given an immediate Moslem burial. Many of the bodies had abdomen filled colonic fluids—internal diarrhea. Unusual cellulose macromolecules were found in each of the biopsies. Samples of all food were analyzed. Some partially, not yet completely degraded, intact cellulose nanotech molecular systems were identified in a dessert, chocolate truffles."

"It is not understood why this mass murder was carried out. The most logical answer seems to involve oil rich member family rivalries. Investigations are continuing."

Case #3 – Casablanca – Morocco – "OPEC, the Organization of Petroleum Exporting Countries held a non-official meeting in the exclusive Vichy Celestins Spa Hotel in Casablanca, Morocco. This was not the normal annual meeting, but a conference focusing on new and developing special high energy technology from renewable or sustainable energy sources. Representatives from each of the 13 members were present. They brought in several high tech 'western' scientists to brief or update various areas of energy supply and energy demand including solar energy, hydro energy, wind energy, geothermal energy, biomass, and the sun's sonic irradiation. Seven well known European scientists spoke and agreed to help the OPEC 'brothers' to co-develop some renewal energy to complement their finite sources of oil."

"They held an excellent two-day conference. On the first day they listened to the new sciences, exchanged energy ideas, shared professional contact addresses, enjoyed a touristic visit to the second largest mosque in the world, and then ate a large Moroccan banquet dinner that evening. The second day, they listened to another sets of ideas for sustainable energy sources. In the afternoon, most of the participants returned to their temporary homes in Vienna, home of OPEC. On the way to their airplanes each attendee was given a five-pound box of famous Morocco sweets. The Moroccan people are known to have the biggest sweet tooth in the world. Everyone was informed that the sweets were to be eaten after a large evening dinner."

"A couple of days later many of the attendees and their families had failed to leave their beds. They were warm, dead, and gave off terrible smells. Because of the nature of the deaths, possible contagion was declared and Austrian laws required that the deceased be refrigerated for 4-6 days. Austria notified WHO, who notified Michael Gaines, the American Attorney General, and myself as Chairman of the Committee of Nanotechnology. We sent a nanotech-literate team to Vienna to the appropriate government forensics people, and to the doors of many of the OPEC Morocco Conference attendees. Where possible we obtained permission from families, autopsied as many victims as possible, brought the specimens back to the USA, and analyzed them."

"This led to the unusual sequence of events in which we obtained biopsy samples from over twenty nanotech victims in one day. Our analysis concluded. The active substance was most probably a possible cellulose nanotech molecular system. We will soon know for certain. Only two days after death and with continuous refrigeration, the bodies were in good physical condition. From each victim, where permission was received, we took 1 liter of colonic leaked abdominal fluids and 10 grams of colonic tissues. We concentrated the fluids and freeze dried them. These were next stored in liquid nitrogen such that we now have several months of the soluble forms of the nanotech system for future studies. All tissues were sub-cell sequenced and re-suspended or dissolved and freeze dried so we also now have both soluble and membrane bound forms of the nanotech system for future studies. More than ten years of trying to obtain viable nanotech samples, and suddenly it fell from the desert."

"If one looks for motives, there are many older conservative and powerful members of some of the OPEC countries who do not want change. There were several who protested this secret 'traitorous' meeting. They simply prefer things as they are and are willing to prevent any innovation. Some think that murder is not too far to go to maintain the status quo."

Case # 4 – Democratic Republic of Congo – "With no shots being fired, there was the elimination of an entire military army camp in the Congo. Apparently, more than 300 soldiers were killed with a possible nanotechnical system. Local natives discovered the atrocity from the powerful terrible and very macabre smell, plus the accumulation of numerous predatory animals in the area. The Big Black Looper military camp was located along the Kasai River, between the deep savannah and the rainforest. Loopers are normal sized blacks who were provided with military weapons and paid to kill off the tribes of black pygmy villagers who fought only with their historically primitive weapons. A European company was bankrolling the 'tribal' war in the belief that there was oil on the land historically owned by the pygmy people."

"Word of the killings reached the 'outside' world in several days. We learned about it a week later. And we sent a small forensic team to the area. We learned from the locals that the pygmies somehow obtained a 'magic poison' and placed it into the food which was going up river to the Looper's camp. This 'magic poison', killed every soldier and all of their military attack dogs, overnight. The story told to us was that the Loopers all had terrible diarrhea, inside and outside. Locals, fearful of black spirits, immediately buried the bodies and destroyed the foods."

"So, by the time we got there and talked to the local natives, there were no samples of human tissues nor foods to bring back and analyze. We talked with the pygmy chief. Some of his comments were: 'yes, we used a magic poison, purchased it from a foreigner, placed it in the Looper's food, buried all to hide the bodies, killed every one of them, killed none of us, I am better than a West Point General'. They also claimed that they would do this again. This was a new modern weapon, and it was now a new pygmy military tactic."

"Our conclusion: the 'magic poison' was probably a cellulose nanotech molecular system produced in Europe and now is being used in Africa."

Mr. Murphy finished his presentation. "In a general summary, it would appear that we are facing a new type of nanotech molecular system that is amenable to group or mass type usages. It can be distributed in the food. One can only begin to imagine how many ways such a weapon can be used—single targets or mass targets. This is a new approach using these new nanotech weapons."

"Only a few years have passed and some industrialists have really enhanced the success of the organic nanotech molecular killing systems. Now the cellulose nanotech molecular killing system is rapidly becoming popular. This latter system is more useful/practical for multiple or mass killings as with large land acquisition, creative genocide, future aerospace, cyber weapons, military weapons, and local or mini civil wars. And it all began as a mechanism within economic competition—market control."

Mr. Fermer, official historian of the committee, spoke, "Looking through the recent past 150 years, there have been 10 major and 81 mini- and maxi-wars on this planet we call earth. More than 400 million earthlings have been killed. 50,000 villages and cities, millions of bridges and tunnels have been destroyed. Most have been rebuilt. Two major cities were made uninhabitable for 50 years due to massive radiation. Seventy five percent of all graves were occupied by victims of related violence, especially some type of so-called war. I realize that nanotech systems can kill, but it does not destroy. Is this better?"

Mr. Dagda Murphy, having had 14-years-experience dealing with these nanotech killing systems, spoke up, "Let us stop here, think for a while, and focus on the future from this most recent past. Have nanotech weapons become available to anyone-anywhere today? One or many? If so, how can we fight it? Is it to become the international opiates of the future?"

He thought quietly to himself, 'Maybe the boys can be of help again. I will have a talk with Jamie and his musketeer buddies.'

Mr. Reasoner, the Chairman, deemed it time to start closing down the meeting. He said, "Please return to me the originals of those small packets which contain a list of the names and some information concerning our newly proposed choices for nanotech killer candidates. Make what notes you want from them and please return them to me. Remember our 'Need to Know' policy. OK. I think we are reaching saturation levels and it is time for some questions. Now does anyone have any specific questions?"

And indeed, the hands quickly flew up. Some difficult questions would soon be coming forward. There were a lot of new info and data and unanswered questions to consider, so might as well get started. Dr. William Walker, Chief of INTERPOL was the first to ask…

[Mr. Murphy sat back and thought to himself, 'The switch to the new cellulose nanotech molecular system as a major weapon was totally unexpected. Also, Korrectorizer chose to begin using it in African villages. Why? Was this a clever change, or an accident? He knows we are beginning to understand his systems. Apparently a one trigger mechanism is now being favored. So why not a single blocker mechanism? Time to contact one of our boys—probably Li.']

8

THE MUSKETEERS ARE READY

Four boy musketeers, from four different continents, were coming out of their educational shells—college plus supplemental training. When they first faced the nanotech world, they were pre-teenagers at play in a summer camp playground in Switzerland. Over the next few years, they lost several friends and their fathers because of nanotech killers. They worked with governmental committees, recruited several professional witches, and obtained some revenge by eliminating a few nanotech killers. Each had chosen professions which hopefully would allow them to help eliminate the international nano killing system. And they were starting to blend into a successful team. Children were becoming men with a purpose.

They were Jamie O'Reilly in Boston, USA, Li Jiang in Nanking, China and Los Angeles, USA, Kef Legoase in Cape Town and Johannesburg, South Africa, and Aykut Turan in Istanbul, Turkey. They held their first unique conference computer system which was especially encrypted using their own newly modified version of the reverse Avatar re-language, during these past many years. They had each finished or almost finished their colleges and post graduate education/training programs and wanted to talk about the future.

So, Jamie initiated the call and spoke, "This is Ey'tuka. Who is there?"

Li said, "This is Tsu'teye."

Kef said, "This is Na'via."

Aykut said, "This is Mo'ata."

"How are all of you doing?" Jamie continued.

"Things are great!" Aykut responded. "We won our international law suit, and Amber won first prize in the Turkish Dog Classic."

"You guys remember the problem, Aykut said, "My baby sister turned sixteen and mother purchased her a car. Our upper floor, ten living rooms, condo building was allowed only one underground parking space per condo. So, we sued the building owner, won, received permission for a second parking space, and now I will not have to compete with my sister every evening for a parking space."

"My 180-pound dog Amber won the Heracles award at the annual Turkish Dog Classic. I had been working-out with him every week at the Bosphorus University Dog Club. And we worked very hard. Amber pulled his first wagon with 192 pounds of rock. His second pull was with 248 pounds, a winner. And his third pull was 332 pounds, the winning pull. This is more than I can pull. It was the super championship pull. A new Turkish record. Amber was declared the Turkish National Champion. It was great."

Li spoke up, "And I won first place in the senior class Nanotech Design Club at the California Institute of Technology. My design looked like a fat snowman riding a tall skinny giraffe. Everything was made in atoms and molecules of course. HA!"

"As we were playing with the plastic model, two 'atoms' fell off. One of my buddies said it had a bad smell. From the end of the 'giraffe' which it fell, and with the proper coloring, we declared it probably came from inside not outside. The only solution was another round of Heineken beer. So, we sacrificed to science, China, and America, and drank another round. We were good patriots."

And of course, Li's on-line team got their round of chuckles. None of the three understood molecules, but each imagined they would probably be cool.

"Hey Kef, how has your life been? Asked Jamie.

All was quiet for a few moments, then Kef finally spoke up, "Well, the University of Johannesburg is great, and I will get the cast taken off my ankle next week."

Then the questions flew. "What did you do? How did you do it? I'll bet your new girlfriend did it. We warned you about that silly sport in which you won the African National Black Panther award several years ago."

They all had their round of laughing, except Kef. He was still in some pain.

And the correct question was finally formulated. "You were not going to play more soccer, but you did, and you broke your ankle. Right?" Asked Jamie.

Kef admitted it. "Well, you all know. You can take the boy away from playing soccer on Saturdays; but you cannot take him away from thinking soccer all week long; which then, if not careful, leads the boy back to playing soccer on Wednesdays. And sometimes when those Wednesday matches get too rough for pseudo-amateurs, the boy breaks a bone somewhere—so he temporarily stops playing this beautiful game—for a while. No, I'm kidding. I am truly going to stop playing as I will soon be 23. Plus, I am playing against teenagers.—that is an unfair advantage!"

Li spoke out, "Unfair advantage for who? The teenagers or the 20+ year boy?"

Kef came back, "No, I am really going to study Public Management. Nothing else in the world will distract me, not even girls."

Jamie continued, "It is really, really, good to hear your voices again. I feel like I have been living inside a zoo learning from all these stiff-backed-animals called lawyers-professors. Every animal was a different size, shape, color, vocalizations, plus different hooves, feet, hands, rear end, skin texture, ears, teeth, and appetites. I missed you guys a lot. But after that assassination attempt on the four of us in Geneva five years ago, we were indeed wise to disappear for a few years, and spend our time in colleges and schools in studying/training. Now a little revenge will be great. And Harvard University Law School has prepared me well. I will begin to work part time with my uncle's law firm and international import/export company next week. And I will work in the international-comparative legal area involving smuggling and terrorism. As you know. Nano-actions are now legally compared to terrorism-actions. I am really looking forward to it."

Aykut spoke up, "Congratulations. This is a major area we have to cover to even be able to attempt to identify transportation of nanotechnical systems. As I remember in my Aleppo and Istanbul ventures, and Li's Chinese travels, all nanotech weapons were produced in one or more countries, and then used as a death weapon in second or even a third country. International travel is a major player for these guys. It is a place we have to spend more time trying to understand, and to also get into an observation and controlling position."

"Yes," Li responded. "And my experience tells me that just by following the many types of macabre deaths shows that there are many variations in the nanotechnical systems now being produced. Therefore, there has to be several scientists designing them, probably in different countries. I have finished all of my atomic/molecular biology coursework at the California Institute of Technology, and started my doctoral research in nanotech science design. If necessary, I can go to my father's company, now my newly inherited nanotech company, and expand the degree of sophistication of the research. I can pursue my dissertation research, and my experienced company post docs and technicians can create new designs that the nano-killers may be using. And one of the first things that I want to look at—how difficult is it to shift from one nanotech design to another. Plus are they all really so different as each must enter the body, escape the body security system, lay low for a while, do their killing thing, and then disappear. There must be a limited number of possibilities for these nanotech molecular systems."

Jamie replied, "Yes, you are correct. Uncle Dagda mentioned to me that there are now several new nanotech molecular systems available to many buyers. Apparently, these are both minor variations of past systems, and completely new types of designs. So, I think your approach is the right one."

"I want to attack the weakness of the designs if there is such a thing," said Li. "At least that would cut down the volume of production, after a design is functional. I think. I have continuously focused on it. We need a direct anti-nano system, a blocking anti-nano system, and a counter anti-nano system."

And he smiled, as his buddies produced blank looks which said 'of course'. But they also smiled and pretended to really know about nano-molecules.

"That is sort of what I had in mind," replied Aykut. As he laughed.

Then Aykut continued, "As for me, I will continue my banking studies in Istanbul, then go to Harvard University in Boston. I will major in international banking, majoring in money smuggling, money laundering and movement, and electronic banking systems. International banking cybersecurity is a very important area for us. The O'Reilly Foundation offered me a scholarship for my financial support. Only Jamie knows this. I will stay in an apartment near the law school. Jamie will be working with his uncles, part time. It is better that we live separately, study separately, and see each other only occasionally. In this way, until we can develop and initiate an attack plan on these nano-killers, we will not be tempted to play time. And thank you Jamie."

Jamie replied, "You earned it. The foundation scholarship committee selected you based on your discovery of the methods used by the nano-killers in Aleppo and Istanbul. In your application you proposed both an excellent approach for a career study and continued pursuit of the nano-killers. You had the best application. Period."

All Aykut could do was to squeak. "And thank you.'

Li laughed and said, "I remember how you used your electronic magic thumb to hack into the human nano-testing center in the cemetery within the old fortress inside the mountain of the assassins in Syria. It is not really funny. In fact, it was great. That was what first opened the door to the methodology that the nanotech-killers were using in their targeting and killing. In reality, that was anti-cybersecurity before there was cybersecurity."

Jamie came back again, "You do realize, any identification of illegal monies movement or excess accumulation by members of the nanotechnology criminals, whether nanotech scientist or trafficker, is very helpful. It might not help us, but it will be useful for the Committee on Nanotechnology Control to guide the proper legal authority to those people. That could help take some of these guys out of action. And this will help us at the psych revenge level. Right?"

Li was in a good mood and he commented, "This time Aykut will need a long-distance double electronic magic thumb, not just few centimeters."

All passed on responding to that remark. Too heavy!

And there was no verbalization among the very close but very different brothers. The eyes all said yes, let's go! Only forward! They hoped!

Jamie asked, "I continued my study of Irish witchcraft during these last few years in Boston. Kef, did you continue to study voodooism when you came home and during college?"

"I certainly did," answered Kef. "I liked it a lot. But I am not sure yet just how I can use it in our nanotech quest."

"I may have your answer," replied Jamie. "Have you heard about the many recent MUSDs in various places in Africa?"

"Yes, I have. It is really bad—several families and villages in just one week," Kef returned.

Jamie asked, "Do you think that those areas which had the MUSDs could be susceptible to voodooism?"

"I do not know. But that is a good idea," replied Kef. "I have been thinking about it. I certainly will inquire. What I understand is that those MUSDs occurred in western and northern Africa. Those regions are predominately black. And that is where Voodooism originated before it moved to the Caribbean Sea area. From my studies at the Priestess Cleopatra Humfo in Haiti, I developed several African friends who planned to return here and set up voodoo practices. I can check with them."

"During my first years at Harvard University, I met several black Africans," said Jamie. "I too became good friends with one from Nigeria and one from Libya. If you need additional contacts from either of those countries, let me know. I am certain that they would welcome an opportunity to help in our nanotech war."

Jamie continued, "Such that we do not keep our conference too long, I want to offer some advice. You remember my uncle Dagda Murphy. We recently talked in my private home office. He is still Co-Chairman of the Committee on Nanotechnology Control. He said he would be pleased if we continued the nanotech war against Korrectorizer or whomever. He implied to me that there have been major changes in nanotech molecular design in the last 3-4 years. One must be very careful. We have been targets and remain so. In addition, there is information that Korrectorizer may control his nanotech molecular systems program from Washington, DC and an island in the Caribbean Sea. So, again, be careful. Uncle Dagda will help us in any way that he can, legally."

"Here are his suggestions. We will need much of the following information before we can develop a comprehensive attack plan:

1) Some characterization of the latest nanotech molecular system in use,

2) An idea of where and who designed this system,

3) An idea where and who manufactured this system in quantity,

4) By whom and by what means of transport are being used,

5) Targeted areas and/or targeted peoples,

6) Where possible, money flow—nanotech scientists, organizers, sellers and buyers.

Jamie closed off. "Good-bye for now. For future problems or questions let us continue to use the 'need to know', and our reverse Avatar re-language e-mail and skytype-V. Take care!"

9

KEF IN NIGERIA I

Several months later there was data from the World Health Organization that at least eleven villages in Nigeria were recently found to have numerous MUSDs each. Nigeria has a federal republic of government similar to the USA. The elected President and executive Department of Health and Human Services contacted the World Health Organization for assistance in fighting this new 'disease'. WHO contacted the President of the USA—Department of Health and Human Services—Division of High Technology—Committee of Nanotechnology Control Decisions made and decisions carried in reverse sequence back to the Nigerian Department of Health and Human Services. Assistance would be given.

What were those decisions? The USA, WHO, and Nigeria would each financially contribute to efforts to establish an office which would focus on these MUSD deaths. It would be housed within the Nigerian Department of Health and Human Services and would regularly report to each of the three contributors. Recruitment for a Director and staff was difficult because MUSDs and nanotech molecular systems were new to Nigeria. Kefentse Legoase's name came up as his father was killed by the nanotech killers, and he was the only African to have more than ten years of experience with this new 'disease'. Plus, recommendations came from the Chairman and Co-Chairman of the American Committee of Nanotechnology Control, and from the law firm O'Reilly, O'Reilly, and O'Reilly (Jamie), which was noted for its successful efforts in control of illegal and contraband international shipping. Certainly, all the American references helped support his nomination.

When Kef received the appointment, he immediately sent a reverse e-mail to the musketeers and told them. They each congratulated him. Jamie did not tell him about his family's efforts in the decisions. And he recommended his college friend, Aminu Adebayo, to work with him. Jamie knew that Aminu had an excellent education at Harvard U., was of the proper frame of mind to accept the challenge of this new Nigerian 'disease', and would not challenge Kef, same age and different ethnicity. And it so happened that a Yoruba and a Zulu did become close friends.

A few weeks later Kef was on a South African Airlines flight #328 from Cape Town, South Africa to Abuja, in the State of the Federal Capital Territory, Nigeria. Kef was riding economy class and struggling to give comfort to his 6ft 4in and 200lb. frame—a tight fit. He tried to lay back and began to day dream about his life and recent past events.

'This physical size has been a curse and a blessing. It seems that I no longer fit into real clothes or real beds. But it certainly gave me a super soccer career. In my senior year I won the National Outstanding Athlete of the year award. That was good because it resulted in my new 'permanent' name the Black Panther. Because I wanted to go to college, I was allowed to play 'part-time' in the 8-team minor soccer league in Johannesburg. That league allowed its players to go to college, practice soccer, and play matches on two Saturdays each month, not four, six months of the year not nine months of the year. It was good. And also working as a salesman at the Great Elephant Clothes, in the Giant Mall, selling in the boys and men's section, I sold well. All young guys wanted to buy their clothes from the 'Black Panther'. The two salaries allowed me to attend college and graduate in five years.'

'And then returning home to Cape Town to take an Administrator level II position at the South African Dockyards was a good thing. My physical size was helpful in the office and on the docks. More than once I needed to use my English and a strong demeanor to prevent a problem between local and foreign stevedores. And now I will probably have to occasionally go into the villages. Again, both my size and demeanor may be needed.'

It was a long seven-hour flight. So, he slept a little, ate a little, talked to neighbors a little, played with his i-pad, on and off on-line, and finally opened up the summary of his two-week study of Nigeria, Lagos, Abuja, and the more than 500 ethnic groups living in the country. That was the largest quantity of human heterogeneity/ diversity within one polity in the world. One African historian professor called it the all-in-a-pot without a mixer.

The modern age of Nigeria really began with colonialism by the Europeans, especially the British, in the early 19th century. Lagos, a kingship colony, and trying to follow England, was established as the capital from 1800 to 1901 as a British protectorate, then it became a member of the British Empire. Christianity was established in the West and Islam in the North. After World War II Nigeria developed self-rule. The First Republic (1960-66), civil war (1967-79), several military juntas (1970-90), and finally elections and a democracy until today.

Lagos is located on the Atlantic Ocean and is one of the largest sea ports in the world with nearly 12 million people in the surrounding area. It is situated on several semi-connected island-peninsula areas surrounding a 100 sq. mi. Lagos Lagoon is a large body of water in the center. There are several miles of shipping docks. It grew as a sprawl over many years and today it is badly over crowded with thousands of poor people living in minimum housing, terrible environmental pollution, poorly constructed roads and bridges so continuously congested traffic, much crime with many street gangs, homicides, numerous small illegal shops and factories, slave trade, shipping cargo theft, drugs, and on and on. Add to that the multiple white-collar crimes of graft, bank fraud, political corruption, money laundering, ship modification, racketeering, bribery, and on and on. The current crime rate is within the top 10% of world cities.

Abuja became the new capital in 1991. It now has more than two million people. A large savanna-rain forest mosaic area, in central Nigeria, had been chosen. Using an excellent master plan, over a 15-year period, a very modern city called the Federal Capital Territory (FCT) was built. The newly established Federal Republic of Nigeria was divided into 36 states and the FCT. The government was patterned after the USA with a two times 4 year democratically elected President who was in complete control of the Executive branch, an elected Legislative Branch with a Senate and House of Representatives, and Federal and Supreme Courts. It has excellent infrastructure, transportation, and communication systems.

Inside the belt-way there are several super-ways (highways) which are similar to Japan with two tier roads, the upper is limited to 80 miles per hour, the lower limited to 30 miles per hour. The entire city is divided into many multi districts named as based on the time built and their function: example—districts for major government buildings and federal buildings, housing for foreign ambassadors and foreign diplomats, housing for upper level government officials, and general housing; areas of executive-business offices, business and shopping centers, restaurants, personal services, health care, transportation, small shops and factories, education, parks, and sport areas. Rapid light rail transportation from center city to nearby satellite suburbs is excellent and has allowed for the development of green suburbs. Population is currently two million people. Current crime rate is near 10% of world cities—excellent.

Population in Nigeria has one of the highest growth rates in the world. Currently 250 million, expected to reach 400 million by 2060. Median age is 19 years. Long life is 61 years. There are more than 240 tribes, 210 languages, 220 ethnic groups. English is the official language and is taught in schools from 10 years onward. The three most common ethnic groups/languages/religions are: **Hausa** (40%)-Islam-North; **Yoruba** (26%)-Christianity – West; **Igbo** (17%) – Christianity-South; Traditional African groups/languages/religions (15%)-these latter are scattered all over the country; others.

Nigerians share three religions: Catholic or Protestant Christianity; Islam; native faith (Voodoosim). Many people share two faiths—most common is Christianity and Voodooism. All three faiths have one god, only the methods of worship vary.

Other important things:

    International membership – Organization of Petroleum Exporting Companies; Organization of African Unity; African Non-Aligned Movement; International Criminal Court; Commonwealth of Nations; Served as military peacekeepers of several intra African conflicts.

    Education – 15 universities – public and private.

Sports – football/soccer is the national sport and they regularly play in the world cup, won African cup many times, and the only African country to win the Olympic gold-metal in football/soccer. Also, college and professional basketball, cricket, track and field. Basketball and football are major professional sports.

Major Crimes – networks of organized crime; drug trafficking (heroin and cocaine), confraternities are college campus cults; bank fraud; political corruption; bribery; embezzlement; cybercrimes.

Human Rights – in Lagos it is bad; excessive police force; judicial corruption; harsh prisons; human trafficking; child labor; domestic violence; much discrimination based on ethnic groups and religion; in Abuja it is quiet with little human rights problems—mostly white-collar crimes, and ethnic and religious disagreements dominate.

Kef began thinking, 'It seems to me that Nigeria has come a long way in the past two generations, but they still have a long way to go. I know they have oil (hence OPEC), I am certain that must have helped. But the country is growing so very fast—and has a major population below 20 years—lots of energy that needs channeling—history of much crime from every direction, ethnicity and religion difficulties. Where do I begin to look for motives and efforts for minimizing your enemy? There is an enemy everywhere.'

As the South African Airlines flight #328 landed at the Nnamdi Azikiwe International Airport in Abuja, Kef began thinking about Jamie's college friend, Aminu Adebayo, who was going to meet him. They had exchanged several e-mails and Aminu had arranged a one-month apartment rental unit near where he would be working. Later he would select a more permanent location. Jamie recommended him very highly and thought he could be trusted, on a need to know basis. So, they agreed to a six-month trial working arrangement. Aminu was already an analyst in the Department of Health and Human Services. And Kef's three offices would be in the same Department, hence same building. This would make it easy to move around and recruit when and where needed for select investigative efforts. Kef visualized more than one such effort at a time as there was already substantial data to begin to follow.

Kef and Aminu met in the airport terminal, shook hands, said their routine positive professional remarks and headed toward Aminu's car. Center city would be a 30-minute drive. They hopped in the car and took off on the Airport Highway.

Aminu inquired, "How do you feel about this nano-challenge in another country? An exciting adventure but a difficult task?"

Kef replied, "Yes and no. The people who are now running the nanotechnology systems are a major international 'disease' and have been here for more than a decade. In 2032, my father and all the men in his work crew in the Saatfordam Diamond Mine, near Bloemfontein, South Africa, were nano-killed. I have been working with people in the USA for the past twenty years trying to identify the people involved in using these new high-tech systems and neutralize them. We have only eliminated a few. They have also killed family of those of us who are seeking them out. So later, I will explain how our quest could result in a deadly adventure. I know you have a wife and a little boy. We can talk about any possible risk to them as we get into our investigative efforts. But believe me, there will be a risk."

Groaning Aminu stated, "My wife is a western type, Swiss educated, so she has an understanding of where our country is trying to go—modern and west. She works for a Senator in the National Assembly. If you want, we can talk about her work areas later. Basically, it is natural gas-petroleum problems in the oil producing states down south. Her Senator was elected from the state of Delta."

"Thank you," said Kef. "This is my first such efforts on my own in beginning as a detective to find and catch a bunch of killers. I cannot yet predict where it will lead us and who we will need to recruit to help seek out the trail back to the international supplier. There is one certainty, all nanotech molecular systems are produced in the USA, Canada, Europe, and possibly some in China. Most nanotech targets are in less developed countries in Africa, South America and Latin America. Hence international shipping and several locals play a middle man. We want to find the locals, the cargo vessels, and possibly identify the manufacturers. Then we must be able to incarcerate those involved, and pass the information about the vessel and manufacturer to select international authorities. During the past few years these authorities have been established on each continent."

"Then we will probably need to carefully look at the criminal elements in Lagos," said Aminu. "It has the most corrupt shipping and certainly plenty of gangs which, for a small fee, would 'assassinate' entire villages."

"OK," responded Kef. I do want to learn about Lagos anyway."

"I have your work history and I realize that you are an Aruba from Lagos. Do you still have family living there?"

"Oh yes. My mother and father, uncles, aunts, cousins, and on, still live there. Only one of my two brothers lives here in Abuja, the other lives up north in Hausa."

Kef asked, "Is travel difficult going into and 'exploring' that area of Nigeria? I do want to spend a couple of weeks in Moslem Nigeria. That part of the north is all Moslem, is it not?"

"Yes, and this can be arranged."

And the two young well educated African public managers continued talking about everything related to the upward movement of Africa on the world scene, and how they could play an important role.

Driving through the Center City and into the WUSA 2 district, Kef was settled into a small apartment on NE 15th Street and Aminu went a little further to an apartment on NE 8nd Street. Their apartments were about 10 blocks walking to the National Assembly, Supreme Court, and the Presidential Complex where their offices were located in the neighboring Executive Office buildings. Tomorrow Aminu would walk to Kef's apartment. Then the two of them would go to a nearby breakfast restaurant. Afterward they would take a walking tour of the Three Arms Zone and end up in the Presidential and Executive Buildings Complex.

Kef slept very well. He was very excited. He was the athletic type and if war tomorrow, then sleep while sharpening the spears tonight.

The next morning Kef and Aminu were having breakfast at a nearby International House of Pancakes, a popular American restaurant. Pancakes were popular in the Nigerian cities as was the Big Mac. Always the American Bigs around the corner.

Aminu said, "I brought with me a tourist map of the center of Abuja. The downtown area is a long rectangle with numerous buildings and small parks. The rectangle is about 4 blocks wide and 16 blocks long. At the east end are government buildings which are enclosed within a 5-block diameter circle. At the west end is the national soccer stadium. In between is Center City (businesses, offices, shops, apartments, condos, and recreational green parks). The middle region is laid out very much like a chess board, groups of business, groups of shops, etc. However, we have planted hundreds of trees and shrubs, and the numerous buildings vary by many meters in height versus width; plus, there are numerous variations of modern and ultra-modern building designs. The tallest buildings range from 12 to 15 floors."

"The center of Abuja was designed similar to the Smithsonian Mall with the multitude of government buildings in Washington, DC. And it even works pretty good for us.—HaHa."

"So even with this map, I frequently get lost when walking around. Taxis yes, but expensive. Automobile parking is very difficult both above and below ground. Where we work, I think you will find it easier to walk to the office, other government offices, and nearby Center City locations for business or shopping. We will walk through some of this area when we go to the Three Arms Zone (the circle) from here. Most government offices are in the Three Arms Zone, which is directly in front of the gigantic Aso Rock. I will try to point out some of these things as we walk toward the government office buildings."

Kef responded, "Thank you. I'm sure a good walking map will help prevent me from getting lost. Of course, I read some things about the Nigerian government when I learned that we would be working here in Abuja. But seeing is believing. I knew that most of the government was inside a partially enclosed-secured area, and that you had many ultra-modern buildings nearby. But without a good map, it was hard to visualize everything. I remember and I did identify the National Sports Stadium and the famous football battlefield." And he laughed.

Aminu laughed with him. "I already knew that I would be working with the black panther from S.A. who beat us in overtime in the final playoff game for the World Cup XLI, even I know your name. And I am not a soccer fanatic like every male in Abuja."

A proud smile crossed the face of a person whose only claim to fame was a famous unusual name. He had just finished the last bite of his total berry topped pancake, drank his last few drops of milk, and motioned that they should be moving on. Kef really did not want to get involved in a discussion of that last 'famous' match for the 100th time. Especially at the site of that match.

As they walked away from the restaurant Aminu pointed toward the south and east. Toward the east, they could see the Aso Rock, and the Three Arms Zone was directly west in front of it, only a few blocks in front of them. So, they started walking in that general direction. Aminu guided them toward the front of the government 'battle' zones and commented on the nearby surrounding areas.

After a couple of minutes walking, they stopped and Aminu said, "Now look at your map. You can imagine that this large government area is a reverse free throw shooting line or a horseshoe with a diameter of 5 blocks. Look directly straight ahead or east and up at the Aso Rock. This famous granite Rock is nearly one kilometer in diameter and 350 meters high. On this side of the Rock is the Three Arms Zone. Pretend that at the top of the circle is the large 'basketball net corridor' called National Assembly, home of the Senate and House of Representatives, or Capital Building. On this side of that building are several office buildings for the 60 senators and 230 representatives. Over to your left or north, you can see the President's Complex which includes the Presidential State House and the buildings of the various 13 Executive Departments. And over to your right or south, is the Supreme Court Building and the buildings you can see house the three federal courts."

"Surrounding the entire Three Arms Zone area is one continuous road, Circle Drive. The government buildings are surrounded by a 3 meter high ornamental black steel fence. Just outside of the fence is a 2 meter wide sidewalk, 6 meter wide road, and no parking. The three major government buildings face the fence with their front doors; and there is a 'tourist' entry to each from outside the fence. There are three above-below ground visitor parking garages on the outside of the Circle Drive. Several government special police locations and numerous scanning security cameras are located on both sides of Circle Drive. We are standing on the inside or back side of the complex where you can see several parking lots for senior members of the government. The line that we 'pretend' to be standing on goes from left-north to right-south five blocks long and connects to the Circle Drive on both sides. So, the Three Arms Zone contains 20 plus square blocks of most major Nigerian government office buildings, all less than six floors high. And where we will work.

"And yes, the Three Arms Zone connects behind us to the National Sports Stadium some 20-blocks to the west. Independence Avenue connects them on the south and Constitution Avenue connects them on the north side. Most of Center City lies between the two avenues. Half way between the Zone and Stadium are located the two national houses of worship. On the south side of Independence Avenue is the Nigerian National Mosque. On the north side of Constitution Avenue is the Nigerian National Church."

Kef asked, "Are the two major religions treated so equally everywhere?"

"Almost, there are more Moslem citizens than Christian citizens in Nigeria," answered Aminu. "If the two components in a trial agree, the laws allow the case to be tried by the Sharia. Otherwise, the Swiss-Christian legal systems prevail."

Kef thought to himself, 'I am amazed at such equality, at least within the legal structure. Socially, I wonder?'

"You have accomplished all of this in what, less than 30 years?"

"Thirty very difficult years!" Aminu responded. "If you wish some of the personal history of people who were involved in this effort, it was not bloodless, just say so. I can provide them. Many are still alive and live here."

Kef responded, "Thank you. I will keep that in mind, depending upon which way our initial investigations take us. And thank you for the virtual tour. At least now if I get lost, I have a good chance of getting un-lost. Take me to our thinking chambers."

Thus, Kef and Aminu smiled, and began a long-term relationship. They entered the Three Arms Zone and headed toward the Presidential Complex and the Executive Office Building housing the Department of Health and Human Relations.

They first stopped at the Office of the Secretary. Aminu introduced Kef to Mr. Secretary Chimaobi Nkwado, who was an avid football fan, and who remembered that certain unlucky World Cup Playoff match, but would not remember it verbally in Kef's presence. Mr. Nkwado was from a wealthy family, educated in England and was a gentleman.

He had been given Kef's work history which involved a college degree in Public Management at the University of Johannesburg, in English, and a couple of years of on-the-ground experience at the large international dockyards in Cape Town, SA. Otherwise, this young man was simply an attack Zulu warrior. Keep an eye on him.

They all entered the Secretary's office, were served coffee, and immediately began a serious discussion. When introduced to Kef he immediately thanked him. "We appreciate your efforts to help us with this new disease that has suddenly invaded our country. I know that your father was a victim of this nanotech weapon. (He had been briefed.) I am very sorry. We now have more than 300 Nigerian fathers who have suffered the same fate during this past year. Any time and in any way call me personally for assistance. I'm certain that this will not be a simple Lagos street wars gang thing. I feel a new civil war brewing and it must be stopped. I was so happy when our President teamed up with the USA and WHO to investigate. And even happier when your research team was placed here with me/us. It is a human health problem for now. I hope it will not become a military problem."

Kef replied, "We will do our best to not let that happen."

The Secretary continued. "If you do need some military assistance, I will provide Mr. Adelbayo with a short list of senior military officers in various states where you may have to visit. Just tell him the states, and he will have those names in just a few minutes. OK?"

"Thank you. I hope we do not get that close to the 'bad guys', said Kef.

After a few minutes of chatting and getting to know each other, Secretary Nkwado told his secretary to notify one of his senior associates, Sani Abubakar. He said, "I have an excellent 'head hunter' coming to visit." And he chuckled.

The two 'hunters' stepped across the corridor and were introduced to Mr. Sani Abubakar. They entered his office, said hellos, denied a third round of coffee, and sat down to determine the role of Sani, as they were to call him.

"Simple," he said. "I am the Director's 'spy' and 'get what you need' man on the spot. I do not plan to go with you everywhere, but once we determine what and how things can happen, I will be there if you want or need me. I do have the Secretary's authority. So, I can be useful. And that makes things easier for you—one less report to write. See, I am already useful." And he chuckled.

Kef did not chuckle with him, but understood the situation. They were stuck with each other. So might as well get to know him. "I am certain that we will be compatible and useful to each other." And he chuckled. Friends, maybe, someday.

Aminu exchanged looks with Kef. But he said nothing.

So, they spent a few minutes discussing logistics of travel, hotels, meals, contacts, and special needs within the state capitals, and what type of military units were camped where. Sani did have direct access to all of this information, names, telephone numbers, e-mail numbers, and authority over the local and state police. He would give to Aminu the info that was critical for them to travel to their selected states. Would some villages be difficult to travel and visit? Would some tribal groups be difficult to visit? Certain villages were nano-killed. Other villages were accused of these killings. Right or wrong, hatred was in the air in several village areas. Occasionally, continuous presence of military could be necessary.

After a half hour of discussing such critical components of air versus land versus water travel to the massacred villages, Sani asked Kef, "When you have determined which states and villages that you want to investigate and when you want to visit them, let me know. I have prepared folders of each destroyed village and the data and info that our police collected at that time. Here it is."

And he picked up a locked briefcase from his locked desk drawer. "This contains 13 folders of 13 villages where most of the villagers were nanotech killed here in Nigeria, during the past six months. Here is the key. These are all copies. If originals are needed later for reports to USA or WHO, I would need permission from the Secretary, and possibly the President. The President is concerned that this will be more than local Nigerian family murders/massacres. And if other countries or citizens of other countries are found to be involved, things could go to the international courts. One Sub-Court of International Crime is located here in Abuja. So?"

"We are trying to be careful and not 'mess-up' collection, analysis, or interpretation of data from any of the villages. Both the President and Secretary very badly want to apprehend these guys.?

"And so do I," said Kef.

They all stood at the same time, said grim goodbyes, and understood that within a week Kef and Aminu would have a plan—a list of villages and a time frame for inspection of each one. Sani would be the first to see this list.

Aminu took Kef to the second floor of the same building and showed him their new three office 'thinking rooms'.

The offices were furnished—one office for the 'boss', and two offices for two 'workers' each. Kef commented, "I am sure we can have more furniture or space if we ask for it. Certainly, Sani would have them brought here in about two minutes, if we called him." And both he and Aminu laughed.

Kef felt the Nigerian government pressure on him already, and he had not even read all of the death info or data. But he could understand.

Kef started thinking to himself, 'I was nearby when my father and his team of diamond miners were nanotech killed. I felt totally helpless. No one knew anything. No one to turn to and ask questions. And then when it was decided that some deadly moss or fungus or virus or micro-organism killed them, I felt really lost and helpless. Over the years, my Witch-Voodoo friends helped me get some revenge. I know at least one guilty nanotech scientist who is still breathing but not really alive. I am not sorry. He deserved it.'

'Now we have to continue to fight Korrectorizer, as well as help the families of these nanotech massacres obtain a little revenge. I must talk with my Voodoo contacts in Nigeria. I brought with me all of the contact info that I have about the several Voodoo priests/priestesses who are here in west-central Africa. When I spent that summer at the Queen Cleopatra Humfo in Haiti, I met several young Africans in Voodoo trainings. After graduation each had planned to return home to Africa and apply their new craft to help their people. I will e-mail one of the daughters of the Queen and obtain those new African addresses of previous students. I am certain that I can recruit Witchcraft-Voodoo assistance again. They will help me.'

10

MOTION IS MOTION IS MOTION

At 11:00 AM in Boston, Aykut looked into his skype screen and said, "This is Mo'Ata, who else is there?"

Five seconds later he saw and heard a Woolf, Woolf, Woolf,,,,,,,,,,GRRRRR.

So, Aykut immediately replied, "Good Boy! Good Fellow! Stay Down! Relax!"

His 175-pound dog, Amber, his 'little brother' was sitting on Aykut's bed at 6:00 PM in Istanbul and staring at him. He immediately did as Aykut told him to do. Aykut's little sister, Gul, had prearranged him for this first Sunday evening each month skype call from his master. Then Gul sat off to the side so she could watch the action and 'correct' just in case Amber became over excited.

Aykut continued, "How is my big fellow? My big guy? Did you have a good month? Did Gul walk you OK, give you enough food, love you enough, do you miss me? I miss you!"

And there was a loud Woolf – Woolf—from the Istanbul screen.

"I had a good week. I am learning a lot of neat new things. Soon I will be able to rob a bank by standing outside the door, I will not have to go inside with a gun to stick them up and make money. Then, when I come home, you and I can go rent a speed boat spin on the Bosphorus Waterway. But I have to learn a lot more. I need to learn how secret money gets into a bank, and how it travels to other banks and about money laundering houses. Have you ever heard of washing money? They do not use soap. HaHa!"

And there was a loud Woolf—Woolf—from the Istanbul screen.

"Tomorrow I will go to Jamie's house and we will make plans to try to do just that, follow money from laundry to laundry, HA. Jamie's Uncle Dagda suggested that we monitor 'layering' between different banks, laundries, and multiple companies in several countries in Europe and Africa. That means breaking big pieces of money into little pieces of money. Now what do you think of that? From there we will try integration mechanisms such as purchasing center city office buildings and rental properties, historic old mansions, airplanes, bankrupt companies, ships, large pieces of art and paintings, and more. Maybe we could purchase a speed boat of our own so we can go for a ride all the time. Now what do you think of that idea?"

And there was a loud Woolf—Woolf,,,,,GRRRRRRRRRRRRR.

{For the next 15 minutes boy and dog discussed the not-so-legal methodologies of secret electronic banking systems. Amber obviously understood the questions, agreed with the ideas, but was not good with the needed answers. Aykut continued discussing with his little brother the many methods of clandestine movement of money from place to place while avoiding government tax structures. There were many clever ways to accomplish this, and all were constantly in motion. It was fun talking about it, but probably not too much fun when applied to try to identify the money roads used by the nanotech killers. At least Amber and he usually agreed and there were frequent Woolf – Woolf—Woolfs expressing the agreement}

Little sister, Gul, was trying not to develop a stomach ache by trying not to laugh too hard at some of their 'agreements'.

But the 'conversations' had gone smoothly, all had fun and, when Aykut finally said "I have to go now. I will be back, soon."

Amber gave out his Woolfing goodbye and started jumping and dancing up and down on the bed. 120-pound Gul could only sit and watch her bigger brother enjoy himself with her biggest brother. She got as much enjoyment out of this monthly 'secret' conference as the two brothers did.

A couple of months later, Jamie had just hung up a cell-phone call from Uncle Dagda when Aykut rang the doorbell of the O'Reilly Boston house. Aykut had moved to Boston. He was staying at a Harvard University dormitory and going to school most days at Harvard University School of Banking. Jamie was living at home and working most days at his family law firm, O'Reilly, O'Reilly, O'Reilly and Associates. So, they met on pre-selected after evening dinners for coffee and Jamie's mother's homemade apple cobbler dessert—better than any restaurant.

Several years ago, after Jamie's father was nano assassinated, two of Jamie's school buddies were also killed, Jamie was kidnapped, the little finger on his left hand was removed by the nanotech killers, and Jamie securely retreated into the family home. Uncle Dadga convinced him into taking over his father's den-study and study-work there. It was now 'bug' checked regularly by Uncle Dagda's Committee 'bug' specialists. Only then did Jamie and the three other boys feel secure enough to discuss their efforts in battling the Korrectorizer and his associates. The four musketeers, as a group, had also almost been assassinated by these guys a few years ago in Geneva. So special procedures and careful timing had been worked out for any and all such 'business' meetings. This meeting had been established at 7AM this morning via a reverse e-mail system using a special modified Avatar language = Mo'ata to Ey'tuka. It would begin at 7PM in the Boston den-study with only two of the four in presence. Why? The Need to Know!

Aykut entered the lovely old New England house. After entering, he and Jamie double cheek kissed, Turkish style, and Jamie hung Aykut's coat up in the entry corridor. During their mutual greetings they expressed all was well. And they would get caught up on their private lives later.

They went into the salon where Jamie's grandmother was waiting. She also gave Aykut the double cheek-cheek kiss. Her ancestors in Ireland used this greeting, and she considered it to be more aristocratic. And she liked showing off her heritage to the foreign youngsters. She was now in her late eighties and lived with only one full time live in-female caregiver. She was still a handsome lady, in good health, so enjoyed it when Jamie's young male friends visited him. She had raised three sons. One had become the President of the USA. Another was an American Attorney General. And Jamie's father had been the Undersecretary of Higher Technology before he was nano-killed. Jamie was the next generation male and she had high hopes for him. She always wanted to meet and get to know his close friends. So, she demanded and got her fifteen minutes of private conversation with Aykut in the salon, then she let him go with Jamie to his private 'man' cave. This was her best quarter hour of the month.

After settling into the two large arm chairs in the study, and exchanging recent past events on minor college stuff, Mrs. O'Reilly served Irish tea and large portions of apple cobbler. But she was not comfortable enough to sit and converse with the both of them together, so she left in order to allow the fellows to their own 'mischief'.

Jamie began the idea exchange with, "During the past few years we understand that the nanotech molecular systems, of whatever type, appear to all be made by some high technology scientist in a wealthy country with excellent high science technology. And then this system was usually used to kill in another country, modern or just developing, examples are Europe, Middle East, Asia, or Africa. So, we could look for the big action or big money going to the scientist or marketer, probably using land and/or water transportation. Right now, Kef is investigating more than 200 nanotech deaths in Nigeria and several other places in Africa. If we want to complement his efforts, I think we should focus on Europe for big money movement. I remember a Dr. Anneka Andersson from Stockholm, and her African students/ trainees possibly taking some nanotech weapons home with them; a Mr. Faustino Mariniti who has connections to nanotech scientists in Rome and Milan, and extensive shipping into north and west Africa; Dr. Albert Langdon, from London, who was the key nanotech scientist of the first nanotechnology company, Equus Transport International, that manufactured and marketed various 'systems' in Africa; a Mr. Jackson White, also from London, simply buying and selling 'any nanotech-system' to narcotic gangs in Chad and Nigeria, Africa."

"I suggest that we concentrate our initial efforts on the Europeans. At least we do have names and some data that says they connect from nanotech weapons to Africa. We can investigate these shipping routes and money systems. Plus, we need to check on Dr. Langdon, London, as he was a key member of ETI, and many of their members were killed in the Irish Sea last year."

Aykut said, "That is a very good idea. For now, keeping our first series of investigations in Europe and Africa makes it easier for Asu and I, if we should need to travel."

He continued, "Let me then continue by reviewing the possible ways of moving money semi-legally. I will assume that we are following the monies that went to the nanotech scientist or one of the first marketers, hence more than one million dollars per transaction. Common methods are store-value-cross-board-cards, smurfing (large sums divided into small sums), shell companies, on-line gambling, bitcoin, transborder gambling, black currency exchange, Hawale (virtual transfer), and purchase-sell large items such as classic mansions-chateaus-manor houses, real estate, yachts, racing cars and horses, sports betting, casino gambling, and antiques."

"And if you just want to directly clean a large amount of cash (money laundering), many of these previous mentioned methods (certainly buying and selling) plus use of false companies, corrupt banks, corrupt politicians, drug cartels, and street gangs can be used. One can always buy high and sell low if fast laundering is necessary."

"Other areas that we can look at include:

- Low Tax Countries – Andorra, Liechtenstein, Bulgaria, Georgia, Malta, Montenegro.
- Offshore Banks – UBS-AG, Vadian, BSI-SA, Weglin & Co, Sovereign Man.
- Tax Havens – Cayman Islands, Panama, Bahamas, British Islands"

"So, you can see there are many ways and many places to collect, wash, move, hide, store, and reuse illegitimate monies. Some 'professional' hacking would be very helpful, at least in identifying where to begin looking for such money."

Jamie spoke up, "I certainly agree. I had been thinking about this potential problem. Last week I spoke with Li, since he is becoming a PhD nanotech scientist. I asked him what he would do with a large chunk of money coming from a buyer, like Mariniti. What would he do with it, spend it or hide it? If the latter, how and where would he do so. His immediate response was in the conservative direction— offshore bank within a tax haven. I had not really considered that, very clever. Obviously, he also had been thinking about such problems."

"That only leaves us with a dozen or more places to begin looking," Akyut replied. "And that does not consider methods of movement from buyer to tax haven; and from tax haven to spendable positions. Un-spendable money is the same as no money."

"Yes, I agree," said Jamie. "Upfront information about the specific how and where would be very helpful. Any good specific hacking data obtained from any specific nanotech killer candidate and his money movements could give us a good start in tracing those specific monies."

Akyut replied, "If we do not have any good info about a specific candidate and his monies roads, this would cause a lot of hunt and guess. We need Asu."

Aykut spoke up, "It is nearing 8 PM. So I expect Asu Oktem, my cybersecurity partner, to call anytime. You never met Asu, but I am sure you remember him. He is my good Turkish friend who provided me with the hacking magic thumb that I used when I sneaked inside the mountain cave-castle of the Assassins in Syria and recorded the info about the methods that the nanotech killers used. After four years of trying, Uncle Dagda and his international committee did not have such information. And in ten minutes with that little thumb-hacker and a thin mountain wall, we had our first real success."

"Whatever, he finished his computer cybersecurity studies in Istanbul, and went to work with my bank, the International Istanbul Bank. He successfully developed several anti-hacking programs and then studied for a degree in computer programing. The bank next gave him a scholarship to attend a two-year university program in international cybersecurity at the Johns Hopkins University in Baltimore, Maryland. He will soon graduate, return to the IIB. Next year I will also return to the IIB. We will work for the same bank and perform side projects such as involving international nanotechnology crimes. Much of this will be sponsored by the USA Division of High Technology, as in American dollars."

"Now, he will call us on his specially designed Apple IOS-Z-49.6.7 which has a place for a special SIM-card, in fact two of them. What do these special SIM-cards do? Each can be removed and a new one inserted in 5 seconds. When in use any hacking will immediately be detected as you receive a special high frequency sound which temporarily turns off the phone. In general, the cards simply block hackers by using background acute sounds and variable noises. When removed and placed in the dark for 10 hours they 'clean' themselves. In fact, this phone is so popular with the senior administrators and the Board of Directors at the IIB, they want Asu to develop a new generation of such cards. His current training is going in the direction of soft-ware design, and he is working with a couple of John Hopkins University professors who are also software computer engineers. His interests are very broad. He will be great to work with in the future. Certainly, our gang will use his mind."

And of course, Aykut's phone rang and it was Asu. He was calling from Baltimore. Aykut asked him if things were OK to talk about business in the usual way. In other words, they would speak in Turkish now, and later Aykut would translate all for Jamie.

Asu said, "Yes. All is going well and I am looking forward to going home. I want to try some new design ideas that I saw begin to materialize here. But I would like to get some patent rights and make some money for a change. All I have been doing is giving away my brains. HA! HA! How many doctorates do I have? NONE. But if I can help eliminate those nanotech killers, I will be happy."

Aykut commented, "Then you will be happy. Because we need certain critical data that only you can obtain for us. Where are these certain people living, how are they obtaining their tech supplies, who is helping design their primary and secondary nanotech molecular systems, who is manufacturing various molecular programs, who stores their monies, how and with whom are they shipping and marketing their products—names, addresses, telephone numbers, bank numbers, shipping numbers, international codes and customs numbers, and on and on. We have none of these. So, we need your help very badly. OK?"

"I know," Asu replied. "I know this and I will do this. But I do need a couple of hours!"

And he chuckled, along with Aykut and Jamie. They had been trying for several years without success.

Asu continued, "Let me begin with a definition—Cyber Security is the hacking of consumer electronics in an attempt to exploit a computer system or a private network inside a system of computers and take control of it. Hackers have names—White, Gray, Red, Black,—plus

Electronic Chatting, E-Banking, Code Words Systems, Blue Tooth based framework hacking devices, and on. Do you have this?"

Aykut responded, "Yes, I am recording all and will translate later."

"There are several special systems which I think you might want to consider, think about, and get back to me with your questions. These methods include: Mobile Banking Trojans, Phishing, Keyloggers, DoSDo, Waterhole, Fake Wap, Evesdropping, Clickjacking, Cookie Theft, Bait and Switch, and Man Middle Attack. Each of these are defined on-line under—methodsofhacking.com. I suggest that you first consider looking at Phishing and Bait and Switch."

"Look at them all. If you want to focus on money, use Banking Trojans and Phishing. If addresses, use Keyloggers and Bait and Switch. I can use all of them. Plus, that is the area I continue to research. So, I might have some better methods in the near future."

Jamie spoke up, "We have used up our 15-minute limit for this type of call guys."

Asu said, "I understand you are continuously living in the cross-hairs of people who kill for a living. If I can help you in any way, please let me know. When Aykut and I return to Istanbul and work next door to each other, it will be easier to discuss hacking and anti-hacking methods. Like you two can do such in the same 'sterile' room there in Boston."

"But someday you will have to explain to me what is a 'sterile' room—virus free, or girl free?"

And all three friends had their chuckles and a common dangerous quest. They said their thank you and good byes. Asu to Aykut—see you on the Bosphorus Waterway.

"I am now beginning to understand the overall problem," said Jamie. "We need data on the specific candidate, his electronic roads, and his monies roads."

Aykut replied, "And I had the feeling that Asu was asking us to suggest which electronic road he should use on day one for which candidate, so he would not have to do a lot of hunt and guess work. Because I need that data as-soon-as-possible, I will go on-line with methodsofhacking.com. Also, we will both soon be back in Istanbul, working at the same bank, so we can 'silently' talk about our 'special project'. Does that seem reasonable with you?"

"That seems reasonable to me," said Jamie. "Besides, your electronics is much better than mine."

Aykut inquired, "Then how about you informing me about the legal aspects of what we are doing. I am blank here. Is it legal or illegal or non-legal or just para-legal. They are bad guys killers, so does that make us just less than legal?"

"We are certainly less than legal," Jamie replied.

And he laughed. Most of his friends have the same level of understanding of general laws. Somehow, he thought Aykut was pulling his leg.

"There are no hard and fast laws for nano-systems crimes." Jamie said. "Currently, our international laws focus on terrorism. Example: First, a nanotech molecular system can cure certain diseases, such as some cancers. Legally—OK. Second, when a nanotech molecular system kills, it almost always involves trans-national crimes, just as we discussed earlier. The system is usually produced in one country and actions/kills in another country. This is a major legal problem. Not all countries agree or comply with the laws that do exist."

"We are trying to completely-legally link nano-system crimes to terrorism crimes. Terrorism also has a limited criminal law definition at the international level. In general, any violent act which is intended to create fear or terror is considered terrorism. This is especially true if it involves civilians. It can occur for political, religious, ideological, ethnic, or territorial reasons. And it usually targets civilians. Terrorism acts are usually committed by foreign organizations, rebel groups, or just semi-organized groups. They are frequently sponsored by right-wing or left-wing groups, an anarchist state, trans-nationalists, narcoterrorism, cyberterrorism, ethnic violence, religious extremism, maritime terrorism or piracy—pseudo crazies. Nanotech killing does not necessarily fit those criteria of terrorism."

"Because of the similarities between terrorism and nano-system crimes we are in the process of linking them to the same legal systems at the international level. Basically, this is the system used for all **transnational criminal events**. The specific crimes of [murder-rape-theft-kidnapping-violence-prostitution-torture-illegal drugs-hijacking-robbery-autojacking-fraud-extortion-racketeering] are judged under federal, state, or local laws of the country where they are committed. We are following the formula used to develop the legal system for terrorism. Terrorism and nano system crimes now are being positively reviewed together, and we are slowly moving into international legal world."

"The Memorial Institute for the Prevention of Terrorism (2003) is currently being used as a model to develop a Memorial Institute for the Prevention of Nano-Crimes or Nano-Terrorism. The United Nations General Assembly passed two resolutions—the International Convention for Suppression of Acts of Financing Terrorism (1999) and the International Convention of Acts of Financing Nuclear Terrorism (2005). We are trying to introduce a similar resolution for Nano-Crimes or Nano-Terrorism, using the terrorism conventions as a model. The International Court of Justice in the Hague (known as the World Court) judged the first Nano-Crimes or Nano-Terrorism case in 2040." So, the legal world is slowly recognizing and trying to separate the negative and positive aspects of nanotechnology."

Aykut responded, "OK. I have a general understanding where the legal world is going. But let us have another cup of tea, and then I have a bunch of questions. Just as I am sure you have some questions on the possible monies movement possibilities."

11

KEF IN NIGERIA II

In mid-morning, Kef and Aminu were discussing research options in their new offices. They began reviewing the thirteen 'nanotech' massacred villages.

Kef began, "There are seven villages in the South-South part of the country, where the rich oil and natural gas producing fields are located. Three are just north of Lagos. While three were in the north in the states of Kaduna and Niger. There seems to be three groups. So? Did that imply that logically there was similar causes behind/within each of the three groups. It is simply a first working assumption. What do you think? Shall we begin with the southern states?"

"I think you are right in assuming three groups," replied Aminu. "If you look at each region, there are many differences between the three regions, but many similarities within each region."

Kef continued, "OK. Then we should recruit our first team-mate from that South-South region."

And he smiled at the name of the area. For Nigeria, south means oil.

"If you want to begin in the petroleum-oil-gas region, you can discuss the petroleum problems in that region with my wife when we have lunch together, today," said Aminu. "Earlier I mentioned that she is the Administrative Assistant of a famous Senator from Delta, which is the richest oil producing state in the South-South. It is in the middle of the half dozen such states, including Bayelsa. That is my wife, Ajana's home state."

"Good idea. Maybe she can also help us recruit a team mate from there," Kef replied.

The three of them were going to have lunch today in their building which housed the executive offices for the Department of Health and

Human Relations, Department of Commerce, and the Department of Labor. The three large sets of office buildings, President-Executive, Legislative, and Judicial each had their own restaurant-cafeterias. At noon the two of them would meet Arjana downstairs. She would simply walk over from the Legislative Office Buildings, one block away.

Kef spoke, "Because we will have lunch in less than an hour, perhaps you could give to me a brief summary of your wife's personal-professional life."

"Of course," replied Aminu, "You already know my professional history, public schools here in Abuja, four years scholarship studying at Harvard University in Boston, USA, six years employment in government service here in HHS. While working here, I met Arjana here on the government campus. She was working for Senator Adeleki. We fell in love, married, had our son, Nduka, who now attends pre-school one block from our condo-house in WUSE II. We frequently walk here to work together."

"Arjana was born and raised in Yenagoa, capital of the state of Bayelsa in the South-South, probably where we will spend considerable investigation time. It is the center of the oil rich region in Nigeria. Her family owns a substantial amount of petroleum/natural gas rights, in other words they are very rich. She went to schools in Yenagoa and here in Abuja, received high grades, and family money helped her attend the University of Zurich, Switzerland. She speaks English and German, and studied public management and administration. From there she returned and began working for Senator Adeleki after he was elected for his third 6-year term. Both the Senator's family and Arjana's family have known each other for many years—both are oil rich families. Such is not uncommon in Nigeria."

"The South-South region has more than ten states, 250 village governments, and 45 ethnic/tribal groups each with their own dialect/language. So, it really requires an insider, someone who has lived there, to understand what is happening, how, and maybe why. We will need such help in our investigative efforts, even in just taking dispositions from locals. Outsiders are outsiders."

Kef responded. "I think I understand. Your wife's personal life and working life sort of begins and ends in the South-South."

And the two of them enjoyed a smart grin. As they will soon learn, the uneven distribution of oil and natural gas revenues between land owners and non-land owners present a big unsolved problem in the South-South.

An hour later Aminu and Kef were waiting for Arjana in the entry to their office building cafeteria-café when Aminu suddenly looked up and smiled at a young lady coming toward them. She was very pretty with the beginning of a middle age body. There was love in his look, and Kef could see the same look returned. This was a happy couple with good jobs and their first child. Good. She was a little taller than Aminu, but without heels they would look eye to eye, a handsome couple of professionals. Good 'genes' and a solid education. He thought he was lucky to have Aminu referred to him by Jamie. He had a feeling that the project would go well.

Arjana and Aminu kissed. And when Aminu introduced his wife to Kef, Kef commented, "I have seen your son's picture and I do believe that he is yours; Aminu's, I don't know."

And he winked at her. She just blushed. While Aminu smiled and quickly opened the door and led then toward the food line.

While walking Kef asked Arjana, "And has your son decided what he wants to do in life?"

Arjana quickly responded, "Yes. He wants to be a helicopter engineer."

Kef blinked. 'At four years he has big ideas. I must remember not to engage him in a conversation. I might get overrun.'

They quickly dropped the subject of children, took their food, went to and sat in a secluded corner four-person table, and quickly ate with minimum conservation. Arjana only had one hour for lunch. She was not her own boss, like the 'boys' were.

Half an hour later Arjana, Aminu, and Kef had finished their lunch, Aminu picked up the three trays with dishes and carried them to the dirty dish racks near the exit to the dining room. Arjana and Kef moved into the cafe area of the cafeteria and selected a conversation table in a corner of the room. Aminu brought three cups of coffee to the table and the general conversation shifted into the serious world, Nigerian ethnicity, and petrol, the major problems.

Arjana looked Kef in the eye and said, "It is delightful to meet you and know that someone, not politically oriented," and she smiled because her boss was not nearby, "is attacking this new world-wide disease using government monies. It seems this disease is man made so should be man killed. And you are in the vanguard. If there is anything or anyway that I can help, please let me know. Aminu and I have talked about the thirteen villages which were massacred. And I realize that many of them are in the Niger River Delta, my home. This region provides over ninety percent of the foreign exchange via petroleum products for Nigeria. So, for me, it has a double meaning—my ancestors and my field of professional interest."

"Maybe you should brief Kef about some problems that he might encounter when we go there to investigate the nanotech killings," suggested Aminu.

"Kef said, "Yes, please do."

Arjana responded, "OK. If you have questions while I talk, please ask."

"Nigeria is the tenth largest petroleum producer in the world and a major player in OPEC. Most, and certainly the highest quality, petroleum is located in the Niger Delta Basin, on-shore and off-shore. 600 oil fields and more than 3000 oil wells. The highest quality/quantity is not equally distributed to the many ethnicities in the area, but to select groups."

"There are more than 300 ethnic peoples in Nigeria. HAUSA-70 million, Moslem, north, raising cattle and crops; YORUBA-60 million, Christian-Moslem-Traditional, west and central, mixed professionals, culture, arts; IGBO-40 million, Christian, south-west, mixed professional, marginalized in distribution of oil shares; IJAW-25 million, Christians, south, oil traders, also marginalized in distribution of oil shares; KANURI; 4 million, north-east, Sunni-Moslem, produced insurgent militants (Boko Haram), and on and on and on…"

"I grew up in the Niger Delta Basin, therefore Yoruba, Igbo, Ijaw, Ibibo, Tiv, Porto, and Kanusa are my major ethnics. Plus, today I work with Senator Adeleke, who represents the people of the Basin. So, I do know the oil-ethnic problems of South-South Nigeria."

'Shall I continue?'

"Please do." Answered Kef.

Arjana continued, "As I mentioned, the Ijaw and the Igbo peoples believe that they did not receive their share of oil rights after the civil war. So, they are always looking for an excuse to strike out."

"Plus, there are the continuous problems such as: oil spills, pipeline vandalism, crude oil theft from tankers and above/below ground storage pipelines, pollution, kidnapping foreigners, world pricing difficulties, poor pipeline infrastructure, fires, loss of marketable gas from oil wells, poor gas well development, and now maybe we can add nanotech massacres to the list."

Arjana finished, "To summarize a brief overview, as you make your investigation in the Niger Delta Basin, keep in mind the states of Delta, Bayelsa, Rivers, Imo, Uyo, and Cross River, plus the 'permanent' hatred of the Ijaw and Igbo ethnics in the area. Also remember, the ethnics in Nigeria are not isolated in just one or two states. Some states may have predominately one group. But frequently the groups are scattered in an area that involves more than one state, perhaps more than one country."

Continuing, "And please remember in 1800 there were only 20 countries in Africa and more than 1000 ethnic tribes. Today there are 60 countries, 300 states, and more than 900 ethnic tribes. Many ethnic tribes, which were under a single political unit, are now under several political units. How did this happen? American and European colonists came to modernize and Christianize the African black illiterate. In reality, they identified African natural resources such as oil, gold, diamonds, silver, copper, bauxite, uranium, coca-beans, tropical fruits, unique woods, and slaves. With 'modern' pencils they drew 'convenient' new political lines down the rivers. Historically, most ethnic-tribes were living astraddle rivers, mom and dad on one side, and children plus grandchildren on the other side. So, it became common for the families and ethnic tribes to be split into separate political units. Today this is a major problem with the semi attempts at re-distribution of the 'natural wealth in Africa."

Kef responded, "I understand. And I agree. Thank you very much. That information is indeed helpful. Six of the seven nanotech massacres in the South-South involve those states and those ethnic groups. We may need to call upon you to help us, both in selecting working assistants, 'witnesses', and interpreting what/how they respond to questioning. Good dispositions will help us move in the correct investigative direction. Bad dispositions will put us on false trails. And we are beginning our investigation several weeks late for most villages. Can you suggest someone who knows the people, the area, and how to approach questions or problem solving? Or do we need a separate assistant for each village or 'group' of people?"

"Give me a couple of days to think about this," said Arjana. "I will try to find someone who could serve as an overall assistant, but I should also look for one or two names of assistants from several ethnic groups. You might even want to use cross questioning—separately with two assistants. Information which you receive may be biased."

Aminu spoke, "Because we are going to begin our work in the South-South, can you also please suggest two experienced government people from here on campus who are locals from that region? We will probably make this appointment temporary, because when we move to another region, such as up north to Kaduna, we will try to find similar experienced government people who are locals from there."

"Again, you will have to give me a couple of days to think about this," replied Arjana. "I do understand your rationale in using a short-term experienced government management type with the appropriate regional background. And it is good to use him/them only during the duration of your investigative efforts at that specific location. You can indeed change those assistants when you change locations. I even suggest that you consider doing this."

Kef said, "This will allow us to keep more newly gathered information and data 'quiet'. And if we have someone who has management experience and can hopefully contribute to thinking anew with the new info, and he will not just carry luggage."

And that drew a small round of smiles.

"One more question, we will begin at Port Harcourt, Rivers. Can you give to us any information about this area?"

"Of course, I have been there many times," Arjana explained. "It is a well-organized city of more than one million people, a good science-oriented university, and several 4-star hotels with excellent restaurants. Roads and bridges are good. The reason I say bridges is because this is indeed a delta of a major river, the Niger. There are thousands of streams and small rivers, hence hundreds of bridges. For road travel, you must continuously check for 'functioning' bridges. And ocean water travel is good, if the waves are less than 10 feet and you want to go to the off-shore oil rigs, but dangerous for most of the fast-current rivers. Avoid inland water travel if possible, or rent a very competent boat and experienced captain."

"I am running a little late so I had better get back to work. My boss is out of town, so I have to do his work also." HA HA

Kef stood up. They all stood up, shook hands and he said, "Thank you for the information and advice. I am certain that I will need this information. And I am just as certain that I could never obtain it in such a nice clear and compact form from anyone else in the world, certainly not a lovely young lady."

Aminu spoke up, "Hey don't spoil her. She is liable to nominate herself to serve as one of the administrative assistants for our project. She could take a short vacation and visit many of her childhood friends. Then I would have to stay home and baby sit."

"Does she like football?" asked Kef.

And she gave him a funny look and said, "What?"

Aminu changed the subject. And they continued walking toward her building. The 'boys' just pretended they did not hear her last response. At her legislative building's front door, only Arjana had the necessary entry pass. So, she entered and the 'boys' turned toward their executive building.

On route, Aminu explained, "I forgot to tell you. Arjana played basketball in high school. I am no athlete. Hence we 'prefer' a sport called basketball."

Kef responded, "Yes, I have heard about this sport! HA!"

And the two seemed to be enjoying each other.

12

AYKUT AND ASU

In 2039, Aykut and Asu had finished their college education/training and returned to Istanbul. They were both working for the International Istanbul Bank in Taksim, center of business Istanbul on the European side of the Bosporus Waterway, looking from Europe into Asia. They had side by side offices which looked directly down onto the only water transportation route from the Black Sea to the Marmara Sea to the Aegean Sea to the Mediterranean Sea to the Atlantic Ocean. They could count every transit ship (320 semi-trailers per ship) and oil tanker (1000 to 5000 gallons); As many as 45 vessels per day. All going through a city of 10 million people. Amazing!

Aykut was involved in many aspects of the legal and not so legal electronic movement of monies, at the national and international levels. Asu spent most of his working and after working hours hacking and developing ani-hacking methodologies, cyber-interdigitation, cyber-offensive means, cyber-security, cybernetics, and several new types of cybersecurity systems. Because they were also involved in one of the **special projects–nano-systems** funded by the American Committee of Nanotechnology Control, they shared adjacent offices on the tenth floor of the IIB. With shared spectacular views toward the east down into the Waterway, they could talk 'quietly' with each other anytime, day or night. It was an excellent and very secure arrangement. Both offices were electronically checked every week by Turkish security.

One early evening after a light snack and their starter coffee, they sat down in Aykut's office around his small conference table, two arm chairs, computer terminals, cell phones, pertinent I pad files, and began looking at their recent nanotech research data.

Aykut opened up first, "We agreed to begin with the three most obvious candidates who were located in Europe and Africa connected. Right?"

"Yes," responded Asu. "That is where I am with good data."

"Then let us begin with Dr. Anneka Andersson in Stockholm, Sweden and her black African doctoral student/trainees."

"Dr Andersson was easy. I used simple phishing methods, offering her a special five-year interest free credit card and a 30 percent discount on a new Mercedes car. She willingly gave to me her other two email addresses, home and work addresses, bank accounts and credit card numbers, and recommended two of her students for complimentary credit accounts with Olympic bank credits. Checking into her recent past banking maneuvers, she has two shell companies, 'High Tech Corners' and 'Technics of Tomorrow'. And she regularly purchases and sells, with 'Jackson and Jackson Real Estate', classic mansions on the sea shore along the Baltic Sea. I learned that purchase of nanotech supplies is legitimate via Sweden and international grants for research for her students. I can go further but that is all for now."

"She currently has six male African students from Nigeria, Democratic Republic of Congo, and Angola. From what little I could learn from her scientific publications, they each have separate projects, and she reports their data in good medical journals but uses false names for the villages. And from what little nanotech science that I have learned they are indeed killing villagers in various macabre ways. MUSDs in various village in each country are regularly reported by local police."

"So, they are probably testing their nanotech systems with 'human volunteers'? commented Aykut.

"Yes," said Asu. "I am confident of my data should you want to relay it to Jamie and on to Uncle Dagda as well as Kef in Nigeria. Uncle Dagda and his Committee can follow up on Dr. Andersson's attempts to avoid the law, certainly her taxes. Oh! By the way. Kef can find the names and addresses of her students from their research papers on line. If he has problems, let me know. I have other methods."

And they both smiled and chuckled.

Aykut commented, "Nice work fellow. I can add some additional numbers from Dr. Andersson's bank accounts, credit card accounts, and real estate actions. Those shell companies are just false shadows."

"Who do you want to look at now?" Asked Asu. "Let's do Mr. White. He seems like a meaningless guy. But he does get around."

"OK. Let's go."

"Mr. Jackson White apparently is just a simple businessman who learned, somehow, about this new world of nanotechnology, simply buys and sells like all good businessmen. How the product is used is not important. I used two types of hacking with him."

"First, Bait and Switch didn't work as London has a variety of computer anti-hacking walls in place. I went to Banking Trojan by using his wife, brother, and a good buddy of his who owns a casino called Casino World of London. This is one of the world's largest eight floor cement-brick buildings which is all casino, on James Avenue in London, with different gambling systems on each floor, such as three floors of standard gambling with black jack, one armed, slots, craps, baccarat, roulette, all cards gambling—two floors of teams only betting as pai gow poker, let em ride, spread betting, moneyline, parlay betting, prop betting—two floors of on-line gambling variations/singles or two man teams—one floor of sports betting (usually more than 100 live televised games in progress at any 24 hour period anywhere in the world). Mr. White spends much of his non-working time with his friend, Landy McCarthy, Owner, President, and CEO of the Casino World. His wife, Carry White, and his brother, Steven White, also join him in 'their' co-gambling hobby. Between the three of them, and each a close personal friend of the 'boss', this hacking method was capable of slipping past the employee (who accepts generous tips) setting at the desk for special money management for special groups."

"Mr. White has several bank accounts in England and the Bahamas. He sends different amounts of pound sterling to Dr. Albert Langdon in London every few weeks. Do you recognize that name? He is one of the candidates identified by the American Committee. He also sends American dollars to New York City to a Mr. Freidman Bosting, owner of several freighter ships whose routine routes are between New York, London and several places in western Africa including Morocco, Senegal, Ghana, Nigeria, Central African Republic. Mr. Bosting's ships are known to carry munitions to narcotics gangs in this area. Perhaps one should determine if they carry other 'dangerous' things."

Aykut said, "You will have to give to me the bank-credit card and credit ratings info and I will collect his actions in the borrowing and spending within the gambling world of London. And we can give all of this information to Jamie and Uncle Dagda, as well as the African info to Kef. It would seem that the Christian regions of Africa are becoming more critical for Kef's hard look. That is very interesting."

And they stopped for a few moments, finished their copying notes on paper and ipad, and sort of caught their breath. A second cup of coffee?

"Yes. We are doing pretty good, I think; at least for our first serious efforts at seeking these guys out," replied Aykut. "Our fathers will be happy."

After a few minutes, they changed gears to look at the last of these three candidates. Indeed, Dr. Langdon had been killed in that Irish Sea yachting accident a year ago. So, on to look for info on Mr. Faustino Mariniti from Milan/Rome.

Asu began, "I had much difficulty learning about this very well-established businessman, who knows his business, shall I say. I began my hacking efforts with several different methods such as Fake Wap, keyjoggers, evesdropping, black currency entry, and shake and jive. None of these worked using any combination of his name. It turns out that he has several emails, only one in his 'real' name. And he has several credit cards and bank accounts. These are all pseudo fake or illusionary, dead ends. After much digging I learned he had a twin brother who died ten years ago. He uses his brother's everything as if his brother was still alive. He obviously paid off several political entities in their home village, Empoli, just west of Florence and south of Milan, to make this clever double-entendre ploy. There are three 'legal' account systems that he does use. And I did get into two of them. From them, I learned about his bank accounts in Sassari, Sardinia and Valletta, Malta. Both are less than legitimate. Certainly, they are not reported to any international banking authority. Credit cards and all monetary connections are here, I think. You will have fun digging through the entry numbers that I have for you. I did find several recent payments in US dollars to a medical clinic in Milan, to a businessman in Rabat, Morocco, and to a tourism company in Malaga, Spain. Obviously, I can spend a lot of time chasing this guy as he turns a corner every other kilometer. I think I should give to you his 'living numbers', let you see what you find, and then we try again in a week or two."

Aykut agreed. "I have your new info for Dr. Andersson and Mr. White that I can research out. Maybe in a couple of weeks we can jointly open up any new nanotech data on Mr. Mariniti that is more relevant. In the meanwhile, I will send our current info on Dr. Andersson and Mr. White to Jamie and Kef. Not bad but not very good. I am tired so I will roll up the shades and head out."

Asu complied, "Yes, me too. I have another difficult problem to work on for tomorrow. Good night and see you tomorrow, maybe for lunch."

On the way home, Aykut was thinking, 'Uncle Dagda predicted that the bad guys could be identified with less than legal methods, but should be permanently eliminated with legal methods. Maybe he is right. In this way any good info should go to the Committee, and we should not follow up. We shall see.'

13

KORRECTORIZER II

It was 2030, Oliver Johnson (NY), Chief of Staff for Senator Jordon Johnson (NY), his uncle and pseudo-father, was enjoying his luncheon at the Boar's Head Inn on NE 4th Street on Capitol-Hill in Washington, DC. Three of his senatorial colleagues had joined him as they met at noon on the fourth Friday each month at a local Hill-top restaurant for pleasure and comparison of info/data systems of recent projects. Two years earlier, Oliver had arranged this specific group of 30 plus year olds, all in high level Senatorial staff positions, and from very different senators/states. The three were Jim (IA), Mary Jane (TX), and Bill (CA). The purpose, today, was to try to see more than one point of view of the various problems related to American versus universal healthcare programs.

Socialized medicine, similar to the systems in Canada, Great Britain, Spain, Sweden, and Finland, had been called 'free' health care for their people for many years. There were varying degrees of success and non-success among them. During the past year the question of social/free health care for all American citizens had been continuously on the front pages. Many past American governments had tried to move in that direction, but none were successful. So, the four young lawmakers would seek questions and answers and new ideas or options on health care for the American people.

Oliver (NY) had just finished his post lunch key lime pie dessert with coffee, and opened the conversation. "However one splits the picture, healthcare is most critical for children and the elderly. The government should be responsible for this, not the private sector. These two groups require good food and good health care services."

Jim (IA) followed, "Currently, government provides almost free food programs for school children, poverty level women and infants, food stamps for the poor, free food programs for seniors, and emergency food aid. This feeds 13% or nearly three million Americans. One requires a steady food source, availability, and regular deliverance. This must be government controlled. Sudden reductions or cut offs of this critical life source can be tragic. In my opinion, this responsibility belongs to the government, and back up support belongs in the private sector."

"And food banks are places where the private sector volunteers and the government can directly cooperate, depending upon the region and type of people in need," Bill (CA) added.

"Perhaps one could provide 'food growing space'," replied Mary Jane TX). "If properly designed and supported an adult can possibly grow, eat, and sell his 'own'- fruits and vegetables. The government could provide a small piece of loaned or leased land, seeds, and/or beginning plants, water, etc. And here is where the private sector volunteers could help in planting, cultivating and harvesting. Local media also could help 'spread the word'."

Bill (CA) said, "In California, several non-government communities have done just what you are talking about. Volunteer groups provide 'the land for growing food crops.' Poverty level income people and seniors are encouraged to use this land and are taught how to plant and grow. This also decreases demand, in the surrounding area, as some of the food can be sold and provide these needy people with some pocket change."

"You have adequate land space in California," Oliver (NY) responded. "New York City does not have enough 'food growing space' to grow a peanut. Even normal healthy adults have tried using window or balcony plant growing boxes. After a few 'difficult' attempts they usually change to growing flowers."

Bill concluded, "So what I am hearing is that different solutions should continue to be available for different people in different locations around the country."

"What about good medical health care services for these same groups of people?" asked Oliver (NY).

Mary Jane (TX) responded, "Socialized medicine, today, is interpreted as free medical doctors and free hospital care, poor service, and requisite waiting lines. Looking at the quality of medical care success in Canada and Europe, I do not think the American people want to wait in line for nurses and doctor's appointments, plus medical supplies and drugs. Cheap? Free? Maybe? The bills are still paid—taxes! And, there are significant wait-in-line for even emergency medicals. I know because I lived in England for several years"

"What about a new variety of carefully designed medical and health care insurance plans, government or private sector?" said Jim (IA). "Then there could be numerous private sector insurance supplements (eyes, ears, teeth, home care, special diseases or surgery, etc) for government insurance plans. Also, there are now many supplemental co-insurances for Medicare, worker's medical insurance, owner's injury work coverage for employees, travel-auto/truck insurance, dangerous work disability insurance and injury retirement, etc. My Senator favors all of this."

Oliver (NY) added, "Similar to foods/nutrition, many sixteen-year old children get to choose their own car to join the group of family cars. At thirteen they can choose their own clothes and foods, and maybe cook. But are they taught food-nutrition and cooking methods in our schools? I, nor any of my friends, were not. My girl-friends learned from their mothers. I did not learn. And how does this relate to nutrition at the various levels of monied versus non-monied families?"

He quickly laughed and smiled at Mary Jane (TX), who just smiled without comment. All four had become good friends over the past couple of years and would probably work together again someday; after their Senators were un-elected.

"This is America," continued Oliver (NY). "And it is good to compare notes. There are many options available for good food and good health care for all Americans. Distribution is a key government responsibility. And we must encourage the private sector to help support the government systems and maintain lowest possible costs. Or is there a better way?"

Bill had the last word for the day. "Let the adult who knows the better way step forward. He stood up, stepped away from the table and went toward the rest room. And he laughed, "For now, this is the better way."

They also all stood up, stepped away from the table, and headed back to work with a see ya later or next Friday next month, which ever-happens first, and went their better ways after hashing old ideas with new ideas. At the current levels in their professions they were in position to directly influence all ideas, good or bad. All they needed was to eventually replace their bosses when they retired or failed to get re-elected. The game that is played on Capitol-Hill usually results in the latter before the former.

Several days later, the Senator called Oliver into his office. He had some serious talking to do with the young man. Now was the time. He would propose and require answers to certain questions.—Basically, what is lobbying? Where do lobbyists come from? Is lobbying a good or bad thing? He learned that Oliver was curious about this not-very-understood profession.

Oliver entered the plush office and the Senator told him to sit in one of the large plush brown leather arm chairs. He took the other matching chair. One look in his eye, Oliver knew this was going to be something serious. He only hoped he had not screwed up somewhere. But when the Senator gave him his political smile, he knew everything was positive and on the go.

Uncle/father Jordon Johnson began, "I first met you when you were in diapers. You are now thirty-three. I have only known my wife, Marion, longer. Who more intimately? I really don't know."

And he gave his famous guf-off laugh, got up and poured himself a shot of Johnnie Walker Black Label Scotch, offered Oliver, but Oliver never learned to like that foreign stuff. And something told Oliver he might need all of his clarity tonight.

"I have watched and helped you through under-schooling, basketball success, college success, law school success, and now through two levels of 'how to make American laws' successfully. I hope you have enjoyed it because I have enjoyed pushing you through it. Sometimes you were resistant, sometimes you only had the fast gear in action. You have performed very well. I am very proud of you. You have only one weakness. Changing gears and going at slow or medium speeds is sometimes more productive. And you have trouble being really humble. You will not make a good politician. You see things from above, never from below. So today, now, I am going to talk you about another profession—LOBBYING."

Lobbying is a profession where you deal the cards, and always from the top of the deck. Unless the bottom of the deck can provide 'good-surprises'.

"You are very observant and I know that you have been watching me carefully over these recent years. I have three more years as Senator. I do not plan to run for office again. So, in three years you will need to look for a job. A new job, probably without me looking over your shoulder. I know you are now seeing me spending much time at work outside, not directly related to my Senatorial duties, of my New Yorkers. I have been moving into a new role in a new life as a lawyer/LOBBYIST. Let me explain to you how this profession works. It is not described in the university entrance exams, SAT."

"Lobbyists have a not-so-good reputation. They usually come from the professions of law or business. Law background is better. Lawyers make the laws or work closely with select laws, so they understand how certain laws are going to be interpreted or can be manipulated. There are many 'clients' who want/need assistance with the laws. Normal lawyers frequently can't help; their training is not adequate. Most 'clients' are wealthy individuals or represent major companies/corporations/governments/non-legal-military-groups, semi or less than legal international organizations, or even direct foreign government assistance. Occasionally some lobbyists do accept excessive working fees for correction or re-interpretation of select laws, modification of laws in motion, insertion of 'brother' or 'sister' laws when necessary to win a client's case."

"Many Washington lawyers and lobbyists may do basically the same thing. They sell influence. They are influence peddlers. They are in the business of influencing legal decisions for clients for unregulatable monetary fees. Usually these fees are anywhere between one hundred to one thousand USD per hour. An example, one client could be 5 hours/day, at 5 days/weeks, $1,000/hour would be 25,000 USD for one-week work. And a lobbyist may handle two or three clients per week. Very few lawyers make this. But most lobbyists do make this— big money.—We are talking several million USD per year."

"So, if you look around at our lawyer friends versus our lawyer-lobbyist friends, you will see our lawyer-lobbyist friends living 'much higher on the hog'. Do you understand me?"

Oliver swallowed, "I understand you."

"You can compare that with the annual salary of a Senator which is near 200,000 USD, plus another 200,000 USD living expenses for his Washington, DC, and his second home back in his represented state."

"The Lobby Disclosure Act protects this profession and requires people who are acting as lobbyists to register with the government. Official registration offices for this purpose are located in the House and Senate Office Buildings. Four or five of the wealthiest counties in the USA have offices which are located in the suburbs of Washington, DC: Loudoun County, VA, Arlington Co, VA, Howard Co, MD, Fairfax, Co, VA. Highest income areas include Washington, DC area and New York, NY area. The major lobbyist organization of the world is in Washington, DC. It is the U.S. Chamber of Commerce which focuses on law enforcement, financial issues, taxes, and torts. This Chamber annually spends 100 million USD per lawyer/lobbyist and represents more than 10 million businesses per year. It monitors and reports on more than 500 legislative issues per year for most of these business/clients.

"During the past couple of years, the major legislative problem on Capitol-Hill has been healthcare. The second problem was climate and energy. And the third area involved a group of special interest problems.

"Lastly, many law firms hire former senior government officials, especially those with experience on Capitol-Hill. These latter government lawyers are not considered lobbyists, they are 'senior advisors,' even though their work is very lobbyist oriented."

"Now, dollars do not buy votes in Washington. They buy a better shot at access to the people who vote on all new legal-bills, or modification of existing bills-laws."

"Here is where knowledge of the legal processes is less important than friendship with the people or person who want/need the knowledge of the legal processes that are in motion. In Congress, a written document becomes a legal-bill and then becomes a law. These steps are usually modified several times. How does one interpret a new legal-bill before it becomes a law? Can a legal-bill be altered during movement on the Hill? Is modification possible, and how is it done?—with the help of a few friends? Possibly!"

"Therefore, a lobbyist wants to know the people who are interested in buying a space-automobile, and who makes a space-automobile. You may know the former and the latter, and you must learn all associated parameters, especially the key laws, if you want to set up a new unique for-profit corporation in the USA."

"I will spend a lot of my time during the next three years learning who wants to buy, rent, or steal a space-automobile. I will then retire and go into promoting the space-automobile business. I already have in mind a special kind of travel vehicle which can go into and return to both outer and inner space of this planet. But it is not called an automobile. And many trips will be irreversible."

"Think about these words. If you are interested, we can talk more later, any time. And you can come to my in-house dinner parties and meet the 'space-automobile advocates'. Believe me, they have much interest-need-desire and money. You will see."

And Uncle/Father Senator Jordon Johnson again gave his famous guf-aff laugh.

Oliver was a bit puzzled and thought, 'Is Dad serious?'

After a few moments of contemplation Oliver answered. "Yes, I knew that you were now spending more of your working time with non-New York problems. Remember I have been involved with your monthly schedule for many years. And I could tell you had enough of playing with your electorate, most of them expect too much from you. I never thought that you would be able to be 'so nice for so long'. So, I knew you were more serious this time about not making another multi-month pre-election marathon. I love you Dad. I am happy you made this decision. And I am certain that Marion is also happy. I love her too."

He took another close look at his only known father. He was getting older, grayer, more wrinkles, moving around more slowly. But he still had that compassionate look. And he broke tears for a few moments. Then suddenly Dad also broke a few tears for the first time that Oliver could remember. And all sounds slipped into a masculine quietness. Kissing and hugging between two grown men was not possible—especially father and son, real or virtual.

Finally, a couple of minutes later Dad asked, "Will you talk about this possibility with Chole?"

In response Oliver said, "Yes, we have been living together for almost three years and are starting to seriously consider marriage. In addition, the possible changes in my life must be talked over if we are going to also consider children.

The next evening after work, Chole and Oliver had a 'private' dinner at Jack's Hole-In-The Wall restaurant at the Union Train Station. Chole's father was a senior detective for Congressional Security, while Chole worked as a legal administrative-secretary in the Russell Senate Office Building. Oliver worked in the Senator Johnson's offices next door in the Dirkson Senate Office Building. So, Oliver just walked over to Chole's office at 6:00 PM and they walked on to the UTS in five minutes. One of the best things about working and living on Capitol-Hill was the closeness of most life essentials and the absence of rush hour traffic. It had been many happy working years for both bright, politically connected young-uns.

They walked, sat at a private table, ordered, ate, finished, ordered tall dark coffees, and then the time was here.

Chole thought to herself, 'What did 'Uncle' Senator Johnson want from Oliver this time. More work probably. But he loved it, so what could she do?'

She finally said, "Well, are you going to tell me or do I have to beg Uncle Jordon's most recent secrets from you?"

And she gave him her 'wall to wall' smile. Then she beamed at him with her blue-green eyes and dark hair, perfect light honey colored skin. She was a very bright and lovely Irish Catholic lady. Oliver had been snowed from day one. She was near 6 feet, and he was 6 feet 7 inches, so the two of them were always the taller/superior couple in any stand-up cocktail party. Oliver would tease her about having giraffe children. It was only her stubborn resistance that had kept him from pressuring her into marriage. She just had not been ready.

Oliver said, "Dad wants me to work for him as a lobbyist. Do you know what that is? Do you understand the difference between a lawyer and a lobbyist?"

"Are you kidding?" She answered. "Remember I work for a pool of administrative secretaries which spend most of their working time in translation from American English into legal English manuscripts, legal bills, or law drafts. Most lawyers, especially the younger ones cannot speak or write English or law. So yes, I have access to a lot of normal manuscripts to legal-bills which eventually go to laws and then to and from the committees. But I also see a few altered/ manipulated pre-law manuscripts which bypass the normal routes to legal force, for money."

"Good," responded Oliver. "Then what would you think about being married to a lobbyist?"

All sounds disappeared from the table and a 'happy' couple were suddenly very, very quiet.

Chole thought for a few moments and said, "I knew Uncle Jordon was going in that direction at the end of his term. Very few Senatorial secrets escape our group of simple secretaries. He would need you very much, just as he has been depending upon your leading his legal research team for the past decade. And I think you would make a very good lobbyist. But do I want to marry into such a profession?"

She continued, "Are you asking me to marry you?"

"Yes."

"I did not hear it. What did you say?"

"You saw me say it with my eyes every day for the past three years. If I have to translate it—OK—Will you marry me? My professional intent is to switch from a government-lawyer to a private sector lawyer-lobbyist? My personal intent is for us to live together and have two children, a girl and a boy. I will even become a practicing Catholic. And you can continue working if you want to do so. If you do not want to work on Capitol-Hill, that is all right also. Our new legal group could probably use your help. And…"

He looked his potential 'bride' in the eyes, they were telling him, enough, shut-up, just say it."

Oliver swallowed. Dropped his eyes, embarrassed, repeated. "My dearest love. Please marry me!"

She smiled. He must have got it right this time. So, he got up, went over to her chair, and gave her a whopper kiss, as his uncle/ father Uncle Jordon would call it. And then they both relaxed from finally making a two-year old decision, the most difficult in the lives of both of them. That is the problem with perfectionists. They had lived past non perfect marriages of several of their high school and college friends; and they were concerned about not making decisions.

They were both flying high—coffee and life decisions. So, they could not go home. What they had just started they had to virtual finish tonight. Wedding in June, therefore dates for pre-wedding bachelors party and brides party, wedding, and post-wedding honeymoon in England to visit her family. Her uncle was an elected member of the lower house, the House of Commons of the Parliament of the United Kingdom. And a second cousin was a Lord of the upper house in the House of Lords in the Parliament. Both Houses were located in the Palace of Westminister in the City of Westminister on the north bank of the Thames in central London, England. Oliver had lived all of his professional life in the American government center. And now he would have an opportunity to explore the British government center. This would be like going from caramel pecan apple pie to hot melting chocolate orbs. Oliver looked forward to the honeymoon as much as the wedding. Be careful!

As the very happy Chole and Oliver left the Hole-In-The-Wall and walked home, a messenger ran up to them and gave them a special message. It was from Dad/Uncle Jordon. How did he know so soon?

Oliver opened the message which said:—

'I need a yes or no within two days.'

Also—Congratulations—Marion and I welcome you both into the inner core of the family unit. You must now produce new law units and new human babies.'

HAVE FUN!

Our first house-wedding party will be on the first evening in June—guests listed below!

Esq. Senator Jordon Johnson and Marion Johnson, 11111 Stony Brook Road, Great Falls, VA—INVITES—[RSVP – 1-201-955-8787]

Esq. William A. Watson, Secretary of State, USA, and Janet Watson

Esq. Ester Noville, Director of International Monetary Fund, and Donald Watson

Mr. Wayde Nagut, President of the International Society for the Poor, and Bankay Nagut

Esq. Roger Stumper, President of the Council of the European Union, and Mary Ann Stumper

Major General Carlson Black, US Army, and Sylvia Black

Mr. Clay Stevens, Chief Executive Officer of AT&T, and Janise Stevens

Ambassador Olumide Abioye from Nigeria and Ambassadress Titilayo Abioye

Esq. John Beamer, Mayor of New York City, and Susan Beamer

Esq. Oliver Johnson, Chief of Staff, Senator Jordon Johnson, and Chole Johnson

This party is the first of many for our new company—Korrector Com. It is your engagement party and the beginning of your life as a lobbyist. Always keep in mind, you do not have to like these people, you only have to learn to tolerate them. They would not be invited if they did not bring something of mutual financial benefit, either a benefit in motion, or one that can be put into motion in the very near future. Good luck—continue to trust me.

As always with Uncle/Dad, the future would provide many surprises. The first one happened a few months later with the Istanbul massacre. He had begun to realize that it was their new company that did it. He did not dare tell Chole everything about their proposed new life. Maybe he could never tell her some things in their future together, even after they had happened.

14

KEF IN NIGERIA III

Two months after the briefing of the petroleum problems in South-South Nigeria by Arjana, Aminu's wife, a group of five government men checked into the 89Presidential Hotel in Port Harcourt City, state of Rivers, better known as the state of 1000 bridges. It was located in the near center of the multiple deltas of the Niger River on the Atlantic Ocean. Kef had his own room. While Aminu and Banjoho shared rooms, and Abiefume and Kachiside shared rooms. From Abuja, Aminu drove a Toyota Corolla with Kef riding shotgun, and the other three Nigerians took turns driving a Kia Station Wagon. They would maintain this routine because Kef did not who to completely trust. Several of these death sites could easily yield Nigerian murders by Nigerians. He did trust Aminu.

Before he left Abuja, Kef sent several requests. First a thanks to Secretary Nkwado. Then he asked the Military Assistant Abubakar to perform a 'terrorist type' of search of any ship that entered a Nigerian port and which was registered to Freidman Bosting—also, he would soon send a list of male Africans from Swedish universities who try to cross passport control into Nigeria, using terrorism as a holding excuse, and asked them to be detained.

The interstate roads were excellent so it took only eight hours to drive the distance. The petroleum rich city was very modern with several high-rise buildings in the center and had many well-organized business and shopping areas, plus excellent streets and many parks.

Over the years it had been named the Garden City of Nigeria. In 1912 the area was a small fishing village; with the discovery of coal in 1932 it became a large coal export village; and with the discovery of oil in 1956 it became a modern export city in Nigeria and the Center of the Nigerian Petroleum Industry.

Today, the Port Harcourt metropolitan area contained over one million people, and was the largest and fastest growing most prosperous city in South-South Nigeria. Therefore, the five gentlemen entered a city that was filled with wealthy Nigerians and many foreigners living in luxurious housing developments and large mansions with spectacular water views. They settled into the Presidential Hotel where they would remain for the entire 2 or 3 days of onsite investigation. All of the 'death villages' were within an hour or so of driving time from here. They would travel back and forth as necessary. Summary conferences would be held in the evenings in the hotel, as they would go in different directions and work in groups during the day. After settling into their rooms, one single and two doubles, they walked a few minutes, stretched their legs, and entered into a well-publicized restaurant called the Blue Elephant. After an excellent meal, Kef gave a short briefing.

He began, "I know this is a region with an ethnic mixture of Ijaw, Igbo, and Ibibio, the powerful Yoruba, and a mixture of others nearby. And I am aware of the history of the unequal sharing of petroleum and natural gas and the several mini- wars. Also, I understand that there is still a deep-seated hatred in the area which hasn't cooled down over the many years of political growth of the Republic of Nigeria. We have identified nine 'death villages' in the area. We will try to get to all of them but it may not be feasible. So, I propose to begin with Tumba/Bayelsa, Onne/Rivers, Ofe/Abia, Itu/Imo, and Jeyo/Delta. First, when we arrive at our assigned village, approach the local police, show your government official passes, and request to talk to some of the surviving villagers, local people, families of victims, and area locals. Tell them we are interested in learning everything about the day and night of the mini-massacre. Collect the info/data on tape recorders if they will let you. If not, make careful notes. Recopy them but later, as soon as possible.

"We are saying that the cause of death was due to a food poison. Because the poison apparently required several hours of delayed action, many people were killed, possibly by one given dosage. And yes, the cause death was due to both internal and external diarrhea."

Kef continued, "I am handing out to you a list of questions and suggestions for retrieving information from surviving villagers. Here is the list. Let us look at it together."

QUESTIONS FOR SURVIVING VILLAGERS

1) Identify villagers who were not killed, whatever the reasons—question them.

2) Identify near family members, parents, children, near relations who were there that day/night but survived—question them.

3) Obtain the recall of events from survivors, for both day and night.

4) Did any villagers leave and return to the village that day or night?

5) Were there any strangers in the village that day or night?

6) What were the ethnic and tribal units among the survivors versus non-survivors?

7) Were there any personal or family problems which could have led to this level of violence?

8) Foods and meals—Anything new or different about food consumption—special or new foods—local or 'brought in food'.

9) Determine the starting time for meals for children versus adult, noon time or evening.

10) Determine the starting time when the first cases of diarrhea occurred, early eaters or later in the day eaters, children and adults, and what they ate—if possible!

"OK? Do you have any questions for me?"

After a few moments, no questions. So, Kef continued, "If you need another day or two to question certain villagers, we will do this. But a general time of five-six days, or a total of one week here in the Port Harcourt area, is all we have to collect information about these deaths."

"Tomorrow, Aminu and I will go to Tumba/Bayelsa. Banjoho and Abiefume are from the Itu/Imo region, so they will go there. And Kachiside will go to the local commercial port and obtain information and lists of all ships that registered at Port Harcourt over the past two years."

"We will probably require two or maybe three days for our first investigative efforts. Do not worry. It will go easier later with other villages."

Aminu asked. "Do you plan to conference after collecting info and data from one village at a time?"

"Yes, Kef responded. "When we think that we have a reasonable picture of the 'death village', we will have an after-evening dinner conference in my hotel room. OK?"

The group seemed content with the plan. They quit the restaurant and walked back to the hotel. Each had his assignment for tomorrow, so they were now on their own or in pairs. They would all remain in contact via their cell phones.

The next day Kef and Aminu drove toward Tumba/Bayelsa. It took a long hour hit and miss savanna. Hover most settlements and villages seemed to be on the savanna. There were numerous clusters of oil derricks popping up periodically. There were petroleum oil and natural gas units scattered throughout the area.

They drove into a village depleted of most of the human population. About 75% of the villagers had been nano-killed. Bayelsa State Police, Nigerian Military, and remaining villagers, family, friends, and volunteers were all working and slowly rebuilding. Most buildings were intact. Physical construction was minimum—Psychological construction was maximum.

Kef and Aminu pulled up at the Police 'station' and approached the Nigerian military and State police. They got out and directly approached the officer in charge.

"My name is Kefentse Legoase," he said. "This is Aminu Adebayo. We are military researchers attached to the Department of Health and Human Services, directly appointed through the President. Here are our identification papers."

They shook hands and gave their papers to the officer.

The Colonel took the papers inside, spent the next fifteen minutes making several telephone calls. He then returned to the fellows and said, "Your papers are good. Here are identity cards for the State of Bayelsa for one week. Mr. Legoase, you are a Zulu, from South Africa. Mr. Adebayo, you are a Yoruba, from Nigeria. Correct?"

They could only nod. They were nor expecting such discipline. It was good—probably.

"I hope you can help us find the bastards that did this. I assume you do know that Nigerian and international forensic medical teams have already been here, checked the dead, reported their findings to the Abuja authorities, and all bodies are gone. So!? If we can help you, otherwise, please let us know."

Kef nodded. He took the Bayelsa identity cards, and thanked the Colonel. They then slowly walked away toward a nearby outdoor café with several nice big shade trees. He needed something cold to drink. It was already very hot and very humid.

They sat, ordered cold colas on ice. They waited until they were alone again and Kef began. "Let me remind you that I want to keep our investigation quiet. Let us try to minimize any nearby ears. Let me now call Mr. Kamaeu, our Bayelsa government contact here who, hopefully, has organized several of the survivors. Let us start meeting and talking with these people, preferably in a nearby cool air-conditioned room. OK?"

Aminu replied, "That is good for me!"

Mr. Kamaeu was indeed ready to meet with them. He had a list of more than twenty names of survivors. Over the cell phone he read off several names. They selected five. Mr. Kamaeu would immediately start contacting them and arranging a personal, private interview with each one, beginning after lunch today. Depending upon how these talks went, they would probably want to do several more interviews today and tomorrow. But that could be decided later in the afternoon.

After lunch they had a full afternoon of interviews with each survivor, three older men, and two middle aged women. That evening they had a private dinner, re-listened to the recorded testimonies, and talked about the methodology used by the thieves/killers. Indeed, the memory recall by all five survivors was very similar, hence probably true. The next day they tried a different approach.

The night of the mini-massacre at Bayelsa yielded several children who survived. The next morning Kef and Aminu arranged a different approach for a group interview. They arranged an outdoor picnic lunch for several of these children. They were taken aside, separated from the adults, and interviewed after lunch and big pecan-chocolate desserts. Then they were encouraged to use a story telling format, put some pretense into a 'true' story, informally, not recorded. It went as follows:

Kef began his interview with two little girls. Their names were Mali and Kotae. And they were loaded with information. Half crying and half afraid, they began their stories. They wanted to tell it all.

Mali went first, "We were celebrating our annual Osun Osogbo Festival. We dressed up all pretty and had a great time, sang and danced and read our history and re-cited poems and ate lots of good food. No one was hurting no-one. We were not hurting nobody. Our mothers let us stay up late because there was no school the next day. We had just gone to bed when there was screaming coming from several different huts. And then there was this terrible smell coming from those same huts."

Kotae broke in, "And our mothers went to see what was wrong. They soon came back, made us get dressed, and took us to the side of the village. All children were herded into the animal food storage huts. Mali's mother stayed with us and they locked us inside. Several men with spears and rifles came and guarded outside the door. We were very afraid.—terrible smells and terrible screams of pain!"

Kef waited a few minutes. This massacre happened several weeks ago. But to the girls they were suddenly reliving it again. That was what Kef wanted.

He finally asked, "We think that there was some kind of poison placed into the food, and that is what caused the smell, pain, and deaths. Can you tell us anything about the evening meal?"

"I can tell you everything," said Mali. "It was the dates. I do not like dates. Kotae does not like dates. So, we did not eat dates. But our school friends, Little Ji, Dako, and Biti each gobbled up the dates all evening. They even fed our goats. Now they are all dead—boys and goats."

And she broke into sobs. Kotae was trying to hold it back. But she said, "The dates were brought to the party from Lagos. A stranger in a truck delivered them to the village in the late afternoon. He unloaded several big boxes of dates and then left. We were told that no one should eat them until evening dinner's dessert. They were special. I think no one did because we are good-obedient children in this village."

Kef and Aminu exchanged knowing looks. Many of the deceased were younger ones/children, and indeed most of the goats, but no cows who do not like sweet foods. More than half of the villagers were nano-killed, almost all of the children.

The interviews continued with more children and several adults into the late afternoon. No villager remembered any useful events that happened during the day or evening of the festival. The two little girls were the most observant, yet the most punished. Both of their fathers were killed, but their mothers lived through the last Osun Osogbo Festival, ever, in Tumba village.

The two 'government' agents returned to the Presidential Hotel after dark. They were emotionally down, had a bite to eat, and went directly to bed. They could discuss what they learned today, tomorrow.

After several days of interviews, Kef called everyone together in his hotel room to compare all information, notes, tapes, data, and to ask if there was any need for more searching within any of the 'death villages'.

He reported, "In the Tumba death village, we believe that it was a 'food poison' in the fresh fruit, probably the dates, that was brought into the village near-before mealtime by some stranger who immediately left, that probably caused the deaths. It could have been other fruits, but evidence points to the dates, and a late entry into the evening meal."

Aminu nodded in support. And everyone seemed to agree that this idea of a fresh fruit being a carrier of the poison matched their data. So, a major agreement was to always monitor fresh fruits when looking for the 'poison' system.

Bonjoho spoke up, "We had an unusual situation in Ofe/Abia where the major drinking water well system had gone partially dry. So, the villagers ordered a truck load of plastic bottled water for their festival night. This was delivered from Owerri. The driver came, unloaded, and left immediately. None of that water remains. So, we think the poison could have been in the fruit, but don't eliminate other sources. In this village the death rate was over 90%, including most animals."

"There was also a variety of ethnics within some of the villages." said Aminu. "We have a listing which shows that the 'death villages' are a mixture of Yoruba, Edo, Ibibio, and Efik. While the major ethnics in the region are Ijaw and Igbo. However, no Ijaw or Igbo villages were targeted during the past few months. Why? I have no explanation. But it is interesting!"

And Abiefume spoke up, "We found no major unsettled disagreements within families nor between villages, at least not at the level of homicide action. It would appear no local animosity played a role in these monstrous murders. At least not that we have yet to identify."

"I looked at the lists of commercial ships that docked and had a cargo unload/load during the past two years. I found no specific ship of interest," reported Kachiside.

Kef commented, "In summary, we saw only locals attending dinners on the day of a celebrated event in Tumba, Jayo, Ito, Onne, or Ofe. In each village, strangers did enter, delivered products to that village, and immediately left. We think that most villagers remained in their village during the entire day. No local major family quarrels were found within or among village families. While the very old, sick, or injured villagers, who did not eat the evening meal, did not die."

"Does anyone have more to add to our picture here of the massacres in these investigated villages in the South-South?" asked Kef.

There were no comments.

"Overall, for our first effort, I think we did well. Now be sure to write your reports in detail. I am using them along with my report. We have some good data and info that we can possibly use for future prevention and possible therapeutic approaches to this 'food poison'. And it also appears to be possible that ethnics may be involved in the motives for certain of these deaths."

He continued, "Let us close for now. It is too late to start back to Abuja. Use the rest of the day, recopy your notes and summarize what you consider key areas of information. And this evening, at 7:30, I will invite you to dinner at the Old Township Blue Bell Restaurant for kote (horse mackerel) or suya skewer (beef), adalu (white beans), with a mixture of vegetables select, and mixed fruit kabab. With this hot-heat I have ordered iced water or iced beer. Tomorrow, you four can drive back to Abuja in the station wagon. I will drive back later in the day as I have a breakfast-luncheon meeting with an old Nigerian friend who lives in the area. I will meet with you day after tomorrow in our offices to go over this investigative effort and consider where we should go next. Give to me your reports in two days. I will then write our final report for the South-South Nigeria. And request permission to go into the country again, probably north this time. Questions?"

No one spoke up in question or disagreement.

The next day Kef didn't recognize Nwadinkpa Olabamijji as he came in the front door of the hotel and walked into the dining room. They had studied together in the Queen Cleopatra Humbo in Haiti several years ago. Both of them had aged a little. But they both did well in their studies and promised to meet again in Africa. Nwadinkpa was now an African Prince of Voodoo. And Kef was working in Public Management on a Nanotech Project. Kef stood up and looked twice. But Nwadinkpa never hesitated. His first statement was, 'I would recognize that tall skinny soccer body anywhere. Will you sell it?"

And yes, he was a chunky Voodoo Priest. They hugged each other fiercely as there were many good memories to re-discover, hopefully new ones to discover. They sat and ordered a late breakfast. It was mid-morning and Kef needed to get an early start for his drive back to Abuja. Nwadinkpa lived in the area, in more than one place it seemed. They settled into a brief opening of good old times. But this time, Kef had to keep things rather direct and a little fast. During the few weeks that Kef had been in Nigeria the two of them had emailed the problem that Kef was working on. For now, fun discussion time would be short. There were many more bad facts and info to communicate, and they needed to set up a way to quickly/quietly talk anytime, possibly often. Kef wanted to integrate Voodooism into his 'diagnosis and cure' of the Nigerian 'food disease' problem.

Kef said, "We have discovered several villages here in the South-South where the villagers were massacred with a nanotech molecular system (food poison), probably made in Europe and shipped here, put into the villager's food immediately before a festival meal. Men, women, children, and village animals were killed by a macabre internal and external diarrhea. These are your people. Several villages in this area suffered this horror during the past few months."

Nwadinkpa answered, "Of course we knew of those deaths, but did not know what to do. The local authorities told us to not get involved. Our thinking was that there was a civil war brewing. The Ijaw and Igbo are talking and planning to 'take over' some of the rich oil producing regions in their areas, steal the oil—pump it into their own tankers. And we are afraid that they will use whatever weapons are cheap and effective, even food poisons. If Abuja knows or suspects this, they have not informed me."

"But I do want your help from the Voodoo community here in Nigeria," replied Kef. "Remember, I also have had training under Queen Cleopatra, the declared sister of the African Queen of Voodoo in Lagos. Can you tell me about her?"

"Yes and no!" said Nwadinkpa. "I would need several hours just to begin to cite the Queen's history. Briefly, she was born to no-one. At the age of sixteen she was so beautiful, dark shiny skin and blue-green eyes, red hair, lovely and so alive that a very wealthy old man married her. He died two years later and she inherited his fortune. The following year she seduced another wealthy old man who owned the Ikoyi-Victora Island near the center of the Lago Lagoon. Three years later he died and she inherited the entire island and several 'boxes' of diamonds. She then went to study with Queen Cleopatra in Haiti. There she began her Voodoo training with herbs, snakes, and fortune telling. Over the next few years, she visited her declared sister in Haiti several times for 'continued education'.

"The Queen of African Voodoo is very proficient with her herb medicines, utilization of fear with her snakes in the local population, and prediction of sudden deaths/ failures of various high-ranking politicians and military generals, wealthy oil men, and select professors, plus the families of these Nigerian leaders. She takes care of the poor, the needy, and the homeless in certain Lagos suburbs. There she is also Queen of the Nigerian Poor. Those many thousands love her.

"She outlived two more wealthy old men over the next eleven years. Near forty years of age, the Queen decided to have children. She obtained sperm from several Nigerian football players. And using a mixture of herbs, within nine months she delivered five identical baby girls in her 'remodeled' castle on the Lagos Island in the center of the Lagos Lagoon. They were beautiful, genetically identical girls. Identical in that each was a mutant/variant. One of each mutant was lacking in taste, or hearing, or smell, touch, or speaking tongue. By lacking I mean each mutant lacks the sense organs for that specific sense."

"Each, now a lovely 26 year old lady, is named after a specific poison snake that she controls, just as a child does her pet. For example— The Queen's nick name is Cobra. The ladies are called Krait, Viper, Mamba, Jaraca, and Coral. I know them all as I have visited the island several times. You will learn that the Queen is more of a sorceress than just a witch. She is an amazing woman. And it will be good to possibly do, including make your enemies disappear."

"To understand the African Queen, you must first visit and talk with her and her daughters. I will write a letter of introduction for you. Ask her declared sister, Queen Cleopatra in Haiti, to write a letter of introduction for you. Tell her what you see about the beginning tragedy for her people, but only after you have made friends with **'the family'**. You will find that she is really a warm person who came through a difficult lifetime. But she is now the most powerful person in Nigeria. The politicians built a new capital city, inland, Abuja. It is six hours driving time from Lagos, just to escape her. Or so it is told. And her daughters know more about Nigeria than all of the politicians put together. They frequently wear similar/different/unusual clothing and head pieces on the streets. They regularly infiltrate Christian, Islamic, or Native (Voodoo) religious or ethnic/tribal groups or regions. They are their mother's super spies and do carry that secret cold little body guard pet in their pockets, purses, or shopping bags. When you visit, do be careful. I am told there are more than 50 of the most powerful poisonous snakes in the world living on the island. And they all live comfortably with the African Queen and her family. If you get to know the daughters, they can be very human and of some fun. You just have to remember that they are a little more reptile than human. With that in mind, you will not have any troubles."

Kef swallowed a couple of times and replied, "Can I meet the Queen on a boat or at a nearby hotel or somewhere safe?"

"Believe me it will be an experience more remarkable than the time we spent with Queen Cleopatra. Remember those days?"

"But the Queen did not use snakes!"

Nwadinkpa replied, "You will get used to it. Besides they are our people and will want to help. Queen Cleopatra and I will back you up."

And Kef said quietly to himself, 'I really do not like snakes. In fact, I hate snakes. And I am afraid of snakes. But if it is required to help bring down those nanotech killers, anything. I will try. I think.'

15

NANOTECH AND KUNG FU

[Boston had recently established a large high technology research and science developmental complex of more than 100 laboratory companies called the High Technology Center of Life Sciences in Boston (KTC-LSB). Included were three laboratories which focused on nanotechnology. The various companies employed both private and university personnel, had private and government support monies, and were rapidly moving forward with several billion dollars in venture capital. Li had given the name of Dr. George Miller, a long-time friend and director of one of the companies, to Jamie. Dr. Miller was researching on cellulose and cellulase systems. And he had recent data that Li could immediately use in his effort to battle this new cellulose nanotech molecular system being used in the African villages. Jamie met with Dr. Miller and was bringing this new unpublished data to Li. Hopefully these new ideas would be useful, now.]

Jamie O'Reilly (Ey'tuka) was flying from Boston on South Western Airlines into Los Angeles International Airport; arrival time would be 4:00 PM. He was less than an hour out when his mind started drifting back to his previous trips to visit this second most populated (seven million people) city in the USA. He remembered it as the leading American artistic center, a gigantic global entertainment industry, and the most diversified immigration center which covered more than 500 sq mi. It was a sprawl of widely dispersed settlements connected to a 'downtown' which year around had good weather, massive traffic problems, numerous high/low rise central city buildings, and extensive local and foreign ethnic and racial diversity. There were over 600 million tourists each year in what is described as a constellation of microclimates and microcosms of more than one hundred unique collections of everything American past and present. What a city. Almost as good as Boston. HA!

As they landed, Li Jang (Tsu'teye) was waiting for him in the SWA tunnel exiting the incoming planes. They hugged and kissed until tears filled their eyes. A few sniffs later, they headed for the parking lot and Li's yellow Mustang convertible. They had lived together-separately for the past fifteen years. Nanking/ Los Angeles and Boston were still home working stations. Li was seeking within nanotechnology, cures for a variety of diseases. Jamie was focusing on the development of new international laws concerning terrorism, trying to include nano-terrorism into that legal category. Some countries agreed. Some countries did not agree. Both young men were intent in their work.

So, several options were in motion. Jamie was bringing the ideas of Dr. Miller, and some plans and info from Uncle Dagda. Having a doctorate in nano-technology and having inherited his father's nanotech company, Li was the nano-technology expert working on the nanotech molecular system designs to counter Korrectorizer's attacks. The two other musketeers, Kef (Na'via) and Aykut (Mo'ata), complemented their four-person team effort via in-field or on-site investigations of nanotech killings and evaluating banking/monetary accounts of several nanotech killer candidates, respectively. So, the team was trying to cover several investigative fronts simultaneously.

Each of their fathers had been nano-assassinated. And during the past few years they had been working with various international legal authorities and a select group of witches from the World Witches Conclave to try to neutralize a Korrectorizer's group of assassins. They were on a secret time table. They were on a secret schedule. It could happen.

Li said, "It certainly is good to see you again after several years."

Jamie answered, "The last time we were together was in Geneva, the day Korrectorizer tried to assassinate all four of us. Uncle Dagda warned us, remember. We immediately split and each went home.

Then we began and continued our education training programs. Now we are ready to challenge those nanotech killers. I wonder if he/they even know we are still in motion."

"In a sense I will be disappointed if he does not know we are here," said Li. "He owes us big revenge in some way. At the appropriate time, we successfully disappeared from Korectorizer's view. We each carefully disappeared into a university scene for our advanced education and training. Now we are more ready. And we need to find him and eliminate this worldwide nanotech disease that he has initiated."

As they arrived in the parking area and climbed into Li's yellow Mustang convertible, Li lowered the preen-fold down black top and they headed west into the California sun.

Jamie spoke up, "Yes. I can see that you are heading toward the ocean. Great. I would like to feel a cool ocean breeze and drink a cold beer. I have only seen an ocean sun-set once in my life. I look forward to my second such experience. They are a rare occurrence in Boston."

And he laid back his head back into the wind.

They chuckled, and quickly returned to their past buddy-relationship that they had before they escaped the attempted assassination in Geneva. They both knew they would have their revenge.

Li took off for the Santa Monica State Beach and to the Red Beach Cafe. It would be loaded with pre-thirty year 'children', especially the female variety. After all, they were near thirty but still single.

Half an hour later they parked the car in the Café parking lot, parked their bodies in sun chairs under a large golf umbrella, and parked their eyes on the bikinis running up and down the beach not thirty yards distance. Two minutes later they toasted with ice cold beers. Jamie drank John Adams and Li drank Yuengling. Each loyal to his heritage. What a way to finish a long hot day, with a best friend and the common memory of their fathers. At this minute, life was good. Tomorrow would come and the pursuit would continue. But now, they were newly prepared adults, no longer novice teenagers.

The rest of the day was spent talking about their recent plus and minus efforts in schools and with partial families. Li had no parents nor siblings; but he did have a girlfriend. Jamie was living with his mother, no father nor siblings. This was directly a result of the nanotech battles.

They slept the night at Li's two floor, three bed room combo-house in Pasadena. In the morning they arose, drank a glass of cheery-cranberry juice, ate a bowl of honeyed oats and pecan cereal topped with fresh fruit and fat free milk, and drank a follow up cup of green tea—still young enough for natures youth food. Next, they took off for a day of Hollywood tourism. This was something Jamie had always wanted to do, now finally. Second visit to California, but first visit to Hollywood.

They drove to 0001 Hollywood Blvd, parked in paid parking, and climbed into a Mercedes tourism midi-van. At 9:00 AM the bus tour group began their six-hour Great Hollywood Voyage. This tour provided a comfortable ride and a driver/tour leader to point out and describe all sites.

"This is the tour I have always wanted to do since I was a little boy," declared Jamie.

"Me too," added Li. And he laughed as the two hit a high five.

First stop was at the Walk of Fame on Hollywood Blvd which had more than 200 squares, 16in x 16in, names and hand prints of famous movie stars, past and present. Along the boulevard they visited the first ever movie theaters in America, the Dolby Theater, and the famous Chinese Theater.

Next, going toward West Los Angeles and up into Beverly Hills, where if you have a large house/mansion it implies that you are now a famous movie star and making mega dollars per movie. The driver turned on a video screen which showed close ups of many of the houses as they drove past them. Why video? Most houses were enclosed by walls and large shrubs/trees, so a clear view was rarely available. The video helped one guess how many mega dollars this particular star received—related to the size/vastness of the property behind the wall. They saw 'pictures' of houses of more than seventy-five movie stars that they knew or recognized.

Around noon they stopped at John Wayne's Cowboy Beef Parlor on Dale Evans Rodeo Drive. And yes, they had Texas T-bone steaks, baked potatoes with pure butter, and ice-cold Budweiser beers. It was good and unique fun. They were young once again.

The afternoon finish was a one-hour view of the first ever black and white Tarzan movie starring the 1939 American swimming gold medalist Johnnie Weissmuller. Cheta, the monkey, was the hero of course.

To end a very memorable day, and having eaten a filling protein luncheon, they went directly to Dodger Stadium and arrived early enough to watch batting practice. The Boston Red Sox were in town playing the Los Angeles Dodgers in a double header. They watched most of both games. In the fifth inning of game two, they decided they were hungry for a baseball foot long Dodger hot dog with pickle, catsup, mustard, french-fries, and another Budweiser light. They may have begun the day early and gently, and ended in with maybe-sleep-kindly stomachs. But there were no problems sleeping nor entering another day. Does this prove they are still 'young'? They thought so!

The next morning the two of them planned to spend the day in Li's world, talking science with Li's people. His house was on 71126 East California Blvd, near the California Institute of Technology. The CIT is a small private university specializing in natural sciences and engineering. In these areas, it is ranked #4 in the world and educates only 4000 students each year, which included 1000 advanced/graduate students. And it was a ten-minute walk from Lombard Rd where his Jiang Nanotech International building was located. In addition, there were nine other private high technology medical research companies nearby. Each was under the ownership with private partners and supported by both private and government medical grants and contracts. These companies provided projects for the CIT graduate and post-doctoral students, and studied a wide variety of medical problems. The Los Angeles Botanical Gardens and several recreational parks were in the area. So, it was an excellent living location for a young man concentrating on high technology medical sciences and still keeping his physical health and body strength high. Afterall, he was a black belt Kung Fu. This required regular physical activity to maintain his competition.

After a meager breakfast, the two of them walked along a gentle tree lined street to Li's JNI building. Jamie was not science trained, but did recently have a couple of laboratory chemistry and biology courses as optional college classes. He did need some understanding of the high-tech weapon system they were battling. They entered and Li generally explained the layout of the building. Li's father built the six-floor building which had been carefully designed for floor to floor functioning.

Li began, "All of the private medical research company laboratories nearby have similar general designs. And we use only manpower at the advanced university level of MS, PhD, or MD, post-doctoral trainees, and university faculty members. Our building has several floors of laboratory rooms for atomic, molecular, chemical, analytical, and cell/tissue analysis. We have two especially designed floors for analysis and synthesis of genes (DNA), mirror gene copies (RNA), proteins (peptides), lipoproteins (cell membranes), and special organic molecules. Our JNI has six floors, five to six labs per floor. Plus, on select floors there are a total of five dust-free rooms for high tech (expensive) electronic equipment, two sterile labs for tissue culture, one large lab as a master working cold room, and one large working freezer room. Offices are scattered on each floor. The VPs and I have our offices on the first floor. We also have a small library and conference room on the first floor. Currently we have forty-five researchers."

"The building has a sub-basement for car parking. An upper basement level is used for storage, offices for security and maintenance personnel; and there is a small animal facility (mostly mice). The first floor has a visitor-controlled-walk-in entry in front. There are several closed-circuit television cameras inside and outside. Employees can enter via a double monitored entry from the back of the building. Elevators are in front and back—both are employee hand palm coded. We have motion activated cameras on each floor, as we have had theft several times over the years—high security is necessary. We always have several projects and guest workers in motion."

"To give you an idea of some of the expenses, a brief idea of expensive laboratory equipment totaling several million USD would include: UV-Visible-IR analytical spectrophotometer, DNA sequencer and synthesizer, RNA synthesizer, protein sequencer and synthesizer, high precision liquid chromatography, microarray technology system, micro-CT scanner, radioisotope counter for H3, C14, and P32, micro-NMR, gel imaging analyzer, and others. Some of these are so sophisticated and the quantity of use is such we require a full-time expert to run just that one instrument."

Jamie said, "Wow! And you inherited all of this from your father. What responsibility!"

"Not exactly." replied Li. I worked with my father in these labs much of my life. So, it was only natural that I continue to grow his 'baby'. However, when he 'died', there were existing debts in the multi-million-dollar range. So, I had to acquire three venture capital financial partners. This was several years ago, but we are now slowly paying the debt off. Fifteen more years and I will be Owner and President. For now, I am just CEO and President. But I can make all research decisions, and purse the research methodology as I think appropriate. I have two close friends who worked with my father for more than thirty years. They have stuck with me and carry the titles of Co-Vice Presidents. We have continued those profitable projects, cut those that were not seeing profit, and eased into new projects as new money became available."

"It was difficult both studying for my PhD and trying to run a profitable medical research company. My two VPs were the key to our success."

"My father had several excellent associates in his law firm," said Jamie. 'He always used to say 'an excellent worker is worth his weight in gold.' I hope I can learn such someday. What projects do you have in motion?"

Li answered, "Most of our current studies focus on peptide and protein molecules related to specific diseases, example—acinar cells in the pancreas producing proteases that digest foods in the stomach (several stomach diseases), beta cells in the pancreas that manufacture and then secrete upon signal—insulin, four subtypes of small lung cell cancer cells that secrete certain proteins that help them metastasize to other parts of the body, stimulation of select hepatocytes in the liver to secrete precursors of bile salts for digestion in the colon, and of course the nanotech molecular systems which can stimulate or kill a variety of body cells identified with a newly synthesized MoAB (monoclonal homing antibody). We will talk more about this later."

"OK. Here we are. This was my father's nest for more than thirty years. I hope it will be my nest at least as long. Let's go in and let me introduce you to some of my working friends, and also show you around. When you are comfortable with the 'smell' of science, we can go to my office and have some coffee, relax, and I will invite some of my key decision makers to chat for a while. Then we can have lunch at Betty and Bobs just down the street. After lunch we can talk nanotech."

A couple of hours later, after meeting several of Li's scientists, looking at both simple and sophisticated medical research equipment, checking out especially designed rooms for tissue culture to grow human cells, cold rooms versus freezing rooms, toxic chemical protection and radioactivity protection rooms, they returned to Li's office on the first floor.

'Neat people and very dedicated to Li and their sciences,' Jamie thought to himself.

Coffee was hot and ready, both of them needed a caffeine boast. They entered the conversation area of the office and sat in the nice big arm chairs. Coffee was served and Li asked his secretary to invite Walter and Edward, the two vice presidents, to join them. Ten minutes later the four of them were budding friends and discussing research and currently available financial support systems.

At lunch, Li had a surprise for Jamie. A tall, slim, lovely young Chinese lady joined the two of them. Her name was Ting Ting Chong. She met Li in Nanking in the Kung Fu training programs several years ago. After high school in China, she came to the USA to study high technology in molecular and biological chemistries. Currently she was studying for her PhD in nanotechnology and even taking one of Li's courses at the CIT. They had re-fallen in love, now she was here, and next was to tie the knot. Li introduced her as his fiance. And Jamie spotted the engagement ring on her left-hand ring finger.

Jamie jumped up and gave Ting a massive bear hug. He was over 200 pounds to her 105 pounds. But three big smiles were of a super approval nature. The two of them sort of looked each other over, suddenly realizing they were going to be together on a regular basis for a long time, so first opinions were critical.

"Li, when did this happen?" asked Jamie. "I did not know you were ever serious about someone. Especially someone so beautiful. Ting. Do you have a sister?"

Ting answered, "No. But I have two brothers. And they are both bigger than you." And she winked at Li, and laughed.

"Not my style," responded Jamie.

And he also broke down laughing.

Li was suddenly seeing a different view of his finance. She was becoming American-ified. And he joined the chuckles.

Li spoke, "You will have to be careful around my future wife as she is very fast with responses."

They had ordered a lunch of small green salads, cheese, luncheon meats, hot rolls, fresh fruits, and cold coconut milk—it arrived. All fresh and delicious. They dug in.

Li introduced tonight's event. "As teenagers we met in Nanking in the Wu Xing Kung Fu Matches. Our first introduction was when, as early teenagers we fought each other in the Kung Fu match at 35 kilo. But I forgot who won? HA!"

Ting quickly said. "He never forgets. And today Li is a Black Belt and I am still Brown Belt, two notches behind. But tonight, I hope to close the gap."

Li spoke out. "Tonight, Ting is fighting a Red Belt at the Los Angeles Martial Arts Center. If she wins, she will be one step behind me. Is she loses, she will have to fight a Red Belt again, but at another time. One must defeat a degree above you to allow your own advancement."

Ting added, "I am sorry but I must stay in motion all day today. So, I must eat quickly, take an analytical biochemistry exam at 2 PM, then go home and prepare for tonight's fight at the Center—9 PM. I hope you will be there."

Jamie quickly spoke up, "Not even the Blue Dragon of China could stop me. This Kung Fu match was the hidden reason that I came all the way from the Atlantic to the Pacific. Now, can we bet on the matches?"

Li closed the conversation. "There is only one bet. My lovely peacock."

Ting turned red in the face. And sent a questioning look toward Li. While Jamie stood up and cheered. It would be a fun evening—we hope.

"We can explain our personal history to Jamie after you win tonight." Li spoke. 'Current plans are for Li to graduate with her doctorate this summer. We briefly return to Li's family in China and get re-married. Then we will immediately return here and both begin new projects on nanotech molecular designs for that cellulose system. Ting has better visualizations for these types of molecules than I do. She will be employed in our basic nanotech designs group. I think we will be able to work well together. I think. I hope so."

And he gave his fiancé a loving smile. It was immediately returned.

Thus the three of them moved onward…

After lunch, Li and Jamie returned to his office. Walter and Edward joined them and they began a review of the information that Uncle Dagda gave to Jamie. The info was several pages of hand written notes that Uncle Dagda had made during one of the Committee of Nanotechnology Control Meetings in Washington. Jamie was to share the ideas on the notes and then destroy them. He had given them to Li earlier, so Li was ready to share the data with his two VPs.

The four settled in around the small conference table and Li began. "The information begins with a description of the three general types of nanotech molecular systems (NMS) in use today:"

1) NMS for brain area function – organic/protein molecule injected into spinal cord/fluid which will enter and bind to a certain specific region of the brain and inhibit that region of the body so controlled by that brain region,

2) NMS for specific tissue/organ system – organic/protein molecule injected into the blood and with a homing MoAB it will bind to a specific cell in a specific tissue and inhibit that tissue, **OR** it can be consumed and with a digestion blocking component and a homing MoAB it can enter the blood and bind to a specific cell in a specific tissue and inhibit that tissue.

3) NMS for gastrointestinal digestive system only – cellulose/protein molecule consumed in the stomach, travels through the digestive system to the colon where the colonic bacteria digest the cellulose and activate a membrane digestion protein-lipase which ruptures membranes and causes internal diarrhea.

"The first organic NMS is expensive and can only be initiated on one or two people at a time when they are unconscious; before or after construction it must be maintained frozen in dry ice or liquid nitrogen until use.

"The second organic NMS is very expensive and can be used with one or several people; it can be injected or digested if carefully used; it requires a digestion blocker and/or a homing MoAB; before or after construction it must be maintained frozen in dry ice or liquid nitrogen until use."

"The third cellulose NMS is very cheap; it is easily constructed; once it enters the GI tract, digestion and activation will occur automatically in the colon and subsequent colon membrane rupturing; after construction it can be maintained at room temperature."

"In general, proper design of the organic/protein (by using non-digestable synthetic amino acids) can allow a delay of action time of several hours. This cellulose/protein design will automatically cause a delay of several hours. And with most nanotech killings, where forensic examinations were performed, there was a delay of several hours"

"In summary, most NMS utilized a time lag to probably allow the 'killer' to escape. It is suggested that we take advantage of this time lag and develop a NMS blocker, digestor, neutralizer, re-router, or a homing MoAB blocker."

"What do you think?"

Jamie said, "It sounds like a good suggestion. Gentlemen?"

Walter spoke first, "Because each NMS is targeted on a specific cell or tissue, and if our time of counter attack is a few hours after it is placed into the body, we can forget stomach digestion. The NMS would be well past there. The NMS would probably already be attached to or inside the targeted cell. It would be very difficult to develop an early encounter to the NMS. It would be easier to develop a general neutralizer of the action of the organic/protein trigger mechanisms."

"That is an interesting idea," replied Edward. "We usually use a somewhat common organic/protein trigger mechanism. It is the targeting area that is unique in most of our targeting efforts, not the trigger area."

Jamie added, "My uncle told me that the first and second NMS are being used less today. Why? My understanding is the cost ranges in the several hundred thousand to more than one million US dollar range for one such specific NMS. The third NMS, with the cellulose/protein trigger mechanism is cheaper, a few hundred US dollar range for one. I have recently talked with our partner in Nigeria. They have had several hundred nanotech deaths, mostly diarrhea, recently. Hence this suggests the third cellulose NMS as the preferred nano-weapon. Apparently, a civil war has begun there and of course this would be cheaper and have broader military usage. He thinks the third cellulose NMS will be the major weapon there in the near future."

"Then in terms of our priorities, maybe we should look at possible inhibitory mechanisms for the cellulose/protein molecular system," replied Li.

"Edward replied, "That system has minimal specificity, and common activation and destruction mechanisms."

"And there are no cell membranes to enter or go through as that system begins inside the GI tract and its action is inside the GI tract. So, we would have to only target and inhibit one set of cellulose/protein trigger mechanisms," said Walter.

"We have never played with cellulose, but it is a simple six carbon sugar-like molecule," replied Edward. "I can try to design two or three for this week, test them out next week, and start seeking neutralizers for them in a week or two."

Li said. "Do you think the cellulose/protein design will be easy?"

For a moment Walter thought and then responded, "Yes. But we can do this. There are a limited number of ways to covalently bind cellulose to a protein."

Then Li continued, "Let us talk about this a little more, then we can flip a coin to see who gets the honors of playing with the cow. After all, the major component in grass is cellulose. And that is the cow's favorite food."

All laughed, except Jamie. His science was just not quite enough.

————— ❦ —————

After a final decision to pursue a neutralizer for the trigger mechanism of the cellulose/protein NMS, Walter and Edward returned to their laboratories. Li and Jamie were both pleased. Jamie continued updating Kef concerning Kef's Nigerian efforts. He would return to Boston tomorrow. And the two musketeers finished a leisurely afternoon reminiscing in Kef's office, then went downtown, did a little shopping, and ate a substantial evening dinner at the Marriott Marquis Restaurant near the LA Chinese Martial Arts Center.

During the meal Jamie asked, "Because we will shortly go to watch Ting in her Kung Fu match, can you please explain to me what is Wu Xing or Kung Fu?"

Li answered, "Of course. The American Military calls it close quarters defense (CQD). The world-wide types include: akido, hapkido, judo, jujitsu, karate, krav maga, kung fu, muay thai, tae kwon do, and tai chai. These started in several different countries at different times over the past thousand plus years."

"Routinely, kung fu refers to Chinese martial arts. And there are six sub-types of these: eagle claw, hung gar, five animals, monkey, praying mantis, and wing chun."

"Five Animals is Shaolin Kung Fu because it originated in the Shaolin Temple in China, was the first Chinese martial arts, and is the most popular today. Ting and I practice this form."

"The five animals we use are the following: tiger, crane, leopard, snake, and dragon. It began a thousand years ago with 18 techniques, increased to 72 techniques, and now uses 170 techniques. All moves and counter moves are based upon the natural offensive and defensive moves of an animal, one by one, which ever one you choose at that point in the match."

"All animals use a common set of stances such as the forward stance, horse stance, bird stance, cat stance, general fighting stance, and the twist stance."

"Most animals use a common punch move such as jab, hook, uppercut, block, step back, step sideways, and step forward."

"Most animals use the traditional moves of that specific animal such as snake or dragon, tiger or leopard, or crane."

Jamie spoke up, "Wow! I can begin to understand why it takes many years to master and successfully use all of that physical knowledge. You have been practicing kung fu for more than fifteen years. Right?"

Li nodded positively. "And I obtained the highest ranking only two years ago."

"What are the rankings?" asked Jamie.

"There are certificates associated with belts and sashes, answered Li. "A fighter is judged and awarded by a world ranking association called the Martial Arts International Federation."

"One begins with a beginner's white belt (1). Every few months he may try to move up in ranking by fighting a belt grade above him. He may move up only when he defeats an above grade fighter. Above grades are yellow (2), gold (3), orange (4), green (5), blue (6), purple (7), brown (8), red (9), and black (10). Black Belt is the highest belt/ sash grade. Although another super grade, Masters Black Belt, allows one to study and use hand weapons."

"Fascinating!" said Jamie. "And Ting will fight tonight for a possible red belt. Is that correct?"

"Yes," replied Li. "She is fighting a very good fighter who is about twenty pounds heavier than she is. But Ting is not only fast, she is very quick. Quickness frequently wins over physical size. It is agility that is critical, for defense as well as offense. And she does want to be closer to that Black Belt when we are married. She has not said anything. But I know she would like to have a child before she is beyond thirty years. That gives her three more years."

"And your feelings here?" Jamie inquired.

"I would like a child, but I want her and her health first. So? I do help, but not too much?" Li said.

He continued, "Come. Let us finish and go watch some of the earlier matches so you can begin to develop a feel for what the fighters are trying to do to win."

And Jamie was off on another new experience—first making movies, then making high tech drugs, and now fighting a Brown Belt—all in forty-eight hours. What a journey!

As they were walking down the street to the Martial Art Center, Li gave Jamie a small booklet, told him to put it into his pocket, and to read it tomorrow morning while on the plane back to Boston, but not before. Jamie promised.—tomorrow—

When tomorrow came, Jamie was on a United Airlines from Los Angeles to Boston. As they passed over Denver he laid back in his seat and opened the gift booklet that Li gave to him. He read:

THE FIVE MENTAL STATES OF KUNG FU

The journey to self-mastery requires building patience, discipline, and awareness.

1) **Sensual Desire** – intertwined pleasure arising from deep craving involves vision, hearing, smell, touch, and/or taste - **MASTER CONTROL**

2) **III Will** – state of not wanting something or someone - **OVERCOME NEGATIVE EMOTIONS**

3) **Sloth or Torpor** – state of inaction can lead to self-imprisonment – **SET GOALS AND SEEK INSPIRATION**

4) **Restlessness** – continuous movement from X to Z to X - **MEDIATION AND FOCUS**

5) **Skeptical Doubt** – hesitation and questioning forwardness – **CHALLENGE DOUBTS ONE BY ONE**

The journey to fully understanding our purpose and value in life— or achieving self-mastery—begins the second we are born. It requires a commitment to building patience, discipline, and self-awareness. In all future journeys we must focus on the present and the future…

16

KEF IN NIGERIA IV

After returning to Abuja, Kef spent the first week sending an update of his findings to the other musketeers, and to Uncle Dagda through Jamie. Then he thought about how he was going to organize his next moves, both with the African Queen of Voodoo and in the North, the Moslem sector.

Abuja was a clean new city with everything modern, excellent transportation, well-built infrastructure, and both private and rental living accommodations that were well organized. So, Kef sometimes just enjoyed working outside and away from the government office. He easily made friends in the Executive Office Building. But sometimes they interrupted his work concentration, usually wanting to talk soccer. Within a few blocks of the three arms zone, the government offices area, were several parks with a variety of eating stands. They were popular with the government employees. And he had learned that they did indeed serve tasty food. So, he frequently disappeared, 'temporarily out of office', and into a nearby park, just he and his new i-pad XLO. Today, at 1:00 PM, he went five blocks west into a well treed area, near his favorite Water Buffalo Burger stand. He arrived, ordered his burger made with the female buffalo meat steak on a poppy seed bun, loaded with red lettuce, sheep cheese, onion, Dijon mustard, plus potato fries, and a very cold pepsi cola. He found an empty table in the shade, sat, ate his lunch, then opened his i-pad.

He opened a beginning file on the African Queen of Voodoo, but could not get his mind into the problem. He had just assigned each member of his N-4 team key projects which should take each of them a couple of weeks of government archival research. Aminu had been assigned to uncover all he could about the local-personal history of the Voodoo

Queen. Bonjoho was to learn about the Queen's several organizations and finances. Kef had also asked Aykut to investigate the financial picture of the Queen. Abiefume was researching northern Nigeria, the Moslem region. While Kachiside was responsible for learning about the problems in southern Nigeria and the oil interrelationships.

A little bored, he looked up and spotted a beautiful very dark young lady, probably near mid-twenties, sitting at a nearby table. She was wearing a bright red short skirt, a lovely sleeveless red blouse with pink floral designs, red low heel shoes, and shiny crimson lipstick. Being a center forward college soccer athlete Kef was always on the attack. Plus, he never had difficulty meeting young ladies. He approached her and asked, "May I sit here. My new i-pad XLM is becoming difficult to read in the direct sun shine which has now chased me away from my table. And most other shaded tables seem to be occupied!"

She looked at him with that 'but you are a stranger' set of eyes.

He caught the look and quickly introduced himself. "My name is Kefentse Legoase. I am working on a special contract with an American government committee and the Nigerian Department of Health and Human Services. I am from South Africa." And he gave her his best smile.

She responded, "I know. Your picture was in the Nigerian Gazette a couple of weeks ago. It said that you were the soccer player called the Black Panther and beat us in the World Cup Playoffs a few years ago. Is that true?"

Kef said to himself, 'I thought she would be impressed that I am working with the American and Nigerian governments, and here she only remembers from the newspapers that I am just another foreign soccer player.'

"My sixteen year old little brother is totally in love with center field soccer specialists. He is trying so hard to make the Green Jackets so he can try to get a college scholarship."

And of course, that brought back Kef's memories of fighting for the same type of scholarship from the same position on a soccer team—successfully.

Kef replied, "Yes you have me straight. What your brother is trying to do is what I successfully did about ten years ago. It does bring back good memories."

The young lady said, "I am sorry. I did not intend to bring back old memories."

"That is alright," he replied. "The memories were very good. You might say that I am here because those memories were very good. But I am sorry. I will leave if I have disturbed you."

And he stood up, picked up his i-pad, and started to leave.

She quickly grabbed his i-pad and said, "But not before you show me your new i-pad XLQ. I have never seen one."

He did a double take, sat back down, and stuck out his hand to shake hello.

The young lady responded, "My name is Adaeze Okonkwo. I work as a level three judicial associate for Judge Ihejirika in the Department of Justice. This morning I passed the exam for the fourth or senior level judicial associate position. When such a position now becomes available, I can apply. You see I live with my invalid mother and little brother. We only have my income. Therefore, it is very important that I continue doing well. I am celebrating by taking a free afternoon off."

Kef spoke up. "Let me help you celebrate by buying you a big tusked chocolate with marshmallow ice cream cone."

She looked at him as if to say, are you serious?

He looked back at here as if to say, yes, of course I am serious.

They broke down laughing. It was the beginning of a potentially warm and involved relationship. Kef did not get back to doing serious work on his i-pad that afternoon. And the African Queen of Voodoo would just have to wait on him.

A couple of days later Aminu wanted to spend some private time with Kef in his office. So, after lunch the two of them lunched around the small conference table. Aminu began with the problem he was having.

"You assigned me to investigate the life of the African Queen of Voodoo living in Lagos. I do not understand why I am doing this. Should I know the importance of this old lady to our project?"

"No, you should not," answered Kef. "Our nanotech team always works by 'need to know'. At this point in time, you do not need to know. But I will answer your question. This old lady is certainly one of the most powerful Nigerians. It is probable that she will help us in eliminating the nanotech problem here in Nigeria, and possibly a couple of other problems that are beginning to simmer. She is the most powerful sorceress/voodoo priestess in Africa. She uses snakes and poisonous herbs as weapons. Go learn about her. That is enough for now. We will talk more later."

Aminu was stunned, and could not respond. But would certainly do as requested.

Kef continued, "Obviously what you have uncovered did not go very deep into Lagos and the Queen's personal history. Look at the wealthy old men she married and 'lost', the enemies she fought and destroyed, the many friends that somehow were elevated to higher levels of life because their enemies had disappeared, the role of her daughters in the family businesses, and just how wealthy the family really is today compared to thirty years ago."

Kef finished and stood up. "Do you understand me? When you have heard and followed me more closely, come back and we will talk again. Possibly by then we can increase your 'need to know'."

Aminu apologized, stood, and left the office. Kef just smiled as the door closed.

Two weeks later Kef had a 'date' with his new friend, Adaeze Okonkwo. It was a beautiful Saturday morning and he drove his rented car, stopped, and parked near her apartment. She lived in the East Jako district which was an area close to the Department of Justice Building. Many of the government departments had special 'free' rental apartments units assigned to employees near their work place. Adaeze lived about five blocks from work. She promised him an afternoon playout, a common practice for newly met young couples.

He arrived just before lunchtime. She was waiting at the door, and quickly let him in. She was anxious to have her mother meet this foreigner.

Kef spoke first, " It is going to be hot this afternoon but cool this evening on the water. You probably should bring a sweater."

Suddenly from the other room an older voice called out. "That is what I told her. I hope she hears you!"

Adaeze winked at Kef and said, "Yes, I will pick one up on the way out. First let introduce you to my mother."

"Mother, this is Kef, a South African citizen who is working on a joint project for Nigeria and the United States. He is working in the Department of Health and Human Resources. We have had lunch twice over the past couple of weeks. And today we are going to the Nigerian Boat Club, courtesy of the President. Later we will attend the American Jazz Festival at the Club. So, we should not be home late."

"I know you will be home early," Mother said as she gave Kef a stern look.

"Of course," responded Kef. What else could he say. And he gave mother a big smile.

Suddenly from the back of the apartment came a loud 'younger' voice. Adaeze's younger brother, Olasupo. "Don't let him get away. I want to meet him and make arrangements for my first lesson."

And big sister turned reddish, raised her shoulders in a what can I do gesture?

Olasupo burst into the room, rushed up to Kef, gave him a players-handshake, and said, "Are you really the Black Panther?"

Kef looked at Adaeze, raised his shoulder in the same what can I do gesture, laughed, and responded, "Some people call me that. But then they are football players."

"Then I can call you that because I am the best fifteen year old center fielder in all of Nigeria. But I could always use some good advice and pointers on the back switch and opposite foot shoot. I know you are good at that shot because I saw you score with it on television."

"You will have to show me your moves, soon," Kef answered.

"OK! In two weeks, we play the Red Rinos in the Stadium. I will learn more about the exact time, tell sis, and she can bring you so you can watch me, then later you can teach me. OK." Little brother was flying high.

Kef said, "You have a deal. Now we will be late if we do not hurry to the Club."

He grabbed Adaeze by the arm who grabbed a jacket. He gave her mother a quick cheek kiss and said, "It was nice to meet you. And I hope to come by again soon when we can have time to chat. I know the President is waiting at the Club so we don't want to be late."

And he glanced at Olasupo, "See you next week."

And mom responded, 'I know you will not be late!" And she winked at him.

The young couple looked each other in the eyes and headed out the door, down the stairs, into the car, and away for a Nigerian playout.

Kef now knew his way around central Abuja. They took the Circle Drive, east and north, which went around the Three Arms Zone that enclosed most of the buildings for the three civilian departments of the Nigerian government. As they semi-circled the area the gigantic Aso Rock appeared on the right. At one square mile and over 800 feet tall, in the mornings it certainly overshadowed the entire government area. It was solid granite, but did have a few tourists oriented tunnels.

They picked up the A234 motorway and went west for twenty miles to the large Li Lake, where the Nigerian Boat Club was located. The Club had special membership only for high level government employees and wealthy business people—a carefully designed 'watering hole'.

Kef had a temporary membership thanks to the Nigerian President's select foreigner's protocol. He would enjoy it often in the hot summer months. They pulled up to the front entry of a large rectangular building facing west and overlooking a large lake, gave the electronic keys and Club pass to the doorman, and went inside to their assigned table for a light lunch. Sitting, glancing over the lunch menu, they ordered sandwiches and salad. Later they would go boating.

They sat quietly for several moments. Adaeze stared out at the lake and said, "Just let me sit here all day and stare at this fabulous deep blue. Abuja has only red, crimson, yellow, brown, green, and of course, black." And she laughed.

She continued, "Blue is my favorite color. I only see it when I come here. I think this is my third or fourth visit. It is really beautiful."

Kef replied, I grew up in Cape Town, South Africa, on two oceans. So, I have all shades of blues in my childhood memory bank. Yes, it is a most beautiful color."

He continued, "I guess we grew up on different sides of the street. I had unlimited waters and sea food to eat. I lived in a poor crowded neighborhood with seven brothers and sisters. All families in the area had many children. So, I continuously had numerous brothers and sisters to play with and learn from. And I certainly never had any private free time."

Adaeze responded, "Yes, you are right. Growing up by myself for the first ten years, until Olasupo came, I only had myself to play with. From my family history I know that we were living in the village of Abuja when the Lagos government decided to build a capital here. My grandfather was a building contractor and was killed in a fall from the tenth floor of a high-rise building. My father was a government worker and died of a heart attack when Olasupo was two years old and I was,,aha,, a beginning teenager. Believe me, young boy and girl teenager do not necessarily become close friends, nor even play together very much. We are closer now, as we are older. Mother was also a government worker, but she also had a stroke four years ago. The government did not give much insurance in those days, but our health coverage was and is still good. So, I became the family's major financial supporter. I worked hard, did well, and my superiors promoted every two or three years. With the free rental apartment close to work, and Olasupo going to a nearby high school which is free to children of government employees, mother's major health problems are covered with government insurance, we are doing OK."

"And I thought I had growth problems," said Kef. "I had too many childhood friends, and you did not have enough. We did not grow up on opposite sides of the street. There was not even a street between our youth-lives—I think."

"And here I am a support follower," replied Adaeze. You are a leader."

Kef responded, "But I am several years older than you."

"And how old is that?"

"How can I tell you how much older I am if I do not have your starting number?'

"Oh! That was tricky. OK, I am twenty-six."

"Then I must be twenty-nine," Kef had carefully calculated on the fingers of both hands.

And they both looked each other in the eyes and laughed. They were becoming honest and sincere already.

The food arrived, and they settled down to nibble and chat for the next couple of hours. At two o'clock they went down to the boat docks, identified the boat named the Green Turtle, checked to learn that this was indeed their boat for a 'round the lake' boating excursion this afternoon. They boarded, selected a small table with a second floor deep blue water view, settled down again, and ordered a couple of alcohol-less Bloody Marys.

Soon they cleared the dock area and were out into the middle of the dark blue lake. The lake was nearly three miles wide and more than twenty miles long. The mountains were near seven hundred feet high on the north and west sides; so, one could see the beautiful water in front of the mountains and the setting sun on the western mountain tops at the same time. The mountains were covered with large old eucalyptus trees, contrasting with their light pale green colors.

The Green Turtle was the only boat, one hundred feet long, two levels, snow white with a light blue and green interior, designed for local short distance travels, and with simple entertainment facilities for fifty to one hundred people, second level. It only served mixed and non-mixed drinks and snack foods. A three soft piece band continuously provided relaxing music over the waveless water. A perfect setting for a gentle—get to know you...

Kef and Adaeze had twenty-five years plus of personal life history that they seemed to want to immediately share. This was the proper setting for passing unspoken messages. They certainly talked more and more future, even long term. Suddenly the boat horn blared. Without noticing it, more than two hours shot by and they had re-docked. They de-barked, returned to shore, and returned to their reserved table in the dining room. The table had been cleared, beautified, and a bottle of French champagne was sitting in an ice bucket. It was compliments of the President of Nigeria. The two 'happy' ones just looked at each other and broke down laughing.

"Once in a life time—we certainly can never forget this day," so Kef managed to say, even with some tears in his eyes. Macho?

They saluted the Li Blue Lake Waters of Nigeria and said, 'We will return to the Deep Blue. Soon."

At seven-thirty they went next door to the adjacent semi covered semi-crab shaped auditorium facing the setting sun over the water and looking down at a moving platform stage. The open-air facility had two seating areas. The lower twenty rows of soft seats were for

Club members only and one entered it from below. The upper fifty rows of hard seats were for non-members, or for those others who paid, and one entered it from above via three separate stairways. Kef had the necessary Club membership pass for tonight, so they went below and settled into the softer seats. Nice!

The American Jazz Festival would last more than three hours. Kef suggested they leave at the mid-show break. In this way he could get Adaeze home 'early'. He was already thinking of keeping on the good side of a possible future mother-in-law.

The program was all American: Arianna Neikrug, Chris Beck, Camila Meza, Jaime Branch, and Sasha Mesakowski. It was full of highly talented jazz musicians who wanted to show their best; translated that meant an hour or more—hence five times five ended after midnight. Kef was thinking properly for an early leaving time.

They did not get home toooo early. Mother was in bed, not asleep, but she did not complain out loudly. She just let the children know she was there, and alert. It was OK. It had been a positive evening.

A couple of weeks later Aminu was ready. He requested an appointment with Kef to try again to present his collected info on the African Queen of Voodoo. They met in Kef's office after lunch.

Aminu looked sheepishly at Kef, again apologized for a not very good beginning research effort, and hoped this time would be better.

Kef responded with, "I hope so too."

Aminu began. "Because you are new to our country, I will begin my review with Lagos, go to Abuja, and discuss the info on the African Queen of Voodoo. In 1427, Portuguese explorers settled in what is now Lagos. It is a collection of islands and peninsulas, interlaced with numerous small rivers and creeks, surrounding a large lagoon, and connecting directly into the Atlantic Ocean. In the mid-twentieth century, the area was administrated by the British as a Nigerian colony. However, Lagos declared independence in 1960 and became the capital of Nigeria. Soon the Federation of Nigeria was established with twelve states, Lagos as the old capital. The new capital city, Abuja, was in the center of the country. The Nigerian capital moved there in 1991."

"Sometime around 1970, a female child was born in the desolate Ajegunle area of Lagos to someone. No one knew who the mother was, but a homeless middle-aged lady, who had recently lost her child, picked her up and breast fed her. She took in the homeless, parentless little girl, who was badly malnourished and feverish. Neighbors assumed the baby would die, so ignored the situation. She did not. In fact, the child drank any liquid they gave her and ate all foods. She was beautiful with dark shiny skin, blue-green eyes, and red hair. She had a smile that caught your heart and drew you to her. She was simply very lovely, without any abnormal body areas. All reproductive age and older women came by just to hold her and wish for such a gift—from heaven?"

Exactly how and where she grew up is not known. It is clear that with that beautiful face she was continuously attractive to men. But she was very intelligent, and always managed to escape male clutches. Early in life she learned that she had a certain enchantment with snakes. Because the Lagos area was inundated with them, she easily attracted and learned to control them. Anyone, e.g. males, would have to very careful in her presence. As she grew up and males tried to force themselves on her, they usually found themselves seeking an emergency snake doctor with a variety of anti-snake venoms. More than once, as a teenager, she was in the courts being charged with such things from assault and battery, attempted murder, or even murder. People would go to the court proceedings to watch and laugh at the plaintiffs who never ever won a case against her. She was simply too beautiful and cunning. And she could be rather entertaining when she wanted to be."

"Three years later a wealthy old 'oil' man, Jaju Wachuku, fell in love with her and married her. Within six months he was found dead by a snake bite, while he was working in the couple's lovely garden. No criminal charges. No trial. But she did inherit several oil fields, a couple of oil wells, and five distribution pipe lines."

"Five years later she got pregnant by another wealthy husband businessman, Shenu Amaechi. She miscarried. The following year she got pregnant by him again. She miscarried again. The night of the second miscarriage the husband committed suicide by sleeping in bed with several poisonous snakes. She was in the hospital at the time, so no court charges were filed against her. This time she inherited the entire Lagos Island in the middle of the Lagos Lagoon, and several other pieces of real estate in the Lagoon area. She quickly re-built the English manor/castle in the center of the unoccupied island, but left the surrounding jungle-like area and jungle of trees intact.

"Piers were built along the east and south sides of the island to allow boating access for family, guests, and house deliveries, and to help avoid snakes."

"She established a security force of more than fifty very poisonous snakes and a dozen snake handlers near the piers and the walls of the castle."

"It is wise to arrange appointments to see the Queen a few days before you wish to boat to the island. She will help you out during your 'transit'.

Kef broke in, "I know this woman has five daughters, and is living with all of these poisonous snakes, and people go into that mansion building to see her. Does she not come out and meet people, at least sometimes. I cannot go in there and talk with her."

Aminu looked at Kef, "I do not understand. What do you want me to do?"

Kef answered "I have had some training in Voodooism in Haiti. So, I am somewhat qualified to talk to her and might even understand her. I could even ask for her help. These people are her people."

Aminu continued, "I know she has a sister in Haiti. And she went there several times to learn and compare Voodoo ideas, techniques, methods, and whatever they do for good or bad."

"According to a university sociologist-psychologist whom I have talked with, the Voodoo Queen can conjure, spiritualize, perform magic rootwork, intervene in problem solving, protect against evil, provide excellent marital advice, solve domestic disputes, handle judicial affairs, aid in childbearing, cure various female health problems, perform good luck rituals at weddings or anniversaries, among other magic."

"She provides (sells) magic amulets known as gris-gris. They are composed of snake skin, copper coins, fresh rose petals, fresh lavender flowers rolled into a chamois cloth and placed into a leather bag with various snake heads imprinted on the front."

"A couple of years later she married again. Esquire Bukola Ngumaha, a wealthy retired federal judge wanted to give her, and himself, a child. After two years of trying, it was determined that he was too old; he did not have a high enough sperm count. She fed him one of her special herb mixes that mimicked Cobra venom. It did kill him, quickly and surely. It was thought that she loved him. But I did not find out if herb-venom comparisons were 'scientifically recorded."

Kef just grinned.

"The Voodoo Queen regularly performs special services several times a year. 1) the Congo Circle which is a public park gathering for free and ex-slave peoples: 2) Sunday night worship which mixes Voodooism and Catholicism; 3) a free lake front occasionally performs very special black magic (for big money)."

"She is total owner and controller of four different companies and a surburb of Lagos which houses many homeless, very poor, and destitute people to whom she provides everything. Each company is not for profit and includes: the Good Shall Rise.com, the Great Zombi.com, Justice for Truth.com, the Bad Shall Go Down.com. I was not able to find out anything about her many bank accounts."

Kef thought to himself. "This will give Aykut and Asu, in Istanbul, a real challenge.

Aminu finished, "This one more piece of info is all I have. I will give it to you, and you can decide if it's interesting."

"The Voodoo Queen had always wanted to have her own children. So she collected sperm from young soccer athletes, prepared several different combinations of herbs, treated the sperm, and tested the viability under a microscope. Apparently, some group of physicians helped her—no records of who or where or what was done. Probably in the basement of her mansion. There are medical facilities there. Overall results were five identical baby girl mutant variants. Each girl was genetically the same, except each lacked a different sense. An example is: loss of hearing, touch, speech, taste, and smell. And each is named after their favorite poisonous snake. An example is : Viper, Krait, Mamba, Jaraca, and Coral. The Queen uses the name of Cobra. Each of these are favorite playmates and routinely travel with their mothers.

'For now, that is the best I can do. If you need more, give me some time, point in which direction to go, and I will continue looking."

Kef said, "Extremely well done. This nicely completes what knowledge I already have. And yes, later, after I share this information with certain musketeer team members, I will have more questions for you. Does that make you happy?"

All Aminu could say was, "Thank you. Something told me that you would have more."

And he looked Kef in the eye, smiled, and shook his head.

17

THE NANOTECH LABORATORY

{The heart of the nanotech molecular system is the protein molecule. Each protein is composed of ten to several hundred amino acids. There are twenty-two natural ones, two more that Li's father created and synthesized several years ago, and one that Li created and synthesized during his dissertation (PhD) research. All amino acids are small molecules, about the size of sugar molecules (20 to 30 atoms in size)}.

{In biology, the twenty-two natural amino acids are bound together on a rubber string like a beaded necklace in what are called peptide-N bonds. Hence, they are protein necklaces. The synthetic amino acids are similarly bound together in what are called peptide-S bonds. And the natural plus synthetic amino acids can be bound together in what are called peptide-Q bonds. All beaded amino acid chains twist into three dimensional formations like beaded spaghetti on rather stiff rubber springs.}

{The body's digestive system easily digests the normal peptide-N bonds and converts the protein back into its many amino acids which separately enter the blood and travel to all body cells for future use in protein re-construction. But it has difficulty digesting the peptide-S bonds, and cannot digest the peptide-Q bonds. Therefore, one can design and synthesize proteins with combinations of natural and synthetic amino acids. In this way new proteins can be synthesized which have both modified function and rates of digestion. Such proteins are called **dual** or **hybrid proteins**—like hybrid cars—and they may or may not necessarily be part of a nanotech molecular system, but may be simply associated components.}

It was 9:00 AM on Monday morning when Li and his five senior associates met in Li's office. They were sitting around the conference table, sipping coffee, and waiting for Li to start the show.

Li began, "I want to discuss two areas today. **First**, how can we develop a **dual protein** to interfere with or block the action of an **active organic nanotech molecular system**? Let us assume this active system has entered a person, moved within the body to reach its target cells or tissue. Consider that it may or may not be bound to the 'molecular target' within the target cell or on the target cell's membrane. How do we do this?

"**Second**, then I want to discuss how can we develop a **dual protein** to interfere or block the action of an **active cellulose nanotech molecular system**? Let us assume this active system has entered a person, moved within the body to reach its target cells or tissue. Consider that it may or may not be bound to the 'molecular target' within the target cell or on the target cell's membrane. How do we do this?"

"So, similar but different problems. Time to the target and location of target may be similar, but the target would be different. Cellulose is a sugar-like molecule (fifteen to twenty atoms), not an amino acid type molecule. Blocking or binding to a sugar-like molecule is not the same as blocking or binding to an amino acid."

"Can we use a dual protein directly? Remember it must travel through the body rapidly, in just a few minutes. Keep in mind, most general infection agents require hours to days to act once it enters the body. Most of our designed nanotech molecular systems reach their target site within six to twelve hours. One can assume that there are five to ten hours maximum to interfere with or block this active system. So, a counter system must happen with minutes to hours. OK. Give me your ideas!

Walter, the oldest and most experienced in nanotechnology, close friend of Li's father, spoke first. "One option would be to use one separate dual protein, without nanotech molecular actions. Maybe one could use a snake venom protein for homing purposes. These venom poison proteins are small in size—twenty to fifty amino acids. A monoclonal antibody (MoAB) is a large protein—five thousand amino acids—not good—too big. Small sizes would be faster traveling, have easier membrane transport, and probably would be more active."

Edward added, "I had thoughts along the same lines. A small blocking dual protein with a small active region; plus, a snake venom protein or the active region of a snake venom protein. Hence two small proteins, one for homing and one for blocking, bound together as one complete stopping system."

"One also needs to consider mode of entry to the body," said Jackson. "You need to introduce the dual protein near the targeted site of the active nanotech molecular system. If in the brain, spinal fluids. If GI tract, possibly through the stomach. If in the lungs, of course through the nose."

Li spoke up, "You are suggesting that we have to take into account the location of the nanotech molecular system's target inside the body, as the dual protein design would need to be different with different body cell targets.—This is not going to be simple."

"What you are saying," said Rodger, "is that we may need to design and synthesize a dual protein for each active system based upon the bodily target location, components of the system, and it must reach and act on this system fast—minutes if possible."

Edward asked, "This approach would require that you have a pre-designed dual protein ready at the bedside of the patient, and it must be both fast traveling in the body and fast acting at the target site. Right?"

Li said, "What I am hearing is that we cannot design and synthesize a dual protein, go to the patient, which-ever continent that might be, treat him, cure him, all within a few hours. Well then, we must seek a different approach."

"Maybe we should think of a general protein for general blocking purposes," suggested Walter." For example, a dual protein which could block action of all nanotech molecular systems which have an organic (amino acid) trigger mechanism. Or a dual system which could block action of all nanotech molecular systems which have a cellulose trigger mechanism.—two distinct blocking systems!"

"Good idea," Li replied. "This approach would narrow it down to two major dual proteins—one for organic (amino-acids) and one for cellulose. I think this is more practical, and maybe even possible."

Walter continued, "I really like the possibility of two types of dual systems."

"Let us play with this idea for a while," said Li. "Walter, you worked with snake venom several years ago. I ask you to review your work and to be prepared to give us a brief review of its relationship to our nanotech molecular systems. Can you do this, next week?"

Walter responded, "Yes, not long ago it was a pleasure to review my first work with your father. This data was used to develop one of our multicomponent systems. OK. Let me open some of my old summary data books."

"I do remember," Walter continued, "Salivary venoms, from the salivary glands of snakes, scorpions, insects, jellyfish, and snails, are composed of several groups of toxic proteins. Five to ten different toxic proteins may be found in any one snake's venom. These venoms, and many viruses, contain proteins which will home-in on certain molecular and cellular targets in the body. Plus, they contain proteins which will act directly on certain pre-identified target cells, similar to MoABs. General examples are toxic proteins which bind/attack nerve and brain cells, blood cells, muscle cells, lung cells, mini blood coagulates, and specific single cell types. Many of these proteins have been purified and are available to work within the lab. Let me give you some examples."

"I also remember several purified proteins that were available to use in laboratory settings which included phospholipase A2, phosphodiesterase 4, phosphomonoesterase, myotoxins, amino acid oxidases, disintegrins, small DNA-RNA units, several small unknown peptides, morphine-like killer proteins, nerve/brain toxins, and others."

"And the snakes that have the largest quantity and most potent combination of these toxic proteins include: cobra, tiger snake, krait, rattlesnake, viper, black mamba, adder, and belcher sea snake."

Li spoke up, "It appears that there is an abundance of knowledge of the composition of venoms. I assume that the more important snakes, such as the cobra, have a published, detailed amino acid composition of their specific venom proteins. And that we could readily obtain any of these snakes, insects, or even scorpions for study if we wanted to try some experiments with their venom and some of our nanotech molecular systems."

"Yes," answered Walter. "I am certain herpetologists could provide us with almost any poisonous snake, fresh intact venom, or various types of toxic protein extracts from the venom."

"All right, said Li, "Edward, I am going to give this idea to you. Look at the composition of various venoms, check with a herpetologist to see what is currently available for laboratory use. Present this information to us in two weeks. We can then decide if combined working with venom toxic proteins and our nanotech molecular systems would be useful. If so, where do we start with our experiments."

"Now, let us continue with these two questions. 1) What amino acid sequence in a dual protein would best block an **organic** sequence containing an active system already in place in a person. 2) And compare this with the amino acid sequence of a dual protein that would best block a **cellulose** sequence containing an active system already in place in a person. In other words, I want to block the 'killing system' before it acts and kills that person? Organic or cellulose? Jim, what do you think?"

Jim thought for a few moments and then began to try to answer...

Li interrupted, "Wait a minute. Let us separate the two types of activated systems and look at them separately. The organic activating system obviously has many possible problems and answers, because we can recognize several venoms which use this type of mechanism. Let us think about these systems one by one. Each of you select one venom, tell me which one you want to work on, literature research it out, and we will look there at our next meeting."

"Again, let me slightly change the subject. Let us talk biochemistry for a little while. Let me introduce this gentleman who is a friend of mine, Dr. Jon Haskson. He is a Professor of Biochemistry at the University of Los Angeles. Plus, he is a specialist in digestive biochemistry. I think he can help help us with the cellulose activating system in the GI tract."

Dr. Haskson spoke up, "Thank you. There are so very few people who want to learn about the human digestion system, especially in the colon. I am certainly very happy to share one of my favorite subjects with you today—colonic actions—HA! HA!"

"I think I understand the problem you are facing is probably two-fold. The people who are dying have a delayed initiation time from eating certain foods, and the resulting membrane holes or leakages in the colon caused death by leaked colonic bacterial infections into the abdominal cavity."

"First, venoms do not enter the digestive tract. They directly enter the blood vascular system. The GI is mostly the mouth, stomach, small intestine, and the colon. You are finding people dying from leaky colons. Let us first look there. That is where the problems and answers are located."

Continuing, "The colon is the only location in the body for colonic bacteria which provide the cellulase that can digest cellulose and activate cellulose trigger containing molecular systems. But the body, including the colon, naturally does not have a molecule that can digest itself. If we had such a molecule, we would continuously digest leaks or holes in our own colon walls/membranes, leak colonic fluids into our abdominal cavity, and infect-kill ourselves very fast, within minutes to hours. This could occur in babyhood. Such a molecule would be called a colonesterase. Colonesterases are not normal body proteins. They have to be created—synthetic."

"In my opinion, the active cellulose nanotech molecular system is a type of colonesterase. It is activated by cellulose/cellulases inside the colon. Upon activation it then digests tiny leaks and small holes in the colonic wall/membrane. Such digestions would require only minutes-hours to travel from the stomach to the colon, for colonic fluid with bacteria to enter the intestinal cavity and anus, and for death to occur."

Li spoke up, "If I understand. Your theory is as follows:

- The nanotech molecular system is a colonesterase which, when activated, cuts leaks/holes in the walls of the colon,

- This colonesterase is activated by cellulose from the food and cellulase from intestinal bacteria which digest the cellulose,

- The components of digested cellulose directly activate the colonesterase."

Dr. Haskson responded, "Two attack points – 1) block activity of the colonesterase; – OR 2) block the activity of the cellulose-cellulase complex activation of the colonesterase.

Li understood, "Yes. Blocking either control point should prevent digestion resulting in leaks/holes in the colonic walls/membranes.

Dr. Haskson followed up, "I suggest you explore either potential inhibitor point. Your major preventive/cure target should focus on colonesterase activity!"

"Do you have any questions?"

—Yes—New Ideas!—Hands flew up!!!—

18

KEF IN NIGERIA V

[There are five great lakes in Africa—Victoria, Congo, Chad, Tanganyika, and Malawi. Lake Chad, which is shared by Nigeria, Chad, Niger, and Cameroon, is fed by several rivers. The two in northeast Nigeria are Komadugu Yobe and Ngadda.

In 1970, Lake Chad was 10,000 square miles. Today it is 3,000 square miles. It has a depth of ten to thirty feet; previously it had a depth of more than one hundred feet. And it provides water, inadequately, for thirty million people. This area is near the center of the entire Sahara Dessert of northern Africa. And it pays the price of a brief monsoon and lengthy drought each year. There are no dams or canals to control or conserve the water. Each country claims direct access.

In 2010 a civil war began in northeast Nigeria and created major destruction of basic social services from clean water to foods to health care to education to security. It created more than eight million homeless people, mostly women and children, requiring urgent life-saving assistance from local and international private and government sources. Small independent gangs and armies strived to establish an independent military base in the north-west, but were not successful. Today, unrest is still a major problem in the area.]

Kef was sitting in his office and reading the latest government reports from the Nigerian state of Borno, where all of the Nigerian part of Lake Chad is located. The highlights were focusing upon a two-month old major military uprising between the state capital of Borno, Maiduguri, and the Lake. Nigerian, Cameroon and Niger 'retired' military, ex-military from several African countries, foreign mercenaries, and a variety of African gangs moved in coordination from the lake east to west and captured land on both sides of the Komadugu Yobe and Ngadda Rivers. No one seemed to know where the support monies were coming from, nor what the objectives of the leaders of the movement were. But what caught Kef's eye was the statement—'**The villagers from many of the villages just west of Lake Chad were killed with some kind of a food poison that caused macabre deaths with excessive diarrhea. These villages are now thought to be haunted as a family of evil spirits has been released into the area.**'

Kef could only moan, 'It appears that we have nanotech killings in both the north and the south of Nigeria. Where do I go, first? I will call and inform the musketeers, report this new info, and ask for advice. Uncle Dagda could probably also offer good advice.'

Suddenly, Kef's cell phone beeped three-one-two-one times. By the ringing mechanism he could tell it was the modified Avatar re-language encrypted system. It was Jamie, and he knew there was a message from Uncle Dagda. He said, "I was just thinking about the devil and you appear."

Jamie laughed and said, "And I felt you dreaming about us. My Irish witchcraft is good and getting better. But 8 AM in Boston translates into 1 PM in Abuja. The time factor screws things up in the final interpretation."

Kef returned, "When are you going to come and visit me. We have beautiful 80-degree weather here. What do you have, one hundred below?"

"Just because you have never seen snow," Jamie replied.

They all knew better and laughed in return. With more than fifteen years of international communicating, the 'boys' were very internationally oriented. And, of course, Uncle Dagda already knew about the nanotech killings in northeast Nigeria via the Committee of Nanotech Control in Washington. They had sent a nanotech trained team into the area, but were not being given adequate access. The Nigerian army was not large and they did not want to start a bigger war, so it was being rumored.

Jamie said, "Uncle Dadga informed me that our 'International-American' Committee tried to send a forensic team into the region one week ago, but the unknown military forces in the area would not let anyone enter. We probably do not know much more than you do. It is possible a new civil war has started, and this 'new' military is using nanotech molecular systems as part of their attack weapons. We have heard that this new macabre form of killing is creating major social turmoil in the area. Villages are not even trying to fight back. They are giving up and even helping the invading military forces. The leaders of this military spread word of new evil spirits. Hence this new evil form of death. You are on the ground there; you will have to re-orient your work load and high tail it to the Lake Chad region of Nigeria. We need current info, fast. Our committee cannot recommend anything without more accurate info. And village deaths seem to be occurring almost every day in the Borno state."

Kef said, "I understand. I have a good Nigerian Associate managing the work in southern Nigeria. We can continue our investigation there. Plus, I was already in motion to visit and evaluate current events in northeast Nigeria. I will contact you just as soon as I have any good data, or one week at the most. Jamie, see you later. Bye for now."

Jamie responded, "I am sending to you some 'personal' stuff from my Uncle. It should arrive within 20 hours by All-Express. Bye–Bye."

Kef had previously arranged for two special work conferences that same day; one for continuing the investigation in the south; one for going to the north. The first one which concerned the South-South included Aminu and Nwadinpa. At 2 PM the two Associates came to the office, were invited in, and settled into chairs around the conference table. No leisure coffee this time, only quick and solid decision making. The two Nigerian fellows knew each other over the years from various conferences and get to know you parties with government friends. The Voodoo Prince of Africa was also known by social reputation to many government employees of the Department of Health and Human Services, Voodoo orientation or not. He regularly mixed with the villagers in the Christian regions of Nigeria as a normal Nigerian as well as a Voodoo Priest. As the big eared mouse in the corner, he continuously monitored good and bad social events in the South, and occasionally informed certain government friends. He could frequently tell you who did what to whom, long before any government employee living in Abuja could even make a lucky guess.

Kef began the conversation, "I assume that you have heard of the fighting in the northeast. These invaders are using nanotech weapons. Therefore, I am being 'advised' to go north and try to find out what is happening near Lake Chad. You two will have to continue the investigation on the nanotech massacres in the south."

"Aminu, to bring you within another ring of **need to know**: I had voodoo training with the Voodoo Queen Cleopatra in Haiti. That is where Nwadinpa and I met. He is going to introduce me to the African Queen of Voodoo in Lagos. We plan to ask her to help us solve the Nigerian problems. As you know, she is a sorcerer-witch as she uses animals/snakes and herbs in addition to spirits/souls in her Voodoo practices. I ask you and Nwadinpa to go south to the areas of the most recent nanotech killings. We think a Professor in Sweden is producing the nanotech molecular system that is being used in Nigeria. And that three of her Nigerian doctoral students are bringing them here, perhaps through Lagos. They are probably either giving them to friends or selling them to other ethnics. But that is just a guess."

"A nanotech science colleague of mine in California, recently went on-line and found this doctor and her associate's names. They are: Tariya Ayebaidobamo, Brasin Perekeme, and Ngozi Okoroafor. I think they are not married but living at home when they return for visits. But you will have to confirm that."

Aminu spoke up, "Those names are Ijaw and Igbo, our suspect tribal/ethnics."

"All right," responded Kef. "I want you to trace them out. Find them. Find their families. Check and determine where they are staying now. Learn when they entered Nigeria and from where. Check their passports for travels outside of Nigeria. Interview them and record recent histories, especially travels. Identify local personal friends and enemies. Ask about their work with nanotech systems. What? Where? How? See if they connect to times immediately before any recent village massacres. Find out if and or when they plan to return to Sweden. And on and on…"

"And Nwadinpa, please look through your friends, pupils, and Voodoo followers concerning these three Nigerians. Learn what you can about them and their families. Is there a major hatred or even serious enough animosity between the fellows and their families against members of the nanotech death villages which could lead to such lethal actions? In other words, try to identify any possible leads between members of Ijaw and Igbo and the recent mass murders."

"I understand the direction you are going," said Nwadinpa. "I shall start 'snooping' around right away."

Aminu agreed, "Yes, I too will start immediately here in the passport and customs records departments to learn their exit and entry in the past couple of years, immediate family addresses, names and addresses of other family members, and then go south. I will stay in touch by cell phone."

"Excellent," responded Kef. "If there are no more questions. Communication via cell phones will be adequate, I think. No one knows us nor exactly what we are doing, yet. It is usually 'beneficial' to talk quietly."

At 4 PM, two different gentlemen knocked on Kef's door, entered, and sat at Kef's conversation table. These were new Associates. And Kef was just getting to know them. They were recommended by both Secretary Chimaobi Nkwado and his close senior associate Mr. Sani Akubakar. Both were Moslems from the northeast region of Nigeria, and worked here in the Department of Health and Human Resourses.

Mr. Hamzah Sheriff was Hausa, the largest ethnic group in the Sub-Saharan Africa. He was from the Fulani tribe in the state of Borno. Mr. Zubaydah Murtaya was Kanuri, not tribal and from the state of Kano. Both were dedicated Moslems and had worked in the Department of HHR for many years. So even though they were going into their home lands, the Secretary trusted them enough to send them with Kef in an attempt to try to understand what was happening near the Lake Chad region, especially concerning the military killings and village takeovers and massacres.

Kef welcomed them, "I am sure you have read about the war-type uprising on the Komadugu Yobe and Ngadda Rivers at Lake

Chad. We have been assigned to go to that region immediately and learn all we can about these actions. If either of you have a problem with entering your homeland states of Borno and Yobe during war actions, please let me know. I would like to travel through much of the area, but such things could be difficult. We will have Presidential permits, and a three special military guard escort. Also, we can call up helicopter assistance from a local military base near Maiduguri. I realize the problem. I can outrun a soccer ball, but not a bullet. SO?"

Knowing the soccer reputation of the Black Panther, Kef got his appropriate laugh, and waited for a response/answer. Both gave him an approval nod of the head, which he assumed/hoped meant they could handle military type actions, emergency style.

"This is what I understand via the Nigerian President as given to me by Secretary Nkwado and his senior associate, Mr. Akubakar, who will be joining us in Maiduguri in a couple of days. We may not be allowed an opportunity to go very far into the danger zone, as the area between Naiduguri and Lake Chad is now being labeled. We may have to gather much of our info from the more than a dozen refugee camps located north and east of the city. There are about five hundred Nigerian soldiers in Naiduguri, hence closer to the city is 'safer' for Abuja civilians. Like Us!"

"When we get there, we can select which of these camps and villages to visit and which people to question based on both ethnic groups and tribal units. I want a broad base of opinions from different directions, even women and possibly some elderly. Children also see a lot more than we realize and frequently are not afraid to tell 'important' strangers about it. We need to know who these militant invaders are. Where do they come from? They seem to have ground to air missiles, rifles, hand munitions, and some kind of food poison. Do they have other weapons? If possible, where are they going and what do they want? If they do have some kind of food poison, where did they get it, how do they dispense it, what does it do? Follow up and learn everything you can. Direct eye witness and village survivors should be good talkers. And on and on!"

"General Makalo will meet us and brief us on the fighting, intensity, and current location. He has provided accommodations for us at the nearby military base, all meals are in house or possible take-outs, three jeeps with drivers for each day for one week, and international communication services if needed. Any other services that we might require, he will try to provide."

Mr. Murtaya asked, "If during our investigations we run into problems with regard to our tribal/ethnic backgrounds, will we be permitted to return to Abuja?"

"Of course," replied Kef. "However, you should know that the President considers this important enough that five people were selected to come here to work with me. So, you will be replaced, immediately. Understand?"

"I guess that means we should carefully select which refugee camp we spend time investigating such that we minimize the possibility of overlapping negative histories." said Mr. Sheriff.

Kef just smiled. The populations, in 'his' homeland, South Africa, were predominately one major race/ethnic, Black African Zulu, who speak isi-Zulu.

During the flight to Maiduguri, Kef opened his laptop and turned to his downloaded cyle of the history of Maiduguri and the Borno region. He read:

'Borno is the most distant state with Maiduguri as the capital (600 miles or 13 hours driving time from Abuja). The population includes several ethnic groups and scattered tribes. The Kanuri are the largest and dominate. Borno has four million Shuwa Arab descendants, mostly practicing Sharia. They serve as the foundation for most Moslem social forms of life, and the civic codes and laws. The Moslem emirs held power during the mid-twentieth century. But Borno returned to civilian rule in 1979. Today the Abuja government is now the dominant government and the emirs are paid advisors.'

'In 2009, a rebel military group, Boko Haram, attempted to establish an Islamic government in the area. It was eventually defeated and the leaders were killed. But the fighting caused major social losses including destruction of schools and churches, kidnapping of school girls and women, abuse of females, food insecurity, and loss of civilian lives, especially among school teachers.'

'The capital has over two million population. It straddles the Nagadda River which enters the west side of Lake Chad. The region is hot, semi-arid. Temperatures range from 70 to 115 F. The city has six Moslem ethnic groups: Kanuri, Hausa, Bura, Fulani, Marghi, and Shuwa; and three Christian ethnic groups: Igbo, Ijaw, and Yoruba.'

'During the many years of unrest more than fifty internally displaced persons camps were functional nearby and in the suburbs. There were several Shagari camps each with fifty households per camp, and many Seraphim camps with seventy households per camp. The National Youth Service of Maiduguri housed and fed more than 10,000 people. While all total, seven languages were spoken in those camps.'

'The city is well laid out with good streets, excellent flood control management, grid connected electricity, adequate septic systems, and some solar power. Most buildings are concrete, brick, stone, and concrete block. They are one to five floors. A dozen highrise buildings are present in the very center which house government offices and key businesses. There are several shopping centers sprawling here and there. Not a wealthy city. Many of the suburbs house only the poor. But the city is rapidly modernizing.'

'The economy is based on farming, ranching, and fishing. Major crops are cotton, millet, beans, peanuts, rice, and wheat. However, the major income derives from sheep and cattle raising. Borno provides nearly half of the meat for consumption in Nigeria. And for Nigerians, meat is eaten two meals every day.'

'Hence, Maiduguri is a cattle city.'

Kef's final thoughts were, 'I wonder if this major income is part of the reason for militant actions.'

A few hours later they were all on the ground, settled into their bedrooms in the military barracks, and having a noon brunch in the cafeteria of the Borno military camp. General Makalo was called away, and a Lieutenant Colonel Nwaoloko was assigned to work with the group. He had joined them and was giving a brief summary of the fighting problems in the Lake Chad area.

He said, "The fighting or rather killing of villagers began near Lake Chad, but quickly moved up the two rivers, up the Ngadda River toward Maiduguri, up the Komadugu Yobe River toward Diffa in Niger, and possibly up one of several rivers going into Cameroon. So, we are probably dealing with military action in three or four places, three rivers, and three countries. And that is the simple part of the problem. Simultaneously, there are several villages being destroyed and villagers killed. Along the Komadugu Yobe River and the Ngadda river one village in three are not destroyed. Why? It is not understood, and the villagers are killed by some kind of food poison. This poison causes both an internal and external diarrhea. Men, women, and children are all affected. It is a terrible macabre thing. I visited one such village. And just the smell does make you think about bad or terrible spirits. The invaders are sending out messages that these are bad spirits from their ancestors. Oh! It is not surprising that the villagers believe them."

"And further up the rivers and in the savanna areas between the rivers, many villagers are either fleeing or just directly giving up. The village men are taken somewhere in the direction of the Lake. While the women and girls are used by the killers. Children are herded with the women and used as hostages. And the livestock are stolen. We have near one thousand Nigerian military in the area to cover more than 20,000 square miles. We estimate they have three to four thousand mercenaries, but scattered, on the rivers and in the savannah. And we estimate possibly four or five attack groups. American satellite pictures are not helpful as these groups are spread out, dressed in local attire, and travel in single small trucks or cars with weapons hidden under blankets. They use different small campsites for only one or two nights. Otherwise, they stay in local villages and mix with the villagers."

Lieutenant Colonel Nwaoloko continued describing the situation in the fighting regions. Mr. Sheriff and Mr. Murtaya had many questions about their 'homeland' and the care of various ethnic groups and tribes. They asked away, as the Colonel was also from a village in Borno. Kef just sat back and listened and learned. This was going to be a real problem, worse than the South-South.

The next day Mr. Murtaya went into a large refugee camp three miles north; and Mr. Sheriff spent the day in a smaller refugee camp down river several miles toward the lake. Each had two extra military guards.

Kef, with his extra guards, entered the city to look, talk, and question. Kef had lived his life only in the modern Christian cities of Cape Town, Johannesburg, and Abuja. He wanted to 'explore' a less developed Moslem city and try to separate the common nationals from the culture traditionists. Maiduguri was modernizing, but the family unit was still pretty much under control of the elderly males, Moslem style.

As he walked down the streets, he saw only a very few women wearing the nijab (covering of head, neck, and face, not the eyes), several wearing the hijab (only head and neck, not the face), but most were wearing multicolored African style dresses. Most men wore western jeans and regular shirts and t-shirts. Again, all clothing, on men and women, were of numerous colors, very bright, and frequently worn in layers with outer vests or jacket like coverings. Head coverings were common for women, but not men. They did not follow Arab dress tradition, but dressed and lived African style.

He walked down the street, checking out the people, old and young, window shopping, and talking with locals whom he heard speaking English. He simply did not speak any local languages so he did not try to make the effort to communicate with the non-English-educated. After walking for a couple of hours, he signaled to his bodyguards that he was going to sit at a table in an outdoor café, they should locate at a nearby table.

He chose a café, sat, and ordered a giant orange ice crushy. As he was drinking, a boy, probably just teen, green shorts, no shirt, sneakers, sun glasses, and wearing a New York Yankees baseball cap, stopped beside him and asked, "Are you an American? You are a man wearing a Boston Red Sox baseball cap. I would like to tell you about the Lake Chad cattle war."

Kef was startled. The boy's English was good. He was probably educated in a local English language school.

The boy continued, "Do you know American Cowboys and Indians, wild horses and long horned cattle? Our cattle are also long horned, very long horned and beautiful golden color. My father had hundreds of these beautiful cattle until they killed him, and stole our cattle from our village last month."

He looked away as tears formed on his face and he looked down in shame.

Kef believed him, reached up, took him by the shoulder, comforted him and said, "I am sorry. My father was also killed when I was a teenager. It is terrible. You will never forget. And you should not. Maybe if you tell me about it, I can help a little."

Kef always believed that kids knew more and could put two and two together faster and better than adults. And he could sense a major lead into the investigations of this 'foreign invasion'.

"Let me buy another ice crushy. What flavor do you like?"

"I like the giant orange ice crushy too."

Kef ordered it. It was brought to the table immediately. Then Kef said, "Drink slowly. And tell me—How did you learn such good English? Is your mother here in the city? Where do you stay now? Did you tell the police about your father and the stolen cattle? Were you there when this happened? Just tell me what you told the police."

So little Kiy started his story. "It was my birthday and I always go to sleep on the mountain above the village on my birthday night. It keeps me strong. Trigger, my horse, and I were sleeping soundly when, at early sunrise, gun shooting and much noise occurred below in the village. I crawled to the big rock and looked down. Six small trucks were driving through the village with men riding in the back and carrying many guns. These were strangers, but dressed like villagers. They were shooting into the air and they set two huts on fire. People ran out. But no one was killed. They took half of the men to the animal pens, opened the gates, and many of my male village friends drove the cattle out and down the road. Four trucks followed. All of the women and children and some of the older men remained behind. Two trucks and several armed men also stayed in the village. My family and friends were placed into several huts and kept under guard all day and night. They were only given water, no food."

"I stayed on the mountain top and watched the village. My mother and father, and my sisters were locked up there. So, I did not follow the cattle thieves down the road to the river. I learned later that there were cattle barges waiting to take them down river to larger cattle ships. And later, I learned that all of my male friends who helped drive the cattle to the river were killed."

"The cattle thieves who remained in the village overnight, did feed the villagers the next day around noon. What did they feed them? One truck had many types of fruit such as watermelon, cantaloupe, pineapple, mangos, bananas, and paw paw. Everyone was very hungry so all ate ravishly. A few hours later all of the thieves left. But one truck stopped on the only road into the village. Four men in the truck blocked the road and let no one in or out. They finally left sometime during the night. I do not know when. Restlessly, I slept."

"The next morning Trigger and I tried to enter the village. When we got close to the huts, a terrible smell hit us. Trigger bucked and jumped and would not go further. I jumped off of him and walked in by myself. There was no noise, only silence. The smell was so terrible I tied my shirt around my nose and face, but it did not help. I walked around the village. But I had difficulty recognizing my family and lifelong friends. Everywhere were bloated smelling bodies. I found my father, almost unrecognizable. My mother was missing. Later I found my mother and several girls and women were locked up in a hut. But they were all dead in a similar way."

And then Kiy broke down and cried. Kef held him and let him cry for several minutes. Kef thought it the best, perhaps the only therapy. And he remembered his father's body taken from the Saatford Diamond Mine in South Africa when he was a boy. He would certainly help this little fellow!

Over the next several days the 'government' investigators, military, and Kef discussed what they heard, saw, and thought was the situation in north and eastern Borno State. Kef had a picture of the problem in his mind, and thought about several ideas concerning potential solutions. He simply had to talk to Li and Uncle Dagda, first.

19

KORRECTORIZER III

It was now 2044, Washington, DC. The major nanotech massacre had been executed perfectly twelve years ago by Korrectorizer in Istanbul. More than 400 international high-tech scientists and their financial supporters were simultaneously executed in a very macabre fashion. It sent the reputation of the 'invisible' company business skyrocketing, and the nanotech business sales had taken off, domestically and internationally. Oliver Johnson did not really know what he was getting into by following in the footsteps of his uncle/father Senator (lawyer-lobbyist) Jordon Johnson. Every year for the past several years, their companies had signed several multi-million-dollar contracts to provide both a cure type and/or kill type nanotech molecular systems to select buyers. Some of the contracts were for treatment or cure efforts of sick people, especially for cancer patients within the USA. However, many of these contracts were for 'assassination' of selected enemies of a buyer 'living' outside the United States. The buyer was usually a member of an international conservative industrialist's club. While the nanotech scientists were recruited from several places in Europe and the USA to both design and manufacture nanotechnical molecular systems for both curing or killing.

As the science of nanotechnology evolved and expanded, two nanotech areas developed in different directions. Jordon Johnson and his nephew/son, Oliver, had established and controlled one American company, Korrector Com I. The designers, manufacturers, distributors, and sales were all legally American. KCI focused on curing diseases such as cancers, sickle cell disease, and other single cell diseases either internationally and or within the USA. The second 'international only' company was established as Korrector Com II. It was less than legal and operated from the British Virgin Islands and several places in Europe. KCII focused on providing custom designed nanotech molecular systems for the 'assassination' contracts of buyers 'outside' the USA who wished to eliminate select 'competitors', and in the beginning was controlled by Senator Jordon (lawyer-lobbyist) Johnson.

Korrector Com I was fully controlled from Washington, DC by both men; while Korrector Com II was established and controlled out of the British Virgin Islands only by the Senator. Oliver was not involved, at least in the beginning in KCII.

While the ex-Senator was alive, all ownerships were registered in his name. When he suddenly died of a massive heart attack in January 2046, Oliver inherited both companies. KCI was now owned only by Oliver Johnson, American citizen, living in Washington, DC. But KCII had been owned by Jordon Johnson Canadian/American citizen, living in Washington, DC and in the British Virgin Islands. With proper remunerations, Oliver acquired this name. He declared he was the legal son of Jordon Johnson who had been born in Canada. So, Oliver was now Oliver Johnson in the USA, and Jordon (Oliver) Johnson in BVI. Oliver owned KCI. Jordon (Oliver) Johnson owned KCII. And later he took over the now famous name, Korrectorizer.

True to heredity, Jordon and Oliver were both very tall with dark brown skin coloring, black eyes, sandy light-colored hair, and large ears—Father and Son??

When both Uncle Jordon and, one year later, his wife died, Oliver also inherited a monetary fortune and the Great Falls, Virginia mansion. He became Owner, CEO, and Chairman of the Board of Korrector Com I and II, and Senior Partner of the law firm Jordon, Williams, Caldor, and Kristcomer. The law firm and KCI, which handled nanotech systems for curing several diseases, were located on the top floor at 2271 M Street NW. These offices were close to super financial resources, the US State Department, World Bank, International Monetary Fund, and five international banks all close to the White House. He was chauffeured by family limousine from Great Falls to the D.C. law firm most days.

The M Street office was his major legal law firm location with his three partners, eight legal associates, and more than thirty support employees. Jordon used this downtown office for most legitimate national and international legal transactions and standard contracts which focused on nanotechnology. His registered lobbyist office was also located here.

In his new Great Falls home Oliver maintained a double office. He set up a second legal location for his law firm, KCI, and some lobbying work. And he also used the home office and two offices in the British Virgin Islands, for tax havens, less-than-legal and outside the USA offices for KCII. This was the control center for the kill type nanotech molecular systems. All such nanotech actions, employees, and monetary transactions for KCII were kept outside the USA. Jordon/Oliver traveled abroad a couple times a year in order to keep all aspects of KCII outside the USA. He never took the family to the BVI. This external USA unique science-legal business was maintained simply as a foreign consultation business endeavor for which he was the senior, and only, American consultant. While abroad, he usually travelled as Jordon Johnson.

Oliver, his wife Chole, and the two children, Condor and Catherine had moved into the Great Falls mansion. From there he continued regular contacts with the 'important' Washington ones—temporary or semi-permanent, American or international, male or female, and even some 'youth' groups. The youth parties were the most fun.

The Great Falls, Virginia mansion had nine large bedrooms/ bathrooms, large dining room, and two kitchens. It totaled more than 4,500 square feet and twenty rooms in a stone-stucco New York style design setting on twelve acres overlooking the Potomac River Rock Basin. Numerous trees, flowering shrubs, and flower gardens created a beautiful welcome spring through autumn. Three large and small salons with two indoor-outdoor patios, a swimming pool, party gaming-gazebo, green house with several very old Japanese bonsai, and a tennis court completed the outdoor entertainment area. Both early-teenage children were already outstanding tennis players and had participated in the Virginia-Fairfax Country Club tennis and horse- riding tournaments. Neither won, but they placed at the top their sex/age groups. They were doing well in school. Chole was a very good Mother. Dad was simply not there much of the time. He was tending his lawyer/lobbyist businesses in the USA, the Caribbean, and in Europe.

April 24 was Condor's birthday. But his little sister wanted to surprise big brother on the evening before. So, mother helped her arrange a surprise.

Cathy walked into the kitchen and said, "Mother, you promised that you would make Condor's favorite key lime pie for his birthday party tonight. Where is it?"

Mother replied, "Did you look on the bottom shelf of the refrigerator?"

"Oh! And did the cook make his favorite foods, white bean casserole, and red lettuce-tomato-cucumber salad with red ranch dressing."

"Yes"

"And did the two special boxes arrive by Fed Express?"

"They arrived. And they are A-OK, all fifty pounds each." replied Mom.

"Can I see them?"

Disgustedly she answered, "NO. I need someone to help finish setting the plates, glasses, silverware, and all on the patio table. Your father will be a little late. He called and tennis practice was running late plus the roads were crowded. They are picking up Condor in the family limousine. And Condor's friends will be here soon. Oh! There is the door-bell. Answer it and take the boys to the swimming pool patio, and tell them about the Fed Express special presents. But do not open them. The boys can swim if they want to. They can change in the gazebo, and there are plenty of towels in there. Hurry and go."

Cathy took off. She knew all of Condor's friends. Most were only one or two years older. She even kind of liked one of them. But she would never show it. All five were there. They must have all come in James or Riley's family limousine. This was going to be a fun surprise on big brother (eleven months older). He is most difficult to surprise. Maybe just once she can out do him.

At the door she counted. William, Lawrence, Landry, James, and Riley hopped out of the big black car, pointed toward the pool on the down river side of the house and ran directly toward it. Cathy nodded, smiled, and hurried to catch up with them. They had been here often enough to know the house grounds as well as she did. But she just laughed and followed them. It was a good group. And Condor needed such a group around him as he was a little wild.

Within five minutes all five had changed into swimming suits and were in the pool. William then challenged James to a game of table tennis. Cathy just sat on a lounge chair and watched. They were too young to have bodies. But Landry was showing some shoulder muscles, as he was already lifting weights in an attempt to try to make the football team next year. And of course, her favorite was Riley who was the tall skinny one, sort of like her father. She thought about it and decided he would best fit into the family as Dad was well over six feet. Mom and Condor were both near six foot, and she knew she would make it to that six-foot mark soon. She was just waiting on the hormones. When Condor got them, he grew more than one foot the following year.

Suddenly, Lawrence left the water and sat down beside Cathy. He said, "I understand that you got a perfect score in the Calculus I exam last week. I did not do well. I want to be an engineer. Dad wants me to be an engineer. Mom wants me to be an engineer. But I need some help. Could you?"

All of the children went to the Thomas Jefferson School which placed students into a class year according to their age, but in subject classes according to their yearly class scores. So, Cathy and Lawrence were in the same Math and Science classes.

Cathy agreed, "But you must teach me to play the piano. I am in love with the crimson colored baby grand piano at school. That will be my after-school challenge."

Lawrence replied, "Oh, OK."

Suddenly a loud TJ yell went up from the sidewalk leading to the pool. Immediately a loud multi TJ yell was returned from the pool side. Condor had announced his arrival. And his buddies had welcomed him. He ran and dived into the pool, clothes and all. He was happy to have a birthday a day early. Maybe he could talk mom into a second one tomorrow. This was great as he was immediately joined by the other five. Three on each side of the net and the first volleyball game was underway. Everyone wanted to be on the birthday boys' side. Why? He was the only six-foot tall thirteen-year old in the school. And volleyball was a tall person's sport. Plus, it was his ball! And the game was on. Condor had just stripped down to his briefs. Cathy knew what he looked like. No big deal.

After half an hour of play, Condor, Landry, and William were leading two games to one. Suddenly Cathy came running from the house screaming—LOOK OUT—HERE COME THE DOGS!

Everyone looked over. Directly behind her were two large— puppies? The two dogs were indeed 50-pound three-month old puppies. Both were all white with two or three large black spots, a black and white panda-like face, and a long curly over the back tail. [Later Cathy would announce that they were European Continental Landseer Dogs (ancestors were the Viking Black Bear Dog) and that they would hit the two-hundred-pound mark by the time they were two years old.] Cathy had changed into her bathing suit, ran, and jumped into the pool. The dogs did not hesitate, they ran and jumped in right behind her. Condor and the boys were stunned—for two seconds. Then they dove and swam after them. The dogs were good swimmers as their ancestors were Viking boat, work, and war dogs. The noise the children and dogs made could have been heard at the 'White House'. So repeated the Father to his law partners the next day. And Condor will always remember it as the best party he ever had. Cathy proved she could out do her big brother if she wanted to do so. The seven young ones did not make it to school the next day.

The British Virgin Islands of Tortola, Virgin Gorda, Anegada, Jost Van Dyke and forty-five other smaller islands was the home of an international legal shadow consultant company K II. Uncle/father Senator Jordon Johnson established this law-science-business firm outside the USA. Oliver inherited the Tortola house and law firm when 'Dad' died. It was the **central control location for the nanotech**

systems research efforts. And Oliver, outside the USA and using the name Jordon Johnson, spent a couple of months here and in Europe during the calendar year, setting up all necessary components of select nanotech hit systems and managing the finances through BVI Banks.

The firm had a large modern designed house with an over-wall swimming pool which faced north into the Atlantic Ocean on Tortola. It was near the peak of Hawks Nest mountain, fifteen minutes from the Beef Island International Airport, and ten minutes from the downtown area, called Road Town, on the south side of the island. The roads were slow as everything was up-down, two lane curves, numerous trees and flowering shrubs. But all was 'tourism' beautiful with many bays for yacht anchorages, diving, swimming, and sea bus excursions around all of the many small islands.

He flew from Tortola to various places in Europe, Africa, Middle East, and Asia to make face to face contact with many of the nano tech scientists, transporters, and a few distributors. He never met any of his business associates in Tortola. He always met them abroad in a public place for lunch/dinner. And he used a hidden electronic recorder for later confirmation of what he said. His name was now Jordon Johnson, Canadian citizen with a Canadian passport.

The British Virgin Islands had several types of tax havens and provided a variety of other 'safe' banking and monetary accounts for live-in (one month per year) land owners. The Korrector Com II used several local banks including the National Bank of the Virgin Islands, First Caribbean International Bank, PVI International (private and offshore), and the Toronto-Dominion Bank.

Jordon arrived at the Tortola house late in the evening as the air route was Washington to Miami to Tortola (with a three-hour layover in Miami). He went directly to bed. He had glanced around and everything was in perfect shape. A local company, Main-Purr (Maintenance Perfect), provided twelve months of maintenance service on house and grounds. They had a partner company, Purr-Lif (Perfect Life), which provided all required services for specific Nanotech people when they were here on a brief live-in. The refrigerator/freezer/bar were stocked. And a note was left that told him he would be picked up at 8:00 AM, and taken down to his one-week yacht rental in Lambert Bay. He usually rented a 27ft Luhrs

Cabin Cruiser if he was going to cruise alone, or a 42ft Nordlund Raised Pilot House with pilot and attendant, if he wanted company. Jordon liked to spend a few days sailing/recovering from Washington, re-analyzing the state of the recent international nanotech sales, and developing a new strategy for future **nanotech research** efforts. He brought his favorite i-pad XL and two flash drives. That was all he needed. His father/uncle had taught him to keep it simple. He tried.

At 7:30 AM he entered the kitchen, noticed Julio waiting beside the coffee pot, and he smelled the Columbian coffee in the air. Julio had been with Purr-Lif several years, and he was an easy fellow to deal with. He liked him.

Jordon spoke first, "How is life Julio. Your son is now on the soccer team, so you are happy?"

Julio replied, "Yes and he is scoring almost one goal every game."

"So, should I start to bet on him, or just bet on the team?"

"No. No. Do not bet. You only lose money."

He laughed, turned around, poured Jordon a cup of coffee with one spoonful of sugar. He knew from experience with this boss.

A car was waiting outside and Jordon would have breakfast on the yacht. So, they chatted for a couple of minutes about meals later in the week, sipped coffee, nibbled on cinnamon breakfast rolls, and headed for the car. He only needed his computer and flash drives. All necessary clothes were already on board. Jordon was German enough that when he found a pattern he liked, he used it consistently—daily sequences of events, clothes, food, drinks, work and play routines. For now, three days and nights in the boat, three days back in the house, three or four weeks in Europe, back for a couple more days in BVI with sunshine, and then return to Washington. But first, a little piece of floating paradise.

He began with a light breakfast prepared by Jack, the pilot and cook. The next few hours he scanned the sales areas on disc one. Spending a couple hours of studying recent nanotech info sent from his data collectors in Europe, he decided which area needed inducement. He opened the employee directory of Korrector Com II, which contained all personal and professional info, on disc two. He had made several new appointments in Europe, Africa, and South America. Then he arranged for airline tickets for different days over the next month in

Europe and Africa. Jordon was content with his **research company which was listed in the international listings as a legal consulting firm in nanotechnology.** He down dressed, took a quick swim, had a late lunch, and emptied his mind for the next twenty-four hours.

He would be directly communicating, eye to eye, with: 'Dr. Anneka Andersson (Stockholm), Dr. Jackson White (London), Dr. Wilbur Sanchez (Madrid), Mr. Faustino Mariniti (Rome), Dr. Wolfstein Wolff (Vienna), Mr. Henry Harrison (London), Mr. Andre DeBoire (Tripoli), and a couple of others.

A few days later he began to make the rounds in Europe of individuals who were on the Korrector Com II payroll, designing, manufacturing, shipping, distributing, and selling nanotech molecular systems, usually to areas of 'extreme social unrest.' He had decided to focus on the nanotech cellulose molecular system and the mass activity in large groups, military style. It would go well. He knew it to be so.

The research groups from the Committee of Nanotechnology Control in Washington, DC, were now routinely following, and monitoring the movements, 24/7, of several of the potential nanotech killer candidates. They were spread into five 3 person teams in Europe.

Dr. Anneka Anderson was having lunch with a very tall dark brown skinned, light haired, well dressed man on the Viking Dockside Lounge in Stockholm on a Tuesday noon. All of the team's high-ultra tech video units were collecting everything they were saying. Much of the discussion seemed to involve nanotechnology of varying dimensions. She was a nanotech scientist, and his share of the conversation almost matched hers. He certainly had an excellent understanding of the technology. They were discussing new nanotech molecular systems that she was developing and the high research costs for such efforts. Because of this the prices per system had increased considerably. He argued that the numerous little battles in the many 'difficult' social areas in Africa would allow for a 'McDonalds type' of sales and everything would be great. She backed down for now, and compromised on the price per unit. But she wanted to test her new system first. When the visitor left the area, they followed him. But he was evasive and disappeared.

Three days later one of the Committee's research team was monitoring and recording the conversation of the luncheon of Dr. Harrison at the Four Lords Shield on the Thames River in London. Dr. Harrison was a nanotech scientist with his own research laboratory and clinics on N. Edgar Street. His luncheon guest seemed to know a lot about nanotechnology. Most of their three-hour luncheon focused on nanotech molecular systems which could be used by military units, were ambient weather stable, and still provided a macabre effect. They were discussing prices and available dates for north Africa deliveries.

When the very tall dark brown skinned gentleman left, he was successfully followed to his hotel room. Bribing hotel management with a five hundred euro bill, the researchers learned much about the man. The man was named Jordon Johnson, a businessman and lawyer from the British Virgin Islands. Nanotechnology was his specialty. Comparing with the data and pictures of the man who recently had the luncheon with Dr. Anderson, and matching the voice patterns, it was probably the same person. So, immediately the research team following Dr White switched, and began to follow a new candidate. Also, back in Washington they started several levels of computer searches about this Mr. Johnson.

Over the next few weeks, Mr. Jordon Johnson was successfully monitored as he traveled and visited several nanotech scientists, businessmen, shippers, and arms dealers in Rome, Vienna, Madrid, Tripoli, Rabat, Dakar, Freetown, and Lagos. They also learned later that in some of the African countries, the military often made purchases, kept some of the systems, and sold the rest to pseudo-military neighbors and friends.

When Mr. Johnson returned to the British Virgin Islands, he declared that this trip was the most successful yet. Nanotechnology was becoming more recognized as a simple way to kill your non-friends and enemy. It did not require significant training, and left a very macabre effect. What a way to die? OH!

After summing all of his sales numbers, Jordon Johnson saw a beautiful 1,989.5 million in American dollars appear as 'profit', a new Korrector Com II record. He would be even more comfortable in retirement, and the children would be able to select whatever university and profession they wanted. If one could just ignore that ultimate product that was being sold! It did kill badly!

And the Committee of Nanotechnology Control had a mass of video and audio data from several meetings of a newly identified very tall, dark brown skin coloring, black eyes, sandy light-colored hair, and large ears, and very well dressed gentleman. They identified him as Canadian Jordon Johnson, businessman from the British Virgin Islands. This Mr. Johnson appeared to know very well several of the European and African candidates on the potential nanotech killer list. And in initial analysis of their information, it appeared the committee may have hit the jackpot. There was extensive data about nanotech designs, manufacture, sales, and future African regions for distribution. Excellent! Fascinating! Great!

20

KEF AND THE AFRICAN QUEEN OF VOODOO

Kef and Nwadinkpa took a taxi seaboat from the pier at the Lagos International Airport immediately after flying in from Abuja. They had an appointment with the African Queen of Voodoo in her castle, which was located on the Ikoyi-Victoria Island in the south-middle of the Lagos Lagoon.

Zipping along Kef glanced out the window and commented, "The area is not really very nice and the water is certainly not clean. Do they really eat fish from here?"

Nwadinkpa responded, "Of course. You have to realize that much of Lagos is imbedded in poverty. And when you are hungry, germs can be 'cooked out' of some foods."

Kef asked, "I can imagine that when the government moved to Abuja, and transferred most government employees there, poverty here increased dramatically. Is this true?"

"I do not think so," answered Nwadinkpa. "The salaries of government employees here in Nigeria are not high. Like many countries there are 'benefits' given to these employees that help compensate for the differences between public versus private sector incomes—free housing, food discounts, school scholarships, health insurances, etc. Over the years I don't think government employees were major contributors to help feed and house the Lagos poor. There is a large wealthy private sector here. I would think they and the church contributed the most."

"Would you consider someone like the Queen as one of those contributors?" asked Kef.

"Definitely. It is said that she has one or maybe two shanty town areas in which she is the major contributor to housing, schools, and food. Now that is an area of social endeavor nobody wants to look at closely because those who have done so have disappeared."

"Do you mean as in dead?

"No, I mean as in gone."

"Oh!"

When suddenly the driver swerved to the left and there was the Queen's island with the castrum/castle in the middle peeking through the numerous trees.

Nwadinkpa continued, "Let me briefly tell you about this area of the world! I have been here several times. And you might have to go on by yourself, if she says no to me."

And he laughed at himself. Indeed, it was an unusual part of the world that Kef and he were seriously entering, or re-entering. Always a bit scary.

He began: "Let me think this through. OK."

"Lagos is one of the largest seaports in the world, twelve million people in the State of Lagos. Most populated areas are clustered around several semi connected island-peninsulas. In the center is this large lake-like body of water, the Lagos Lagoon. The periphery has several miles of shipping docks, private and public, local and international. To the north and east are several regions of home-less people living in poverty. To the north and west are suburbs of middle income and wealthy people, industries and major business establishments. To the west and south are peninsulas with numerous shipping conglomerates. From the island, most of the lagoon is on the north and the ocean is on the south."

"In the south center of the Lagos Lagoon is this one square mile island. It is known as the Queens Island. There is one castle/castrum/ fortified fortress on the island. It is inhabited by the African Queen of Voodoo, her five daughters, acolyte trainees, several select friends, a few invitees, several servants, and security guards. The island is predominately swamp and low marsh, plus many marsh loving plants such as cyprus, tupelo, wax myrtle, and Spanish moss. The only entry to the castrum is via a wooden pier for boat docking along the shoreline, and a small wooden helicopter landing platform. These connect to a rock road and board walk leading inland from the pier to a small drawbridge, raise-steel gates and a massive door (two small doors within one large door). Boat pier to drawbridge is over two hundred feet. Doors and gates are in a two-foot wide, twelve-foot high outer stone wall topped in rolled razor wire. This wall surrounds the entire castle. Presence of the wall, razor wire, swamp-marsh, and the Queen's snakes, the castle has never been successfully 'invaded."

"Immediately inside the wall is a fifty-foot wide courtyard. Next is a four walled rectangular housing stone structure, three floors above and one floor below ground. The structure has four tall turrets, one on each corner. No windows on the first floor, but several windows on the second and third floors. The interior is probably more than 100,000 sq. ft. It encloses a large entry, great hall, several salons and visitor rooms, two kitchens, a large library, several work rooms, many bed chambers with private toilets. It was modernized by the Queen when she moved into it, many years ago. It is said that it can house more than one hundred people. Of course, the Queen and her daughters have separate living facilities on the second floor. I am told that the third floor and the basement have many multiple-use rooms."

"To enter the castrum you may have to walk from the boat pier to the drawbridge through any number of accompanying semi-sleeping snakes. While walking to the castrum you will be filmed and voice recorded. At the drawbridge, remote cameras will continue to take your picture. If tentatively approved, a speaker will ask your name and business. The speaker will relay this info to someone, and respond to you in a couple of minutes, yes or no. If no, that is that. If yes, you will be let in through one of the small doors and someone will meet you and check you for weapons or electronics. He will then take you to one of several visitors meeting rooms. The corridors leading to these rooms have audio/video cameras and several cages filled with snakes. Do not worry. The gates of the cages are locked. In the meeting rooms there will be several chairs and coffee or tea, and more cameras. In a short while, another person will come and take you to the person to whom you have requested to see. There are three 'business' secretaries. So, it is possible one may have to wait his turn to see the Queen. One should prepare oneself for short waiting intervals. Today we have an appointment with her at 11:00 A.M. I do not expect she will keep us waiting."

As the taxi seaboat slowed down and glided into the pier Kef looked out the window. What should he see, but several 'beautiful' small snakes.

Kef thought, 'Is this really necessary. I think I need more time to consider. Maybe I should go back to Abuja and return later. I could get sick as an excuse. But tomorrow would not be better than today. It is something like trying to break through a three-man soccer defense line in trying to score with a left foot kick (he was a right footer). I can and will do it, right now!'

Nwadinkpa paid the driver, grabbed Kef by the arm, and hauled him from the taxi seaboat. He looked back and waved. They had already told the driver, if needed, they would call him later in the day.

Kef just stood there, looking, but unable to move. He heard someone say, "Don't worry. They eat and come out here on the pier and digest everything while lying in the sun. If they are in the sun, they have full tummies and are not hungry. So, you are safe."

Kef looked to his right. Sitting on a support post was a pre-teen boy who was looking at him and grinning.

Kef glanced at Nwadinkpa who also just smiled. If something was funny, he did not see it.

Then the little boy spoke up, "If you would like a safe journey to the big door, one American dollar and I guarantee the entire distance with less than one bite from less than one snake."

Nwadinkpa went to the boy, gave him an American dollar, and the three of them, snakes free, started walking the 200 plus feet up the road/boardwalk to the door. They chose the boardwalk which was two feet above the ground.

Kef asked the boy. "Why are there two parallel roads here, rock and board-walks?"

The boy replied, "Look at that end of the docks (he pointed to the left) and you see a larger dock area covered with a small roof. It is directly connected to the rock road going to the big door. You cannot see it but there is a building at the end of the road which contains a small truck. When the Queen orders supplies, they are shipped to here (he pointed to the left) and unloaded onto the dock. Later two men bring the truck out and pick up the supplies. They take them over the bridge, through the big door, inside the walls, around the inner courtyard, and to the back-kitchen doors. So, the rock road is for delivery of castrum supplies."

Kef asked again, "And why the board walk?"

"It is nearly snake free. It is slightly elevated, so more difficult for the snakes to climb on. Plus, the Queen places snake-off in those little pots (he pointed to the pots positioned every few feet) that gives off a strong smell which snakes do not like, so most of them stay away."

Having walked half way to the big door, Kef commented, "Are you saying we did not have to pay you to protect us from the snakes when the smell is already doing that protection?"

The boy smiled and said, "But you did not know this, and double protection against a poison snake is a good thing. YES?"

Kef backed down, reached into his pocket, pulled out another dollar and gave it to him, and also smiled.

They arrived at the drawbridge/big-door area. From video they requested entry. Kef thought that it was easier than he anticipated, until Nwadinkpa told him, "That is one of several boy scampers that scam people like you. These snakes on the pier are harmless, but the boy saw you were afraid, so he 'protected' you."

The boy spoke up again, "And if you want to know what is in those pots that keeps the snakes away, I will only need one more dollar."

This time Kef smiled and handed the boy another dollar.

"Dried garlic or plant camphor extracts are inside those breathing pots. The Queen is very good with herbs. For snakes—certainly—strong smells! Carry one of those pots with you and you will be 'reasonably' safe."

And the two grown up boys laughed, thanked the younger boy, and had to admit this scam was a neat 'reasonable' trick, and similar to the games they used to play when they were younger.

What they did not know was that they were continuously being video viewed, audio recorded, and evaluated. Remote videos were not only on top of the wall but also at many hidden locations in the trees.

Kef and Nwadinkpa successfully worked their way through the several check points between the outside of the castrum to the inside of the Queens drawing room. It took almost an hour. But the Queen was observing them, so time was not important. Kef looked around. This room was probably the most beautiful room in the castrum. It was decorated with many floral draperies and floor carpets, many paintings of famous Nigerians, large antique arm chairs, couches, and tea tables. All were basically red, yellow, green, and crimson. Nature at its brightest. No windows. But one 'secretary' was setting in a corner at a beautiful black ebony table with snake legs.

They approached her and Nwadinkpa said. "Ms. Anyanwu, it is a pleasure to see you again. I hope everything is well."

Ms. Anyanwu responded, "Yes and No. Mr. Olabamiji. As you know we try to help the no become a yes. That is a never-ending task. But the Queen is experienced and skilled at this, so we just try to keep up with her. Thank you."

Nwadinkpa continued, "This is Kefentse Legoase."

"Yes, we know," replied Ms. Anyanwu. "It is nice to meet you. We know you are from South Africa and working on a Nanotech project with the Americans and Abuja. The Queen is interested in your project. So, she will see you. Please sit and she will be with you shortly."

Several minutes later the African Queen of Voodoo entered the room, regally dressed in a bright red and green gown. She was wearing her hair in mohawk-like goddess braids up on the top of her head, bright red finger nails and toe nails with open shoes. Facial make up was extensive with emphasis of green colors around the eyes. She had blue-green eyes. The fellows knew she was in her eighties, but she certainly looked to be in her fifties. She approached them and nodded. They quickly stood up and bowed in return.

Her first words were, "Gentlemen!"

In response, Nwadinkpa replied, "Your Majesty!"

Kef did not know what to say. Was she really royalty, or was Nwadinkpa being overly careful? To be safe he also said, "Your Majesty!"

The Queen responded, "Thank you Nwadinkpa. But you do not need to play your games with me." And she moved forward, hugged him, took him by the arm, walked away, and laughed.

She turned to Kef and said, "Nwadinkpa and I have been friends for many years. I am more than a Queen to him. I am his god. Without me he would not have any of his Voodoo followers. When he pretends that I am great, I send more South-South believers to him. And that is life and money and the pleasure of accomplishment. So, we have our understandings, and we are both happy."

She routed them to a nearby table and chairs, ordered tea, waited one minute as the hot water was delivered, placed two tea leaves into each cup, and sat back to wait for the conversation to continue.

Nwadinkpa smiled and just nodded.

The Queen motioned for them to sit and she asked, "Mr. Kefentse Legoase from South Africa, and connected to the Americans. What do you want from me today?"

Embarrassingly, Kef understood the spot to where he was being placed.

He replied, "I want to ask you to help me save your people. There are major problems in the South-South and also in north east of Nigeria. Abuja does not really know what to do. And the Americans have an interest because the weapons being used are produced in the western worlds' laboratories. They feel guilty. But they also want to learn about the most recent versions and develop counter or blocking mechanisms for these weapons."

The Queen commented, "I am aware of these problems, but I do not understand these weapons. They are man made molecules. Correct?—chemistry, not physics."

Kef said, "I am not a scientist but I will try to explain these molecules."

Continuing, "I know that you do understand chemical-biological extracts containing proteins, venoms and herbs. These weapons are called nanotech because they are synthetic molecules which mimic natural proteins. When placed into the body they can inhibit the function of certain body tissues such as heart or brain, or they can digest body tissues or vessels. What I understand is as follows: The nano-system which is being used here in Nigeria causes digestion of the colon in the body resulting in internal and external diarrhea. Usually death occurs within several hours, and may be very macabre in character."

The Queen replied. "Yes, I have talked with family members who have recently had their loved ones killed with these nanotech weapons. Terrible!"

"We are working on a non-protein blocker which will be ready soon, we hope. The scientist designing it is a close personal friend of mine. We plan to test it, this month, in the north east regions of Nigeria after people have been 'infected' or placed into 'pre-kill' states."

"We usually do not know in advance which village or who is going to be attacked and killed. However, we are currently learning about key leaders who have access to these nanotech systems. It could be possible, very soon, to eliminate some of these individuals. But there we would certainly need your help. Or perhaps the help of your little friends."

"Let us talk more after lunch. I want you to meet my daughters and their little friends."

What could Kef say, "Yes. I would love to meet your family."

They finished their tea and stood up. Nwadinkpa took the Queen by the arm and walked to the door and down the corridor to a large dining room. Kef fell in behind them. As they entered the yellow-orange-green decorated room, Kef looked up toward the center ceiling at a beautiful Austrian chandelier. Under it was a large very black ebony table and chairs, all with hand carved snake legs. The table was set with Japanese china and German silver-ware. He thought, 'very nice, very expensive.'

As they entered the room and looked around, from a side door came five young ladies. Two of them went to Nwadinkpa, took him by the arms and led him to pre-selected chairs on one side of the table. Two others went to Kef, took him by the arms and led him to pre-selected chairs on the other side of the table. While the fifth young lady took mother by the arm and led her to pre-selected chairs at the end of the table. Kef was very nervous and started to sweat a little.

The ladies, all unmarried, near forty years, had different hair styles and long dresses of many bright colors. They were not beautiful, more like handsome, or academic, as in professor. Over the years, Mother had imported several teachers for 'in house' education. And apparently, each did have a 'permanent' hobby such as painting, poetry, sculpture, jewelry design, and gardening. Two of them also learned additional languages, Russian and Japanese. All of them spoke some British English. Kef had already so learned all of this from Nwadinkpa a few weeks ago.

They sat and the Queen raised her wine glass, with French Chardonnay. "Cheers, and a welcome to the two men with a wish for a successful venture," said the lady at the head of the table. "I believe it is a very important project, and I will support it with both my brains and bran."

And they all had a good chuckle. Even though the guys were not sure if bran was muscle or money. But they laughed anyway, just to be safe.

Lunch was served. It was a light version dodorishi (beef stew), white and black beans, mashed plantain, ojojo (yam balls), and fruit dessert kabab. Small portions—delicious.

Now the Queen nodded, which gave the daughters permission to invade the minds of the male guests.

The natural leader of the group, sitting to the left of Kef, was Viper. She inquired, "We do not travel often, so one area which is always on our minds is travel. What is out there? You are from South Africa. Can you tell us something about your homeland?"

Kef swallowed. He did not come prepared for this and quickly jogged his mind.

He responded, "Of course. The southern tip of Africa was settled 10,000 years ago and went through many re-settlings by many foreign tribes, groups, ethnics, etc. In the twentieth century several peoples established chieftains, kingdoms, and semi-countries. Foreigners from Europe established military superiority and apartheid began in 1978. Numerous civil 'battles/wars' continued until elections of 1994, 1999, 2004, and 2009, finally a majority republican government was securely founded. Today we have three capitals.—Pretoria for an Executive government, Bloemfontein for a Judicial government, and Cape Town for a Legislative government."

"The Republic of South Africa is physically the largest country in Africa and one of the richest because of several very valuable natural resources—gold, silver, diamonds, copper, iron, platinum, and uranium. There are two **major** cities. Cape Town is far south, the major shipping center for South Africa, and is the connection point of the Indian and Atlantic Oceans. Johannesburg is far north and is ranked 47th out of the 50 cities in the world as a center of commerce. It is the major mining center and produces most of the heavy industrial products in all of Africa, such as steel and cement."

"One suburb, Soweto of Johannesburg, was where the apartheid wars played out. Nelson Mandela and the African National Congress led the successful battles (political and military) over racial oppression during a period of twenty to thirty years. Mr. Mandela spent much of that time in prison. A new multi-racial republic with majority rule eventually prevailed at the beginning of twenty-first century. Mr. Mandela became the South Africa President, won the Nobel Prize of Peace, and is certainly the most famous South African. OK. Any questions?"

Viper asked, "So, like Nigeria, South Africa had many non-democratic governments which included foreigners and Black Africans, yes? Only in this century have you achieved a multi-racial democracy where the natives have begun to control their own fate."

Kef replied, "That is one way to look at it. One must include in that analysis of history the monetary means to accomplish our democracies. The valuable natural resources in South Africa helped us get our heads above water. Just as the petroleum resources helped you get your heads above water. Who do we thank for this, the European foreigners? I do not know. I am not a historian, nor a politician. And I try to avoid questions like that which will get me into trouble."

So, for the next couple of hours, Kef and the 'snake' ladies analyzed the similar versus different roads that their countries, and other African countries, took to finally find 'stable' multi-racial democracies. And the many newly established countries yet looking for republic stature. All countries were different, but yet similar. The Queen (Mother) just sat back and enjoyed watching her 'educated' daughters in motion. Maybe the five collars and leashes could be loosened, a little.

Mid-afternoon, the Queen changed the subject to the South-South problems in Nigeria. Most of her Voodoo followers were in southern Nigeria. And she definitely wanted to be involved with her people. She had to leave for a wedding soon, so they needed to be brief.

"Again, please explain the situation of the nanotech killing in the South-South. The people 'belong' to Nwandinkpa and myself," stated the Queen.

Kef nodded to Nwandinkpa who began, "We have been evaluating the recent killings in more than ten villages in the petroleum rich region of the South-South. We think we have identified the leaders of the killers. They are three students who are studying nanotechnological sciences at the Karlinsky Institute in Sweden. They study the sciences associated with these biological weapons. When they come home to see family and friends, they bring some of these nanotech molecular systems, or food poisons as we call them publicly. In some villages these poisons are placed in the fruit which is eaten at evening celebration dinners where the entire village participates. The students either sell the nanotech systems or use them in pre-planned targets in certain villages. We do not know if these massacres are ethnic or petroleum related killings. In other words, we do not yet know the motives. All three students are now home, and we are monitoring their individual movements. I think we will have enough evidence/data in a week or ten days to recommend some kind of 'corrective action'.

Kef finished by saying, "This morning you asked me what I wanted from you. I now ask you to help us correct the wrongs being done to your people in the north and the south. The murderers need corrective therapy. One such mechanism is for your daughters to introduce them to their little cold friends. We will know for certain who the leaders are within one month. Nwadinkpa has the names and families of the South-South science students. And he is the senior investigator of this region. He may have new data before I do. Please contact him if there is information or problems for 'his' region. I am responsible for the Lake Chad killings. I may have to go there to arrange an official arrest plan. If you think your daughters could help us there also, please contact me and give to me your ideas. Or if you have other mechanisms of corrective therapy that could be used, please let me know."

He looked around at the Queen and her ladies. "Is everything understood?"

The Queen smiled, stood up, and said, "We must finish preparing for the special wedding tonight. I assume that you are coming?"

Kef replied, "Of course. How else can I determine if you are better than your sister in voodoo ceremonies?"

They both laughed. She knew he was referring to the Caribbean. A friendship was developing.

That night the wedding was taking place at the White Pavilion in the large park on the water in the suburb of Oauba Agbay. It was a large circular 'capped' facility used for special events and festivals. Tonight, it would be completely filled with nearly 2000 people. Why? Because the Queen was going to perform a voodoo wedding ceremony for the son of the Chief of the General Staff (from Abuja) and the daughter of a wealthy oil baron from Bayelsa. Plus, during the extensive ceremony, the first of two sons for the two to-be grandfathers would be begotten. The Queen had performed many voodoo ceremonies here, but never simultaneously a marriage and double conception.

All seats were packed full of families, honored guests, friends, and anyone who could sneak into the open aired gazebo styled facility. As sunset approached the drums began beating louder and faster, and the singing grew in intensity. It was time to bring forth the spirits of the cult of LOA (Voodoo God). Several groups of drums, the arara, manman, segond, yourba, and bula, from two to six feet tall, were all beating near maximum. Three heavily muscled male dancers had been performing a modern version of dancing-gymnastics for fifteen minutes and were sweating profusely. They withdrew from the center stage area, and were replaced by ten women and ten man dressed only in lion cloths and copper ankle bracelets. They danced without a specific formation, but anti-clockwise in interlocking circles, no formation forward, no formation backward. As the dancing progressed various males and females partnered, danced closely, and pretended to make love. First there was simulated copulation lying down, then standing up, then front to side, then front to back, then up to down, then down to down and then up to up with other couples. After an exhausting half hour, all dancers were sweating and they drifted from the center area. As they left, they passed beside the elevated rear stage podium where the bride and groom were sitting and watching. On the way out, male dancers kissed the pre-bride, female dancers kissed the pre-groom.

The more than one hundred singers that had been continuously singing over the past hour suddenly stopped singing. All drums stopped playing. All people went silent. Nature stopped. And the eight 10-foot tall flare-posts, which circled the center stage area, suddenly flamed to hot yellow life. Everyone gasped as from five different directions came a tall slim lovely lady, a daughter of the Queen. Each was naked and their bodies were painted in orange, green, blue, and yellow. The faces were red with green eyes. They entered together with identical snake/serpent dance movements—slithering on their bellies. The giant maomao drum started beating, at first slow rhythms, then after a few minutes the pace began to continuously increase. Each lady had her own style of voodoo dancing—naga-chaud, yanvalu-dos-bas, venka-nolu, mahi data, and mahi japata. Each dance was very different yet very much the same due of the presence of the black African historical rhythm and beat.

After about fifteen minutes five little naked girls came onto the stage area. Each carried a basket which was set beside one of the dancers. They opened the lids and quickly left. Each dancer had crawled up to her basket, lied on the floor with her arms around her basket, from which two snakes crawled up and out of each basket. Each snake seemed to know how to select which arm to climb because one went left and the other went right. Each dancer stood and returned to her voodoo dance while holding, playing, and fondling her life-long pets. Five lovely women, five beautiful cold creatures, all happily dancing together. Impossible? Yes! No! Maybe?

Finally, the big drum stopped beating and the ladies and their pets, each thoroughly dripping in sweat, ran in five different directions from the centrum.

Everything was quiet for several minutes. Suddenly, a single small drum beat began. Five minutes later the rada-rada drums began at a faster beat. Two men came into the center area. They were carrying one basket each which they placed on the floor. They took off the lids and left the area. The drum beating increased in intensity. Suddenly a hooded head appeared above the opening of each basket. From one basket a shiny jade-green cobra snake exited. From the other basket a shiny topaz-yellow cobra snake exited. Down the isle leading from the front to the center of the podium area came a pole-sling chair, carried by four muscular men. The elegant lady in the chair was totally dressed in see-through silk, white in color, which semi-hid her entire body. Her hair was still in mohawk-like goddess braids and she had red finger nails and toe nails. She wore extensive make up with green around her blue green eyes. The African Queen of Voodoo stood and shouted "May the Gods Run Before Us".

And the people stood and shouted, "May the Gods Run Before Us"

The men set the chair down and lifted the Queen to the floor. She walked over to her pets, and began singing to them. They both quickly stood up, and slithered to her. For several minutes she walked around the area, singing in the ancient voodoo dialect. The snakes simply followed her. They were historically older than African voodoo. People moved aside and gave the three of them plenty of room to pass. Then for the next fifteen minutes she sang Nigerian wedding songs, while her associates prepared the center of the stage area for the wedding ceremony.

The stage was properly transformed for matrimony, a small black ebony table, and five designated areas around the table were established. The Queen stood in front of the table, bride on her left, facing her, mother and father standing behind her. Groom on her right, facing her, mother and father standing behind him. She asked the couple and parents to quietly take their places.

She then turned to her pets and spoke to them. They turned, went directly to their baskets, and climbed into them. They then stood up and watched the ceremony. She now re-faced the couple and began singing again in the ancient Voodoo dialect. She sang the official wedding poem. Only two or three 'older Voodoo Royalty' knew this ancient powerful music which was based in the spiritual past of the two about to unite in marriage. When special or select future events were associated with this music by a voodoo wedding ceremony, the projected event always happened and in a very powerful way.

The Queen gave several ancient voodoo words to the bride, and she gave several 'different' ancient voodoo words to the groom. They were to repeat those words just before they went to bed every night for two months. She declared their union, and gave to each of them a series of six vials. They were to each drink one vial today, and one vial each on day 3, day 5, day 8, day 9, and day 4x4. If you do this several things will happen to you as a couple—super luck, wealth, happiness, one son in sixteen months and one son in thirty- two months. The daughters of the Queen then took the bride into a back room in the Pavilion, and examined/talked to her. Next, five of the Queen's male attendants took the groom into another back room in the Pavilion, and examined/talked to him.

On a nod from the 'examiners', the Queen produced the necessary spell to allow the specific requested LWA/God to complete the future as today ordained.

LEBA:

OPEN THE GATES FOR ME,

SO THAT I MAY GO THROUGH,

UPON MY RETURN I SHALL GREET THE LWA.

VOODOO LEGBA,

OPEN THE GATE FOR ME,

SO THAT I MAY COME TO YOU.

AMEN

The next day, the newly voodoo linked couple went to the Nigerian Cathedral in Lagos and were married (again) under the eyes of a Cardinal who was flown in from the Vatican of Rome.

The Queen's fees for various services varied from a few thousand American dollars for simple 'guarantee happy' birthday/anniversaries, to a few million American dollars for a business 'guarantee' arrangement possibly including elimination of any specific negative components. The recent wedding which guaranteed two sons 'on time' cost five million American dollars from each father of the bridal couple, the Chief of General Staff of Nigeria and the very wealthy Oil Baron from the South-South of Nigeria.

21

BORNO AND LAKE CHAD

Mohammad was born in the sixth century in Mecca, and his revealed faith of Islam spread from Medina throughout the Arabian Peninsula. From there his followers moved east into Asia, and west into northern Africa and the Mediterranean Sea. In the eighth century, joining with the Berbers, from Morocco they moved into Spain and dominated commerce, culture, and religion in the Iberian Peninsula for five hundred years. Over those years several Moslem empires were established in northern Africa: Tokur, Mauritania and Western Mali; Kanem-Chad, Nigeria, and Libya; Borno; Ghana; Mali; Songhay. Now they have broken into numerous Moslem countries/republics across Africa.

During the last three centuries Moslem teachers and imams relocated from the Mediterranean Sea region south into the central African towns. Both East and West African rulers were the first to accept Islam. Traveling scholars carried the language to the Atlantic Ocean villages on the African coast. Islam became de-Arabized and Africanized. In the nineteenth century the Yoruba people adopted Islam in what is today's Nigeria.

In the seventeenth century, particularly along the Atlantic Sea, the Europeans began colonizing the African continent. Therefore, much of the western seaboard of Africa lived through several centuries of the mixing of local religions, Islam and Christianity. Nigeria is a good example. In the twenty first century, one of the first multi-ethnic, multi-religion republics in the world was successfully established here. The two religions did not truly clash. Both believed in one all-powerful God. In some areas today Nigeria is 55% Moslem, 45 % Christian, and 10-12% practice native Voodooism. Federal laws have been developed and made functional for 'both' religions. Legal national buildings and social systems co-exist for Islam, Christianity, and ancient beliefs.

Kef had to make changes in his thinking as he moved from Voodooism-Christianity to Islam-Voodooism. All 'three' religions worship a single god, but the believers will tell you that their Gods are not the same. Kef would return to the South-South problem a couple of weeks later. First, he needed to implement his plan for the northeast Nigerian problem. It was ready in his mind. So, when he returned from Lagos to Abuja, he quickly flew on to Maiduguri. He was to rendezvous with the Nigerian military, one American military unit, Borno police, the African Voodoo Queen, and his boy spies. And Li promised he would soon be ready with his anti-nanotech system. Now, how best to use the latter, he was still thinking.

On the plane he re-read the encrypted Avatar re-language note from Li. It read: 'We have tested several systems to interfere with the cellulose-cellulase bacterial enzyme system present in the human body because of the nanotech intake. I will try to explain the science.'

'The cellulose nanotech molecular system, probably a colonesterase, when activated by colonic bacterial cellulase, digests holes in the walls of the colon. This allows digestive fluids and bacteria to leak into the abdominal cavity—internal diarrhea. Such will cause death in a few hours. Acid (pH 4.5 to 5.0) inhibits the bacterial cellulase. Hence the cellulose nanotech molecular system is not activated, but harmlessly excreted. Therefore, we are developing a blocking system by decreasing the body pH (acid) to inhibit the bacterial cellulase activity.'

'Theocratically, this will be accomplished with an acid-based sleeping gas which will travel via the lungs to the blood to the colon in a few seconds, and put the person to sleep. Such a system should cause a couple of hours of sleep. Hence the change in body blood acidity should not be very uncomfortable for a long period of time. Currently we are studying BZ, halothane vapor (fluothane), and methoxyflurane (penthrane). Each gas has plus and minus side effects. And each gas causes partial external diarrhea, prevents internal diarrhea, and any activated enzymes are soon expelled. So hopefully, usually, death is avoided. We do not yet have good numbers for dosage levels. So, there is a risk about how much gas to spray onto a group of people. This is still an estimated guess. Let me know what you think. Plus, when do you want to test? We will send it in 30 pounds tanks. I hope that the Nigerians can work with this. It could be a life saver.'

As Kef landed in Maiduguri, he was met by Kiy, his special little buddy, who greeted him with their favorite orange drinks. He welcomed Kiy's presence as the boy was very anxious and ready to go. He had already located two of the invaders' military camp sites and wanted to show Kef immediately—by map of course. First, a quick lunch and then a conference with Colonel Nwaoloko and his selected soldiers from the Nigerian army, Captain Greenstein, newly arrived American drone squadron commander and his three assistants, Mr. Ajubea, Borno state police and regional deputies. The group totaled a special controlling command force of nearly thirty military and civilians, all government authorized to develop and commit battle plans against the foreign invaders. Kef had a role in mind for each group. He expected that they each had been studying the maps of the region and were all ready to go.

America was funding some of this military effort. They would be testing Li's new anti-nano system designed to block the powerful nanotech molecular system in live human testing. They would also evaluate how to protect their own drone military research efforts in desert-like conditions. Because Kef was the only one with experience in nano-weapon fighting, the two countries placed him temporarily in-charge of the first operation. He was not military, so he had to be satisfied with that.

Kef opened the meeting, "Colonel, please update us concerning the methods that the invaders are currently using to attack the villages."

Colonel Nwaoloko complied, "Little Kiy's verbal report was quite correct. These foreign soldiers/mercenaries/invaders work in several scattered groups of thirty or forty. They have grenades, cheap Indian and Iranian made assault rifles, and possibly a couple of ground to air missiles per group. So only a real army can stop them. And we are talking about canvasing over 1,000 square miles. They drive into a village in three or four small trucks, each carrying about five to six men, early in the morning hours in a surprise attack. Usually, they meet little resistance. The villagers will have only a couple of hunting rifles, machetes, long knives, spears, and a few bows and arrows. So, the 'raid' is quickly accomplished. Older people, women and children are placed into a large hut. The younger males are used to help drive the cattle down the road to a place on the river where cattle barges are waiting to load the animals. Once the cattle are loaded, a few village men help row the barges down the stream. Somewhere on route the cattle are loaded onto ships. The ships containing the cattle continue, apparently towards Lake Chad and international territory. The village men are taken to slave markets in a neighboring country, or killed, depending upon their age and physical size."

"Back in the village, a few of the invaders remain as guards. The children, women, and older ones are locked in one or two large huts. They are given only water for the next 36 hours. At noon the second day a truck drives into the village. It is loaded with food and much fruit, such as variety of melons, pomegranate, mangos, bananas, citrus fruit, figs, and many types of nuts. Apparently, the nanotech killer system (food poison) is in the fruit. Everyone is very hungry and thirsty, so they gorge themselves on the food and liquids. The effect of the nanotech 'poison', initiates the diarrhea, and begins a few hours after they start eating. No one survives this. The guards leave as soon as a terrible smell starts to emanate from the village."

Kef said, "Thank you. Kiy, is that how you remember that day when your mother, father, family, and neighbors were killed?

Kiy just lowered his head and nodded affirmatively.

Kef continued, "Does anyone know about a semi-permanent headquarters or temporary camps from which these men attack? Kiy has identified several. Anyone else who knows where any of these camps were or are now, please show us on the maps."

Mr. Ajubea spoke up, "We think that they move around every week or soon after they have made a successful raid. They do not stay in a central location. This is why our army has trouble locating them. We occasionally see strangers in Maiduguri and the larger villages especially along the rivers. Friends of mine also see strangers in the larger villages and some cities near the northern and eastern country borders. But we are a democratic republic. We cannot just arrest someone without some evidence that would later hold up in Nigerian courts."

Colonel Nwaoloko added, "Even using spy satellite pictures from the Americans does not help much. After a raid, the various groups separate into one or two or three truck units, and move around between raids. I think they even re-organize in new groups of trucks for the next set of raids. Obviously, there are only two or three people making decisions and giving orders to the others. And they have some means of telecommunication as they do not have regular organization-decision making meetings, even out in the savanna. Someone decides who will go with whom on which raid. They must have a couple hundred active invaders. Where possible, they go into larger villages far from the rivers to 'rest' between raids, and to make it more difficult to identify who is a militant versus who is just a wandering nomad. Official passports are not that common out there."

"What I am hearing," said Kef. "We have many problems. Where are they between raids? Who is making the decisions? How can we save or rescue the villagers from their own 'jails' Can we get the cattle back before they leave the area? Can we stop them from kidnapping or killing the village males?"

"Some potential questions need answers are: A few raiders must remain with the cattle. Where are the cattle and the cattle food temporarily maintained? They need diesel for their trucks, from where? How do they get the nanotech molecular system (human food poison) from abroad, probably Europe? Where does the fresh fruit come from, and how? The latter must be recent or somewhat fresh. And if the 'food poison' does comes from Europe, does it come through some airport in the north, through Niger or Chad?"

"Several possibilities come to mind," said the Colonel. "Diffa, Niger, is on the northern Nigeria border. It is a medium sized city, has good resources, and a local airport. It is two-three truck hours away from the 'raiding-zone' villages area. Hence easy transportation for much of the necessary human requirements from food to petrol could probably be obtained via Diffa."

"Baga, Nigeria, and Baga Sol, Chad are rivers feeding into Lake Chad. N'jamena, Chad, is a large city near the lake and has many available resources, including international air travel," said Mr. Ajubea.

Colonel Nwaoloko added, "I see where you are going. We can set up road blocks between Diffa and the raiding-zone, and monitor for non-Nigerian citizens, trucks carrying men with military type guns, foods such as fruit, and of course tanker trucks carrying small truck diesel fuel."

Kef said, "I assume there could be freighter ships in Lake Chad which could carry cattle to one or more of these cities. Would N'jamena, being the largest city in that area, have facilities for trans-shipping and slaughter of cattle for market?"

And little Kiy jumped in, "Yes, I have been there with my father. There is a slaughter house for cattle in N'jamena. And they bought our cattle, and our neighbor's cattle too. I have seen it."

"So here is another place to investigate," said Kef. "Perhaps a couple of military river patrol boats in the area where the rivers enter Lake Chad. A couple of boats at the south end of the lake, near N'jamena, watching for 'drug-runners' would be good. Of course, they could also watch for cows walking on the water."

And they all broke the strain with a nice chuckle.

Kef stood up, went to the map of northeastern Nigeria on the wall and began laying out a plan. "1) set up road-blockages from Diffa, Niger into the raiding villages area; 2) stop, search, and confiscate all guns not identified as villagers' hunting rifles; 3) monitor Lake Chad for freight ships carrying cattle with Nigeria markings; 4) identify any temporary campsites that the raiding groups might use for re-fueling and the picking up any supplies such as food, water, and their 'food-poison'; 5) send and help our boy-spies to locate, follow the raiders, regularly notify us where they are, what they are doing, and in what direction they are going."

"We already have permission for our military to temporarily 'borrow' several different types of American drones," Kef added. "I think they have just arrived. Is that correct Colonel?"

Colonel Nwaoloko nodded in the affirmative.

"Later, Captain Greenstein can describe how the American drones work and how we will use them."

"Now here is what I want you, Kiy, and your buddies to do. Only take with you five or six other boys who lived in the region, know certain areas, and who lost family members in the food-poison raids. Work in three groups of two. Use the roads and village trails, when possible, which are not very accessible by cars or trucks. Do not go close to the raiders. We will provide you with good binocular scopes, so you can 'spy' from a distance. We will provide you with silent electric Honda motor bikes. You have already driven them, so you know their limitations on and off the roads. Watch and follow the raiders from a distance. Most villages that have been raided are near waterways, streams or rivers. This is for immediate and rapid cattle transfer onto small animal raft-boats. They then quickly leave the area."

"We will give you legal permits to use with the villagers. You can use them as a government 'credit' card for unlimited food, water, and electricity for your bikes. Re-charge your bikes overnight. All villages have electricity. We will also give you throw away cell phones. They will be only programed to call Colonel Nwaoloko when you press number 1 three times. Keep the Colonel informed every two days. After a positive usage, you must immediately bury the phone in the sand or throw it into the river—use it only two or three times. When we are finished, I will give to all of you and your buddies an up-to-date-real-cell-phone to use as your own."

"Kiy quickly spoke up, "Who will pay for the monthly phone fees?"

Kef laughed. "The Nigerian government, of course."

And that made the boy a very happy young man.

'Kef reminded himself the motto of the musketeers 'need to know'. All Nigerian military action would be carried out at night to minimize the missiles of the raiders. He purposely did not have Mr. Hamzah Sheriff or Mr. Zubaydah Murtaya in the 'need to know' category. He did not invite them to this meeting. There was just too much local-ethnic killing going on, and more to come. He did not know them well enough to trust them. Besides, both were recommended by higher political-ups. Sometimes that can become a problem. So, the sleeping gas tanks and Queen's snake actions will remain temporally classified on site. And I need to organize a Snake Drop Team with Viper, her chosen sisters, the Nigerian military reptile squad, and practice the Queen's castle to invader's campsite runs using helicopters, planes, and drones. We need to practice this run several times to successfully and quietly accomplish these actions when needed. Afterall, we may be transferring 10 to 15 very fast and deadly snakes in containers during a single plane trip. I am glad I am not going. Wow!'

Kef looked at Captain Greenstein, "Captain, would you please brief us about the drones, what they are and how we will use them.

The Captain replied, "With pleasure. Before we get into military actions, let me tell you about the USA Military Drones or unmanned aerial vehicles (UAVs). We have 22 UAVs in our arsenal. Because the Nigerian Military are planning to purchase one or more types of drones, and later you will be asked to help make that selection, I will briefly review many of these automatic guys."

"UAVs are true game changers in military operations. Drones offer many advantages over traditional warfare tactics, especially with the ultimate goal of reducing soldier fatalities. And current military and commercial spending on the continued development of these UAVs is well over $100 billion, and going up each year. One key is that they keep ground troops out of harms way during deliverance of reconnaissance and surveillance, in addition to aerial fire support. Because of time, I will mention only a few of these guys so you can see the big picture. Watch the video screen behind me and we will continuously show illustrations of the UAVs as I describe them."

1) Avenger (General Atomics) – 450mph, 44'x70', 15,000mi, turban engines internal weapons, ground control of two,

2) AAI-RQ-7- Shadow – 100mph, 12'x14', 75mi, reconnaissance and surveillance, trail mounted catapult launch,

3) MQ-9-Reaper – 200mph, 35'x65', 1,200mi, high altitude and long endurance for surveillance,

4) MQ-1-Predator–100mph, 25'x50', 750mi, medium altitude, many high- powered high-resolution video sensors and cameras,

5) MQ-8-Fire Scout – 100mph, 25'x25', 50mi, low noise, excellent reconnaissance, aerial fire support, precision targeting, situation awareness, high lift capacity,

6) RQ-12-Wasp – 40mph, 2'x2', 10mi, 60 pounds, 2 onboard cameras which deliver on-time intelligence and beyond-line-of-sight-awareness,

7) RQ-20-Puma – 50mph, 5'x10', 40mi, 30pounds, battery powered, hand launched, used for surveillance and intelligence gathering, has infra-red and electro-optical cameras,

8) RQ-31-Fast Ant – 100mph, 1'x2', 20mi, 20pounds, hand launched, battery powered, surveillance, plus delivery of a variety of weapon systems.

"The bodies of our modern UAVs are made mostly of composite materials. At our Aeronautics Factory we have large high-tech laboratories for developing new composite materials for UAV structure framework and skins. The inorganic chemistry and organic chemistry basis for this include the 17 heavy atoms and rare earth elements such as: lanthanum, scandium, yttrium, europium, cerium, neodymin, samarium, and on. These are combined to create solid pieces of the drone's air frame and skin, and associated components."

"At least 10 countries now produce more than 25 types of drones. Hence a wide variety of composites are now being used for military and commercial functions. It is probable that several hundred UAVs are manufactured each year by USA, China, Russia, Germany, and more. These include multi-rotors such as tri-coptors, quad-coptors, hexo-coptors, and octo-coptors. One observes both winged and wingless aircraft everywhere in all UVA factories."

"All drones are controlled from the ground using a drone transmitter which has left and right stick control, plus a variety of buttons and switches. These assign the throttle and yaw control to the left stick, and pitch and roll to the right stick."

"The drone's brain is the flight controller or inertial measurement unit (IMU). It houses very sensitive gyroscopes, accelerometers, and barometric pressure sensors."

"I will not take time to describe more drone components. I realize that unless you are trained in aerodynamics, this is impossible to understand. Suffice it to say the pilot also learns use of brushed or brushless sensor type motors and electronic speed. Most pilots understand how to use this complementary equipment, but they certainly do not know how to cook up a drone framework."

"Basically, you pilot your flying aircraft from the ground, near-by or from a few miles away. Or you fly it from a distance, several hundred miles or several thousand miles away."

Captain Greenstein closed his note book. And the room turned quiet. There were very few pilots of any kind in the audience. Hence there was a general buzzing with numerous blank looks. Only a few intelligent looks came forth.

Little Kiy added his comments, "One of the Americans told me that I could ride on a drone. Maybe trade my bike for a drone. Who do I talk to about this exchange?"

And that opened the conversation to start comparisons with high tech transportation systems in military actions—and a few chuckles.

After a few minutes discussing the importance of military technology in today's wars, everything quieted down. "I will not take questions right now. My objective was to introduce you to military drones, UAVs. Over the next few weeks, we can arrange teaching and training periods and my associates can establish time periods for the Nigerian military who will, hopefully later, work with the drones more permanently."

"With your permission, Mr. Kef Legoase," Captain Greenstein looked over and winked at Kef, "I will try to brief our groups about how we will use the drones over the next few weeks. Is this OK?"

The two senior leaders were indeed becoming good friends. Kef nodded a quick affirmative.

Captain Greenstein continued. "Nigeria has agreed to allow the USA to test and employ three squadrons of drones in these desert or savanna climates. We have selected two Ravens, two Wasps, and two Pumas. The drones that we chose are small in size, light in weight, quiet, and have various combinations of attachments such as visual, sound, transport, communications, and/or weapon systems. Our three squadrons have these six drones, and three suburban panel vehicles with interior laboratory and working space to transport, conceal, and maintain two drones within each. Three men can reside, and work actually, inside each vehicle. All power systems are electric, and the roof of the vehicle has a high-tech solar panel system which provides most necessary drone energy. Only the vehicle uses gasoline. For general security, such as in red areas, we usually have a single marine commando unit assigned for special support that travels in a second SUV associated panel. We have three such units. Now each drone can travel 10 to 50 miles. When at rest, the drone will be continuously covered with a special small tent while it is being readied for action. They are off-limits to all except the American members of the Drone teams, and special selected Nigerian trainees, I am sorry. We also are required to follow orders."

"We plan to test out the drones for these short distances. Later we can possibly increase to long distance scouting, delivering and also picking up packages, functioning in bad weather, and avoidance of military actions such as guns or missiles. I am sorry but most of our maneuvering will be classified and we cannot show or teach you more about these remarkable auto-electronic guys."

Kef then continued, "Now let me finish up and briefly explain a couple of other ways which we will use these drones. We may not use the drones for direct military action. 1) We will be dropping poisonous desert snakes into invader-campsites. The snakes will be provided by the Queen and her daughters. 2) And we will drop tanks of sleeping gas into villages where villagers, who ate the 'poisoned food', were located. We hope the gas will help prevent the food poison from working. At present, this sleeping gas has never been used. It is experimental and can only be used as a scientific test. Let me briefly explain a little more."

"The African Queen of Voodoo, is currently living in her castle on the island in the center the Lagos Lagoon. She lives there with her five daughter-ladies and their more than fifty types of poisonous snakes. Each daughter is named after a specific snake with whom she continuously lives, day and night. When we have an invader-target campsite identified, and ready to strike, the Queen will be informed. She will have her oldest daughter, Viper, chose two of her sisters. They will select several Saw Scaled Vipers and Nubian Spitting Cobras, which are the best desert-savanna snakes, travel from Lagos to Maiduguri via military aircraft, and continue by helicopter on to one of our drone units near the strike site. The daughters will bring the snakes enclosed in secure containers. Later they will transfer the snakes, under control of the Nigerian military, into special baskets which will rupture when dropped from 100 feet or more. One reptile knowledgeable military squadron unit will attach those baskets to a drone and drop them over the site. A satchel will also open releasing leaflets with a picture of an **ouroboros,** which is a snake eating its tail. It reads."

"Snakes prefer snakes, but will consume people when necessary!"

"Does everyone understand? The Queen's daughters are very nice ladies, but rather scary and certainly, for me, a little dangerous. I don't like snakes. So, I insisted that the daughters accompany the snakes all the way to the drone take off." HAHA!

Colonel Nwaoloko added, "Thank you. I am certain all of my people will be very happy with that decision!"

Captain Greenstein quickly responded, "We also thank you very much."

The meeting followed up with a couple of hours of questions and answers, then a 'nice-tasty' military dinner in the dining room. Kef wanted to be certain that the group understood the overall approach. So, he and the Captain did answer more questions during dinner. Specific details would have to be decided during their daily decision making, as he would not be available during most days. He needed to simultaneously monitor events in both north and south Nigeria. And now, he needed to catch a late evening military plane to Abuja. He was also thinking about seeing Adaeze again.

Kef was re-playing his proposed plan in his mind as the Nigerian Air Force jet took him quickly back to his temporary home in Abuja. He was confident that their plans would bring in positive results. And he was close enough to return to the 'battlefield' in a few hours, if something went wrong. This plan should capture or neutralize some of the invaders. He knew that many of them were afraid of snakes. So, a couple of successful gifts of the Queen's little cold children, dropping out of the sky, leaflets of ouroboros, dropping out of the sky, these should quickly create a bit of chaotic behavior among those brave invaders who were killing old men, women and children in outlying villages with poison-macabre foods. He had learned that the invaders paychecks were one cow per militant per raid. At least that was what one of the fleeing villagers had told him. Was one cow worth several vipers and cobras running around a campsite? He doubted it. Certainly not for him!

22

BATTLE ACTION

A couple of weeks later, Kef was up early, drank a big glass of pomegranate juice, ate a bowl of muesli cereal with whole milk, and headed for work. In his office he immediately initiated an Avatar re-language encrypted cell call to his three musketeer buddies, which would connect everyone in ten hours, reasonably convenient for everyone from Istanbul to Los Angeles. He used the new key words, rain storm alive, which informed them he wanted an update of all actions in motion. He then organized his most recent info and data on the two Nigerian problems, north and south, made a list of questions, and prepared for the evening musketeer conference.

When the time rolled around, he glanced at his conductivity connector, there were three contacts, so he began some modified Avatar talk. "This is Na'via. Who is there?"

Li said, "This is Tsu'teye."

Jamie said, "This is Ey'tuka."

Aykut said, "This is Mo'ata."

Kef asked, "Is everyone in good health? And do you have a lot of good info for me? We have initiated our attack plans in the north and the south of Nigeria. If it is all right, I will explain the north Nigeria plan first. Please give to me any info you have concerning the Borno-Lake Chad region. Let me have anything you think might be critical to our current attack plans. I don't think so, but it could become necessary to modify our current plan. OK? Then I will tell you about the plan for south Nigeria."

They each complied.

Kef began, "The mini-war that is occurring in the Lake Chad region of Nigeria probably involves a few hundred foreign invaders or mercenaries who have Chinese military-army weapons and a few ground to air missiles. They attack at night using five or six small trucks with several men in each. The villagers have no modern weapons, so are easily overcome. The invaders steal the village's cattle, kidnap the younger men, and jail the older men, women, and children in large huts. Cattle are driven to the nearest stream or river, loaded onto cattle barges, taken down river, re-loaded onto cargo vessels and shipped into Lake Chad and onto some further destination involving intact animal sales or slaughter houses and the sales of beef. The young village men are then later sold into slavery or killed. Twenty to thirty hours after the attack, the villagers who were locked up, are fed fruit and nuts. The fruit contains the cellulase nanotech molecular system, or as we are now thinking of it as a colonic enzyme called colonesterase. The effects hit everyone a few hours later. No one survives the 'food poison'. And yes, the macabre deaths, do occur."

"Our current attack plan for the north is to attempt to locate the invaders' campsites, which seem to continuously change, and to identify the villages on the day of an attack. We are setting up routine blockades on roads in the hostile areas. We are confiscating all military weapons, identify, arrest, and seize illegal cattle and possible thieves on the roads and in river-lake boats."

"We also have a new collaborator, the Queen of Africa Voodoo, her five mutant daughters, and their pet poisonous snakes. They will provide us with some of their pets which we shall drop into the invader's campsites. The Queen is both witch and charlatan as she uses spirits/souls and biologicals in her practice. Her daughters will handle the logistics of transferring the snakes to the battle areas."

"And Li is providing us with a neutralizing tear-sleeping gas to spray on the villagers who have eaten the fruit, hence consumed the nanotech system. Hopefully the gas will prevent the cellulase digestive enzyme activity in the colon from functioning, and thus prevent the colonesterase from causing the diarrhea and morbid deaths. This is our beginning on the northern front. Any questions?"

Jamie asked, "Do you know from where and how the nanotech system gets into Nigeria."

Kef answered, "Yes, we think it is flown into Diffa, Niger, and then trucked overland into the Lake Chad region. We are setting up special road-blocks to try to intercept these shipments. Is it coming from Europe, probably? But we do not know for certain."

"Hey," said Aykut. "If you can provide me with names of companies, such as air cargo, camping supplies, truck fuel, land or shipping transportation, cattle sales centers, slaughter houses, and so forth, I can explore the finances, locations, and senior management of these companies over the past few months. Any monetary spikes or large payments to these companies from a European source should make them a suspect."

"I can do that," said Kef. "The Nigerian government is giving excellent assistance for our investigative efforts, and the Nigerian military will be giving us occasional potent firepower, including both Nigerian helicopter and US drone assistance drops of the poisonous snakes into the enemy camps."

"Now let me give to you a brief first report, which recently arrived, of the first couple of weeks of pursuing these military efforts. We have had quite good success, as follows."

"We think that in recent months, the invaders did not expect any sudden organized armed resistance. They were set up for only offense, and paid no attention to defense positions when setting up campsites and selecting villages to raid. Almost immediately we killed and captured more than 120 of them and confiscated 61 rifles, and two ground to air missiles from three separate road blocks/ambushes. One large cargo ship containing 165 cattle was captured, 25 invaders arrested, and 17 automatic weapons were confiscated. In addition, we managed to save 172 villagers in one village using Li's gas counter actant. The gas did reverse/prevent the nanotech cellulase action (colonesterase activation) in the colons of most children and women, but not with the older men. One night we also managed to use a drone to drop a basket of the Queen's snakes into an invaders' campsite. And checking the site next day we observed that of the 50 to 100 men we expected to find, we found the site empty, but there were 32 bodies containing snake bites. It would appear that the Queen's little friends/children enjoyed themselves."

And the group got a good round of smiles. Things then became quiet.

Slowly Kef continued. "Now let me talk for a couple of minutes about our battle plan for southern Nigeria. We have located the homes and travel patterns of the three doctoral students who are currently studying with Dr. Anneka Andersson in Stockholm. All three had returned home for the summer. Seven villages, in the areas near their home villages, had been struck with the cellulose nanotech molecular system (colonesterase) in the past few weeks. Plus, several outlying individual families have suffered the same fate."

"Nwadinkpa, my key friend and Voodoo Priest of southern Nigeria, and several of the Queen Voodoo's followers have been providing direct eyesight within the villages in the area. Both have confirmed the presence of those three students in their home villages. Apparently, the students often meet at a truck stop/restaurant in one of the central villages, Jayo, late at night after it closes."

"The three are part of a gang of nearly 20-25 young rebels. It would seem to be a gang of friends with 'common' ideas to make money for the family units by siphoning oil from existing pipelines in the delta area. Our calculations on oil siphoning show one can make a few hundred thousand dollars in cash in one week with such efforts, if a foreign tanker is available for several days to rapidly and properly re-load. Properly means a small foreign tanker with oil pumps which can move the oil from a shore-based pipeline to the small tanker at a rate of 50 gallon per minute, and there is nearby a commercial tanker immediately available to transfer all of it into the international flow pool."

"At the same time this village attack provides a distraction in a nearby village with their harsh military-like raid which closes down the village, locks the women and children in a couple of large huts, and takes the men to a second large hut somewhere out in the savanna. All are maintained imprisoned for 24 to 36 hours. They are then fed food containing a cellulose nanotech molecular system (again probably colonesterse). After the cellulose system starts to show its effect on the villagers, the gang members quickly leave the area, letting the nearby oil pump siphoning system continue on its own. Two or three days later when the distraction with police is maximum, they quietly return and retrieve the small ship with the oil pumps, sail to a large tanker, fill it, and get paid cash. The international larger tanker then just sails away. There are more than 100 river tributaries and numerous foreign tankers of all sizes sailing the delta waters of the Niger River every day. We have been checking out this group, the three Swedish-African students and gang friends, and their role with the village massacres. We believe there is a direct relationship between the siphoning of oil and the killing with nanotech systems."

"We think the macabre form of death is used both as a distraction and as a warning to other villagers in the area—This is not your business!"

"We are often talking with the Queen. She is evaluating the exact role of the lives of these three students in their villages and in the region. If she is convinced that they were directly involved in the village massacres, she will have her daughters deliver some of her special small cold damp children as gifts into the homes of each of these men before they return to Sweden to school. If the Queen is not convinced, we have a problem. We are waiting on her decision and assistance. Aykut, what do you have concerning these students bank accounts?"

Aykut replied, "Yes, each has a simple bank account in the National Bank of Stockholm. Their accounts show several deposits of five thousand Euros each over the past couple of years. And deposits of one hundred thousand Euros each just before they arrived for vacation in Nigeria in June.

Kef continued Aykut's thoughts. "Now these are students from non-wealthy villages! Where did the money come from? And why? How? Is it oil money? Does anyone have any comments or questions?"

Kef suddenly stopped and changed direction. "Wait a moment please. I have just received a report from one of my associates in the South-South Nigeria. The report is from Nwadinkpa, my Voodoo

Priest Africa friend, and an associate of the Voodoo Queen of Africa. The Priest and I studied together with the Queen Cleopatra of Haiti a few years ago. So, we are very good friends."

"Recently I sent Aykut's new information on the three African-Swedish graduate students to both the Queen and Nwadinkpa. I thought Nwadinka would send to me regular update reports. He has not done so. Maybe this is why."

"This last evening there was a police raid on a certain truck stop/restaurant in that location where I have just mentioned. The report reads that the local police raided a truck stop/restaurant in Jayo and discovered fourteen men dead, each killed by snake bites, yet no snakes were found. Several windows were open so the snakes may have 'escaped'. There are many snakes in the area, so such killing is not abnormal. And on and on.'

"An extra-private note in the Voodoo dialect says that only one of the Nigerian students from Sweden was among the dead. The other two must have survived.—Soooo!"

After several moments of quietness, Kef spoke up. "Well, I guess the Queen decided that these guys are guilty of some of the massacres of her voodoo followers in this part of the South. Not surprising. I just expected to be notified before she initiated such punishments. However, I guess this is her land and her people, and she certainly does not need my permission to control Nigerian life and death. The Queen is a doer, not a follower. I suppose that I should have anticipated such action."

And there were a few more moments of silence. Kef was a little shook up, and could not come up with any smart remarks.

He finally continued, "The Queen is many years older, wiser, very experienced, and has much control of her people. She made that decision on her own. I certainly cannot express my feelings to her in any way. Nwadinkpa must have not been told, or told not to tell me. Either way, perhaps some of the South's problems are going to be solved without my help. If this group was a major cause of the massacres and oil theft, it is good. But during the past months there have also been several oil thefts which did not have associate nanotech killings. No doors can be closed yet."

Jamie spoke up, "Allow me to contribute some new ideas to our efforts. Kef, you rest a minute. After Kef set up this conference, I contacted Uncle Dagda and got the latest info from the Committee of Nanotechnology Control. Aykut and I also talked earlier today. Aykut."

"Jamie is correct," said Aykut. "We have monetary data and info on several of the nanotech killer candidates, including Dr. Andersson. She has several bank accounts in Sweden, Switzerland, Luxemburg, and the British Virgin Islands. Her accounts in the Luxemburg Bank of the People and the First Caribbean International Bank regularly have a couple of deposits of several hundred thousand dollars each per year. She then generally transfers some of this to the Switzerland National Bank account. The money sources are always from the USA, Canada, or the British Virgin Islands. This money is not related to her professor's salary."

"OK," said Jamie. "Now, let me relay to you some recent info direct from Uncle Dagda. The Committee had previously authorized 24/7 monitoring of several of the nanotech killer candidates. About one week ago, Dr. Jackson White met with a very tall, slim, dark brown skin, black eyes, light hair, well dressed gentleman at the Southbys Street-side Restaurant in London. High tech voice recordings and an almost three hour conversation was obtained. Many pictures of this man were taken. Upon checking him out, the man turned out to probably be a Canadian who was coming from the British Virgin Islands. During the one-hour lunch period, the word nano was used more than twenty times. Along with this word were the words— production, shipping, costs, and several place names in Africa. Something illegal was being marketed"

"It took a couple of hours using several American intelligence systems to more precisely determine just who this man could be. He travels under the name of Jordon Johnson, a Canadian citizen. Mr. Johnson is a lawyer who lives part time in an isolated house on 65 acres, 35729 Gooden Road, Jackmire, a suburb of Toronto, Canada. He travels to his second home in the Caribbean, and on business to Europe and Africa."

"However, I understand that Jordon Johnson is also the name of a rather famous American Senator. First analysis determined that this person at the table in London was also Oliver Johnson, Jordon Johnson's nephew and adopted son, lawyer and lobbyist out of Washington, DC. And they do look very much alike. He is an American citizen who often travels under a pseudo-correct Canadian identity. Currently there is identity confusion concerning this/these Canadian-Americans."

"Two days later, this same man was lunching with Dr. Anneka Andersson in the gardens of the Aroura Restaurant in Stockholm. Again, many pictures and a distant high tech video recording was made of the entire two-hour luncheon. And yes, similar information was obtained by the investigators of the American Office of National Security Agency. Mr. Jordon Johnson, alias possibly Mr. Oliver Johnson, was discussing nano tech systems with a nanotech scientist who seemed to be receiving deposits in her foreign bank accounts from non-traceable sources. She also mentioned several of her African students who were doing an excellent job of testing some of their nanotech molecular systems. And she was bragging about how much money for pleasure she was giving to them, but it was university tuition money.—HA HA."

"During the next week Mr. Johnson met with a Dr. John Wholemart in Dublin, Ireland, and couple of days later with a Dr. Eagart Natle in Brussels, Belgium. Both of these recorded conversations involved contracts to design some new types of nanotech molecular systems which focused upon brain function. Because business was good, Mr. Johnson said he was willing to pay very well. And he wanted the new system capable of entering the body through breathing, nose or mouth. He also wanted it capable of being transported and stored at ambient temperature. Dr. Natle promised he would have a human trial model in five to six months. Dr. Wholemart was already working on brain function, but he would not have a potential model for human testing for at least one year. Agreements were made."

"During several days of continued travel time the Committee of Nanotechnology Control obtained several additional high-tech video recordings of Mr. Johnson and several of his contacts, each recording discussed the design of nanotech systems, production, transportation, sales, and possible legal cover-ups."

"One week later, Mr. Jordon Johnson was having a luncheon with Mr. Faustino Mariniti on the outdoor patio of the Bono Bogetta restaurant in Rome. High tech pictures and video recordings were obtained. Previous data was confirmed. Nanotech systems were discussed in detail with regard to northern African countries. However, costs became a factor in the negotiations. After all, Mr. Mariniti had his own nanotech scientists on payroll in Milan. In addition, he was always having International Maritime Organization violations with his shipping. He routinely placed his ships with flags of convenience, most of them were flagged in non-European, distant countries. He avoided taxes, gave sub-levels of personnel wages, performed illegal mid-ocean ship to ship transfers, declared bankruptcy and abandoned old ships, and on and on. It is obvious that Mr. Johnson and Mr. Mariniti really did not want to continue a business partnership. We will follow this relationship, but expect it to fade away."

"The Committee is currently thinking that the very tall well-dressed Canadian lawyer, who is running around Europe making contacts with nanotech oriented people, and is named Jordon and/or Oliver Johnson, could be our Mr. Korrectorizer. I know Aykut is also checking out this Mr. Johnson. So, the man's life and working background are being very thoroughly checked from North America and from Europe. I do not know what will happen. It depends upon what the Committee learns about this man. Will they want us to continue working with nanotech control, or have us leave him alone so they can deal with him? There certainly is an important new face in the picture. Each of you let me know your feelings. Is he Korrectorizer, the killer of our fathers, and whom we have been dueling for the past almost twenty years? If it is determined to be so, and he is in some way punished by someone else, such as official circles, will this be enough 'revenge' for us?

"Think seriously about it. We may or may not have the American political and science systems to help if we decide to continue trying to neutralize the negative aspects of the nanotech systems by focusing on our father's killer. They may want us to back out and let them pursue this Johnson without us." What I am trying to say is if he is the organizer of the assassination of our fathers and more than 1000 other people, should we, can we just walk away?

No one could respond!

23

THE END?

Over the next several weeks, Oliver-Jordon Johnson, American, or Jordon-Oliver Johnson, Canadian, was placed under the American social-security-political-judicial microscope, and examined in detail. Aykut and his cybertech hacking friend, Asu, from Europe dug deeply, semi-legally, into all Jordon Johnson and Oliver Johnson information sites in Europe, Asia, and Africa. Where did he really come from? How did he get to be where he is? Where is he going? Was it possible that this man was responsible for several hundred macabre deaths worldwide during the past 10-15 years? If so, he had certainly covered his tracks well. He was not even under major suspicion.

Uncle Dagda and the four musketeers compared and jogged their memory banks. They talked and talked. This guy was not directly found. Korrectorizer was there, somewhere, but not a Jordon/Oliver Johnson. There was not a lot of good evidence for immediate criminal indictments. The nano-weapons were made in country A, used to kill in countries B or C, and traveled via international carriers a, b, or c. The macabre deaths were usually in countries B or C or D, hence evidence of the assassinations, murders, killers, homicides, or executions were not directly found in the USA. Americans were not directly involved. So American laws were not directly involved. All evidence had to be gathered through second country or international laws and permissions. Often such was not feasible, nor even possible. Access in Asia, Africa, and South America were not always easy to obtain, especially if a non-American was not directly involved.

A 'ton' of printed information was produced about the real 'persons' of Jordon Johnson and Oliver Johnson. They were indeed genetically related, somehow. And they sort of grew up together, worked side by side for many years on Capitol Hill in Washington, DC, and in a law-lobby set of companies involved with nanotechnology. If one, or both, of them was the Korrectorizer, was he organizer/leader, manufacturing/transport coordinator, promotor/ salesman, or what of the mass killings which had been happening around the world during the past 10+ years. He/they certainly was/were deeply involved in nanotechnology, cure or kill!

The Committee of Nanotechnology Control in Washington, DC was meeting to discuss this Oliver or Jordon Johnson person(s) and to resolve which way to go with reviewing his past. It could be criminal charges of murdering several hundred people, or dropping the charges, temporarily, and putting him 'on ice'. One major problem— every lawyer and lobbyist in Washington, DC, knew Jordon Johnson and Oliver Johnson and was his (their) friend! All new detailed information and recent government data would be presented to the committee members today, hopefully.

All twelve committee members were present at their routine Washington meeting site. Therefore, Mr. John Reasoner brought the committee to order and opened the meeting. He welcomed everyone and then turned over the presentation to Mr. Dagda Murphy, who had been making the daily decisions concerning the nanotech investigative events in all countries for nearly twenty plus years.

Mr. Murphy began, "Welcome to our last meeting of this year. Much has happened during the past year. One of our boys, now grown up, has successfully established a winning formula on two fronts in Nigeria. I will first briefly describe each of them."

"In northeastern Nigeria there have been numerous cattle raids by a large group of foreign invaders/mercenaries. Some of these, mostly non-Nigerians, have now been intercepted by the Nigerian military. Such efforts required assistance of the African Queen of Voodoo (and her trained poisonous snakes). The Queen is Nigerian, living in western Nigeria, and readily cooperated with the Nigerian military. The military dropped baskets of her pet snakes from our military drones into the invaders' campsites. In addition, the nanotech system which was used by these invaders on the villagers during their village raids was inhibited by a neutralizing chemical which was provided by another one of our boys. Therefore, the combination of gifts from the Queen, which were dropped onto the campsites, plus the anti-cellulose gas in the villages, sprayed on the 'exposed' villagers, resulted in disruption of several invader groups."

"In southern Nigeria the oil theft and nanotech killings have decreased in number. We think this is because some of the probable leaders of the nanotech system attacks also met with the African Queen of Voodoo's mutant daughters and their pet poisonous snakes. At a nightly meeting of the leaders, who were coordinating the siphoning oil from oil pipelines and then using the nanotech poisoning of the villages to distract the police, many of them met their snake fates from Voodoo sources. Needless to say, the leaders who lost the battle, did not return to Sweden for schooling. At least temporarily they lost some of the petroleum war, which apparently had also begun in several other regions of the South-South."

"Now, another piece of information, as 'carefully' researched by one of our other musketeers, was collected and later relayed to us. It involved some excellent electronic information sent to us concerning Mr. Jordon Johnson's several bank accounts. Outside of the USA, the Canadian-American has six bank accounts in four different banks, all non-American. There is more than 1.3 billion Euro all total. He has paid no taxes in the USA or Canada during the past several years. The summaries of this new information are being forwarded to the Committee."

"This temporarily ends a brief information report from our musketeers."

"Now most importantly, we have identified this Canadian-American (or American-Canadian) who just might be the Korrectorizer that we have been seeking for so long. He is probably an American living here in Washington, DC. He has taken his adopted uncle/father's name, Jordon Johnson, and has a citizenship/passport from Canada. This he uses to routinely go to and from his other house on Tortola Island in the British Virgin Islands. From there, away from his lawyer colleagues and family, he focuses on his nanotech killing program. And from there he travels to meet with his contact associates, nanotech scientists, transporters, and salesmen, mostly in Europe, Africa, and South America. He spends one or two months each year working in the British Virgin Islands."

"One conclusion we are making," added Mr. Reasoner, "is that we have a situation where most components of these international killings, using nanotech systems, is predominately controlled from outside the USA by a 'legal' Canadian citizen. Therefore, obtaining data on a 'non-American', is difficult. Also, many of the countries where the killings occur, do not cooperate in our attempts at a 'complete' investigation of their citizens."

Continuing, "What we need is to discuss the possible ways and means as to how we can obtain more, complete, and targeted information and data concerning the 'lawyer advisor/consult façade' that Mr. Johnson uses, American or Canadian. And we definitely want to keep him in the center of the picture. Let us please focus on this for a few minutes, and consider other geological facts."

"Please look at this map of downtown Washington, District of Columbia, USA:—1600 Pennsylvania Avenue, NW, White House – 1818 H Street, NW, World Bank Headquarters – 700 19th Street, NW – International Monetary Fund Headquarters – the center of a major control of world currencies – 2219 I Street, NW, Offices of the Nanotech Com I – 2021 Pennsylvania Avenue, office of Dagda's Washington Center of Nanotech Research. You will note that several key players are physically within a couple of blocks of each other. We think that one of the two Mr. Johnsons has used this location, hired the proper people, and continuously milked information from our research plans and efforts. We even have two of these people identified and hope soon to use them for future reverse spying."

"Now we will try to answer questions from committee members."

The day following the Committee meeting Uncle Dagda was sitting in Joe's Organic Lunch Café at 2025 Pennsylvania avenue, NW. This was near his small Washington condo-office at 1903 K Street, NW, which he used when in DC on business. He was sitting at a single private table eating a large tuna salad and drinking fat-free milk. Suddenly glancing up, he met eye to eye with a very tall, slim, medium aged, dark brown skin, black eyes, light color hair, very well-dressed, obviously a lawyer, entering the restaurant. In the recent Johnson info, he had seen many pictures of Oliver Johnson. Yes, this was him. He was now looking directly at the possible 'killer' that he had been chasing for many years. He knew that Johnson's law firm was only a couple blocks away at 2219 I Street, NW. And he often thought he might accidently meet this Oliver Johnson here someday. But he was still shocked when he did so. The two of them exchanged 'knowing' looks, as if each was the sudden enemy returning form the dead. Was this supposition, fictitious, or reality? Was he hallucinating? He would know soon as he had already started considering which psychological pressures to use.

But he had made his final decision about this man. He deserved to be punished. And he convinced the musketeers to be involved. They were preparing to implement a strip down search psychological-psychiatric treatment to help Mr. Johnson see just what he had done with his life—kill several hundred people.

It was March 10, 2048, in Great Falls, Virginia, the home of the Johnson family, Oliver, Chole, Condor, Catherine, and two dogs, Git and Go, were all in fast motion. Tonight, was Dad's fiftieth birthday. The once in a lifetime celebration was about to begin. Invited were only family and several personal friends of Dad.

Oliver Johnson, born and raised by a non-married mother in the Brooklyn, New York ghetto was left with no family or friends behind when she died ten years ago. Uncle/father and his wife/second mother did not have any children; so, when they went, there was a large genetic gap in Oliver's family. Chole, being several years younger, arranged full time health care for her elderly parents in the Great Falls house. Chole's two sisters, husbands, and their five children had arrived for the party. The children were already in the games room playing double pool. And Oliver had three close male friends, one was an ex-President of the USA, one was a Chief Justice of the American Supreme Court, the other was a lawyer/lobbyist law partner who held a permanent contract with the Club of American Senators, and their wives, all who would soon arrive. It would be a large exclusive party of twelve adults and seven teenage high schoolers, plus two 200-pound dogs. But they had adequate space in their 5,000 sq ft mansion. Tonight, they had also retained three extra cooks and waiters. It is frequently said, always save the most and best for last. Maybe tonight there was a possibility this would begin.

By 8:00 PM, all guests had arrived. Each was served white wine and began circulating in and out of the large and small salons, and the games room. Men were talking in a group with men about European and African politics, the armed rebels in Brazil, new government efforts to fight carbon pollution, weather predictions for this winter, and Oliver's favorite sport—college basketball playoffs. The women were talking in a group comparing children's schools, new French dessert recipes, new Swarovski crystal jewelry, and Mediterranean vacations for this summer. Soon all were seated, food was served and a glass of red wine was added for a meal of leg of lamb, carrot-peas-squash casserole, beet tower salad with mint, hot pain d'or, and for dessert, mousse au chocolate and fresh Brazilian coffee.

After dinner the children brought in the stack of presents with Dad's name on them. He always passed his presents around so everyone could enjoy the surprises inside. This year it included a Rolex pocket watch-micro-recorder, new i-padXLZ, gold cuff-links, personalized bottle of 35-year old Jack Daniels, vinyl of Everything Johnny Cash, book on Chinese bonsai, and a digital photo album. His son, Condor gave him a new baseball glove because his other one was worn out. His daughter, Catherine gave him a new thumb print double touch lock briefcase. And his wife, Chole gave him a custom designed Giorgo Armani deep blue, three piece all wool suit from Saks Fifth Avenue in New York City. Each male friend brought to him nice expensive camping gifts. Yes, Oliver had a very good family and friends who loved him.

One of the waiters gave him a bottle of Dom Perignon champagne which he immediately popped open. He then motioned that son and daughter should open the next two bottles. All children and adults were over sixteen. Besides sleeping on the floor can be fun. And there were lots of beds and waiters to help you.

As things began to get merry, there was the doorbell. Fed Ex delivered what looked to be a package containing a very large painting. Everyone sang Happy Birthday again as Dad opened it. He then held it up and showed it to everyone. What was it? All stared and stared and stared. What was it?

A letter accompanied the painting/picture said:

'This is a picture of five of the three hundred murdered high-tech scientists at the Istanbul Massacre in 2032. Do you recognize any of them?'

When one looked carefully one could distinguish five pink body bag sized balloon like things with what could be two dark eyes in what could be an upper head area. Directly under each balloon was a grave stone. On each stone it gave a person's name and birth-death dates. It was gross. It was awful. One could almost smell stench coming from the picture.

Everyone stared at Oliver while silently asking what and why? The men knew. The women thought they knew. The children did not know. It was best to keep it that way. Was it an appropriate time for everyone to disappear?

Oliver could not meet anyone's eyes. So, he quickly re-wrapped the present and took it upstairs to his bedroom, shut and locked the door. He did not come back down. Obviously, the birthday party was over. Without saying a word, everyone just took their jackets and coats and went home.

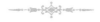

Mr. Dagda Murphy, as father of his fatherless four musketeers from four different parts of the world, had regularly exchanged ideas and potential points of attack on who they now believed was the true murderer of the boys' fathers, and probably several hundred others. They considered the possibility that this man may have entered the nanotech molecular system of weapons by following in his uncle/father's footsteps. However, when he really understood what the nanotech systems were doing to people, not just killing them but destroying them and their families, he still did not stop the nanotechnology. The money was just too good. They determined that he was easily banking several hundred million tax-free euros each year.

So, the 'last' war effort would be to bomb Mr. Oliver-Jordan Johnson with viscous psychiatric and psychological attacks—**VICTIMS**—pictures and headlines in newspapers, magazines, colored prints and various sizes of types published with dates, photographs before and after deaths. Mr. Murphy had five filing cabinets full of newspaper clippings and published articles of the stories and pictures of the many nanotech killings and dated official information. All of this and more could be sent by hand, and various professional carriers such as USPS, and FEDX. All could be delivered directly to the Johnson offices, to his post boxes, and to his Great Falls house. Some could even be delivered to his wife and children!

Dagda Murphy would organize and direct all psychological efforts of guilt. The boys would be only indirectly involved. Mr. Murphy lived almost next door to the Nanotech Com I Offices. It was easy to control what and where delivery could be easily carried out any day. But he was technically a government employee. He had to be very careful. The boys were far away, if legal problems should backfire on them.

Over the next several weeks, Oliver Johnson continuously received pictures and explanations of those pictures regularly by post, e-mail, cell phone attachments, land line telephone, messengers, written notes or envelopes containing pictures of the nanotech dead which were placed in his office building where he would see them, under his office door which the janitors saw and read, office in-mail boxes, under the car windshield wipers, and in the home post-box. Oliver soon developed an elevated heart rate and abnormal pulse condition, acid stomach, lost weight, was having trouble concentrating on his work, suddenly started greying, and of course avoided his colleagues and friends as much as possible. He even had two light strokes.

After a few weeks of this psyco-warefare, he developed defibrillation migraine headaches, which would not go away. But he could not see a doctor. He could not explain his problem to anyone. It was all his BIG secret.

Just when he thought he could handle this 'blackmail', the pictures started coming every day by e-mail, cartoon post, spam, land line phone, and personal messengers. The sender(s) even threatened to send death pictures directly to the house, to his wife. If so, he would not be able to adequately explain those twenty plus years living with her. They had been married most of the time that Uncle Jordon had been organizing and developing the nanotech company. And he had founded it outside of the United States, without him, so he, Oliver, was legally innocent. Only when he inherited the company did he also inherit a British Virgins Island Company that successfully sold death as the major product. He knew this, so he then became legally guilty.

When the sender(s) threatened to send nasty macabre pictures to the children, he panicked and cried for help. He did not know 'to whom'. But the 'to whom' knew.

A message was sent to him telling him to go to his house on Tortola Island for a work break and short vacation. He replied by purchasing his British Virgin Islands plane tickets for the coming weekend, letting his island house-office caregiver know he was coming, but he would not need him. Then he reserved the smaller Luhrs cruiser for himself for a few of days of leisure cruising.

After that Commission's meeting a few weeks ago, Dagda had contacted his cousin, the High Priestess of Irish Witchcraft, who contacted her international witch colleagues of the World Witches Conclave. She discussed the situation concerning Oliver-Jordon Johnson with them. And then the Priestess asked her two special friends what should be done? They gave her their opinions. There was only one possible solution. The Priestess told Dagda who relayed that info to Jamie, and that solution had been immediately placed into action. Hence the regular delivery of the pictures and descriptions of the many macabre nanotech killings had begun in earnest. Jamie later contacted his three musketeer buddies and explained a new plan. He then sent them to the British Virgin Islands to make further suggested special preparations. They would arrive, hotel, taxi, and work separately. Now it was only a matter of time.

The combination of flights from Washington to Tortola Island required one long day of travel such that arrival time was late evening. Upon arrival, 'Jordon' Johnson took a taxi directly to the house, entered the back way into the kitchen, from the refrigerator took and drank a complete bottle of pineapple juice, his favorite, and fell into an exhausted sleep.

He awoke the next morning near noon. Somewhat refreshed, he grabbed another bottle of pineapple juice, turned on the coffee machine, and opened a package of sesame rolls. Suddenly, as he looked around, he saw that the walls were filled with pictures. He looked. Yes, they were the same macabre pictures that the family had been receiving during the past several weeks. He could not handle it. He broke down again into a sobbing cry. Did he really kill all of those people? No! It was not possible. Uncle/father did it! And he went back to bed. He laid down. But as he looked at the ceiling he read:

CONGRATULATIONS – 1000 DEATHS—
A NEW WORLD RECORD
NO GUNS – NO BULLETS
AMAZING

And he cried himself to sleep, again. Waking late afternoon, and calling the boat renters and a taxi, picked up his daughter's gift i-pad XLZ plus three flash- drives, and the taxi took him to the main pier control office. He obtained the keys and checked the boat out for five days. At slip 432 he boarded his red and white Luhrs Cruiser, checked the kitchen shelves to verify adequate provisions, and embarked into the waters north of Tortola Island. He entered a very large area of more than fifty large and small islands scattered just north of the British Virgin Islands. He loved the gray-blue wide-open ocean with no living two legged entities anywhere. He always thought of it as '**Mr. Comfort**'.

Sitting on a rock-tree projection of land on the Hawks Nest/Bahan Ghut Mountain top and looking into the north from Tortola Island, now together, the four musketeers sat on and leaned back in the grass and hard rocks and stared out into the Atlantic Ocean. They were seeking a small red and white Luhrs cruiser. They spotted it going north into the Atlantic. And were carefully following it.

Kef spoke up, 'I'm sure that the vial of sedative herbal extract, which the African Queen of Voodoo gave to me, and which I placed into his bottles of pineapple juice, will allow him to have a comfortable sleep such that he can be at peace with himself. Now can we really be at peace with ourselves?"

"He was a good businessman, a good lawyer, and a very good father."

"But he was a very terrible human being."

And Ey'tuka, Tsu'teye, Na'via, and Mo'ata looked up into the ocean's sun set. However, they could not look each other in the eyes.

The red-white boat slowly disappeared behind one of the small islands. Suddenly their lives were gone. For twenty years, they had chased the man who killed their fathers. Now he was gone. There was nothing left. What would they do?

The 150 mph hurricane Dagda hit the British Virgin Islands two days later.

The red and white Luhrs Cruiser was never seen again.

Mr. Oliver–Jordon Johnson was never seen again.

NANO TRILOGY

SYNOPSIS

NANO TRILOGY – III
NANOTARGETED VILLAGES

DEVELOPMENT OF A NEW type of super macabre nanotech molecular system for group use; new system proves to be very powerful and difficult to control; this offensive system is used to attack several villages and kill hundreds of people; the boys, by now grown professionals, develop their own counter molecular weapons program; battles in African villages now employ American high-tech military weapons, including special molecular counter weapons, US military mini drones, witch's herbs and trained poisonous snakes, all of which allow critical victories for the musketeers; the industrial leader, named Korrectorizer, is traced from New York to Washington, D.C., to the Caribbean and to Europe; he is trapped by the musketeer team; they learn he was their fathers' killer; revenge was initiated; however, a body was never found.

Printed in the USA
CPSIA information can be obtained
at www.ICGtesting.com
LVHW051918210924
791652LV00019B/272

enjoy and while outside of the gym she always returned to her imperious, demanding, sadistic self, inside it at least she became again someone it was nice to be with.

And still Barry Williams and she continued to invent horrible items of torture…

The latest in that series was based on your normal home stationary bike although their model was absolutely diabolical in how it tortured us.

Basically, it had the same components as such an exercising aid although with certain critical modifications. There were no handlebars as the hands were required to be held up behind the head as in the first position of slavery. And similarly, there was no saddle.

Let me describe my first session on it. As I was ordered to this new room and stood in the doorway looking at this machine, I was immediately struck with horror for the implications were very apparent. She pushed me over to it and ordered me to climb up, placing my left foot into the lockable pedal and then swing my right leg over the frame and rear wheel to be similarly locked into the other one. Below me I could see the mechanism that would drive the wheel behind and below me and to which were attached four long, very thin strips of leather.

The other part was driven by a vertical crank shaft encased in a couple of journals that held it securely and allowed it to move smoothly up and down. Screwed onto its threaded top piece was a large, cigar-shaped plug, clearly destined for my backside. And just in front of that was yet another vertical shaft similarly attached to the frame that had a small noose attached to its top. Both of the shafts could be easily extended or retracted by means of a knurled screw that when loosened, allowed the inner shaft in each case to be adjusted and then the screw tightened again.

The despicable Williams was on hand to attend to the fine details of my being mounted on this rather fearful instrument. I could see that once he had adjusted the first of those two of the shafts so that with the crank at its topmost point, he extended the cigar-shaped object up and into my anus so that when the shaft retracted to its lowest point it couldn't drop out.

The other shaft with its little plastic loop at the top was destined for my testicles and he first unscrewed the locking collar and raised the inner shaft until the tip was near my balls then carefully secured the cord around their root.

He now directed me to pedal slowly so he could check out that both these adjustments were working satisfactorily, the one to repeatedly fuck my arse and the other to stretch my balls.

But that was only half the story. I mentioned the wheel and its four leather thongs. These of course were destined for my bottom and once I got up to speed, they would extend out and whip my buttocks, both of them in a somewhat random attack that would eventually develop horrible welts all over the two cheeks.

There was one final component of this machine that really set off its horrible function. Williams had attached a small dynamo to the frame that was driven by the rear wheel and the power it generated was used to regulate an electric current whose electrodes were that cigar shaped plug up my backside and what I had thought was plastic but was in fact a highly conductive material wrapped around the root of my balls.

She explained it to me in her usual glee at outlining a new and horrible pain for Roger and me. He incidentally had been perched on a pedestal with a massive buttplug at its tip, being hoisted up and over it and then lowered down onto it to suffer his own pain at the intrusion while watching me generate mine by my own efforts.

"You are shortly going to pedal, scum." And then she pointed up to a large meter on the wall facing me that had two needles. One was red; the other black. "The red needle indicates the speed you are required to pedal at, whilst the other indicates your current speed. If, once you have achieved that minimum speed, and the device is activated, if you then let your speed drop below the minimum, you will receive a particularly nasty shock between your arse and your balls…"

She smiled sweetly at me while explaining all this and standing at the console that controlled all of its workings. "Start pedalling, scum. You have five seconds to get up to speed and then I will switch on the punishment device."

I didn't hesitate, applying all of my strength to those pedals so as to get that black needle up past the red one. I almost made it but then just as the needle was hovering over the other one the most horrible pain erupted down at my middle. Fortunately it only took just one last thrust with my feet to get it past the needle and that horrible shock disappeared.

I now knew that I was in for one awful day. She hadn't mentioned how long I was going to be kept on this machine although I assumed that Roger would also have his stint on it before she called it quits.

The effort was not impossible but it was considerable and I knew that as I pedalled, my body would be moving sinuously to counterbalance each successive thrust of my legs and of course this was what she wanted. Oh she delighted in seeing me suffer but it was just as much the sight of the muscles of my body moving that pleased her so much.

She left the console then and strolled up beside me, watching avidly as my thigh on that side strained and then relaxed with each revolution of the pedals and then she reached out and let her fingers rove over them.

She then let her other hand stray down to my buttocks, now being lashed quite hard by those four very thin strips of leather. They had been purposely designed to require many, many applications before the effects of those thin lashes would really begin to tell, however in stroking my buttocks as they assisted in the pedalling motion, her hands came under the lash of those strips and she pulled it back swiftly but then smiled as she realised that the pain she was now feeling in her hand was being delivered by those four lashes with every revolution of the wheel.

But then she smiled in glee as she recognised that my buttocks not to mention my anus and testicles were soon going to be very, very sore indeed.

I wanted desperately to ask her, 'How long?' But I managed to stifle the plea. But she anticipated my question anyway. "You want to know how long I'm going to leave you on this, don't you, scum?"

"Yes, Mistress. My buttocks and anus and testicles are already in great pain. I hope you're not going to leave me on this machine for too long?"

"Oh, you're going to have plenty of time to consider your sins, boy," she said with patently obvious glee. "You can have the whole day on it… Enjoy!"

I slumped down in defeat but continued to pedal as that first shock had been really horrible. It's a case of the lesser of two evils, isn't it?

As it happened, she had been lying as usual and had Roger and I exchanged after an hour pedalling away at that horrible machine. And then I had to watch as he was installed onto it and began his hour of horror. I have to say though that as I stood, now impaled on that standard he had previously been occupying, and stared up at his magnificent body pedalling away just as I had done, I was startled to 'hear' thoughts from him. I actually looked hard at him to see if his lips were moving for I couldn't believe that he was actually communicating with me mentally rather than verbally.

I concentrated everything on replying to him in the same way and I then noted him turn to look at me from his perch up there on that dastardly machine and we both smiled at one another.

If we were right, this might be yet another tool in our small arsenal of defences against that bitch's mad vendetta against me.

Chapter 5

This new power, very possibly activated by a desperation born of our treatment on that island, rapidly grew from vague ideas to coherent words and then real sentences and so from then on we were very much more able to actually plan our next moves.

He spoke of his framing and how he knew where the evidence of it was, but in my case, we were both very aware that only Frederica's confession could possibly clear me for there had only been the two of us in her room at the time of the alleged offence and all the rest of the evidence had been circumstantial.

Rape is a horrible offence and in my understanding permanently damages the psyche of most women who suffer it. I knew I hadn't been guilty of it but I know that every single one of my friends and my parents and other relations all believed her and not me.

This had hurt me terribly, especially as I was totally innocent. But I couldn't even blame the legal system. As I sat in the court and listened to her evidence, she oozed sincerity and even showed a modicum of sympathy for me which added to her credence and therefore assisted in the judge sentencing me to slavery for the rest of my life. I think what distressed me most was that not a single one of my family or friends took into account my past behaviour and my willingness to help and assist others whenever it was possible.

But to return to the ESP that had now manifested itself between Roger and me, it now grew to the point that even if we were separated by quite a few kilometres. It still seemed to work with the same strength as if we were standing next to each other. It became possible to test this a couple of days later when she decided to take me for a run across to the mainland and the supermarket there.

This was an instance of her sanity coming and going. It was not ever evident during our workouts in her gymnasium, for example. And yet when we finished those and resumed our normal activities, once again she became the despot, delighting in torturing Roger and/or me and of course she had retained Barry Williams and I suspect that when she was consulting with or joining him in fabricating some new horrible device, her madness may have been at its peak.

Surely the most ardent and dedicated sadist does not spend a major portion of their time inventing ways of administering spectacular but horrible forms of pain simply because they want to get back at a person for a conceived slight?

As we became more and more adept at 'thinking' to one another, Roger and I pondered this question almost endlessly – but never came up with an answer that satisfied us.

So far I have outlined some of the so-called punishments that she or he or both of them invented, first of all for me alone, but then including Roger, and finally the other slaves, now all male, you will recall.

It seemed as if she spent her time either devising or helping Williams to build new devices but then delighted in watching her slaves bodies suffering horribly as they were forced to endure what ever it was that particular implement delivered.

Sometimes, instead of waiting for a new device to be finished, she would return to one of the others and you must understand that by no means have I so far described all of them. What I have done in this short account is to try and show just how depraved that woman was and that the fact that she was one of the wealthiest people in the whole of Australia seemed to insulate her from any hope of escape or relief from those trials and tribulations.

But even if it had been possible for Roger and me to somehow escape her clutches, we wouldn't have contemplated it unless it involved the whole slave herd. Why didn't we appeal to Mr Havers, you wonder? The short answer to that is that we didn't dare. He and his wife were still proving as a very welcome buffer between her worst excesses and ourselves and as the pair of them had been very loyal retainers to Frederica's parents and therefore the family, although they very definitely helped us all, we didn't dare risk involving the other slaves in even worst excesses if we had judged them wrongly.

I think perhaps I will now briefly mention some of her other torture machines and how they were used on Roger and me and then turn to the last days and how we escaped her clutches.

The rack is an ancient instrument of torture apparently much favoured in mediaeval times, having been used in the Tower of London from 1447 when it was called the Duke of Exeter's Daughter.

I have now discovered that many modern slave owners who favour exotic methods of punishing their slaves' wrongdoings have equipped their punishment room with such a device. Out of curiosity I researched this use (once I was free of Frederica's domination) and discovered that while some owners favoured a wooden version similar to the mediaeval models, others used stainless steel and modern electrics and electronics in their construction.

Our hated owner favoured the mediaeval model and even dressed Barry Williams up in a brief leather codpiece and mask of the same material over his head to simulate an ancient torturer.

Apart from its basic hardwood rectangular frame supported on four sturdy legs of the same material, it featured an inner frame capable of being raised and lowered between the floor and the outer horizontal frame of the instrument. This inner frame included a grid of smaller timbers that formed the initial bed for the victim.

And yes, of course it was me whom she chose to christen it.

On the day in question, I had been cleaning and polishing her little gig when one of the household slaves rushed up and told me breathlessly that I was required in the slave cellars. I gulped, aware that it had been a few days since I had been 'punished' for some spurious offence and that no doubt now was the time to the next one. But I didn't hesitate, well aware that if she thought for one second that I had not responded instantly to her imperious demand, the 'punishment' so-called might well be doubled.

He pointed me in the direction of the Rack

Room and as I entered and made the appropriate obeisance to her, I also noted that Williams was now dressed up as I described above and was busying himself positioning the leather manacles that would shortly be adorning my wrists and ankles.

"You were most unsatisfactory as my bed-buck last night, slave," she said witheringly. "I think a few hours on the rack may well ginger up your efforts to please me with your body."

Of course I responded appropriately but as she hadn't used either Roger or me as her sexual stooge last night, the point was rather moot. Nevertheless I didn't think about that aspect very much at all as by now, she more often than not didn't even bother creating an excuse to torture one or more of us simply because she felt like it.

Neither of the Havers was present and for some reason I was pleased because more and more lately when they were made to witness such events as this, the expression on their faces were beginning to lead me to believe that they had had enough and weren't far off packing their bags and leaving her employ.

In my mind, this would be far, far worse than their staying because they were still able to exert a degree of restraint at times and anything was better than nothing. I couldn't imagine how bad it might be if she made Barry Williams her slave overseer over all the other slaves and in her present state of mind Roger and I thought that was the most likely result if the Havers' did depart.

Anyway, she gestured towards the bed of the rack and I obediently climbed onto it and spread my arms and legs out towards the four corners, allowing

Williams to secure them in the leather cuffs and then returned to the manually powered winch anchored to the centre of the outer timber frame, around the drum of which had been wound a length of rope so that its two ends reached out towards the pulleys at the top corners and thence down to my wrists. Rotating the handle activated the drum drawing both ends of that rope inwards and thus tightening it and stretching my body until it was just short of being painful.

"And now the inner frame if you please, Barry."

"Yes, Mistress," he said unctuously in his usual fawning tones, but then moved to the side where was situated a wooden wheel with a handle which he then rotated and I felt the bed on which I was lying drop down from under me. The various joints in my body from wrists, elbows, shoulders, hips, knees and ankles were all now under a strain from the weight of my body and the pain became very noticeable.

Above me, she stared down at my naked body in pleasure. Apparently, stretched out as it now was, the muscles gave it a new aspect for her and she reached down to lightly run her fingertips over them all from the biceps in my right arm down over the shoulder muscles, the pectorals and all the rest of them.

This was very possible because Williams had constructed the whole instrument so that she would have easy access to every part of my body. The inner frame was thus only thirty centimetres wide although the outer frame thirty-five centimetres so that her fingertips could easily reach any part of my body.

I hung there sagging just a little at the middle but this didn't please her one little bit. "It's much too slack, Barry. Just look how much he's sagging…"

He didn't hesitate and as he now rotated that handle and its ratchet clicked ominously and quite loudly (made so on purpose by him) the pain in my joints, all of them, increased almost exponentially and I screamed and moaned appropriately, well aware that she wouldn't be satisfied until I did. Again she ran her fingers over my whole body leaving my genitals until last but then feeling and fondling them until I was rampantly erect when she imperiously held out her hand towards Williams who jumped in response and guessing her requirement fetched a small rubber-tailed whip and handed to her.

Of course she didn't thank him. She rarely thanked anyone for anything, but took the whip and then lashed at my cock and balls a few times screaming at me about my ancestry, my uselessness, my rudeness in refusing her attentions and of course the non-existent rape by which she had engineered my conviction and sentence to slavery for the rest of my life.

The pain of my suspension was now sending horrible barbs all over my body and my unsupported head must have been flailing this way and that as I attempted to cope with that pain as well as the growing agony in my genitals.

What I feared at first in these horrible moments was that she would lose her reason completely and, in this case, order Williams to continue operating the winch until my arms or possibly my thighs would be torn from my body. But the part of her brain that was still sane seemed to step in just in time and save me from possible death, and that's what happened at that moment.

"Bring the bed backup, Barry," she said and then went on: "and you can then release him. But it's a very good machine. You have done very well." And at that point, she turned on her heel and walked out and just as quickly, Mr Havers appeared as he didn't trust Barry Williams one iota and he oversaw my careful release by the de-tensioning of the ropes and my removal entirely from the instrument, after which he led me up to her suite, ordering me in a quite loud voice to sort through all her clothes seeking out those that needed cleaning or any repairs. But when we arrived he had me move each of the joints in my body, starting with my right ankle and moving up to the knee, hip, shoulder, et cetera on both sides and nodding when all seem to be in perfect working order.

"You were lucky this time, Peter. And you may be sure that I really do feel for you but I can tell you now that Mary and I are just about ready to pack our bags. I know it's far worse for you and your slave companions but she is responding less and less to my pleadings on your behalf in the pair of us are sick to our stomachs at having to witness her madness."

"You agree she is mad, Mr Havers?" I knew I was taking a risk in phrasing that statement the way I did but I had finally decided that enough was enough.

I was lucky. He responded as I had hoped.

93

"Yes, I do now. It has taken me a long time and in hindsight, I should have seen it earlier. But the problem is, as I have no doubt that you are well aware, she is perfectly entitled with the full backing of the law to do everything she has already done to you all but you and Roger in particular." He looked at me shrewdly for a few seconds and then went on: "You didn't violate her, did you, boy?"

"No sir, I didn't. She had prepared a small container with her vaginal juices and the moment she got me into her room smeared them all over my cock and then screamed that terrible word – and you are well aware of the result.

"No one. Not even my parents or my best friends believe my story which, I have to admit, is pretty unbelievable anyway…"

"For what it's worth, Peter, I believe you. But I can't see that being much use to you. The only way you are going to be able to get free of her is for her to admit to her own guilt and I can't see that as a very likely possibility, can you?"

I shook my head but smiled tenuously at him. "No I can't, sir, but your vote of confidence has really bucked me up and I'm sure Roger will be just as pleased if I am able to communicate your confidence to him."

You will note I was still being very careful and certainly hadn't revealed that I could interact with my friend mentally.

"Be careful, boy. She is vigilant and if she once suspects your loyalty, I hate to think what the consequences might be. As to Roger, I have an inner feeling that he is as innocent of his crime as you are. Am I right?"

94

I nodded. "Yes, indeed, sir. I believe he was framed..." I didn't go into any more detail because you will recall we were not supposed to be communicating with another slave at all and although I wanted to believe that the butler and his wife were on our side, they had been loyal retainers to her mother and father virtually all their working lives and to switch camps as seemed to be the case could just as easily be a ploy on her part to uncover resistance or, horror of horrors, a slave rebellion.

He left me then and while I began to check through her clothes, I also communicated to Roger all that had occurred since I had been stretched on the rack. He was both sympathetic and horrified but he also agreed that the butler was on our side, commenting that we had both noticed that the pair of them were more and more appalled at what their employer was doing to we slaves – all of us, now.

But of course, as we both agreed, they were still powerless to help us in any material way. As we all knew, she was perfectly entitled to do almost anything she damned well liked to and with us and we had no recourse at law, or in any other way to counter her.

To my mind, this was a major defect in the *Slavery Act* and it needed rectifying. God knows how many slave owners were abusing their property in the same way she was. I'm not saying for one moment that the institution had not been a wonderful saviour for the planet as a whole or even that the draconian nature of it hadn't been necessary in those early days, but I think that the time may now be ripe for a review of the worst aspects of the institution with a view to avoiding the excesses as I have described them in this little account.

The days continued with each passing one making both Roger and I more and more nervous about which of us was going to be singled out next for one of her diabolical punishments and what its nature might be.

But we also decided to try and communicate mentally with somebody in high places with a view to making them aware just how bad things were in some situations involving slaves and slavery.

Yes, I will admit that in our case our owner was in all probability insane but although her paid employees were well aware of that, there was no-one to whom they could turn to relieve the situation since everything she had done to us was perfectly legal. The only way we were going to obtain any alleviation of our terrible situation was for her to be stopped in her tracks and with all her resources I had no idea whatsoever as to how that might be achieved.

But enough of all this soliloquising. No matter how I looked at it I couldn't for the life of me dream up any solution that might have even a glimmering of a chance. And so Roger and I continued attempting to contact others outside the island and perhaps in a position of influence but to no avail.

How and why the pair of us had managed to achieve something no human being before us had experienced, we had no idea. Yes I have heard and read of instances in wartime when a mother has sat up in bed in the middle of the night and sensed that her son had died – and later investigation had revealed that it had been at that moment but that is the only type of extrasensory perception that has ever been given very much credence at all.

And so he and I continued to develop this new talent by practising it, especially when we were apart such as when I was galloping Frederica around the streets of Southport in her gig – and still we waited for the next horror she and Williams could come up with. And the more we did so, the more accurate and detailed it became. But still we were unable to make contact in this way with other people, not even William or Mary Havers with whom we now felt were very much on our side.

Nevertheless, we felt sure that it was therefore a purpose even if we didn't yet understand what that might be.

One of the last devices Williams created for her was a larger version of her little gig, this one designed for two – and yes, Roger was now to be my partner on her little excursions across the bridge to the mainland.

Actually, I suspect it may have been the similarity between our two physiques as well as the contrast of our two skin colours that may have prompted her to suggest it to him, but it matters little either way.

The new vehicle was very much more elaborate and comfortable for her than the original model although of course the basic design was still the same. In order to accommodate two human ponies instead of one, Williams retained the original single pole but bifurcated it a metre out from its front but of course retained the butt-plug and cuff system of harnessing us to it.

She was delighted with the new vehicle and lost

no time in ordering us to begin our new joint training. It was nothing new to me of course but Roger found it pretty uncomfortable at first. And from the very first steps we both realised that trotting or otherwise running as a pair required us to synchronise our steps because if we didn't, the movement in our backsides became very uncomfortable indeed. Nevertheless, we were both natural athletes and we soon found our rhythm and once that was achieved, we could gradually increase our speed until we were virtually galloping around the track that ran right around the island and, while you may find this difficult to believe, we actually began to exult in that duty.

The wind in our faces, our close proximity to each other and the fact that while we were aware that she was sitting in her beautiful new gig behind us, she was out of sight and we could therefore, at least to some extent put her out of our minds.

The time came when she decided we were sufficiently trained to take us across to the mainland and I'm sure you won't be surprised to hear that we created quite a furore as we now galloped her along the Esplanade towards the shopping centre at Southport, both our cocks at full mast and slamming violently from side to side with each step, and when she ordered us into its car park and we found a spot to park, a quite large crowd gathered around us, half of which stood around Roger and me whilst the others congratulated her on such a wonderful equipage.

Williams had provided this vehicle with a parking brake system which she could lock on and protect us from theft but I suspect this journey was more to test the water so to speak as to public acceptance of the new idea than any real need for her to shop.

The answer to that was patently obvious for there were approbations all-round and not a single hint of criticism from any of them and Mr Havers later whispered to me that not only was she being applauded by the locals but the media had caught on to the idea and the newspapers and television stations had all featured us in their local news coverage.

This had a very positive effect on her attitude to the pair of us and for quite a while she left off punishing me for perceived faults and even extended her gymnastics sessions and that meant that he and I also had more time there.

This was wonderful for you will recall when we were in that mode, she was actually quite civil to me and I actually dared to think that perhaps it may have been a turning point in her madness but in that I was to be sorely disappointed and she soon returned to devising new ways of giving me grief.

The last of her 'punishments' I shall describe involved what I believe are called penal enemas. Most people will know that an enema is simply the insertion of water at various temperatures and with a large range of additives into the anus and rectum once considered a remedy for all manner of human ailments and was even reportedly used in the treatment of the so-called madness that afflicted King George III.

That belief has now been largely discredited but the process has lingered on with the BDSM

(Bondage and Discipline; Sado-Masochism) aficionados when extremely large doses are administered and then the 'bottom', whose belly is probably now distended as if he was carrying twins, is forced to perform a series of exercises with or without a butt-plug to keep the dose inside him. Sometimes the addition of chemicals to cause effervescence to take place which will create gases that will bloat him even more may be added.

I believe it was Barry Williams who put her up to this horrible variety of BDSM activity, no doubt expounding on the extreme discomfort being forced to perform such exercises as sit-ups while holding in a litre or more of hot liquid which may be churning away inside one's belly.

As usual, she had allocated yet another of the small rooms in the basement of the mansion for this 'punishment', for she still harboured and promoted the myth that each of these tortures was a perfectly legitimate punishment for perceived wrongs. Roger and I were sent for and directed to this new room and while I stared at the set up in mystification, I sensed that Roger, beside me, was aware of what it meant and in a few seconds he was mentally describing to me what it all meant. I can tell you, it took all of my willpower to remain with that innocent expression on my face but from what Roger was describing, I would rather have taken a dozen powerful strokes of the cane to my buttocks than face what he was implying in the message he was sending me.

Alas, it was all too true!

By now, and with the continued use of the Electric Bed, our two bodies were still at their absolute peak of perfection. Again I stress not overly muscled but each one finely wrought and without even a milligram of fat to blur the sharpness of their definition and as usual when we entered her presence, she took time to run her fingertips over the both of us examining each muscle group in great detail and commenting to Williams how well she had honed and toned our muscles so as to present probably the finest example of male slavery in Australia – and even perhaps the world.

Her words implied that we had nothing to do with this development. We were simply animals whom she had taken in hand and trained to be the best.

Now I know that the institution of criminal slavery had been designed largely with this intention so as to make it the most feared form of criminal punishment ever devised. But in my understanding, very few slave owners took that policy to the lengths she did so far as it related to Roger and me.

Yes, her discipline over the other slaves had hardened and they now went in fear of her but with us she took it to lengths I find it difficult to describe. For example caning the anus whilst we are required to lay on our backs, grasp our knees from behind and draw them up and out to expose it thus offering the anus perfectly for the attentions of her cane which she then lashes down on the anal ring with full force.

Yes I'm sure you are shuddering and may even be feeling nauseous as you read these lines but I assure you that such an order was certainly not beyond the pale and I can only thank my lucky stars and the incredible fitness of my circulatory system that the healing blood quickly mended any wounds she might inflict although the pain which is possibly the worst I have ever felt, took longer to go away.

But to return to the enemas, Williams had created a perfect 'bath' in which we could be secured on a hands and knees but then with our upper bodies forced down onto the floor of the bath so that our buttocks and anus were perfectly exposed, especially as there were straps to secure our knees as wide as they could get them.

He had also created a rather intricate looking plumbing system over the top of the bath and this included a row of inverted glass bottles containing all manner of additives including irritants and substances designed to create the gaseous effect I mentioned above. This enabled him to adjust the flow of the basic water as well as its temperature – anything from 40°C to near freezing.

The contents of individual or multiple bottles could also easily be added to the mix by means of precisely accurate little valves and as we entered and I was directed to climb into the bath to have my limbs secured in the position described above, he was explaining to her what each of the various liquids were and how they affected my bowels.

He was talking in rather low tones and I only caught a few words but the gist was there: I was about to be in for a few hours of hell.

He also showed her the main plug which would be the means by which the water and other ingredients were introduced into my body, pointing out the conical shape that allowed easy entry but would require considerable effort to expel it and in fact it also possessed an inflatable ring behind that large swelling that would make pushing it out by one's own efforts, virtually impossible.

I knelt there in that bath that was wider than your normal domestic bath tub and considerably longer allowing Williams to get in beside me and see to my imprisonment in the bonds and then once he had pushed that large plastic conical plug into my anus, he climbed out of it again to rejoin her at the control panel.

"You see, Mistress, that I can set all the appropriate adjustments including the water flow and its temperature and the additives but none of them will take effect until I turn this final valve that allows the mixture to squirt into his belly…"

She was clearly excited about my coming distress and asked him which was more painful, a rapid filling of my belly or a slow trickle. He grinned gleefully but as I said earlier any smile he put on was more a grimace and such was the case now.

"Both are distinctly uncomfortable but I suspect the gradual build-up of a small flow would be more enjoyable for you as the pain will mount until it is so bad that he will suspect his belly is about to burst. That will be the time to add a measure of sodium bicarbonate that will increase the gaseous effect."

She grinned in that maniacal way she had when contemplating some severe trial for me (and these days Roger, as well) and nodded. "Right, then make it slow."

He made the appropriate adjustments and then pointed to the master valve which was in the form of one of those ball valves with a single handle that moves in a 90° arc.

I could see her face and she was watching me carefully and so as she turned that valve to begin the flow, I grimaced although there was really no pain at all at that point. Nevertheless, as I have tried to show throughout this account, everything I did in relation to her was designed to pander to her desire to see me suffer and the more I could do this – as long as I kept it realistic, the more I could obviate the worst excesses of her trials.

I think that island and her regime on it had turned me into a master showman which Roger already was. Anyway, just as he had taken a leaf out of my book in the pain management stakes, so had I in learning how to fool her as to the degree of pain I was suffering.

In any case, the discomfort as my rectum and lower intestine is began to fill soon began to bite and I fidgeted and moaned and groaned in real discomfort, which of course pleased her no end.

One of the meters on that console kept Williams informed as to the total amount of liquid he had injected inside me as well as the pressure and when these figures indicated no more was advisable, he so informed her and then showed her how to jerk that plug from my anus and at the same time step well clear because she could expect a quite spectacular first jet.

And he wasn't wrong! He first shutdown the various valves that fed the ingredients to the main inlet and then closed that valve as well. He then nodded to her and invited her to do the deed.

The initial shock was the extreme pain as my

anus was rudely stretched wide open by the base of that conical plug but then I could feel the liquids spurting out behind me. By twisting my head I could just see her face and the horrible smile of triumph as she watched the smelly now brown liquid squirt out and form into a puddle at the bottom of the bath because he had inserted the plug so as to add to my horror by the fact that I was now kneeling in my own near liquid faeces.

Fifth As the liquid exited my body, so the flow reduced but eventually it was time to insert clean water in order to flush out any remaining chemicals. This she didn't find nearly as entertaining and curtly informed Williams that he could finish the session himself.

Chapter 6

The end, when it came, was very sudden.

Without any warning at all, her malady suddenly disappeared – totally. This was no temporary lifting such as when we worked out in the gymnasium and not only did it mean that she ceased to harbour that unreasoning resentment of me but became extremely pleasant to everyone on the island even down to the other slaves, that is all of them except Roger and me.

So far as we were concerned, she kept apologising for her behaviour and attitudes and while we were suspicious, thinking this was just another of her horrible ploys to manoeuvre us into positions where she could justifiably (to herself) punish us in one or another of the ways I have attempted to describe in the foregoing pages, we eventually began to realise that she had indeed changed for the better and hoped it was permanent.

The atmosphere on the island slowly began to return to its former state before her parents died and now Roger and I began to wonder what she was going to do about me.

She must have realised just how bad was her framing of me with that spurious cry of rape that had landed me here on this island as a slave to the rest of my life. Of course we didn't mention it to her, scared silly that such a move might well rekindle her madness and then a return to those terrible former days.

So far as Roger was concerned, there was no point in him conjecturing as to how he might turn the tables on those people who had framed him for until he regained his freedom, it was impossible.

We did see a recurrence of her lawyer and investment advisers visits, though, and assumed she was again running her own affairs properly but that's about as far as any thoughts on that subject might go.

So far as Roger and I were concerned, she no longer kept us in her suite and we simply became normal household slaves, sleeping with the others in a virtual cell painted onto the floor of the slave dormitory in the basement.

And then it happened. In the normal course of events we were aroused at 5:30 a.m., hosed down, fed and passed our wastes and to the ground floor and begin our days toil were hard at it (whatever 'it' was) by 6 a.m. But on this occasion, just as we were about to move upstairs, there was an unholy scream from the region of her suite and her new personal slave, a very becoming young female who had replaced Roger and me, came running out to find Mr Havers and to blurt out the news that her mistress was lifeless in her bed.

He gestured for us to accompany him (I wondered then if he had intuitively guessed that it was important for the pair of us to be with him at that time) and when we arrived in her bedroom, saw her lying serenely, dressed uncharacteristically in a charming nightie and with her hand holding a note.

The butler checked her carotid artery for a pulse and shook his head then used the phone beside her bed to call her doctor. He was there within fifteen minutes and checking her mouth indicated that he thought she had taken cyanide but that would have to be confirmed by an autopsy.

The butler then called her solicitor, told him the news and asked if he could call around immediately as he had no idea of who her heir or the executor of her estate was. He told us the solicitor hadn't been informative except to say he would be there as soon as he could get dressed and be on his way. He also added that he would inform the police as this is necessary in the case of suicide or suspected suicide.

As luck would have it the police inspector who arrived was the same one who had conducted the enquiry into my so-called rape of Frederica Masters and I think he had come with the preconceived notion that I had probably somehow managed to murder her and despite the fact that her new personal slave and the butler had both confirmed that I had been nowhere near her or could possibly have tampered with her food, he still looked at me suspiciously – until he was handed the note that explained it all:

I wish to put on record my utter shame and sorrow of the way I have treated Peter Franklin because he refused my invitation to become my boyfriend back in high school. I don't know if I can claim insanity for this but I do know that I am very culpable of engineering and charging him with a non-existent rape during a Sunday barbecue at my home to which I had invited all my school friends. Having secured him as my slave I subjected him to untold horrors all of which were totally un-earned and certainly undeserved. And further seeing that he was interested in Roger Scott, I added him to my revenge and then ensured that from then on he too was treated abominably. Accordingly I apologise to the pair of them and know that only my death will allow them any relief and accordingly have made them joint heirs to my whole estate, excepting only a bequest to my most faithful William and Mary Havers. Having written this, I intend to take cyanide and so end a useless and vindictive life.

After reading this, and verifying the signature at its base, the inspector apologised profusely to me for being so ready to believe her during his investigation of her so-called rape by me. I was polite and civil to him but I still thought he had been far too ready to listen to her and not properly investigate that allegation. He left soon after that and the doctor then saw to the removal of her body while her solicitor confirmed the news in that little note that Roger and I were the principal beneficiaries and that both William and Mary Havers would receive a million dollars each. There were no other beneficiaries but her solicitor then indicated that she had deposited with him a sealed document only to be opened upon her death and he had brought that with him.

It contained a sworn affidavit confirming that

she had lied about her so-called rape and that I was totally guiltless of any crime against her.

The solicitor indicated that this document when presented to the District Court of Queensland would guarantee my freedom but then looked at Roger who immediately confided in him the whereabouts of the evidence that would exonerate him from the false charges laid that had resulted in his slavery and subsequent purchase by Frederica. The solicitor asked the pair of us to give him a couple of days to effect these corrections to our citizenship after which he would lodge her will for probate and from then on we would have effective control of her estate as she had named us both as joint executors with her solicitor.

We were of course utterly stunned by these events. When you have been enslaved for over a year and particularly under the regime she imposed on me and then later, Roger, the almost instant transition back to freedom and even more incredible, the inheritance of her twenty billion dollar estate between us seemed unbelievable.

But when we had jointly come down to Earth, the first thing we did was to go and find William and Mary and apprise them of their and our good fortune and furthermore to ask them to stay on at least until we could find suitable replacements but really indefinitely as we recognised just how important they had been in tempering her mad schemes to punish me and by extension, Roger, particularly over the last few weeks when her madness had seemed to peak.

They had looked at one another and nodded.

"We would enjoy staying on, Peter and Roger and while we certainly have no knowledge or experience about financial management, we do know this house and how it runs and would love to assist you both in returning it to the happy times that we all, and that includes the slaves, used to enjoy under Miss Frederica's parents' regime here.

"Now I imagine that the solicitor is seeing to your freedom but has he suggested that you stay on the island for the moment. Is that correct?"

We nodded. "Yes it is but he said that considering the seriousness of her actions against us, the courts would move swiftly in rectifying both my wrongful conviction for rape and in Roger's case the tampering of examination results."

"Right! Then that will be a perfect time for you to become used to wearing clothing again, won't it?" He was grinning broadly at this and gesturing towards our continued nakedness which of course had totally escaped us.

We had become so used to going everywhere stark naked and nude that it hadn't even occurred to us to go seeking clothing. In fact, that became quite a bit of a problem as her father and mother's clothing had all been taken to the Salvation Army depot and apart from William Havers whose build was nothing like ours, there were no males on the island who wore clothing.

He promised to pop across and purchased some temporary shorts and T-shirts as well as underwear for us until we were legally free and again citizens and could safely venture out as such and do our own shopping.

The solicitor had promised to arrange

111

appropriate financial adjustments so that we could manage this house and of course her other financial affairs until probate was granted and we would legally become the owners of this estate and all her other assets.

But once we were alone the most important matter for the pair of us was what we were going to do with our lives and how we were going to spend them.

"Well Peter, I for one want to spend it with you. I now know that I love you and I want to be with you for the rest of my life…"

He looked at me enquiringly but I didn't say anything for the moment, simply rising and going over to his chair, leaning down and kissing him. "Does that answer your implied question, my friend?"

He grinned and nodded. "It does!"

"So that leaves us with the other question: What are we going to do with our lives? Learning to run this house and the island will be interesting for a few weeks. I'm not at all sure about managing a twenty billion dollar investment portfolio but as for resuming my cadetship as a journalist, well that just seems rather ridiculous, much and all as I really had enjoyed it as a career."

"And the same goes for me. The one thing that I would like to pursue though, is seeing if we can overcome the difficulties in modifying the Electric Bed so as to achieve its extraordinary function to develop the human body to perfection but without that terrible pain that accompanied each session we had on it.

"Just imagine if we were successful and could

manufacture the unit in its changed function, if they were cheap enough to be a part of just about every household and even if not, in every gym around the world, the end results in the human race would be absolutely incredible, wouldn't they?"

"They certainly would. And I had forgotten that idea of ours so yes, let's see if we can find trustworthy colleagues to properly investigate the idea – perhaps set up a limited liability company with them as members so as to protect the design against predators."

And so that's what we did.

As soon as we had adjusted to our new enormous wealth, seen to any necessary changes to the island and its house and had countless meetings with the solicitor and Frederica's investment advisers, we did indeed go seeking other expert advice with regard to the Electric Bed and the pair of us funded the ongoing research as to the possibility or not of achieving a workable model that does not involve the horrible pain.

And almost as a footnote, let me say that it was with great delight that we achieved two things with immediate effect:

We ruthlessly dismantled every single part of every one of her horrible torture chambers that she and Williams had so lovingly created; and,

We sold Barry Williams to a quarry owner after investigating the very worst possible employment we could find for him. He would be spending his remaining days with a pick and sledgehammer, endlessly breaking up larger stones into smaller ones for the rest of his life.

I believe this is an appropriate point to end my tale. It started out with me having a career in journalism developed into a horrible year in which I was subjected to the most horrible existence possible for a human being; but then met the man who was to become the love of my life and finally ended up as the co-beneficiary of an enormous estate with which the pair of us are hopefully going to do some good in the world.